BEGGAR HOME LANE

J. D. JONES

Copyright © 2024 by J. D. Jones

All rights reserved.

No part of this book may be reproduced in any form or by any electronic or mechanical means, including information storage and retrieval systems, without written permission from the author, except for the use of brief quotations in a book review.

Illustration © Tom Edwards

TomEdwardsDesign.com

ALSO BY J. D. JONES

The Chaos Legacies

Book 1: The Zion Tower

Book 2: The Fallen Empire

All are available on the Amazon Kindle Store in Kindle and paperback format. Read for free on Kindle Unlimited.

For Mum and Dad - thank you for always encouraging and believing in me.

Dad - a throwaway comment about the cold frame you were building for the garden gave me the inspiration for this book. I'm forever grateful.
Mum - I imagine you'll find this book far too dark for your liking, but I'm dedicating it to you nonetheless.
Love you both very much.

J x

DISCLAIMER

This book contains adult themes including violence, abduction, strong language and sexual abuse.

GRAND PARADE, YORK
2012

ONE

I THINK it's a fact of life that weird shit happens. And more often than not, this aforementioned shit is utterly atrocious. People disappear and die, families fall apart, and cats get run over by reckless drivers. Sadly, this has all been the case with my life, right down to my cat being murdered. The world is full of messed up people who like to try and make it even more messed up. Cue the absolute car crash that is my life.

Gab and I were about as boring as 16-year-old twins can get when it all started. We didn't overcomplicate anything, we just got on with it. We woke up, maybe did our paper round, got yelled at by the mother for being too slow getting ready, pulled ourselves into our crinkled school uniforms and rushed out of the house, just in time to not be late. At school, we went our separate ways, each with our own group of friends. Neither of us was particularly popular, but we weren't really disliked either. We were just normal school kids. We fell into the traditional ebb and flow of a mid-Yorkshire comprehensive, producing a bang-average performance - we weren't going to be clever enough to change the world, but we weren't going to end up in prison either. We were just normal.

If you think about it, it's pretty impressive that two twins of our age got on so well. Most siblings like us would be at odds. I don't know if it was an inbuilt tolerance that we were born with, but in general, we got on like a house on fire. We were genuine mates. That's rare if you ask me.

Thinking about where to start this story, I properly started to get involved in events one Tuesday afternoon in early March. It was typical York weather for that time of year - bloody freezing. The winter that we had supposedly left behind along with Christmas, New Year and all that rubbish had suddenly made a dramatic return, bringing frost and the occasional fall of snow. It pissed me off, to be honest. I hated being cold. I still do.

Let me paint the picture for you. I was in Spanish class (I hated Spanish almost as much as the cold), paying as little attention as possible, and sat midway to the back of the room next to the window. I was with Paul, probably my closest friend at school (not that I talk to him now, especially in my current situation, and *especially* after everything that happened. I suppose most of the friends we make at school are just that - friends we made at school. You don't speak to them for years and don't really give a shit what happened to them, and they probably feel the same way about you. There's no big fallout or anything - you just drift apart. That's what happens after school. It's some weird-arse fairytale bubble where everyone knows everyone and everyone bitches about everyone and then it ends and you never see most of them again). Paul was a bit of a prick if we're being perfectly honest, but I got on with him well. At the point where we'll start our story, we were using the compasses from our pencil cases to carve a few obscene drawings into the side of the desk, hoping that Isherham (the absolute witch of a Spanish teacher) wouldn't notice.

'Chris Keeler!' Isherham's piercing voice suddenly echoed across the room. I dropped the compass to my knee immediately, quietly praying that she hadn't noticed my casual vandalism. 'If you would like to pay attention instead of staring at the floor,' (thank God for that!) 'You might be able to answer my question.'

Shit, there's a question?

My eyes raced across the whiteboard behind her, where I saw various words related to animals. *Gato... gato means cat... I have a cat...*

'Tengo un gato…' I began. Amazingly, an encouraging smile began to spread across Isherham's face. I carried on. 'Tengo un gato en mi pantalones.'

A few sniggers arose from members of the class. Isherham's face turned stony. 'You have a cat in your pants?' She asked, incredulously.

The classroom fell into fits of laughter, myself and Paul included.

'You're a twat,' Paul managed, guffawing.

A ghost of a smile crossed Isherham's face as she saw the funny side of my sentence that was accidentally on purpose lost in translation. 'Thank you for sharing that with us, Mr Keeler, I'll enjoy seeing you and your companion in my office at the end of the day.' She approached our desk, as Paul began to shout in protest.

'Oi, what have I done?'

'Both of you,' Isherham continued, 'can spend an hour after school sanding down the edge of your desks.' She reached us and pointed to the graffiti left by our compasses. The all-knowing eyes of the Spanish teacher met ours with an intrusive intensity. 'And I'll thank you for not doodling on the desks in my class again.'

'Bollocks,' I muttered. My dad would not be impressed.

TWO

PAUL DIDN'T TURN up for detention, so it ended up being just me, using a worn sanding block that Isherham had sourced from the DT classrooms for my convenience. I sent my compatriot an irritated text. *Can't believe you skived this, you knob.* No reply. I continued to scrape away at the penis I'd expertly drawn with my compass on the edge of the desk. Work of art, if you ask me.

Thanks to Isherham (and Paul, who, by extension, I now blamed for my misfortune), I missed the main school bus home, so had to wait for the 41 outside the main gates. It was even colder than it had been earlier, and I had neglected to bring a coat, as I hadn't anticipated standing around waiting for a stupid bus.

I grumbled at the bus driver as he arrived and dropped 50p into his tray, before taking a seat near the back of the bus, warming my hands in my armpits. Dad - and Mum for that matter, although she rarely gave much of a shit - would be bloody furious with me. Dad had wanted me to help with his latest woodwork project that night (not that I'd had much of a choice, slave labour if you ask me). My Dad had, for as long as I could remember, been obsessed with building things out of what was essentially crap he found on the street. He regularly scoured skips and bins and the back alleys behind pubs to find planks of wood, crates, pallets, and other useless paraphernalia. He would then spend hours sawing these apart and screwing them together to make equally useless items. Recent projects had resulted in a box to keep the cat's food and water in, a flowerbed in the middle of the garden (which remained empty) and an abnormally sized coat rack, which he still hadn't put up anywhere.

His most recent project had been to create a cold frame for the garden. What is a cold frame you ask? Well, I'll happily explain. It's basically a poor man's greenhouse. Dad planned to box off an area of ground in the garden with wooden planks, within which he would put down compost and grow plants and vegetables. The pièce de résistance of this would be a lid on top of the box with a window in, allowing sunlight to enter and heat to be trapped inside. Hence, he would have created a warm environment for his precious plants to grow in. Load of bollocks if you ask me.

Anyway, there wouldn't be any helping Dad that night. Not when it was nearly 5.30 pm and tea would be due on the table shortly. He would not be impressed.

'And where the fuck have you been?' Dad predictably berated me the second I walked through the door.

'I got a detention,' I grumbled, honestly. No point hiding the truth. Not that he cared much anyway. He just wanted his bloody cold frame building.

'We had work to do, you little prick,' he hissed, before stalking away from the front door and into the lounge. I glanced in to see he was working his way through a can of Stella (his fourth, by the look of the empties on the floor), watching the football.

'Don't even think about sitting down to watch the game, young man,' he said in between swigs of lager. 'You don't get to watch anything if you don't get the work done. Have I taught you nothing?'

I remained silent and sauntered into the kitchen, where Mum was finishing up tea. Standard Tuesday night dinner - sausage and mash. Mum looked tired. There were bags under her eyes.

'Where's your sister?' She asked, half-heartedly.

'Dunno,' I mumbled, helping myself to a Coke from the fridge and sitting at the table. 'We didn't come home together.'

'Gabby!' She shouted immediately, calling out aimlessly to get her daughter's attention. From somewhere upstairs, Gab's voice materialised.

'What?' Came the slightly rude reply.

'Tea's ready!' Mum bellowed back. 'Go get your father, would you, Chris?'

'I don't think he's going to want to talk to me.'

'Don't be a baby. Go tell him food's ready.'

'Bloody hell,' I muttered, under my breath.

'Language,' Mum reminded me half-heartedly.

Begrudgingly, I wandered towards the lounge, where I saw my Dad draining the remains of his fourth can.

'Dad?' I began, slightly cautiously.

'I know, I know tea's ready, I heard your mother's foghorn of a voice.' He swore loudly and pulled himself up, following me as I scarpered back to the kitchen.

Gab had made it downstairs by this point and was already tucking into her sausage and mash, ignoring Mum's feeble protests to wait for the others.

'What happened to you?' Gab asked me, trying to be subtle and not let Mum and Dad hear.

'He got a bloody detention, didn't he?' My Dad mocked, demolishing one of his sausages. 'What did you do, boy, beat up a Year 7?'

'No,' I grumbled, irritated at his implication that I was a thug. Not all sons are like their fathers. 'I drew on the desk in Spanish.'

Gab chortled. 'What did you draw?'

I stifled a grin. 'A penis.'

'Fucking gayboy,' my Dad spat, unkindly. He pulled a face as he tried Mum's mash, examining it carefully on his fork. 'Karen, this mash is absolute dogshite.'

'Thanks, Len, I made it myself,' my Mum's mildly sarcastic reply came.

Dad huffed. 'I don't want it.'

With that, Len Keeler stood up, abandoned his plate, liberated a fifth can of lager from the fridge and disappeared back to the lounge.

I rolled my eyes at Gab. Mum seemed uninterested in my Dad's abusive departure. If anything, she seemed to relish the fact that he'd left the room.

We ate the rest of our meal quietly, before Gab and I offered to clear the table. Mum murmured some words of thanks before retiring upstairs for a bath.

'He's in a right foul mood tonight,' Gab observed whilst washing a plate.

'What's new?'

'He was really pissed you weren't here to help him with that frigging hot box thing.'

'It's a cold frame.'

Gab rolled her eyes. 'Is it now?' She mocked.

'He could try and be a bit nicer to me and I might actually want to help.'

'Don't be silly, Chris, we both know Dad's a prick.'

'You got that right.'

THREE

PAUL WASN'T at school the next day, obviously. I guessed he'd pulled a sicky, too scared to face the wrath of Isherham when she questioned him on not turning up for detention. The day went by as normal, with no notable events to report.

I caught up with Gab in the canteen and we both joined the queue for the pasta counter. Neither of us had much interesting to say to each other and spent most of the wait discussing which pasta dish we'd go for.

'One pound sixty please, son,' the dinner lady on the counter announced.

'One sixty?' I asked, confused. 'It was only one twenty last week?'

'Gone up, hasn't it lad? There's a recession you know.'

'Shit,' I grumbled, reluctantly handing over more change than I wanted to.

'We sitting together?' Gab enquired, after being similarly extorted.

'I suppose.'

'Bloody hell, don't sound too excited about it.'

Some people would call me a loser sitting with my twin sister. It wasn't like I didn't have friends at school - but with various lunchtime activity clubs, people going to the canteen at different times and a fair bit of truancy, my options were limited. And I didn't mind sitting with Gab, we got on well.

'You'd better get home in time today. Dad'll be after you otherwise.'

'Don't worry, I've been on my best behaviour today.'

We had an assembly that afternoon, where all of Year 11 came together in the hall for our compulsory moral lesson of the week, delivered by Head-of-Year, Mrs Taylor. We were treated to a delightful talk on the dangers of unprotected sex, in which our 45-year-old Head-of-Year stoically explained the various options available for safe sex, all whilst keeping a remarkably straight face and doing a stand-up job of ignoring the inevitable hecklers.

The slightly raucous atmosphere was subdued at the end of assembly when Deputy Head Mr Arnold stepped forward to deliver his foreboding message.

'Some of you may be aware that a student has not been seen since the weekend. Some of you know Ellie James, and we know that some of you saw her this weekend at a party. Thanks to all who have already spoken to us and the police about when you last saw her. We're sure she will be found soon and is probably messing about, maybe with some other friends. But it's imperative that if anyone hears, sees or knows anything, you come and speak to me immediately. My office is always open.'

'Was that the party you were at?' I asked Gab, as the assembly drew to a close. The traditional end-of-assembly rigmarole included the normal spiel: announcements about various sports club fixtures, drama society rehearsals and the crowning of this week's "Pupil of the Week" - predictably awarded to Cameron Hopkins, the absolute brown-noser of the year and every teacher's favourite little loser.

'Hm,' Gab murmured in response. 'She was drinking a lot... I hope she hasn't ended up in trouble.'

'Me too,' I murmured. I'd met Ellie a few times and quite liked her. She was pretty fit and always had a chat with me. 'I hope she didn't end up like Molly.'

'Bloody hell, no.' Gab's face turned dark at the reminder of Molly Atkinson. Molly had been in the year above us and out drinking in the park with some mates at the back end of the previous year. She had disappeared and never been seen again. Everybody assumed she had fallen into the river right next to the park. Divers had searched for her and parts of the river had even been drained, but her body had never been found. In the end, the police had said her body must have washed downriver and was lost forever. I personally thought they had given up a little too easily, but what did I know? I was sixteen.

'She'll turn up,' I smiled, reassuringly. Kids around our neighbourhood were always disappearing and reappearing. It was commonplace amongst the community that kids would start drinking and doing a bit of weed anywhere from the age of fourteen to sixteen. It was almost a rite of passage. I regularly partook in an evening park trip where we shared a few bottles of cheap cider, and house parties were a common occurrence in the homes of those with more tolerant parents who were happy to turn a blind eye. It wasn't unusual for kids to vanish for a couple of days on a bender, before being found in a bush somewhere, looking rough as shit but generally without injury. Hell, it had even happened to me once or twice. Grand Parade was the rough end of York, after all.

That night, however, my hope of Ellie turning up diminished a little. For the first time, she appeared on the TV.

Unusually for the Keeler family, we were *all* sat in the lounge, watching the six-o-clock news. Dad had been drinking since lunchtime and had henceforth decided he didn't have the energy to build the cold frame that night. Lucky me. *It'll never get bloody built.*

I sat and watched as the newsreader on BBC Yorkshire officially declared Ellie missing. He then kindly reminded viewers that Ellie was just the latest in a long line of people to disappear from the west side of York over the past several years. If he wasn't careful, people would start getting the wrong idea about Grand Parade. Not that it had a particularly sterling reputation.

'All these bloody kids running off. Bet they're all on the piss.' As always, Dad showed buckets of empathy.

None of us said anything, we just watched the news solemnly. I should have known something was wrong that evening, but I got distracted. You see, that was the night that our cat got run over.

FOUR

STEVE from across the road (an irritating, annoying bloke if I ever met one) knocked on the door at about 8 pm. It was Gab who answered. Immediately, a cry of horror came from the front door and I leapt to my feet.

It broke my heart to see Tigger - our overweight tabby cat of twelve years - lying crippled in Steve the neighbour's arms. Tigger's legs had been twisted into horrendous-looking angles, patches of fur were missing and he was quietly meowing sorrowfully. He had never really been a vocal cat until that very moment. My legs felt weak as my beloved feline friend was presented to me, mortally wounded.

'What the hell happened?' My Mum demanded, showing the first bit of passion I'd seen in years.

As was typical for Steve, he was pretty useless. 'Dunno. Found him on the corner, near where that house is being done up on Beggar Home Lane. Guess he was run over.'

'Thank you, Captain Obvious,' Gab spat venomously, liberating Tigger from Steve's arms.

Steve didn't seem to notice Gab's annoyance or sarcasm. As well as being useless and annoying, he was also as thick as pig shit.

Mum moved forward, thanking Steve for retrieving the poor cat and ushering the neighbour away. Steve seemed to hesitate as if expecting some form of reward or thanks before Gab angrily slammed the door in his face.

'Shit,' I whispered, examining the poor cat. If animals could display emotion, I could have sworn I could see agony and sadness on Tigger's tired little face. 'He's not in a good way, Mum.'

'He's not,' Mum agreed, immediately reaching for her coat and car keys. 'We'll get him to the vets.' She approached the door, shouting behind her, myself and Gab in hot pursuit. 'Len, we're going to the vets! I think Tigger got run over!'

'Like fuck you are!' Len's slightly slurred reply came as he waddled over from his position in the lounge. 'Why the hell are you doing that?'

I felt a surge of anger burn through me. I loved Tigger and had known him for as long as I could remember. I didn't need my cock of a father making this any more difficult than it needed to be.

'Because he's been run over, idiot!' I shouted, not brave enough to call my father anything more extreme.

'Watch your mouth, boy,' Dad retorted, swaying slightly as he neared the three of us. 'The vet's going to cost a bloody fortune and we all know how it's going to end up. The bastard's done for, look at him.'

I couldn't argue with Dad's assessment of Tigger's condition. Even the cat's breathing was laboured. His little face was looking more and more haggard.

'Nah,' Dad continued, stepping closer and closer to Gab. 'I'm not paying some pretentious over-educated prick with too many letters after his name to put it down. Waste of money. The rich get richer, and we'll be without a cat.'

'Dad, he's in pain!' Gab cried, tears streaming down her face.

'Len, please,' Mum said calmly, stepping towards her tipsy husband. 'Think of the kids. He needs to be... *dealt with*... properly. Professionally.'

'Bullshit,' Dad spat, unkindly. He moved closer to Gab. My sister whimpered, holding the mutilated animal to her chest tightly. Tigger meowed again, quietly, as if protesting the whole situation around him. How simple life must seem as a cat.

I wasn't entirely sure what possessed me to stand in front of my

Dad at that point, but I never regretted it. I knew what Len Keeler was like. He was a drunk who cared very little about anyone apart from himself, least of all his family. He did things his way and fought tooth and nail if anyone opposed him. It hadn't been an uncommon appearance for him to turn violent towards Mum, although she always hid it well from us and never seemed to do much about it. I fully knew at that moment that I might end up with a black eye, or worse, but I still did it. I loved my sister and that bloody cat. I wasn't going to let Dad dictate the outcome of this situation without a fight.

'Move, boy,' Dad grumbled indifferently, trying to sidestep around me. 'It'll be out of its misery soon enough. I'm just not paying a vet to do what I could do myself for free.'

'Dad!' Gab yelled, horrified and incredulous at the revelation of our father's true plan.

'Gabrielle, he won't feel a thing!' Dad's roaring response could almost be mistaken for having a tinge of sympathy to it. Almost.

'Bullshit.' It was my turn to respond thus. Unfortunately, that was the final straw.

Len Keeler's meaty fist connected with my jaw, knocking me side-on and throwing me to the right. Mum howled in protest, jumping to my aid and cushioning my fall to the floor. Gab screamed, overwhelmed by the dramatically escalating situation.

'Give it to me,' Dad murmured, darkly, rounding on Gab.

'Don't you touch her!' I spat blood to the ground, shouting in defence of my sister.

Dad spun and rounded on me again. The effect of the alcohol seemed to have vanished from his system. He was focused, on the warpath and unbelievably dangerous.

'I won't hurt her if the bitch hands over the fucking cat!' He bellowed, his foul-smelling breath berating my face.

Dad turned back to my sister, and at this point, Gab gave in. Meekly, she extended her arms and presented him with the cat. To my surprise, he was rather gentle in taking the mangled remains of Tigger from her. He held the cat to his chest closely, cradling his head in one hand.

'Right then,' he grumbled. With that, he spun around and headed towards the garage door. The three of us remained in the hallway, stunned. The past few minutes had taken it out of all of us. Gab was crying silently, my Mum shaking her head in dismay. I examined my mouth and wiped away blood from my split lip.

No sound could be heard from the garage and Dad didn't reappear for the rest of the night. The next morning, as we always did in the Keeler family when Len kicked off, we carried on as if nothing had happened. No one dared mention Tigger and for a long time, no one ever did.

FIVE

I DON'T REALLY BELIEVE in magic, and I don't think you could describe this story as one about magic. I think there are supernatural things in this world, that's for certain - I've seen them. But magic... no, I wouldn't call it that. I look at the world we live in nowadays, decades since the events I'm recounting for you. In today's world, the existence of supernatural forces cannot be denied. It's shaped our culture. I know that, even from where I am now.

I don't know what you would call the things I went through, but it certainly wasn't magic. It was way too dark to be magic.

Paul still wasn't back at school and he wasn't responding to my texts. I'd given up by Friday. I'd had a shitty week. Detention, boring lessons, relentless homework, Tigger's untimely demise, Dad's punch to the face and Mum's most recent promise that I wasn't going out this Saturday had topped it all off. Clearly, she'd got herself all in a tizz about Ellie James' disappearance last weekend and was anything but comfortable with the idea of Gab and I going to a party on Saturday night. I also suspected she was a little oversensitive after Dad's recent outburst - I mean, who could blame her?

But it didn't mean we wouldn't go, it just meant we had to be a bit more subtle with it, especially if we planned to steal Dad's booze. So,

Saturday night came and Mum went out to the gym, as she often did on a Saturday night. Afterwards, she would probably go to the Homestead for a few glasses of wine with the gym girls. Dad hadn't been seen since lunchtime, probably at the Homestead himself, thoroughly inebriated. Neither of them made it difficult to sneak out. They probably wouldn't even notice we were gone.

We unlocked the garage and climbed over Dad's half-finished woodwork projects, towards some shelves. There, we liberated a box of Carling and a cheap bottle of Vodka from Dad's impressive stash, loaded our goods into our backpacks and set out walking to Vicky's. Vicky was in Gab's form at school and had invited most of Year 11 to her house that evening, whilst her parents were away for the weekend in London. We both liked Vicky's house. She lived on Calvary Avenue, one of the nicer roads in Grand Parade and even had a hot tub in the garden. Unfortunately, it meant it was a good half an hour walk, and we had to go through the shittiest of council estates.

'What do you think Dad did to him?' Gab quietly wondered aloud, interrupting an otherwise silent walk.

'What do you mean?'

'To Tigger.'

'I don't like to think about it, Gab. We know he's a sadistic pig, so who knows? He could have chopped the poor bugger's head off for all we know.'

'Fuck's sake, Chris,' Gab sighed, looking at me with sad eyes.

Shit, that was insensitive. 'Sorry,' I mumbled, looking away from her grief-stricken face. She had loved that cat even more than I had. 'I guess he took Tigger off you quite gently... maybe he was humane about it.'

'Talking bollocks is even worse,' Gab responded as we walked onto Beggar Home Lane: the very place where useless Steve had found our poor cat.

We meandered around a few construction vans that had been left by the side of the road. One of the old ladies was apparently having some work done. Number 130 had a skip on the drive and scaffolding around the walls of the house. I decided to have a nosy.

'What are you doing?' Gab implored as I started rooting around the edges of the skip and construction vans.

'Trying my luck,' I muttered, peering at the floor carefully. 'Construction lads are careless and always leaving stuff lying around, like... bingo!' I held up my find - a half-empty packet of cigarettes, clearly dropped by a clumsy builder. 'There's ten fags in here - we'll be well loved at the party!'

'Wow, they'll go far,' Gab grumbled sarcastically, before continuing our journey. 'Come on, I'm bloody freezing.' She crossed the road, past a poorly parked little red car (one wheel on the curb, the rest on the road) and I caught up with her easily. I was pretty pleased with the find. It was easy enough to rob alcohol from Dad, but neither he nor Mum smoked - neither did I for that matter. But it was a party, we were sixteen, and I knew it was cool. The fact that cigarettes were a recipe for lung cancer never even occurred to me.

We arrived at the party just after 9 pm, to find dozens of schoolmates running around an already trashed house. The sofas had been ripped, all manner of drinks had been spilt over the carpets, and half-empty pizza boxes were strewn across every surface. Vicky half noticed our arrival and was happy to relieve us of our bottle of vodka, kindly leaving us with the crate of Carling. With that, we got to drinking.

Gab and I drifted apart as we hung out with our respective friendship groups. To my annoyance, I couldn't find Paul anywhere. He deserved a good punch when I next saw him, going AWOL like that.

Anyway, I soon forgot about Paul. Within a few hours, I'd found myself in the hot tub (now dyed green with something I didn't want to know about), appropriately pissed. With me were Adam and John, two lads I knocked about with, and two girls, Lucy and Meg. Both were pretty good-looking and all three of us were trying our best to flirt with them. It was going horrendously.

Somehow, I was then back in the kitchen, going to town on a cold pizza. I'm pretty sure I was still in my swimming trunks. Vicky and a boy shoved past me, both dressed in very little, heading upstairs.

Then I was on a sofa, lying on my back with a blanket over me. A bottle of wine was in my hand, and I happily sipped on it every few minutes. A game of spin the bottle was taking place near me. I think I was involved for a few turns.

A little later, my clothes were back on, my swimming trunks lost to the carnage, and a hefty pair of hands were helping me to the door. As soon as I was out in the street, I promptly vomited and began the long walk home. I was vaguely aware that Gab was stumbling along with me, equally hammered. Somehow, we made it out of Vicky's street.

'What on earth are you two doing?'

A stern voice brought an ounce of sobriety to my thoroughly inebriated state. I managed to look up at the speaker, trying hard to focus on my vision.

'Fuck…' I managed, recognising Mr Arnold, the Deputy Head. What the hell was he doing here? I slurred my question at the teacher. 'Why you here, Sir?'

'I live down the road from here, not that it's any of your business, Keeler.'

'Sorry Sir,' I burped, before throwing up all over his shoes.

'Bloody hell, Chris,' Mr Arnold sighed, catching me as I swayed dangerously. 'We'd better get you home. And you, Gabrielle. I'll call you a taxi. I'd drive you, but I've had a few myself, and clearly need to give you both an example of responsible drinking. Honestly, what would your parents think?'

'They wouldn't give a shit, Sir,' Gab belched, managing to maintain her balance better than me.

'I assume you don't have cash on you?' Mr Arnold asked as he finished calling a taxi.

'No Sir,' I managed, still unbalanced holding on to the Deputy Head for dear life. 'But I can give you a cigarette.' I produced the packet I had salvaged on Begger Home Lane earlier, bringing an exacerbated sigh from my more sober sister.

Mr Arnold seemed to stifle a laugh, before taking the packet from me. 'I'll take these, Keeler, it's a shocking habit. Especially for someone of your age.' He examined the packet, extracting the remaining cigarette. Apparently, either my friends or I had smoked the rest.

The taxi arrived a few minutes later and Mr Arnold helped us in. Luckily, Gab was able to tell the driver an address.

'We'll need to have a word about this on Monday,' Mr Arnold said as we clambered into the back seats. 'You can't be behaving like this, you two, especially at your age.'

'Please don't tell our parents, Sir,' Gab pleaded, as Mr Arnold handed the driver a tenner and assured him that we wouldn't be sick in his car.

'No, I won't this time,' Mr Arnold replied, with an understanding smile. 'We were all sixteen once. And I don't expect your Dad would be impressed.' He said it almost knowingly, as if aware of how Len Keeler could often be. 'But this is a one-off, you two. Don't expect favours from me. I'm still your teacher, and I can't have the pair of you running around like this.'

'You were always one of the good ones, Sir,' I slurred, trying to reach out and shake his hand only to hit the closed door.

Mr Arnold chuckled through the window. 'Goodnight you two. Don't let this happen again.'

With that, the taxi began its journey across Grand Parade and I passed out, most of the night blurring into a bizarre, drunken memory.

SIX

THE REST of that weekend disappeared into nothingness. I spent most of Sunday cooped up in bed, nursing the worst hangover of my life. My mouth had felt as dry as the Sahara, the unpleasant taste of cheap cigarettes dominating my every sense.

By the grace of God, my Mum had either been out or asleep herself, and Dad was passed out on the sofa surrounded by empty lager cans when we got home on that Saturday night. As a result, my drunken escapades went unnoticed, and I was simply considered a lazy teenager throughout Sunday.

Monday rolled around, and Gab and I kept our promise, turning up at Mr Arnold's office at the start of the school day. He quietly and calmly talked us through the dangers of excessive drinking (nothing we hadn't heard before) and reminded us that alcohol was something to be enjoyed in moderation, otherwise it would ruin our lives. A subtle reference to our father suggested he knew far more about our home situation than we had realised.

As our friendly disciplining came to a close, I felt it the appropriate time to return Mr Arnold's £10, which he had kindly lent us for our taxi. The Deputy Head graciously declined the offer, but still asked me to stay in the office, whilst encouraging Gab to leave.

Something was off.

'Chris, when was the last time you saw Paul Thornton?'

The question caught me off guard. Paul? Why was he suddenly involved?

'I...' I stammered, confused by the question. 'Tuesday I think. We were in Spanish together.'

'That's right,' Mr Arnold nodded, sitting down behind his desk and flicking through a few papers piled up there. 'And you were both due for detention in Mrs Isherham's room after school, is that right?'

'Yes Sir, and I said I'm sorry, I shouldn't have drawn anything on the desk.'

'I'm not interrogating you about what you did or didn't do, Chris,' Mr Arnold replied, kindly. 'You've served your punishment and I don't see the need to go over it... although I can't guarantee your Spanish teacher will feel the same way.' He winked at me knowingly, as if silently acknowledging that he knew Isherham was a battle-axe. 'No, I want to know why Paul didn't turn up.'

'I dunno, Sir,' I admitted, glumly. 'I haven't seen him since. He wasn't even at that party on Saturday, you know, the one you...'

'I remember, Chris,' Mr Arnold interrupted firmly, not without betraying a small, bemused smile. 'Has he texted or called you?'

'No, Sir. He's been ghosting me.'

'Excuse me?'

'Ignoring me, Sir.'

'I see. Do you have your mobile phone on you? Would I be able to see your texts to him?'

'Um...' I hesitated, aware that my texts contained a lot more swearing than Mr Arnold was likely to be impressed with.

'Don't worry about what you've written,' the teacher smiled as if reading my mind. 'We were all sixteen once.' The same thing he'd said to me on Saturday.

Reluctantly, I extracted my mobile phone from the breast pocket of my blazer and handed it to Mr Arnold, unlocking it as I did so. The Deputy Head took a few moments perusing the messages I had sent to Paul, before checking my call history, to see several failed attempts to reach my friend. He did all of this with the screen in my view, so I could see he wasn't looking at anything else.

Eventually, Mr Arnold sighed and passed the phone back to me. 'You can go, Chris. Thanks for coming to see me.'

'Sir?' I asked, not moving from my seat, 'why all the questions about Paul?'

Mr Arnold sighed heavily, leaning back in his chair. 'Paul's mum called us on Thursday saying he hadn't come home for a few days. "Nothing to worry about," she told me, "he's probably off drinking with his friends somewhere and will turn up soon." But when he didn't reappear at this party over the weekend, people started to get worried. He's about to join a long list of people who have disappeared over the past few months.'

'Shit,' I murmured, for a moment lost in Mr Arnold's revelation.

'Try not to worry, Chris,' Mr Arnold said, cheerily. 'This is Grand Parade. Kids run off all the time and reappear a few days or weeks later after an underaged bender. I haven't forgotten that your mother found you in a park after a few days not so long ago.'

I nodded regretfully and began to take my leave.

'We'll be announcing this in assembly tomorrow, Chris, if Paul still hasn't turned up. I suggest you keep it quiet until then. We don't want rumours circulating the school.'

'No Sir,' I replied on autopilot, wandering out of his office. I felt shell-shocked. Something weird was going on. Too many kids were disappearing. Too many kids that *I* knew.

What the hell was going on?

SEVEN

MONDAY EVENING finally found my Dad in a good mood. Obviously, it was because his woodwork was finally taking off.

Len Keeler had managed to go a whole day with only a few cans of beer in him and was hence steady enough to do a little woodwork. But it wasn't just his sudden sobriety that had motivated him. No, it was his latest-found piece of crap.

Gab and I walked through the door to be greeted by a window propped up against the radiator, my Dad stood triumphantly next to it, admiring his find.

'Isn't she a beauty?' He boasted, looking at the pair of us. He was like a new person when his creative mind took over. The miserable drunken bastard had temporarily vanished, replaced with a father who actually acknowledged his children had feelings.

Unfortunately for Gab, her interest in Dad's projects had steadily dwindled over the years. As a result, she sighed, ignored her father and headed straight upstairs to her room. That left me alone to hear Dad's dramatic retelling of how he had retrieved such a useless object. Lucky me.

'Found this in a skip down on Beggar Home Lane,' he announced to me, proudly. 'Doing a big extension on that old lady's house.

Gutting it, by the look of it. Thought it would be perfect for the cold frame. What do you think?'

I nodded numbly, slightly amazed my Dad had asked for my humble opinion. I was a little impressed with my father. He must have been quick off the mark - I hadn't remembered seeing a sizeable window in the skip on Saturday night when I had found cigarettes dropped by one of the builders. It must have only made it to the skip in the last day or so. Dad must have taken a break from his weekend bender to track it down. Impressive.

'I've been looking for something like it for bloody ages,' he continued, almost to himself. 'It'll be the perfect roof. Come on, let's get to it.' He said the last sentence gruffly, implying I didn't really have a choice. Reluctantly, I followed him to the garage... Tigger's final destination. Fortunately, I saw no signs of feline remains in the garage.

Aside from Dad's lucrative collection of booze, perfectly organised on shelves that - you guessed it - he had built himself, the garage was a museum of organised chaos. Several bikes, both whole and with crucial parts missing hung on or were leant up against the walls. Cardboard boxes stuffed with old clothes, Christmas decorations and childhood memorabilia were haphazardly piled in one corner of the room. Taking up the majority of the space, however, was Dad's woodwork station.

It consisted of a few wooden benches and desks, all organised surprisingly well for a drunk. A plethora of tools littered the surfaces, including saws, drills, screws and clamps. Sawdust and chips of wood cluttered the floor and desktops, and piles upon piles of salvaged wooden planks, crates and palates adorned the edges of his workstation.

Dad walked the window over to one of the desks and placed it down, before admiring it once again. To me, it looked like a piece of shit. It was a rectangular, wooden window, with six small panes of glass separated by small beams. Once upon a time, the wood looked to have been painted sky blue. Now, it was chipped and dirty. One of the glass panes had a crack running through it, the others were covered in dust and grime. It probably measured three feet by two and sported rusty-looking hinges on one side, one with an angry-looking nail still attached - a threat of tetanus if I ever saw one.

My Dad beamed at the window, clearly overjoyed with his find. I didn't see the appeal, but he seemed happy, and when Len Keeler was happy, everyone was happy. Quite how happy he was overwhelmed me when he walked over to his booze selection, extracted two cans of Budweiser and handed one to me. 'Don't tell your mother,' he winked, before moving back to the workstation. I knew it was only a bribe because most of his projects needed two sets of hands. I didn't complain though, opening the can and sipping the lukewarm lager.

'We need to use these wooden planks,' he motioned to the debris surrounding him, 'to make a rectangular box that fits this window perfectly. Then we'll clean up the window, put some new hinges on it, and attach it to the box as a roof that can be lifted up on one end. Then, we'll take it to the garden and voila! A cold frame for the garden.'

At this point, you may be wondering whether this man was the same bloke who had rudely rejected my Mum's dinner, punched me in the face, and refused to let our cat be humanely dealt with by the vets. As we got to work, these thoughts crossed my mind, but I had a very simple explanation.

The explanation was this: more than anything in the world, my Dad bloody loved building things. He was a shitty, abusive, alcoholic of a father, and the vast majority of the time I wished I had a different Dad. Ninety-nine per cent of the time, he was a grade-A prick. But when a project took over, he transformed. He sobered up (slightly). He swore less. He was... pleasant. Somehow, perversely, I relished these moments. They were the times when I had a real father, not some knobhead who beat us regularly. Even though I hated woodwork and had little to no interest in it, the quiet moments of father-son bonding (if you could call it that) were relished.

Work progressed quietly as it always did. We didn't really say much to each other unless it had directly to do with the build. Dad would give instructions and I would give feedback if he was about to accidentally drill through my hand whilst I held pieces of wood together. I never made creative suggestions. The man had a vision, and who was I to complain?

I took those moments to reflect on how Dad had ended up as he was. To give him credit, he'd had a pretty shitty life - and he wasn't *entirely* to blame for it.

I'd heard all of this from my Mum, so its accuracy may not be perfect, but it gives you a good idea. Leonard Keeler had been a model student at high school before going to Newcastle University to study Medicine in the late 70s. He'd graduated and ended up working in North Yorkshire, where he pursued his lifelong dream of becoming a surgeon. Fast forward a few years through a handful of failed postgraduate exams and training programme rejections and Len's dream to train as a surgeon was slowly slipping away. He became disillusioned with the profession and began drinking heavily. Within a few years, he'd given up medicine completely and relinquished his title of Doctor.

Then the drinking got really bad. At this point, my Mum had tried to stage an intervention, using a friend to help him get a job in construction. He'd always loved building things and fixing things - I guess that's why he had wanted to be a surgeon so badly.

So he started work for a friend's company, operating cranes and helping build apartment complexes. Still, the drinking continued to rear its ugly head, and time after time my Dad was warned about coming to work not entirely sober.

Everything came to a head when he had a withdrawal seizure whilst operating a crane. Thankfully, no one was hurt, but thousands of pounds worth of damage was done as the crane ripped through a half-built apartment block. Len was sacked on the spot but wasn't done there. The drinking and history of failure had turned him into a resentful, vindictive man.

Len managed to find a lawyer and an old medical school friend who worked together to get Len a diagnosis of epilepsy, blaming that, not the booze, for his seizure on the crane. When the lawyer accused the construction company of not screening Len for epilepsy, and allowing a vulnerable man to be exposed to stressful situations with loud noises and flashing lights, the company folded almost immediately. They agreed on an immense payout, which Len took happily.

No more was said. My Dad hadn't worked a day since and had drunk away a good chunk of the compensation.

I don't think Dad would have ended up this way if his original profession hadn't been so damned awkward and if he'd got a little help for his drinking. So in a way, it wasn't his fault. But, it didn't stop the fact that he had become a resentful, unkind alcoholic.

The cold frame only took a few hours. Dad worked meticulously and carefully, planning every measurement to the most acute detail. A few cans of lager later we were carrying the surprisingly heavy piece outside to the garden, where a ready-made patch of the garden sat waiting.

Silently, we lowered the frame onto the soft, loamy soil. Thick wooden planks were set perpendicular to each side of the window. These sides surrounded this soil, which could be seen through the now-clean panes of glass. New hinges adorned one side of the window, meaning it could be opened to access the soil and eventual plants beneath.

Dad stood back to admire our work, claiming that he would begin planting inside the poor man's greenhouse tomorrow.

I stayed bent down, ensuring it was securely tucked into the earth. A reflection flashed past me in one of the panes of glass, startling me. I looked closer to see it had only been my face reflecting back at me.

With that, Dad's latest woodwork project was complete, and he instantly returned to being a miserable, abusive bastard.

EIGHT

MIDWEEK, Paul was officially declared as missing both at school and on the local news channel. Mrs Taylor announced it at an impromptu whole-school assembly. It came as a surprising coincidence when she also announced that Vicky, whose party we had been at on Saturday, had also been missing for the past few days, but had thankfully turned up at her house yesterday, covered in dirt, stinking of booze and looking pretty sorry for herself.

Mrs Taylor was less than impressed with the events of the last few weeks and consequently declared an 'alcohol epidemic' amongst the Year 11s. For the rest of Wednesday afternoon, the entire year came before Mrs Taylor in groups of twenty. She harshly berated each group for fifteen minutes about the dangers of alcohol, how all of us were out of control, and that we all needed to sort ourselves out.

To be fair, she wasn't wrong. Grand Parade was definitely the rough part of York, and underage drinking had been commonplace there for decades. What had recently emerged, however, was a fashion of sixteen-year-olds getting absolutely rat-arsed, disappearing off the face of the earth for a few days, then appearing still half-cut, feeling rather sorry for themselves. That was what happened to most of them anyway; others, like Paul, Ellie James and Molly Atkinson seemed to have disappeared for good. Whether booze was involved in their unexplained absence, nobody knew.

After an afternoon of moral lectures on the dangers of drinking, Gab and I naturally ended up drinking cheap cider in the park with our friends Adam and Lucy - the same two I had sat with in the hot tub at Vicky's house. They'd apparently lost their virginity to each other that same night and had thus decided to become a couple. How long it would last - knowing Adam's track record - was anyone's guess.

The four of us settled on a bench on the cold March afternoon. The sky was clear and bright, and a hesitant ray of sunshine was keeping us moderately warm in our coats. We passed the two-litre bottle of overly strong cider between us periodically, chatting about nothing much, watching as the gardeners in the nearby cemetery went about their business. Cheery place, Grand Parade.

'What do you reckon keeps happening to people?' Lucy enquired, downing a few glugs of cider. 'Do you think everyone is just getting pissed?'

'Getting pissed and falling in the river,' I mumbled, uninterested in serious topics. We'd had enough of that from Mrs Taylor.

'So you think they're dead?' Lucy gasped, incredulously.

'Who?' I responded.

'Paul and Ellie? They've not turned up?'

'I don't know, do I, Lucy? I've not got a frigging crystal ball.' I was getting irritated.

'Alright, dickhead,' she spat back, drinking more cider. Gab took the bottle from her and had a swig herself.

'We might need to move,' Adam suddenly said, eyeing the gardeners who had suddenly decided to pay attention to us.

'What are you kids doing?' A strong Yorkshire accent shouted, as an oversized beefcake of a man waddled over to us, spade in hand. 'You got nothing better to do than sit in our parks and drink shitty cider? How old are you anyway?'

'Fuck off, old man,' Adam retorted, although he stood up as if about to leave the park.

'Watch your tone, boy,' Beefcake responded, leaning on his shovel. 'Come on, all of you, get moving.'

Slowly, we began to shift from the bench.

'Wasn't you digging at these graves was it?'

'What?' Gab responded, clearly confused.

'Graves. Loads of 'em. Dug up, made a mess of. It'll be some of you bloody kids, I'll bet.'

'Not us,' I said simply, shrugging. 'Why the hell would we want to dig up graves?'

'Kids like you are stupid.'

'Cheers,' Gab replied, her sarcasm on point as always.

'Kids think people get buried with their money and jewels and shit. Like it's ancient fucking Egypt. Trying to rob graves.'

'I don't think any of us are stupid enough to think that,' Lucy said, the bottle of cider back in her hand.

'Maybe not, but it'll be someone at that shitty school of yours.' Beefcake began to retreat, clearly happy he had said enough and given plenty of encouragement for us to scarper.

'Surely it was just a dog or something?' I shouted as we walked in the opposite direction of the cemetery.

'If you know a dog that can dig six-foot holes, boy, you bring it to me and I'll put it to work!'

NINE

WEEKEND. Dad's pissed again. Mum's buggered off somewhere - a lucky escape. Gab's bored in her room. And somehow - goodness knows why - I'm in the garden, planting vegetables in Dad's glorious cold frame.

There was something peaceful about doing it. I don't know why. There was a lot on my mind. People disappearing and everyone going off on three-day benders all the time. The shitty treatment my Dad had given us as a family over the past week. Saying goodbye to Tigger. But something about being in that garden, planting and getting my hands dirty - it was soothing.

After a few hours, I noticed Gab had come to sit on one of our garden chairs with a cup of tea. She was playing on her phone, wasting time. She didn't offer to make me a drink.

'What're you doing?' She eventually asked.

'I'm building a fort, what does it look like?'

Gab chuckled. 'Touché.' She paused. Then: 'Seriously though, since when did you like gardening?'

'Since this morning, apparently. It soothes me.'

'Ha. Loser.'

'Cheers. Make me a cup of tea, will you?'

'Make it yourself.'

Gab went back to her phone and I went back to planting. For all the complaining I had done about the cold box, I couldn't argue that it was a clever idea. I had already noticed that the inside of it had become warmer than the air outside. The window from the skip did a good job of letting heat in and stopping it from escaping. It really was a miniature greenhouse.

I finished planting a few courgettes (not entirely sure why, I hate courgettes) and sat back to admire my handiwork. The world around me was quiet. All I could hear was Gab's nails tapping on her phone screen.

I shut the box, pulling the window down from its laid-back position on the hinges. Through the glass, I once again looked upon my crops. Dad wouldn't be doing any planting, I knew that for sure. He liked the building of things, but once it was done he quickly lost interest in the item. He'd once built a container for Tigger's food and water, then immediately stopped caring about it and failed to fill it once. He'd built a coat rack that was still waiting to be hung up. And now the hotbox was done, he didn't care about the plants that would go in it. He just wanted to build stuff, then abandon it. So was his way.

I saw my reflection in the glass before me as I stared at my courgettes. Then, without explanation, I was looking at a house.

I blinked. Then I rubbed my eyes. Once again, I looked into the hotbox.

Clear as day, without any explanation, I wasn't looking at the damp soil and the roots of my plants. I was looking at a house, faint and distant and not entirely solid, but definitely a house. In fact, it was a row of houses - a full street. I was staring at a street, with cars and houses and even people walking past, as if in slow motion. A tiny red car moved across the window, almost elegantly. It was as if I was looking out of my own living room window. The panes of glass before me were alive with ethereal images of a living, breathing community.

'Chris?' Gab's voice floated into my subconscious as I remained kneeling on the ground, slack-jawed at what I could see. I didn't even notice her come over to me. 'Chris?' She repeated.

I closed my eyes and rubbed them, shaking my head violently.

When I opened them, the images were gone. Once again, all I saw was the soil through the window, nothing else. I breathed a sigh of relief. I must have been daydreaming. Maybe I was overtired.

'You alright?' Gab said, shaking me. There was concern in her voice.

'Yeah,' I breathed, standing up and wiping the dirt off my jeans. 'Yeah, fine, thanks. I'm just tired. I might go lie down or watch TV for a bit.'

'Don't go in the lounge,' Gab warned, as she walked with me back into the house. 'Dad's passed out in there with the football on. He'll know you're disturbing him, even if he's pissed.'

'I know,' I grumbled, trudging up to my room. I noticed that Gab was watching me with curiosity. She could tell I wasn't myself. And I wasn't - clearly, I was exhausted, I was having bloody hallucinations!

I collapsed onto my bed and closed my eyes, reminding myself that the window on top of the cold frame was nothing more than a bit of wood with a few panes of glass in it.

TEN

OF COURSE, I'd imagined seeing something in the window. That would make sense, right? There's no such thing as magical windows that show you random images unless you're at a museum or funfair or something like that. No, I was just tired or worn out or hungover.

There wasn't any official party that Saturday night, so a few of the Year 11s decided to meet in the local park at sunset. Wrapped in our coats, we sat around a disposable barbecue that we used for warmth, not cooking. Obviously, drinks were less abundant than at Vicky's house last week, but we had plenty of cheap cider to go around.

There were only about a dozen of us, and we stayed there late into the night. Mum rang my mobile at one point to check I was okay but didn't demand that me and Gab rushed home. I managed to sound sober enough on the phone, I think.

Adam and Lucy decided to go and cop off in one of the bushes, so Gab and I decided we'd take the opportunity to leave. The remaining stragglers had got on to telling ghost stories, which I wasn't particularly in the mood for.

We walked home from the park, which was much closer to our house than Vicky's had been. I was quite proud of myself - I was in a much better state than last Saturday, only mildly buzzed by the booze.

I was even walking in a straight line. Unfortunately, it was Gab's turn to be a little too pissed. This time, as we walked onto Beggar Home Lane, she spewed all over the pavement, just avoiding the bonnet of a nearby car. The little red vehicle in question displayed a tiny flashing red light on the dashboard.

It was just our luck that a police officer happened to drive by - not unusual in Grand Parade, but incredibly bloody unlucky.

'For fuck's sake,' I whispered, stopping as the car pulled over by us. 'Good evening, Sir,' I announced, loudly and clearly, trying my very best to pretend I had not been drinking. There was little I could do to mask this for Gab, who I was now supporting to ensure she stayed upright and didn't fall onto the red car she had very nearly given a new paint job to.

'How old are you, son?' The officer asked as he got out of the driver's seat.

'Eighteen,' I lied.

'You got some ID?'

'Not on me.'

'So how did you buy the booze that you stink of? Or get served in a pub?'

'I just look old enough.'

'Bullshit.'

'Honestly.'

'What's your name?'

I hesitated. 'Paul.'

The officer looked startled. 'Paul who?'

Again I hesitated and thought furiously. I couldn't give Paul's full name - Paul Thornton. He was known to be missing. I'd get in all kinds of shit if I pretended to be him. Unfortunately, few other names were coming to my mind. Eventually, I spat out: 'Arnold. Paul Arnold.'

The policeman frowned. 'Arnold's not a common surname around here,' he grumbled. 'The only other Arnold I know is Mike Arnold, who teaches at Saint Joseph's.'

'That's my Dad.' Idiot. What a stupid lie. Why the hell did I say that? I know why... I was panicked and a little drunk.

'Well, I'd better give him a ring. Me and your Dad know each other from the pub. I'm sure he'll be pleased to know I've been looking out for his son. Although, he never mentioned that he had kids...'

'Shit, sorry Sir, I don't mean that Mr Arnold, I mean...'

'Save it, kid. I know you're bullshitting me.' The policemen sighed and began to move back towards his car. 'I can't be arsed dealing with you two tonight. I've already broken up two pub fights and got punched in the kidney. Do you live nearby?'

'Just off Beggar Home, Sir,' I said, waving vaguely in the direction of our house.

The copper began to get back in his car. 'Don't lie to police officers, lad. You'll end up in real deep shit.'

I nodded, dumbly.

'And get your mate home. She looks a right mess.' On cue, Gab released another torrent of vomit onto the pavement.

The police officer said no more and drove off a few seconds later. Heart racing and completely overwhelmed that I'd escaped the encounter unscathed, I began to drag Gab towards the house.

It occurred to me that we were passing the skip of the old woman's house that was being renovated - the same place I had discovered the cigarettes and Dad had liberated the infamous window.

Something was off.

I looked around.

Immediately, I sobered up. It couldn't be.

I was looking across the road, away from the skip. Before me was the row of houses I walked past nearly every day on my way to school. Never before had they interested me. Until that very moment.

This was the view I had seen through the window on the cold frame, right down to the bright red Citroën C1 - the very car Gab had narrowly avoided vomiting over, with the tiny flashing red light on the dash. The only difference was that the car looked a lot more bruised and tired now than it had in the window. My mouth fell open as I stared across the road. How was this possible?

Gab decided to choose that moment to vomit not only down her front but all over my new trainers. I swore loudly at her as I was torn away from the vision before me.

I must have been hallucinating. I had been tired and traumatised by the previous week. It was just my subconscious projecting the image onto the window - an image I had seen a thousand times before on my daily commute to school down Beggar Home Lane. There was absolutely no way that the window had portrayed an *actual image* of this street.

I shook my head and continued to drag my inebriated sister back home. I hated myself for it, but I couldn't help wondering why the houses and cars I'd seen through the window had looked a lot more modern and fresh than they had this evening… almost as if the version I'd "seen" in the window had been from several years ago.

Bollocks. I hadn't seen anything. I was imagining things.

Still, I found myself unable to sleep that Saturday night after I had shoved Gab into her room. I lay staring up at the ceiling, trying to understand why on earth my imagination had conjured up an image in the window, and why the hell it was of a street I knew so well.

Well ladies and gentlemen, if you think this shit is weird, it's about to get a whole lot weirder. And a whole lot darker, too.

ELEVEN

THE WHOLE of the next day was spent trying not to go and look at the window. I refused to give in to what I *knew* was absolute insanity. But the temptation was immense. What I'd seen in the window… it just wasn't quite right. Something was off.

Mum and Dad did a reasonable job of distracting me from my intrusive thoughts. Gab had decided it would be a splendid idea to get up in the night and vomit down the stairs, the absolute prat. It resulted in Mum being an uncharacteristic disciplinarian, which unfortunately just egged Dad on. An already tender Gab managed to barricade herself in her bedroom to prevent the onslaught of our father, but still received a forty-five-minute verbal berating through closed doors.

Trying to be as subtle as I could, I waited a few hours before slipping out of the front door, noticing Dad sitting in his usual place on the sofa with a can and Mum nursing a glass of wine next to a half-empty bottle in the kitchen on my way out. As I escaped into the street (more for fresh air than anything), I reflected on the fact that alcoholism was clearly a massive issue in my family. My Dad was an abusive drunk, my Mum used drink to cope with the stress of being married to him and his children were teenage delinquents who got pissed in the park - as last night had royally proven.

The thoughts of Beggar Home Lane appearing in the glass of that bloody window kept invading my mind. It was just my imagination. *Just* my imagination. I needed to leave it alone and move on.

So, naturally, I ended up finding myself on Beggar Home Lane a few minutes later.

I stopped by the skip. The old lady's house was well and truly mid-demolition. A few walls were missing and scaffolding towered over the house's feeble remains. I stared at it for a few moments, trying to imagine where the window might have come from. Was it a first-floor window? No... the view of the street I'd seen in the glass had been a ground-level view, just like...

No. Stop it. *I didn't see anything through that bloody window. It's all in my head. Bullshit.*

'You alright, lad?'

The builder's voice startled me and I jumped out of my skin. The man laughed. 'Calm down, lad. Didn't mean to scare you.'

'Sorry,' I grumbled, shakily.

'You alright? You look as white as a sheet.'

'Yeah,' I lied. 'Fine.' I looked up at the bloke. He was considerably taller than me and much wider as well. He had a bald head and a poorly groomed beard. He couldn't look more like a builder if he tried. 'You work on Sundays?' I asked, trying to change the subject and forget the constant onslaught of thoughts surrounding the window.

The builder shrugged. 'They're paying us well. I'll work Sundays if the price is right.' Spoken like a true tradesman.

'What are you doing to it?' I asked.

'What does it look like, lad? Full renovation. Pretty much knocking it down to start again. The couple who bought it liked the plot but hated the house. So we're practically making them a new one. More money than sense if you ask me.'

'I thought an old lady lived here?'

'Yeah, she did. But she got old, senile like.' He pointed at his temple and twisted his finger around like a screwdriver. 'Went downhill pretty quickly by the sounds of it. Started seeing all kinds of weird shit. Demented, you know. That Alzheimers shit. It's a bitch.'

'Yeah,' I murmured, my mind elsewhere. *Seeing things… no. Impossible. Loads of old people get dementia. That's why she was seeing things.*

'Moved her to a home,' the builder continued, oblivious to my inner turmoil. 'So this place went on the market dirt cheap and was snatched up by this young fancy couple in a few days. Shame if you ask me. Can't be doing with these young rich folk. Just make sure you're nice to the little people if you ever get rich, son.'

I nodded and began to sidle away. 'Have a good afternoon,' I muttered, continuing my aimless wander.

'See you, lad,' I just about heard the builder over the sudden roar that enveloped the street. I spun around to see a car heading straight towards me at breakneck speed, just as I was stepping out to cross the otherwise silent road.

'Watch out!' The builder yelled, chasing after me and grabbing me by the scruff of my collar, hauling me back onto the pavement.

The car swerved violently and came to a stop outside a house just opposite. Seemingly oblivious to the fact he had nearly run someone over, a boy not much older than me exited the driver's seat and began to walk towards one of the houses.

'Oi, dickhead!' The builder shouted, releasing my shirt and running across the road after the boy. 'Oi! Who the hell do you think you are, driving like that?'

'Fuck off,' the boy shouted back. 'It's my car and the roads are quiet. I can drive how I want.'

'Don't be a twat. You'll end up killing someone driving like that!'

'Piss off,' the boy spat. I could see arrogance radiating off him even from the other side of the road. 'You're not the boss of me.'

'I'll be having a word with your parents.'

'My parents won't listen to the likes of some uneducated prick like you.'

The builder looked like he was about to throttle the boy. I would have if I was him. Somehow, however, the tradesman kept his cool, clenching his fists tightly. 'I'll be watching you, boy.'

'Whatever,' the boy grumbled, disappearing into the house directly opposite the renovation.

The builder slowly returned to me, seething. He was bright red in the face, his fists still clenched. 'I can't be doing with arrogant pricks like that,' he complained, heading back towards his workplace. 'Watch out for him, lad. He'll end up running you down if you're not careful.'

I nodded, numbly. Even though the boy had indeed been a Grade-A arsehole, it wasn't him I was interested in. It was the car he had driven. I was staring at a bright red Citroën C1. It was just like the one I had seen walking back from the park, just like the one Gab had almost vomited over, and almost identical to the one I thought I'd seen in the window. A little light flashed on a camera attached to the dashboard.

The most concerning feature, however, was a dent in the right front bumper with a few scratches revealing white underneath the red paint…

TWELVE

AND SO IT came to be that on that Sunday afternoon, I found myself sitting in the garden, half-heartedly tending to my vegetables in the cold frame. Every few minutes, I shut the lid and stared into the increasingly dirty glass of the strange window that had found its way into my home. Each time, I saw nothing but earth through the glass.

Something just wasn't right. I'd definitely seen that car in the window. And the marks on its front bumper just didn't sit right with me. To top it all off, the guy had been driving like a prick.

And my cat had been run over and left for dead on Beggar Home Lane.

I'd put two and two together and made five, but I didn't care. I was convinced that idiot had killed my cat. And for some stupid reason, God only knows why, I was using this infernal window to look for some answers.

What a ridiculous situation. I was relying on a bloody window - a pane of glass - to give me answers. What a load of bollocks.

'What the hell are you doing?' Dad's voice floated over from behind as he found me staring at the cold frame.

'Nothing,' I murmured, carefully lifting the lid again and playing around with my trowel.

'At least you're not like your bloody sister, spewing everywhere like a child.'

I ignored him. Sometimes, it was the easiest option.

'Glad to see you're using my cold frame.'

Was that a compliment? Or a slightly positive comment? I quietly shut the lid of the box and turned around to face my father, only to find he had disappeared back into the house. Had he come out just to complain to me about Gab? Or was he genuinely pleased I was using his creation? Sometimes I just didn't understand my father.

I returned my gaze to the cold frame.

Holy shit.

I hadn't imagined it. I *knew* I hadn't. Before me was a living, breathing image.

It was slightly faint, a bizarre and harrowing translucency running through it, but it was there. It was something. There were images within the window.

Initially, it was just in the top left pane of glass, but as I watched, mesmerised, the image transfigured before me, spreading into the neighbouring panes, until all six pieces of glass within the old window were alive with an ethereal yet unnerving image.

What I saw before me was enthralling. Horses dragging carts trotted down the road at a snail's pace. Men dressed in dirty rags and overalls paraded around amongst women wearing full-length, tired-looking dresses. The occasional smart-looking aristocrat prowled through the masses, sporting tails and a top hat. Snow was falling. The houses surrounding them were, whilst sparse, tall and thin, the windows lit with candles. Lampposts sported burning flames and salesmen walked along with mobile, wooden stalls.

Somehow - and I wasn't entirely sure how - I was staring at a Victorian tableau, slowly playing out in front of me, clear as day aside from a light blue glow that surrounded the image. My mouth hung open as I stared, transfixed, unable to tear my eyes away, barely blinking, lost in the impossibility of what was before me.

Nothing indicated that the scene before me was a version of Beggar Home Lane from the 1800s, but that didn't matter. I just *knew* it was.

Somehow, this window was showing me Beggar Home Lane in all stages of history… modern day and now the past.

But it was impossible. It made no sense. The window wouldn't have even been there back then… How could I be looking at the past?

After a few moments, the image began to fade. I gripped the sides of the cold frame, pulling my face closer to the glass, willing it desperately to share more ghostly images with me.

Then, as quickly as it had appeared, it was gone. The window seemed to ripple briefly, before solidifying and returning to normal.

I sat backwards on the cold, wet ground, stunned.

What the hell was this?

I breathed deeply, looking up at the overcast sky, my mind somehow flashing back to Tigger's untimely demise and the scratches on that boy's tiny red car…

THIRTEEN

YORK MINSTER IS a world-famous Cathedral and one of the largest in Europe. It was officially completed in the 1400s but was originally founded centuries before that. The immense, gothic structure serves as the seat of the Archbishop of York and is an image synonymous with the city of York. Even now, as I write these words, decades after the events I describe to you, York Minster still stands. Through hell and high water, the Cathedral has survived countless conflicts and periods of unrest - even the most recent, ultra-catastrophic wars. One of the few photos on my wall these days is one of York Minster. I don't have many pictures… but there is something about the Minster I love. It reminds me of a simpler time. Much more peaceful than the one I know now.

Look at me being all cultured and knowing about York Minster. Well, you'll be surprised to know this about me… I really like cathedrals. I'm not particularly religious, but I do like the buildings. There is a peace to them. A beautiful calm amongst the chaos.

The week after I had seen my second vision in the window (if you could call it that and I wasn't actually going crazy), and nearly two weeks since I'd last seen Paul, the students of Year 11 were "treated" to a guided tour around the famous church. As a Church of England school, Religious Education was a compulsory subject. Thus, the RE staff never missed an opportunity to take us to various houses of worship. In my time I'd seen several Mosques, Hindu and Jewish Temples and even visited an Assembly Hall of Jehovah's Witnesses. We were a rather cultured year group.

This particular Tuesday, Mr Arnold (definitely not my Dad, but definitely called Mike) was accompanied by Ms Dooley and a few others from the RE faculty as they led the trip to the Minster. A lot of my fellow pupils feigned interest or downright ignored the tour guide as we were shown around the Minster's impressive nave and aisles. In order to remain cool amongst my peers, I had to mask my genuine interest.

But as I say, I really liked cathedrals - well, all religious buildings. I was fascinated by their architectural designs, often seeming to defy the laws of physics. Arches and buttresses soared high into the sky around me, suspending tonnes of stone and glass at impossible heights. Intricately detailed stained-glass windows and gargoyles stared down at me from above, entrancing me with their impressive design and beauty. I had been similarly transfixed by the Mosques and Temples we had visited. The gargantuan domed roofs of the Mosques and the ornate designs of the Temples had entranced me, their immensity and complexity captivating. I know it's sad and makes me sound like a loser, but I just loved seeing such places. I like to imagine that buildings like these will survive forever… the last structures standing in the apocalypse…

Hiding my secret passion, I trudged around with the rest of my tour group, laughing along at the quiet banter between my peers, making a particular effort to chortle at comments about the Priests being perverts.

We'd made it over to a large stained glass window at the far end of the Minster. The Great East Window, we were told, was the largest medieval stained glass window in the country. I marvelled at the complex images within each of the panes, representing heaven, hell, biblical stories and the apocalypse. It was a delightfully magnificent work.

Unfortunately, my mind immediately began to wander. My thoughts turned to the much smaller window currently living in my back garden, that, so far, had somehow shown me my own private images - one of Beggar Home Lane and one of a Victorian street. Surely, I must have been imagining things… surely. The idea that images would appear in a broken old window was impossible. Maybe I'd been a bit drunk, or tired, or hungover, or all of the above. I couldn't believe it… I wouldn't.

I felt a nudge to my left, dragging me out of my deep musings. It was Adam, someone I'd always been half-arsed friends with but had got to know a little better since Vicky's party. It seemed now that he was shagging Lucy, he was a little less insufferable.

'Have you seen that?' He whispered, nodding to the other side of the group.

I followed his gaze to see Vicky, the girl who had disappeared after her party before reappearing, safe and sound (if a little bruised), sitting on a bench by one of the nearby chapels. She was crying, silently. I noticed Gab had moved close to her and was about to take a seat by her side.

Strange… I'd never seen Vicky cry. She was a larger-than-life, brash girl who reeked of self-confidence and always put on a cool facade. To see her crying… it was like seeing a different person. I hadn't spoken to her since she'd reappeared from her weekend-long bender. Apparently, it had left her distraught.

I nodded in acknowledgement of Adam and watched as my sister began to comfort Vicky. After a while, Ms Dooley joined the pair and promptly walked them away from the group, obviously to have a quiet word.

Whatever was going on, I knew Gab would share it with me later. That was one of the great things about our relationship. We didn't have secrets, we shared everything. But then… why the hell had I not told her about the window?

I put Gab and Vicky to the back of my mind, continuing on the tour. I managed to forget about the window and the girls for about half an hour, enjoying learning about the complexities of the Cathedral's artwork and architecture, as well as the convoluted steps that went into running and maintaining such an impressive building.

After the tour, I found myself with Adam and Lucy in the Cathedral gift shop. Gab was nowhere to be seen, clearly still with Ms Dooley and Vicky, probably knee-deep in a counselling session. Somehow, with my sister's absence and Paul still being AWOL, I'd ended up the third wheel to Adam and Lucy's ever-more volatile relationship (after they'd got bored of the sex and explored whether their personalities actually matched up, the connection had gone more and more downhill). Regardless, the three of us explored the gift shop for our ten allotted minutes, amused by the prospect of someone paying £25 for a mug in the shape of one of the Cathedral's spires.

'There's a York Minster Monopoly here,' I said, gesturing the pair over, genuinely interested in my find.

'Frigging loser,' Adam sniggered, ignoring the board game I was showing him. 'Look at this though.' Adam pointed to a corner of the gift shop, where an unmanned table stood sporting random paraphernalia: key rings, bags of sweets and woollen hats to name a few. The sign beneath read: '*Village Hall Home Honesty Stall*'.

'What about it?' I grumbled, reluctantly replacing the Monopoly box.

'You can take stuff for free from that table,' Adam explained, a sly smile on his face.

'No you can't,' I corrected him. 'It's an honesty shop. If you want to buy something, you put money in the box and I guess it goes towards the hospice it's raising money for.'

'But there's no one there. So how will anyone know?' Adam winked mischievously, walking over to the Village Hall Home's table. He helped himself to a couple of bags of sweets (mint imperials and gummy worms), before adding a beanie hat to his collection. Glancing around, he quickly stalked away, seemingly without even thinking of paying. Lucy, clearly enamoured by this bad boy approach, grinned broadly and ran after her new boyfriend.

A little saddened by Adam's actions, yet not at all surprised, I sauntered over to the stall, reaching into my pocket. The £10 I had offered Mr Arnold last week for the taxi was still in my jacket pocket. Not entirely sure why I was doing it, I popped the note in the money box and walked away.

Did that make me a good person? No. I don't really think there are good people and bad people in the world. I guess what it did do was it made me a slightly better person than Adam. And realistically, that was enough.

FOURTEEN

IT WASN'T until we were walking home after school that I finally got a chance to speak to Gab alone. I wanted to know what had been going on with Vicky - she had been acting *very* out of character. And to be honest, I was pretty nosy.

'I agreed I wouldn't say anything,' Gab insisted as we walked the familiar route home, our normal twenty-minute commute come rain or shine. 'Ms Dooley made me promise.'

'Come on, who'm I going to tell?'

'It's pretty serious, Chris.'

'I'm not going to say anything. Come on, I promise I'll keep it to myself. You and I tell each other everything, why should this be any different?' I winced internally, thinking of how I hadn't told her about the window... not yet. Was there even anything to tell? I didn't think so.

'Because it's not my business,' Gab implored, obviously struggling with the pressure I was piling on. 'I want to tell you though, Chris, honestly, because I need to offload it, it's pretty messed up.'

'Talk to me,' I said, genuine seriousness in my voice. We stopped walking and looked at each other. I hoped that my eyes showed Gab she could trust me. She knew she could... she always had.

'Fine. But you don't breathe a word to anyone. Least of all Vicky. She'd be furious, and *so* embarrassed.'

'My lips are sealed,' I agreed as we commenced walking again.

Gab sighed deeply and began recounting the tale that Vicky had shared with her. 'She's been seeing this bloke, evidently quite a bit older than us.'

'Hm,' I murmured, already not liking where this was going.

'Nothing too serious, she says, just playing around. She slept with him, which she seemed to enjoy, and he bought her nice things.'

'Sounds dodgy already,' I grumbled.

'I know, but she's a clever girl and she knew full well what she was doing. I guess she was just going along for the ride.'

'Literally.'

Gab threw me daggers, glaring at me harshly. 'If you can't be serious, I'm not telling you anything else.'

'Sorry,' I smiled, amused by my own joke. 'Sorry, I'll be sensible.'

Gab was quiet for a moment before she continued. 'Anyway, she decided she'd had enough of him and broke it off. That was the night before the party. But then, towards the end of the party, he texts her and says he's outside.'

'So it was someone we know? Who was at the party?'

'No idea, I don't think either of us remembers much from that night.'

'You can say that again,' I agreed, barely managing to piece together the memories of vomiting on Mr Arnold's shoes.

'Whether we met or not, it doesn't matter and I doubt we'd remember. But he turned up and persuaded her to go back to his after the party. She went along, they had a good time, then she told him she wanted to leave and didn't want anything else to do with him.'

'I don't really like where this is going.'

'No, I didn't either, but she kept telling me.' Gab's speech had become erratic, and there was a darkness to it. She had been really affected by the story, I could tell. 'He obviously wasn't happy about this…'

'Sounds like a prick.'

'By the sounds of it, he is. Anyway, he wasn't happy and said if she stayed for a few days he'd buy her some presents - a new computer, jewellery, all that sort of stuff.'

'So?'

'So she hung around for that night and the next day then tried to leave again. That's when he became angry. That's when he started hurting her.'

'Shit,' I whispered, as we reached Beggar Home Lane.

Gab nodded. 'It gets worse. He started beating her up and... doing other things that she didn't want.'

'Fucking hell,' I breathed, not wanting to hear the end, yet absorbed by the story.

'So he beat her, but cleverly, so that he didn't leave lots of bruises. He held her down or pulled her hair or something like that. Then he went away and locked her in the house.'

I didn't say anything, too horrified to speak, numbed by the story.

'When he eventually comes back, he seems like a changed person, acting all nice and wanting to hug her and kiss her.'

'Bastard,' I murmured.

Gab nodded. 'Exactly. Anyway, he said he would let her go and she didn't have to see him again, but if she told anyone about it or reported him to the police, he had friends that would kill her and her parents.'

'Bloody hell Gab, this is messed up!'

'I know!' Gab exclaimed. For the first time, I noticed tears trickling down her face. Telling me Vicky's trauma had been considerably painful for her.

'So she told all this to Ms Dooley? Surely she's going to do something?'

'There's not much she can do. She won't say who it is. Won't identify the guy. She's scared he'll make good on his threat.'

'He won't be able to if he's arrested!'

'Didn't you listen, Chris? He said he had *friends* who would kill for him. How the hell can she stop that?'

'Surely he's making that up? A scare tactic? People don't really have friends who would kill people for them.'

'Have you listened to the story? This guy's a psycho! If anyone's going to have killer friends, it'd be him.'

Initially, I didn't reply, overloaded by the story. Then, 'So what did Ms Dooley say?'

'She said she'd report it to the safeguarding lead at school, but said it would be difficult to do much without Vicky identifying the guy. But she's scared shitless, Chris. She's not going to say anything. It took most of today to get the story out of her.'

As we walked past the skip and turned onto our road, thoughts of the window fogged into my mind, trying to distract me from Vicky's horrendous tale. I quickly pushed away these thoughts, trying to forget the window in which I was imagining things.

'We've got to help her,' I murmured, absently.

'How?'

'I have no idea. But I don't like this story… especially not when loads of girls have gone missing from Grand Parade over the last few years.'

Gab gasped. 'I never thought of that.'

'What if it's this perv who's been taking them?'

My sister didn't speak for a few moments as we neared our house. She paused at the end of our driveway, looking at me. 'We've got to find out who this is, Chris. He might be the one terrorising the whole town.'

'This is a dangerous road to go down,' I pointed out, darkly.

'I know. But someone's got to go down it.'

I nodded in acceptance, realising that my life was about to get a whole lot more complicated.

FIFTEEN

VICKY'S STORY had shaken me to my core, and what was even more concerning was that I was about to get neck-deep in a whole lot more trouble. Gab was on the warpath... she wanted to track down whoever this bastard was and read him the riot act - or worse. And I couldn't let my sister do it alone. We were a team, whether I liked it or not. But where we were going to start was anyone's guess.

'Let's think about what we know.' Gab and I were sat in the garden that same evening. It was surprisingly mild and as far out of my Dad's way as humanly possible.

'Not much,' I said, unhelpfully, absently staring towards the cold frame in the corner of the flowerbed. The window... it seemed to glisten in the fading light of day.

'We know Vicky has been seeing someone, probably a moderately well-off bloke quite a bit older than us.'

'And she won't tell us who it is. That would make this whole situation much easier.'

Gab carried on as if she hadn't heard me. 'He's probably decent looking, knowing what Vicky is like. She wouldn't go for an ugly old sap.'

'She got off with Callum Hall a few months ago,' I pointed out, referring to a lad in the sixth form at St Josephs who suffered atrociously from acne.

'I'm pretty sure she was pissed and she only pulled him,' Gab snapped. Apparently, I wasn't allowed to disagree with her train of thought. 'Regardless, we know we're looking for a rich, good-looking bloke from around Grand Parade.'

'Can't be too many knocking around this shithole,' I admitted.

'Exactly.' Gab sat quietly for a minute, looking out into the garden, pondering. 'I'm thinking about what you said,' she murmured, quietly.

'What I said? How kind.'

A glare indicated that my sarcasm was less than appreciated. 'About the other girls going missing.'

'Oh yeah.' I didn't really want to reflect on the point I'd made. It wasn't the cheeriest of subjects.

'Molly Atkinson last year… Ellie James this year. No one knows what happened to them. We just assume they got drunk and fell into the river. That's what the grown-ups tell us.'

'It's not an unrealistic assumption,' I pointed out. 'Plenty of people that live in York have fallen in the river. Bloody hell, it floods the place a few times a year. And most of the cheap bars are somewhere near it. Loads of students have drowned after a few pints.'

'I know, but we're high school kids. If we drink, we're at someone's house or in the park. Grand Parade isn't as close to the river. These girls would have had to go on a decent trek to get anywhere near it.'

'What about Paul?' I asked, my mind suddenly flickering to my still-absent friend.

'Paul?'

'Paul Thornton. You know, he comes to parties and knocks around with me occasionally.'

'What about him?'

'He's still missing. He has been for a few weeks.'

'I don't think it's connected,' Gab dismissed me. 'We're talking about a pervy old bloke who's making girls disappear.'

'He could be batting for the other side as well. Wouldn't be that unusual.'

Gab shook her head. 'I doubt Paul's connected to this. He'll just be on a bender somewhere.'

'It's been two weeks, Gab. That's a hell of a bender.'

'Still, it doesn't make sense.'

'Why not?'

'It just doesn't!' Gab shouted. I backed off. I could see on her face that she was struggling with our discussion. Gab was good friends with Vicky, and she'd got on well with Ellie James. There was a sadness in her heart, I could tell. And it wasn't only about her friends disappearing and being hurt... it was much more than that. Gab was a headstrong, stubborn, independent woman. Even at sixteen, she saw the patriarchy and despised it. She hated misogynists. The idea of an older man taking advantage of and abusing young girls... it made her blood boil. I wasn't too thrilled about the idea either.

And underneath all of that, underneath the bravado and determination and stubbornness, I knew my sister well enough to realise that things went much deeper than that. She was upset and angry but more importantly, she was scared. Fear was driving my sister more than anything, as she dove deeper into her suspicions of a wealthy, powerful predator coming after young girls. She was scared for herself. And I knew, above anything, that was why we needed to do something. Obviously, I was going to help her. I loved Gab more than anyone, and I wasn't going to abandon her.

'So we think Ellie and Molly might be connected to whoever this bloke is,' I eventually summarised, inspiring Gab back to her suspicions. 'Maybe he had a thing with them, broke it off, but it went wrong, just like it would have if Vicky hadn't got herself out.'

Gab nodded, heartened by my encouragement. 'Exactly. They can't all have disappeared into the river and never been found.'

'So how do we track this guy down? Do you think Vicky'll tell us anything else?'

'No,' Gab mumbled, quietly. 'No, I don't think she will. She's too scared. But we could talk to some of the others from the party. See if they saw anything.'

'Everyone was pretty pissed.'

'I know... but all we need is for one person to remember seeing him. He'd have been the only person there that wasn't a teenager. Surely someone saw him.'

'It's worth a try,' I shrugged, finding my eyes drawn over to the window again. I closed my eyes and shook my head, determined not to look at the glass in which I was certain I could see colours dancing. Luckily, Gab wasn't looking at me and didn't notice.

Gab nodded, edified by my agreement. 'You speak with Adam and John. They were there for most of the party. I'll speak to Lucy and Meg tomorrow, and see if we can get anything out of them.'

'And if no one remembers anything?'

'Someone will. I'm sure of it.'

SIXTEEN

GAB WENT INSIDE after a while leaving me alone in the garden. Like an addict, I couldn't take my eyes away from the infernal window that formed the roof of the cold frame.

It's a load of bollocks, I thought furiously. *Victorian streets? Visions of the past? Bullshit. No such thing.*

Naturally, I found myself knelt before the box again as the sun continued to set. Gardening gloves on, I lifted the lid and poked around at my ailing vegetable seedlings. I poured a little water over them and made sure I was happy with the soil, all the while thinking of what would happen when I closed the box this time.

I took a deep breath as that moment arrived. Cautiously and painfully slowly, I reached out and pulled the window towards me on its hinges, bringing it down over the soil and closing the cold frame.

I yelped, jumping out of my skin, shocked and scared by what I saw.

The image was as clear as day. There was no delicate gloss to the picture, no transparency or reflection. No, this time, it was a clear, solid image.

Before me, a living room was presented. It was filthy. Magazines, newspapers and empty food and drink cartons littered the floor. Two large moth-eaten sofas sported piles of miscellaneous objects, including dozens of pairs of glasses, boxes of medication, television remotes, DVD boxes, books and photo frames. For the first time since I had seen things in the window, a sense of smell was associated with the pictures. It *wasn't* pleasant. It was a rank smell, moist and dirty, laced with shit and urine. A tangy metallic taste filled my mouth as if trickles of blood were seeping from my gums. The images were all-encompassing and overwhelming. They were invading every fibre of my being, dragging me into the alternative reality before me.

And there, nestled in the corner of the scene before me was a human being.

The woman sat on one of the sofas, surrounded by a diversified collection of items. She was hunched over, her back bent out of shape by an ageing scoliosis. Her waxy-coloured skin was wrinkled and dry, clinging hopelessly to her osteoporotic bones. Her breathing was laboured and frequent, her thin, grey-white hair swinging back and forwards as her frail body made its respiratory effort.

My eyes were transfixed, staring at this harrowing excuse for a human being, dying slowly amongst her collection of useless paraphernalia.

Suddenly, her chin tilted upwards and eyes, devoid of life and soul, glared up at me, bearing into my very consciousness. I shrieked, throwing myself away from the window and onto my back. I hit the ground hard, the air knocked out of my lungs. Gazing up at the sky, I coughed quietly, trying to breathe deeply and calm my racing heart.

If I'd ever doubted seeing things in that window, it was over now. I *knew* what I had seen. This was no vision or figment of my imagination. This window could see things. It could bloody see things.

I gasped in the air greedily before sitting myself up again and returning to the window. To my surprise, there was still an image present, but it was completely different.

Once again, I was looking at a street. Beggar Home Lane to be precise. I recognised it immediately. And it certainly wasn't from Victorian England.

This was the present day.

I recognised the houses and cars that I walked past every day on the way to school. I could even identify one or two of the local residents, walking the street and going about their business. It seemed to depict rush hour - maybe 8 am or 5 pm, when children made their way to school and adults dragged themselves off to work. The odd car drove quietly down the residential street, careful to avoid any children wandering across the road on their daily school run.

Then I saw it.

The red car.

There was a flash of movement across the road before me. The entire image sped up. Cars and people moved increasingly quickly. The light began to fade and I realised I was looking at the afternoon rush as evening began to set in on the scene before me.

Everything happened so fast.

The red car rushed down the street. I could see people gesturing rudely. I heard faint shouts surrounding my head. For a moment I was tempted to look around and see who was shouting... was it the image, or was it real life? I could barely tell, but I knew I couldn't look away as the tableau played out before me.

An involuntary cry left my mouth as I saw a familiar brown bundle run across the road... *Tigger*... and a bright red little car slam into the mass of fur as the pictures spun before me and started to turn black. I was shouting, feeling sick and faint all at the same time, my entire being submerged in the disturbing images before me.

Then I was on my back again, staring up at the sky, bellowing into nothingness, confused and scared and angry and exhausted.

'What the *fuck* is wrong with you?'

Reality crashed into me like the slam of the red car's door as my father's cruel voice invaded my senses and the world stopped spinning. Suddenly, I was back. The sky had turned a deep blue scarred with amber as the sun finished setting. I dragged oxygen into my lungs and forced myself to sit up, looking as far away from the window as I could and into my Dad's judgemental eyes.

He looked unusually sober, despite the pint-sized tinny in his hand.

'You having a fit or what?' He spat, indifferently.

'I...' I stammered, trying to think of what to say.

'Fucking hell, I raised a retard,' he grumbled, turning on his heels and heading back into the house.

'I was upset my plants weren't growing!' I blurted out. An excuse was probably unnecessary now, as Dad had clearly lost interest in my antics, but I couldn't stop myself. I *had* to drag myself back to reality. Shouting an excuse seemed the natural next step.

Dad turned slowly, an incredulous look on his face, which quickly turned to contempt. In a mocking tone, he imitated me: 'My plants aren't growing? Wah, wah, WAH. What a pussy. I didn't know I'd raised a retard *and* a pussy.'

'Thanks, Dad,' I responded, my sarcasm coming back into play as I came to my senses. 'That means a lot.'

'Huh,' Dad grunted. Then, under his breath, 'scrote.'

'Dickhead,' I murmured.

'The *fuck* did you just say?' Len Keeler span on the spot, rounding on me. I scrambled to my feet, standing my ground.

'Nothing,' I grumbled, pathetically.

'That's what I thought.' Dad's face was within inches of mine. I could smell from his breath that he'd drunk considerably more than one pint can. 'Remember your place, boy.' With that, he walked away, clearly choosing not to fight an unnecessary battle with me. 'If your mother gives a shit, tell her I've gone to the Homestead for the quiz.'

'They do a pub quiz at the Homestead?' I asked, genuinely impressed.

'Obviously. It's a pub.'

'And who the hell do you have on your team?' As far as I was aware, my father wasn't exactly the social type.

'You don't need a bloody team. I can win on my own. Hundred-pound bar tab for the winner.'

'Let's hope you lose.'

Dad turned his face and glared at me, malice in his eyes. 'For your sake, boy, you'd better hope I don't.'

SEVENTEEN

LOOKING BACK, I wish he'd won that bloody quiz. It would have caused a lot less mess if he had.

Whilst Dad was at the pub quiz, almost completely by accident, I got to work on Gab's assignment to question Adam and John. Soon after my encounter with my father, I received a text from Adam to say he had the new Call of Duty game and wanted me to come around and shoot a few terrorists with him. As a sixteen-year-old lad barely interested in school, I had nothing better to do with my evening, so happily accepted the invitation. It would take my mind off all the bizarre shit going on around me, and give me the chance to have a deep chat with Adam, as per Gab's instructions.

I returned to the house to find my Mum bent over the cooker, stirring some pasta. There was a half-empty bottle of wine on the sideboard alongside a near-empty glass.

'Do you want some tea, love?' Mum asked, not looking at me. She was hunched over and tired-looking.

'Thanks, Mum, but I'm good. I'm going to pop out to Adam's for a few hours.'

Mum merely nodded, still not looking at me. Her posture suggested that her balance wasn't perfect that evening.

'Are you okay?' I asked, mildly concerned by my Mum's indifferent behaviour.

'Fine, son, fine. Go see your friend.'

Nothing more was said. Slowly, I left the room, taking a long moment to catch the side of my Mum's face. There were dark bags under her eyes. Silent tears ran down a cheek, where a fresh bruise was displayed.

'Mum, your face…' I began.

'Bloody hell Chris, go out! Go see your friends! You'll be much better with them than with your wreck of a mother!' She was facing me now. I feigned calm despite my insides roaring in surprise as I saw the marks of Len Keeler's fists all over her face and neck. 'And don't look at my face!' She continued, striding towards me aggressively. I slowly backed away. 'My face is none of your *fucking* business!'

The moment I stepped backwards into the hallway, Mum slammed the kitchen door in my face. Wow. I'd never heard her use language like that. My Dad really was a bastard. He ripped apart and ruined even the most kind-hearted and caring people. I tried to ignore the rage bubbling up inside me at the sight of my Mum's bruised face.

At some point that day I think I probably realised that my life was spiralling wildly out of control. Obviously, I notice that only now, looking back, thinking about where I've ended up. But I'm pretty sure it was then, as I embarked on some half-arsed mission to track down missing children and I became acutely aware that Dad was knocking seven bells out of my mother on a semi-regular basis.

But, kids are resilient. I managed to push my fears and despairs away and focus on going to see my mate, Adam, have a few tins and play on the Playstation until we were bored… which would probably be in the early hours of the next morning.

'Alright lad?' Adam greeted me as I arrived at his house. It was only a ten-minute walk from mine, just at the other end of Beggar Home.

'Hi mate,' I mumbled, following Adam into his house. I waved vaguely at my friend's parents as he led me into the kitchen.

'We'll nick a few of these,' Adam whispered, picking out a six-pack of cheap supermarket lager from the fridge. He held them behind his back and sidestepped back through the house, past his parents, whose eyes remained glued to the television, uninterested in the two boys behind them and their underage drinking.

For the next few hours, I sat quite happily sipping the substandard beer and mashing the buttons of my game console controller. We didn't speak much, apart from to compliment or criticise each other's performance. Most of what we said included expletives, so I'll leave it out. We've had enough of them in here.

After we'd finished our three tins each and successfully pummelled each other in an every-man-for-himself death match (played online alongside some international gamers, leading to several slightly racist insults), we decided to take a break. I waited whilst Adam went to try and liberate a few more beverages from his parent's supply. I wasn't disappointed when he came back a few minutes later with a couple of bottles of Carling.

'Thanks,' I muttered, popping the cap off my bottle by using a spoon as a lever. 'Let me ask you a question, Ads.' I was going straight in with it. Gab would be proud. I was a quality detective. And also a little pissed.

'Whatever you like, mate,' Adam slurred a little, relaxing back on his desk chair, his Playstation controller falling onto the ground.

Good, I thought. *He's a bit drunk too. I'll get some honest answers from him.*

'That party the other week,' I began, 'At Vicky's…'

'Absolute quality mate,' Adam grinned, swigging his beer. 'Shagged Lucy, didn't I?'

'Yeah, I know.' I sighed inwardly. Adam was anything but modest.

'Honestly mate, have you seen her tits?' He proceeded to pull out his phone and show me a practically pornographic picture that he had somehow obtained of Lucy.

I looked away, trying not to be distracted. 'That's great mate.'

Adam scoffed. 'Bloody hell, you gay or something? Have you seen them?' He shoved the phone in my face.

'Yeah, they're great mate, well done.'

Adam sneered at me but put his phone away. I tried to get on to the matter at hand. 'Bit weird about Vicky isn't it?'

'Shagging that loser from Year 10? Yeah, absolutely, frigging stupid if you ask me.'

'No mate, about her disappearing.'

'Oh…' Adam looked a little confused as the conversation was finally steered away from sex. 'Yeah, fucking weird.'

'Apparently, she's been going out with some older guy,' I said, trying to sound casual.

'Frigging perv,' Adam belched.

'Yeah, I know.' I paused. Then: 'Did you see anything before she disappeared?' I was asking pretty directly, I knew that. Luckily, Adam didn't seem perturbed.

'Nah mate, but I got her phone didn't I?'

'What?' I didn't understand.

'She ran off at the end of the party, mate. Before she disappeared. Left her phone at home, didn't she?'

'Seriously?'

'Yeah. I had a good look mate. Got some quality shit on there, did I tell you that?'

'What do you mean?'

Adam leant forward, grinning mischievously. 'Nudes mate. Nudes of herself she was sending to someone. Absolute quality mate.'

'I thought you were with Lucy?'

'A man can window-shop!' Adam laughed, revealing just how much of a prick my friend actually was.

'Who was she sending them to?' I asked, trying to keep on topic.

'No idea, lad. She was texting them to someone called Key I think.'

'Key?'

'Like key in a lock,' Adam explained, clearly proud of his intelligent simile.

'Weird.'

'I know mate. But bloody hell, if you thought Lucy's tits were good, these were on another level, I mean…'

'Do you still have that phone?' I interrupted, trying to keep Adam on topic. This information was the only lead we had - I *had* to follow this path further.

'Course not mate, I didn't steal it did I?'

I gave Adam a questioning look.

'Bloody hell mate, I'm not a thief! I just had a little look.' He winked at me. I cringed inwardly. 'No lad, I left the phone at Vicky's house. I'm not going to frigging nick it, am I? Just satisfying my curiosity. I mean honestly, mate, those pics…'

'I've got to get home mate, but thanks for the beer and the game.' I'd heard enough. I was more than happy to run off and avoid any more of Adam's horrendously misogynistic comments. I was a teenage boy just as much as him, and wouldn't mind having sex if the opportunity arose. But I wasn't particularly comfortable with him going over the intricate details of Lucy and Vicky's breasts, especially when he shouldn't have seen Vicky's. Call me traditional, but I wasn't a fan of my so-called friend referring to women as nothing more than trophies he could sleep with.

Anyway, I'd got what I needed.

Key. Whoever Key was, he was the next part of the puzzle. Gab would want to know. Gab would know what to do next… I hoped.

Who the hell was called "Key" anyhow? Sounded like a bloody ridiculous name. But it was a start. And whether I liked it or not, I was beginning down a road that would only lead to darker and darker places…

EIGHTEEN

DAD CAME last in the pub quiz. *Last.* Apparently, I discovered from an onlooker at the Homestead a few days later, he'd got so pissed that he could barely sit up straight let alone write answers down. A few helpful patrons of the pub helped carry Len home, where he got to work terrorising the house.

After stumbling in about half an hour before I got home, he smashed the frosted glass of the front door when he slammed it far too violently. When Mum complained, she got an unapologetic, unbelievably fierce beating, leading to her fleeing upstairs. Gab (who told me all of this the next morning, having watched the events from the landing), remained locked in her room, not making a sound, praying she would avoid her father's wrath. Most uncharacteristically for her, she didn't even go to check on Mum, clearly too scared to venture out of the safety of her room.

I came home to a bomb site.

The house had been upended. Chairs lay in pieces, pictures had been ripped from the wall and broken kitchen crockery littered every surface I could see. A few bloodstains could be seen on the stairs carpet. From the garden, I could hear a ruckus.

Cautiously, I meandered my way through the wreckage of the

house and into the kitchen. More destruction revealed that my father had tried his best to ruin every aspect of the house. One of the cabinets was on the floor and the fridge door lay ajar, letting out a fine beam of light, spilt milk and broken eggs leaking onto the ground. Two empty cans of Stella could be seen on what was left of the sideboard.

I continued my journey into the garden.

There, I found the monster that was my father.

He was in a white-hot rage, his body possessed by an anger so deep and feral that the idea of reasoning with him was absolutely unthinkable. Baseball bat in hand, the drunken beast had driven holes into the garden fence, smashed the windows that looked into the lounge and ripped up whichever flower bed he had come across. Seeing the melee weapon he wielded, I was unsurprised at how he had caused such damage to the house's interior.

Suddenly he saw me. Instantly, he stopped.

I immediately sobered up.

Len Keeler's eyes showed nothing but pure loathing. I was *not* in a good situation…

'There's the little pussy,' my Dad hissed, slurring his words, advancing towards me with his baseball bat primed. I began to back up.

'Dad…' I stammered, ice-cold fear gripping me, choking me, overwhelming me.

'You little piece of *shit*,' he spat, as his proximity to me approached touching distance. The smell of him was repugnant, a mixture of sweat and blood and booze. 'I *fucking lost* because of you.'

'How the hell did I make you lose?' I retorted. Bad move. Why the hell did I challenge him?!

'Little bastard!' He roared, swinging the baseball bat down towards me. I deftly ducked and stepped to the right, leaving his baseball bat to bury itself in the glass of the kitchen door behind me. A cacophony of shattering glass assaulted my senses as I dived out of the way (somehow, maybe intentionally, towards the cold frame and my window… *my* window). From high up in the house, I heard a woman shriek - my Mum or Gab, or both? I couldn't tell.

Dad appeared momentarily disorientated, before spinning around and honing in on my location. His confused face and uneven pupils still managed to focus on my terrified form as I began to back up across the garden.

'You little dirty waste of breath,' my father murmured, quickly advancing on me. He raised his bat again. Once again, I dived away, shielding my face as I felt the rush of the baseball bat flying past me.

A sickening crack echoed around the garden. I looked to my left, back to where I had jumped from, to see my Dad's weapon lodged in the edge of the cold frame.

The window... No!

As if bewitched by the mysterious window and possessed by its will, I dived towards my father, tackling him to the ground. The baseball bat went flying, clattering onto the concrete ground at the other end of the garden. I held my Dad to the floor with strength I didn't know I had.

'Leave my fucking window alone!' I yelled, elbowing him harshly in the face.

Len Keeler roared in frustration, his rage bursting from his very being. He tried to push me off, but somehow I continued to hold the considerably bigger man down.

'Leave me alone!' I then shouted, speaking with courage I never knew I had.

'Little pussy wanting to protect his shitty little flowers!' My Dad mocked, the stench of his breath almost enough to knock me out.

'Go to hell!' I roared. Barely aware of my actions, I punched my Dad hard in the face. Immediately, he went limp and his body stopped struggling against mine.

I rolled off him and lay on the grass, panting heavily. Staring up at the stars above, I wiped blood from my mouth - somehow I'd split my lip - and sucked in oxygen gratefully. I turned to look at my father.

He was still breathing - thank God. There was a thin trickle of blood coming from his temple, and his face looked uneven like he'd had a stroke - although I suspected this was more the effects of the alcohol. But he was breathing. Just out cold.

I pulled myself unsteadily to my feet. Before me, the remains of the cold frame lay. Somehow, miraculously, the window remained unscathed, although its hinges had given way during my father's assault. Gingerly, I reached down and picked up the window. Its hinges came away easily and I had no trouble lifting it into the air, leaving the rest of the cold frame behind in the wreckage, just like my father.

I stared at the window before me. The clear panes of glass showed nothing but the night sky above. Why had I been so desperate to save it? Had I really become obsessed with a piece of old wood and a bit of glass, that I had convinced myself had supernatural powers?

The answer was yes.

Moments later, Beggar Home Lane appeared before me once again. I continued to hold the window in the air, high above me, staring at the glass, now alive with movement and colour.

The image was familiar but zoomed in. The clarity was better than it ever had been. There was no transparency or tinge to it. It was a full, high-definition image, bursting with colour.

And it was on a loop.

The loop was nothing more than a few seconds of familiar footage, but it was enough. A brown bundle, smaller and faster than a human darted across the road in painfully slow motion. Residents shouted in protest and stuck their fingers up rudely at a car speeding along the road. The familiar red car bounded forward, a characteristic little light flashing on the dashboard. Its journey collided with the path of the little bundle of fur.

I watched in horror as Tigger was murdered by the little red car before my very eyes. And I knew what I had to do next.

Without any further thought, I put the window under my arm and carried it inside, leaving my unconscious father alone in the garden with the destroyed cold frame - a fresh reminder that our family was nothing more than a broken group of people, barely staying alive under Len Keeler's reign of terror.

NINETEEN

I IGNORED the wreckage of the house the next morning. Mum hadn't surfaced, so we assumed that she remained barricaded in the relative safety of her bedroom. Dad was nowhere to be found. All that remained was the havoc he had wreaked last night.

Carefully stepping over the shattered glass and other debris littering the floors of the house, Gab and I silently made ourselves some breakfast and slipped out of the family home as quickly as possible.

What an absolute mess of a family. Both of us were shaken, exhausted and pretty terrified, but somehow, over the years, we had grown accustomed to such behaviour. Len Keeler often went on a rampage like this. Noticeably, however, his behaviour had become increasingly more extreme over the past few months, culminating in last night's episode. Last night was the worst ever, no doubt about it.

We walked in silence for a few minutes as we headed along the familiar route to school. As we turned onto Beggar Home Lane, I was about to update Gab about Adam's revelation, and the fact that we were looking for someone called "Key". Unfortunately, my update was put on hold.

There he was.

My mind flashed once again to the images I had seen in my window (now safely stowed under my bed, covered by a sheet). The little red car... the flash that had once been Tigger. Recent memories then resurfaced, as I remembered my encounter with the arrogant prick who owned the car, not much older than me, who had challenged myself and the builder.

And that arrogant little bastard was walking down his driveway, towards his red car.

'Oi!' I shouted, barely aware of what I was doing, possessed by rage and driven by knowledge I shouldn't have been privy to.

The lad looked up at me as he approached his car. His face wore a look of self-entitled contempt. *"Why are you bothering me?"* His expression seemed to shout, laced with pride.

'Oi, you!' I repeated, crossing the road, and heading straight for the boy. He was maybe 18, probably quite a new driver. He had left one of the nicer houses on the road (probably one of the nicer houses in Grand Parade), which immediately made me dislike him. The rich of Grand Parade hated the working class, and, naturally, the working class *really* hated them.

'The hell do you want?' The boy spat, unlocking his car, and making an obvious effort to ignore me.

'You're the little shit that ran over my cat!' I roared, not caring that I was drawing attention from a few passers-by.

'Chris!' Gab shouted in protest, chasing after me. What she said didn't matter. I could barely hear her over the blood rushing through my head.

'Piss off, kid,' the boy responded, laughing as he opened his car door. In the back of my mind, I noticed a tiny flashing camera on his dashboard. 'Stop chatting shit.'

That was it. I saw red. In an instant, all of the aggression and hatred and stress of the last few weeks hit me like a sledgehammer. Images of Tigger's mangled body, my Mum's bruised face and my Dad's unconscious form on the grass slammed into me like a car crash of its own. I felt dizzy, blood pulsing through my head relentlessly.

The window. I need the window. It has all the answers. All the knowledge…

The old woman's face I had seen through the glass appeared in my consciousness, shaking her head disapprovingly, filling me with a sense of dread and fear and hopelessness.

Make him bleed.

It was Gab who described the events of the next few seconds to me that afternoon. Looking back, I can barely remember what happened. It was a blur. But this is how she tells it…

I grabbed the boy by the scruff of his t-shirt and slammed him into the side of his pathetic little car. He roared in protest as I pushed my weight up against him and forced him into the side of the tiny vehicle with as much force as I could muster.

Then my fist took over.

I sent a turbo-charged right hook into the side of the boy's face, releasing a cry of shock from his mouth and a spray of blood into the air. His form crumpled before me as he collapsed sideways onto his knees. Next thing, I was kicking him harshly in his gut, once, twice, three times…

A set of arms enveloped my body and pulled me away.

Gab was screaming.

A small crowd had formed around the commotion. A primal scream left my lips, although I could barely hear it. A hatred unlike anything I had ever known pulsed through me, a force which I had no idea how to control.

Suddenly, I was free… the strong arms surrounding me had evaporated, giving me my only chance of escape. Still mostly unaware of my actions, driven by an impossible fury, I ran to the skip across the road, where construction on the old lady's house was still underway. *The house with the window… my window.*

The next thing I knew, a brick was in my hand.

Then the brick was in the air.

Finally, it was through the window of the small red car.

Shouts of protest and distress echoed around the street as a gentler pair of arms grabbed me and began to pull me away. I heard Gab's voice whisper 'Let's go,' and I was off, dragged away from the bedlam I had created, shaking uncontrollably as wrath and adrenaline coursed through my body, obliterating my senses and overwhelming every instinct.

TWENTY

GAB DECIDED we weren't going to school. Fair enough, considering everything that was going on, and the fact that I'd decided to start World War Three in the middle of the street. Instead, we took a long walk into the city centre and got ourselves a takeaway coffee. We barely spoke on the journey. Once we'd got the coffee, we made our way down to the river, where we found a quiet bench away from the hustle and bustle of York.

Finally, quieter and calmer, with a cup of warm coffee in my hand and the cool breeze of the spring morning washing over me, we began to talk.

'What the *hell* was all that about?' Gab eventually asked. 'Why on earth did you think he killed Tigger?'

I waited before answering, trying to come up with a way to not sound crazy. I failed. 'I just knew, Gab.'

'What does that mean?'

'I just… I *knew* he did. Him and his little red car.'

'How?'

I hesitated. *The window.* 'I saw scratches on the front. Like he'd bashed into something. It was Tigger he ran into.'

'How do you know that? He could have scratched his car a million different ways! And last time I checked, cars are pretty solid and cats are pretty soft. I don't think Tigger would have even made a dent in his car.'

I couldn't argue with the logic, so nodded in sad acceptance. I wasn't going to be able to explain this to her. Not without coming clean about the window.

'He was driving like a prick the other week though.'

'And?'

'He nearly ran me over!'

'Doesn't mean he ran the frigging cat over. Bloody hell Chris, you *assaulted* him! And vandalised his car! You did all that because you have a hunch he ran over Tigger.'

'It's not just a hunch alright!' I shouted, finally breaking. Tears streamed down my eyes. 'I *know* it was him. I can't tell you how, but I know it.'

Gab looked at me with concern in her eyes. 'You can't tell me? Chris, you tell me pretty much everything... why won't you tell me this?'

I shook my head, crying silently. I looked down at my hands, the knuckles of my right hand bruised and cut in places. The events of the last hour washed over me. It was like I had been possessed - like the window had taken ownership of me. I felt like it had controlled my actions, or at least influenced them. It was overpowering me, owning me, speaking to me...

What *was* it?

Gab didn't press me any more. She sat quietly, looking at the river, flowing powerfully. The grass beneath our feet was stained yellow, a sign of the river recently breaking its banks, as was commonplace in York. Floods were something we all got used to around here. Just like Len Keeler being drunk or the window giving me visions. Everything was just a part of life.

'Where the hell were you last night, anyway?'

'I went to Adam's.'

'Oh really?' Gab was now giving me her full attention again. Typical. 'Get anything good?'

I was grateful for the change in subject, so I relayed my conversation with Adam back to her, skipping the bits of discussion that focused on Adam's thorough knowledge of our classmates' breasts. Gab listened with interest, before sitting quietly as I concluded my tale.

'Key?' She eventually asked.

I nodded. 'Key.'

'Who the hell is called Key?'

'Well, I assume it isn't their full name.'

'No shit, Sherlock.' Gab wasn't in the mood for sarcasm. 'Key…' she mused quietly. 'Sounds like a nickname. Something someone picks up at uni or something like that.'

'What do you mean?'

'You know, stories people tell from university. "Oh, Alan lost his room key every week, so he got called Key and it stuck", something like that. Sam Wallace from our school who went to uni last year ended up in an ambulance after drinking too much on his first night. Ever since he's been called "Sambulance".'

'Hilarious,' I grumbled, slightly jealous of my sister's superior knowledge of university and all things cool.

'Key…' she murmured to herself again. 'That's a weird one though.'

We sat quietly again for a while, drinking the rest of our coffees. The odd jogger and dog-walker wandered nearby, paying no heed to the fact that two schoolchildren sat in the middle of the day, still in their uniforms, quite clearly practising truancy.

'Did you stay hidden from Dad the whole of last night?' I tentatively asked, aware that it might be a sensitive subject for Gab.

My twin shrugged, feigning indifference. 'He got home absolutely rat-arsed, as usual, shouting that he'd lost the pub quiz and it was you who was responsible.'

'Naturally.'

Gab continued to speak as if she didn't care, but I could hear the note of fear and sadness in her voice. 'He rampaged around the house, smashing a few glasses and plates, then shouted something about wrecking your flowerbed.'

'He actually said flowerbed?'

'No, he said "stupid fucking gay garden box."'

'Charming.'

'Indeed,' Gab agreed, still looking out at the river. 'Anyway, next thing we knew he'd got a baseball bat from the garage and was heading to the garden. He shoved Mum out of the way and smashed a few things in the kitchen. She protested, got a beating and ran away. I tried to go after her, but she locked herself in the bedroom. I haven't seen her since.'

'He was still running around the garden when I got home. He tried to baseball bat my cold frame to death. So I knocked him out.'

'Ha!' Gab laughed, patting me on my shoulder. 'You knocked him out? Well done, bro.'

'He's getting too much. I don't know how much more Mum can take. I don't know how much more *I* can take.'

Gab shrugged, again pretending not to care. 'It'll be alright. Lots of families in Grand Parade are like ours.'

'Not this bad though.'

Gab said nothing. I knew she understood. We both did.

'What's so special about your bloody cold frame anyway?' Gab asked, suddenly.

I chuckled. 'You wouldn't understand.'

'Try me.'

I couldn't tell her. She would think I was mad. And was I ready to share the window yet? It was *mine*. Only I knew about it… its secrets… its power…

Bloody hell, I sounded like something from Lord of the Rings. I had to tell her. Right then, in that moment I knew, this would only get worse if I didn't share it with Gab.

'It's a long story…'

TWENTY-ONE

AS WAS typical for Gabrielle Keeler, she didn't make any comments initially. In general, apart from being a borderline 16-year-old alcoholic (as we all were), she was a sensible girl. She listened carefully and attentively, saying nothing, simply staring out at the waters.

I told her everything. I started by saying how I'd seen a reflection and thought it was my own. Then I went on to the vision of the street I later identified as Beggar Home Lane, and how this image kept recurring, in several different periods. I talked about the Victorian street, the little red car and the fur ball I just *knew* was Tigger. I told her about the woman I had seen, hoarding rubbish, who had *looked* at me, right at me. I told her about my separate encounter with the red car driver, how he had nearly run me down and how a builder had come to my defence. And I confessed how I realised I was becoming obsessed with the window, almost ruled by it, and that my actions this morning were nothing if not a result of the window taking some form of control over me.

Gab remained quiet throughout my whole tale, only taking an audibly sharp intake of breath when I mentioned the woman turning her gaze directly to me. After I had finished, gasping for breath myself after spilling what felt like my soul to my sister, I waited quietly for her response.

It didn't come for several minutes. Instead, the pair of us continued to watch the world go by. A few more dog walkers sidled past and a couple of recreational kayaks and canoes glided across the river before us. Finally, she uttered two words. 'Show me.'

I didn't hesitate, least of all because it was starting to rain. Walking with an increasing sense of urgency, the pair of us made our way hurriedly back home. Even our walk through Beggar Home Lane was quick, Gab refusing to even acknowledge that this was the very place the window had continually shown me.

It was just before lunchtime when we arrived home. To our surprise, Mum was up and about, moving quietly around the house. It looked considerably better than it had this morning. The destroyed pieces of home decor and kitchen crockery had been removed, a hoover had been set to task and the specks of blood that had dirtied the walls were gone. Holes in the broken windows were boarded up. Mum herself was in the kitchen, sitting at the table, absently watching the news playing on the small television on the counter.

'Mum?' I asked, cautiously. I hadn't seen her since our fiery encounter the previous evening. She looked a lot worse. Her eyes were tired and new bruises were evident on her face, neck and arms.

Mum looked up at us, as if in a trance. It was as if she took a moment to register that we were home. 'Shouldn't...' she paused, looking confused. 'Shouldn't you both be at school?'

'We were pretty shaken up after last night, you know, with Dad and all,' Gab interjected before I could get a word in.

Mum seemed to take this as a good enough reason and gave a half-hearted nod. She didn't mind our truancy. Her gaze returned to the television.

'Are you okay?' Gab enquired.

Our Mum's face slowly turned from the TV once again and looked at us. Her eyes looked empty. There was a sadness and regret there that I hadn't seen before.

'I don't think any of us are, Gabrielle, not anymore. I don't know what we're going to do.'

Mum's words were terrifying. As long as I had known her, she had been a stoic, indifferent woman, immune to Len Keeler's increasingly dramatic and abusive antics. Now… it was almost as if she was broken. She had had enough. She was done. Where that left us… I didn't want to think.

'I didn't know Paul was missing,' Mum murmured, motioning at the news report playing in front of her, changing the subject dramatically.

I followed her stare to the TV screen, where I saw photos of several young people, all of whom were familiar to me. Molly Atkinson, Laurie Openshaw, Ellie James, Paul Thornton and even Vicky (whose photo had the addendum "*found*" underneath) had appeared on the screen, joining the long list of people who had gone missing from Grand Parade over the last few years. A tight knot formed in my stomach when I realised the gravity of the situation. A sinking feeling descended over me even more as I appreciated how most of the pictures in front of me represented individuals from my very school.

'Yeah,' I mumbled, drawn into a trancelike state by the television. 'Yeah, for a few weeks now. I hoped he would have turned up by now.'

'They never seem to,' Mum responded blankly, leaving a foreboding undertone in the kitchen.

'Have you seen Dad?' I asked, more for my own safety than anything. I didn't imagine my punch to the face had gone down well.

My Mum shook her head. 'No, darling.' Her voice was almost dreamlike. It was as if she wasn't there. 'No, but I'm sure he'll turn up. He always does.' There was a dark undertone to her voice, as if foreshadowing a further onslaught that we should be prepared for.

Neither Gab nor I had anything further to say, so we made our way upstairs in order for me to show my sister the fabled window.

'I've never seen her like that,' Gab whispered, speaking to me for the first time since we'd sat at the river. 'Maybe you're right… I don't know if she can take much more.'

'What can we do?' I asked, equally concerned. 'If she was ever going to leave Dad or kick him out, she would have done it years ago. He's been a prick as long as we've been around.'

'Sometimes, when you love someone, it never goes away, no matter how horrible they are to you.'

'Well, it should. How she loves that bastard is beyond me.'

'Do you not love him?' Gab asked as we reached my bedroom.

'Absolutely not. He's an abusive arsehole.'

'But he's our Dad!' Gab exclaimed in a hushed tone.

'You're telling me you do love him?' I responded incredulously.

'Maybe... I don't know. Family is complicated.' She looked abashed and confused.

'No, Gab,' I said, as we entered my room to see the window. 'Family isn't complicated. Dad's a prick. He doesn't deserve our love.'

TWENTY-TWO

I HAD STORED the window under my bed, wrapped in an old bedsheet. With trepidation, I delicately pulled it out from its hiding place and moved it to the middle of my bedroom floor, between myself and Gab. I didn't unwrap it.

'It's big,' Gab whispered, looking at the rectangular shape underneath the sheet.

I began to pull back the sheet and show her the window. As the first pane was revealed, I felt a twinge of sadness to see the tiny crack had widened, clearly a scar of last night's conflict. I paused. I felt confused. Did I want to share this with Gab? A secret that had been exclusively mine? An artefact that was nothing if not *magic*?

'Chris?'

Gab's voice seemed to come from the end of a tunnel. It echoed around my subconscious, feebly attempting to break into my thoughts.

'I...'

'Give it here,' Gab snapped. I felt her reach for the sheet and I threw my arms out to stop her. She recoiled slightly, glaring at me. 'What are you doing?'

'I... I don't know if I can show you,' I whispered, tears forming in my eyes for reasons I didn't quite understand.

'Piss off, let me look.'

With that, Gab ripped the sheet away. I cringed. It felt like ripping off a plaster. For a moment, I couldn't breathe. All of a sudden, my secret was exposed. The window was out in the open. Someone else was looking.

As my mind somersaulted through umpteen emotions, I was barely aware of the window, or the fact that Gab was staring at it, slack-jawed, entranced. Finally, as I managed to breathe again and come to terms with the fact that Gab was now fully my partner in whatever venture this was, I followed her eyes to the panes of glass.

My heart seemed to skip a beat as I saw a familiar image in front of me.

It was the old woman again, surrounded by her hoards of useless appurtenances. The scene seemed different to last time... there was less colour. A dullness seemed to emanate from the whole window, filling my soul with a sense of sadness and tiredness and... frailty. It was more zoomed in. I could see the woman's face more clearly. Wrinkles formed deep canyons in the taut skin of her face. The outline of her jawbone was prominent, and what little hair she had left was sticking out at odd angles, unkempt and greasy.

And she was looking right at us.

Her eyes seemed devoid of life... deep dark pits of soulless despair, where all hope and promise were eaten up and obliterated. It was like looking into the eyes of death.

With a sickeningly cerebral sense of horror, I noticed the woman's hand was now raised and her fingers were extending, flexing, then extending again. She was... beckoning us. She could *see* us. It was a two-way window. She was calling for us, dragging us in, sucking away our lives and souls and pulling us into the deepest recesses of her being...

'Holy shit!' Gab yelled, mercifully breaking the spell. Both of us flung ourselves backwards, landing harshly on the old worn carpet of my bedroom. As I had on the grass last night, I lay on my back, panting heavily, unable to quite believe what was going on.

We both lay on opposite sides of the window for a few minutes, gasping for breath. Luckily, Mum hadn't reacted to Gab's shouting -

not that I imagine she would have done much, in her current state. So we remained undisturbed. Finally, Gab sat up and, seeing this, I did the same.

Neither of us looked at the window immediately. We were looking at each other. Gab's face was white, colour and life drained from it, mimicking the old woman in the window.

'Holy shit,' she repeated, her words coming out as a whispering rasp. 'That was Old Lady Lilly.'

'What?' I coughed in disbelief.

'Old Lady Lilly,' Gab repeated, still greedily gasping for breath. 'The old bat who used to live on Beggar Home. The one whose house is being done up. The one...'

'Who had this window,' I breathed. I could barely believe it... the woman who had lived in the house with this very window was appearing in it. What the hell did it mean? What was going on? 'Did you feel it?' I whispered, afraid of the answer.

'The drag?' Gab responded. 'Like she was trying to pull us in? Call to us?'

'Yeah,' I said softly. It hadn't been a pleasant experience.

'What happens,' Gab continued slowly, 'if we touch the glass when we see the image?'

'What do you mean?' The idea of putting my hand on the image had never occurred to me - I had always been too hypnotised.

'If we touch it, do we... connect? I mean, it felt like she was connecting with *us*.'

'I don't know if I want to find out,' I confessed, more than a bit scared at the prospect of connecting further with Old Lady Lilly.

Gab moved back towards the window, preparing to look once again. 'What if we-'

'Gab,' I interrupted. 'Be careful.'

My sister nodded, giving me a weak smile. 'Always am.'

With my heart still pounding in my chest at what felt like a million beats a minute, we both looked into the glass once again. Amazingly, the image had changed.

This time, it was one I hadn't seen before. Yes, it was Beggar Home Lane, (as it always was, except when Old Lady Lilly made an appearance), but it was dark and dismal. The street was deserted. Rain crashed down in torrents. The sound of an oncoming storm could be heard rumbling in the background. I didn't have to turn and look through my own bedroom window to know that we were currently experiencing a very fair day weather-wise. This soundtrack could *only* be coming from the window before me.

A sickening coldness washed over me, as if the image before us was creating a tiny weather system. I knew Gab could feel it too - she shivered. Was it rainwater I could feel on my forehead or sweat? It was impossible to tell.

Then there was movement.

Someone ran down the street, past the little red car parked in its usual spot, the tiny light flashing on its dash as usual. The images played for us in slow motion, enough for us to see details. The runner was male, around my height and build. His hood was falling back off his head as he ran through the inclement weather. An overwhelming sense of terror seized me in an instant. I knew immediately that it was a personification of the scene before me.

The runner's hood finally fell back and I let out a quiet shout, aghast.

It was Paul. My friend, Paul Thornton, who should have been in detention with me a few weeks ago, after he had drawn an anatomically incorrect version of the external male genitalia on the desk in Spanish class. Without a shadow of a doubt, I knew that the images we were seeing had taken place after that afternoon. How I knew, I couldn't explain, but I just *knew*.

Then we saw why Paul was running.

Bringing up the rear, dressed completely in black, hood covering their entire head and facial features was Paul's pursuer. Someone was chasing him. The terror Paul felt was true and real and being reflected *into* us. I watched with a morbid fascination, begging the images to stop, yet transfixed by their horrific revelations.

The image seemed to speed up as Paul's pursuer closed the distance between them. Moments later, Paul was on the ground, the chaser tackling him expertly and holding him down.

I yelped again, completely flooded by sensory overload. My head recoiled, looking up at Gab for a moment, equally transfixed and horrified by the images before her.

Suddenly, the window went black, before returning to its normal, slightly murky glass. The images were gone, but the reality of them was deeply seated in our hearts.

I stared at the window, then at my sister in awe. She returned the stare.

'Well,' she gasped, for once lost for words. 'That was interesting.'

TWENTY-THREE

BOTH OF US were sufficiently overwhelmed to write off the rest of the day. After our encounter with the window, Gab retreated to her room, uncharacteristically speechless. After she had left, I sat for several minutes before re-covering the window in the old bedsheet and pushing it back under the bed. Then, I lay myself down, stared up at the ceiling for a while and closed my eyes. I was exhausted and shell-shocked. I had no idea how to respond to what I had seen. What was I supposed to do next? And what the hell had happened to poor Paul?

I must have dozed off into a fitful sleep, images of Paul being chased playing over and over in my head. Initially, it was the same image I had seen in the mirror, then it developed to Paul being chased by monsters, lions, demons, and anything my sick mind could imagine. It made the memory even more terrifying.

When my eyes flickered open, the daylight was fading. A noise was rousing me.

A knock on my door...

Dad stepped in.

He looked like shit, his face untidy and unshaven. His hair was stuck up on end, demonstrating how thin and wispy it had become.

Above his right eye, a nasty-looking laceration could be seen, likely caused by my vicious retaliation in the garden last night.

I braced myself for the inevitable beating I was about to receive. Terrifyingly, however, Dad simply smiled.

'I need your help, boy. Got a new project. Get off your arse and come help me.'

His voice was even and calm. There was no anger or hatred there. There was very little indication that he even remembered the events of last night. Had he genuinely forgotten, or just chosen not to acknowledge the atrocious way in which he had behaved? Me getting knocked into next week as revenge for inflicting the impressive gash to his forward seemed an unlikely possibility.

Gingerly, I got up from my bed and followed my father. Even when he was in a relatively good mood, you'd be foolish to disobey him. That certainly wouldn't have gone down well.

The house looked considerably better than it had done this morning. Somebody - presumably Mum - had done a quality job of tidying, fixing broken things and throwing away the rubble of last night's debacle. Everything appeared almost as good as new, if not a little more shabby than normal.

I saw Mum herself sitting in the lounge, absently flicking through television channels. I caught a glimpse of another news report on missing kids in the local area - the story that never seemed to go away.

'Your uncle's over,' Dad grumbled as we made it to the garage.

'Uncle Nev?' I asked, not expecting an answer. Of course it would be Nev. Dad's brother was an equally unsuccessful but slightly more sober version of the man himself. Nev occasionally popped in to see Dad, usually for the two to have a few beers before the pair disappeared off somewhere for the evening. If Dad was mid-woodwork project, Nev would lend a hand (and a critical opinion). As always in our household, when Dad was doing a project, nothing else mattered and the entire world revolved around the work going on inside our house's meagre garage.

Lo and behold, Uncle Nev was sitting in the garage, playing on his old-school Nokia phone, making his way through his second tin of lager (I said he was a slightly more sober version, but he was not *completely* sober). 'Alright little lad!' Nev shouted as he saw me enter. 'How's my favourite nephew?'

Even though Uncle Nev, like Dad, was a bit of a knob, and he only had *one* nephew (thus making me the favourite by default), he was always very pleasant towards Gab, Mum and myself. He seemed to enjoy seeing us and didn't have a default setting turned on to treat us like shit.

'Hi Uncle Nev,' I grumbled, meeting his embrace as he stood to meet me.

'Your Dad tells me you've become quite the carpenter here in his workshop. I wanted to see what you can do!'

Dad threw me an indifferent glance and beckoned me over to his workbench. Unlike our last project, I wasn't offered a beer. I didn't fancy one anyway.

'We're making a storage container for the garden,' Dad huffed, indicating the assortment of random pieces of wood scattered around the workplace. 'A big box to store garden tools, flowerpots, maybe some compost, you know.'

I nodded absently. My Dad was a bizarre man. He had spells of obsession with the garden, dreaming up grand ideas of objects he wanted to build to improve how our outdoor space looked or grow plants more efficiently. He gardened once a year if we were lucky, and usually smashed up his outdoor creations in a fit of drunken rage, as had been demonstrated the previous night. I think he just liked building things. It took him back to his glory days when he was a doctor - when he had made something of himself. Once upon a time he could take out appendixes and fix broken hips. Now, the closest he got to that was screwing a few pieces of wood together to make a vaguely useful structure - I suppose it wasn't *too* different to orthopaedics.

Anyway, I humoured Dad, as I always did, and got to work. I held the planks of wood as instructed and applied pressure in the correct areas. I was even allowed to do some drilling and use the circular saw that evening - lucky me! Throughout the building process, Uncle Nev talked incessantly, as he always did.

'School going okay, Chris?'

'Yeah, it's alright,' I replied, glumly. I gave similarly half-arsed answers to most of his unrelenting questions, particularly the one about girlfriends. I cringed when questions about sex came up from my Uncle who had never had social boundaries, but luckily my father was too caught up in his work to notice my embarrassment and my hurried noncommittal answer.

Nev eventually launched into a rambling soliloquy about his ever-failing love life whilst Dad and I continued to work. The storage box was beginning to take shape and was massive. It measured about six feet in length by two feet wide and was probably a similar depth to width. Inside, storage compartments had been fitted, each with plenty of space for multiple trowels and other tools, watering cans, flowerpots and any other garden implements one may need. One particularly long compartment ran the entire length of the box and was about half a foot wide. This one, my Dad had promised, would be perfect for long spades, hoes, rakes, and other larger pieces of equipment.

As always, I didn't really care about what we had built. The only project of my Dad's I'd ever had an interest in was the window, hidden under my bed upstairs.

Uncle Nev continued his preamble as our building reached its final stages, constantly playing on his retro phone. From afar, I heard the doorbell ring and Mum answered it a few moments later.

The carpentry continued. Nev's voice droned on and on.

Mum entered the garage.

My Dad looked up in shock. Mum *never* came into the garage. It was Dad's space. Sacred. We all knew that. And today of all days, after the horrendous night we'd all experienced, you didn't want to disturb my father's holy of holies.

Mum looked white. Dad looked furious. Nev blurted out a greeting, citing how lovely it was to see his sister-in-law Karen.

'It's the police,' Mum whispered, her voice trembling. I looked at Dad, confused. Had he done something last night after he'd come round? Had he hurt someone? Did he…

'They want to see you, Chris,' Mum managed to say in a shaky tone.

I felt like a lead weight had been dropped on my shoulders. They wanted *me*?

Dad's face turned to meet mine, fury alight in his eyes.

'They…' Mum stammered. Tears were welling up in her eyes. 'They want to take you down to the station. I think they're arresting you.' My heart broke seeing her grief-stricken face. The words seemed to pour from her mouth agonisingly slowly.

I felt Dad's rough hand grab my arm and drag me close to his face. The stench of booze and filth emanated from his entire being. 'What the *fuck* have you done, boy?'

TWENTY-FOUR

I WENT DOWN to the station alone. As I left the house, Gab had appeared at the top of the stairs and looked worried sick. Mum was sobbing - no, wailing - in despair. Dad had a look in his eyes as if he was ready to kill, but Nev had managed to keep him in the garage and away from me.

A pleasant enough Police Officer called Fred introduced himself and told me I was under arrest for assault and destruction of property. I *knew* the events of that morning would come back to haunt me.

When Fred realised I was pretty resigned to my arrest and that I wasn't going to cause any trouble, he didn't even bother to handcuff me as he escorted me down to his police car. He read me my Rights and I settled down into the back of the car for the short journey down to Grand Parade local station. Throughout the journey, I exercised my right to remain silent. I'd watched enough crime films and TV shows to know that I shouldn't say anything without a lawyer present. How long that would last before I broke down was anyone's guess.

Being arrested is pretty bloody terrifying. It feels like your life is over and all control has been snatched away in an instant. That short car journey felt like hours, as my mind rushed through all I would now lose. If I went to prison, I'd waste years of my life. When I finally got out, I wouldn't be able to hold down a proper job. All my friends would have moved on and forgotten me. Dad might have beaten the shit out of Mum enough to kill her. I wouldn't get to see Gab...

I was in a daze as I was taken into the station. The world seemed to slow almost to a standstill. My very being was locked in a cocoon of terror and regret. Conscious thought evaded me. My legs moved by their own accord as I was guided down to an interview room.

The window came back into my mind. Paul. The old woman. The guy who had run over my cat.

And who the hell was Key?

For a while, everything was dark as my thoughts swirled around me. I lost all knowledge of where I was. Nothing made sense. For the first time in my sorry life - which had been pretty shitty, let's be honest - I actually didn't want to live. I didn't feel like there was anything I could live for anymore. It was almost as if...

'Kid, do you want something to eat? I promise, if you say yes we won't use it against you.'

There was a friendliness to the voice. It echoed into my psyche as if from the other side of the world through a tin can. It began to drag me back to reality.

'I get that this is scary, Chris, and we want to help you, but don't make this any more difficult than it needs to be. We've got much more important things to worry about than some teenage bust-up. Just talk to us.'

My vision began to sharpen and my senses slowly started returning to reality. I was in a cold, grey room, with a desk between me and a Policeman - Fred, the one who had picked me up. He had a friendly face and receding black hair with streaks of grey beginning to show. Multiple frown lines contoured his face, displaying a long history of intense police work.

'Do you want a sandwich and a coffee, lad? It'll make you feel better.'

Numbly, I managed to nod. 'Yes.' My voice was rasping, my throat dry and raw. 'Please. Thank you.'

Fred nodded with a brief smile and disappeared from the room. By the time he came back, I'd fully returned to my senses. Aside from my unrelenting fear, the main feeling I had was that of being cold. I hated being cold. The interview room was dingy and dank. It was a place that inspired hopelessness.

'Eat this, lad.' Fred placed a soggy-looking tuna sandwich in a plastic wrap before me, alongside a steaming paper cup. The coffee was cheap and bitter and the sandwich tasted like cardboard, but the combination seemed to help ground me and bring me back to reality.

After he was happy I'd sufficiently sorted myself out, Fred sat down opposite me on the other side of the interview table. He placed a file in front of him and opened it. Inside, I saw numerous documents and a few poor-quality photographs showing a little red car with a smashed window. Another photo showed a brick. A final one showed the slightly bruised face of the boy I had given a decent beating.

'Chris,' Fred began with a sigh, 'this is all something that can go away very easily, but we have to do it properly.' He paused and leant back in his chair. 'There isn't much point of you denying it, we've got multiple witnesses from the scene who describe an assailant matching your description. We've arrested you for assaulting this lad - Aiden Bennet, apparently - and smashing his car window.'

Still feeling slightly in a daze I nodded, glumly. There was no use in denying it. Even if I had a lawyer with me, it wasn't going to change the facts. I wasn't a liar. Barely aware I was saying it, I whispered: 'So I'm going to prison?'

Fred burst out laughing. It brought me back to reality even further. Why was he laughing?

'Prison? For this? Bloody hell, Chris, don't be ridiculous. Prisons are overcrowded as they are, and we're not going to shove you in there for some misdemeanour like this. Don't be stupid. The worst you're going to get is a fine and community service. You've got a decent record, never been in trouble before, and it sounds like you and this lad had a bit of beef anyway, is that right?'

'He ran over my cat,' I grumbled, knowing I had absolutely no proof of that.

'Wow,' Fred replied, raising his eyebrows. 'Are you sure?'

I nodded. 'I saw it,' I half-lied, 'but no one else did.' Then I remembered… 'And he nearly ran me over as well. He drives like a twat.'

Fred smiled in a friendly way. 'There are a lot of people who drive like twats,' he chuckled. 'At some point, he'll get caught by a speeding camera or British Transport Police. Unfortunately, until then, I can't tell him off just for driving like an idiot. Did he look like he hit your cat on purpose?'

I think Fred was humouring me to a degree, but I appreciated it. 'No,' I confessed, being honest about what I had seen, even if it was through the window. 'No, I think he was just driving too fast and my cat got in the way.'

Fred nodded again. 'Again, unfortunately, there is no crime there. That's an "understandable" accident.' He made an inverted commas sign with his hand as he said this. 'Aiden may drive poorly, but he's passed his test and hasn't done anything with malicious intent. Having met him, I understand why you beat him up. He gives off the air of being an arrogant little prick.'

I chuckled. I liked Fred. I felt like he was on my side... sort of.

'You'll need to attend a court date,' Fred went on, beginning to go through the file in front of him again. 'You'll see the judge and you can have a solicitor with you if you so wish. If I were you, I'd say exactly what you've said to me. Tell them you didn't like this guy because of his careless driving, your cat, etcetera. You got angry when you saw him, maybe he insulted you, all that. You've learnt from your mistakes, make a public apology, all should be fine. You'll end up with some community service, maybe a little fine.'

I nodded, glumly. Fred had helped me out a lot. I was grateful.

'Right,' Fred concluded. 'Now that's all done with, you can get home.'

I was taken aback. 'You're letting me go?' I whispered, incredulously.

Fred laughed heartily. 'What do you think, I'm going to chuck you in a cell to wait for the court date? Bollocks to that lad. You think I've got the room or the funding? Ha. You've got to cause much more of a stir than this to get locked up. I can tell you're a decent kid who's just made a mistake.' He paused and chuckled again. 'Anyone who can pick you up?'

'Shit,' I muttered, knowing that Mum would be too upset and Dad would kill me for even asking for a ride. 'I'll ring my Uncle Nev. He's over at the moment.'

'Great,' Fred smiled. 'I will just say though, Chris, that the conditions of your release include you making no contact - directly or indirectly - with the victim of your crime - this Aiden, whoever he is. If you do, that'll really muddy the waters.'

I nodded to show my understanding.

The radio on Fred's police vest crackled for a moment before a voice came through. 'Fred, the body's arrived if you want-'

Fred immediately silenced the radio, swearing quietly. 'Sorry Chris, you shouldn't have heard that.' He sighed, shaking his head. 'Do us a favour and don't mention it? For me?' He winked at me, and I gave him a grateful smile, silently promising my discretion.

The Police Officer hurriedly filled in a few forms and stood up to take his leave. 'One of my deputies will be out to help you with getting in touch with your Uncle. You'll get a letter through the post regarding your court date. And stay out of trouble in the meantime, Chris, I won't be this lenient if you end up back here.' There was sternness to his final words as he left the room.

TWENTY-FIVE

UNCLE NEV WAS MORE than understanding when he picked me up. Why he couldn't have been my Dad, I didn't know. He may have been a drunk like Dad (and considerably over the limit when he picked me up from the police station), but at least he was a pleasant drunk.

'I'd avoid your father, lad,' he said after he had finished feigning sobriety whilst getting me into the car. 'He'll knock the living shit out of you if he sees you.'

I nodded in agreement, before telling Nev how grateful I was for his help.

'Don't mention it, lad,' he replied, cheerily. 'Anything I can do to help. Is everything alright with you? You don't normally act out.'

'Actually…' I began. Should I tell him about Dad's abusive episodes getting more frequent and more extreme? He was so close with my Dad… and would he care? This was the rough end of York. It wasn't unusual for men to knock the shit out of their kids and wives. 'Actually, yeah, it's fine,' I eventually grumbled.

Nev threw me a suspicious glance. 'How did your Dad end up with that busted eyelid?' He asked. It was a leading question.

I shrugged. 'He was pissed last night. Probably got into a fight or something.'

'Hm,' came Nev's reply. No more was said. Could Nev be our saving grace? Someone I could confide in? He'd always been great with Gab, Mum and I. Could he rescue us? Or would he side with Dad?

'You've got my number, Chris,' Nev continued. 'You can always call me. If you're ever in trouble, balls deep, and you don't want your parents to know, I'm always here for you.'

'Thanks,' I muttered. I meant it. For a moment, I thought about spilling everything. The window, Vicky, Key (whoever the hell that was), my boxing matches with my father... everything. Then the moment passed. No. I couldn't tell Nev. Not yet, anyway. If things got worse... maybe. I had his number, didn't I? I could give him a call on his prehistoric Nokia. Whether he would believe half the stuff I wanted to tell him... that was a different matter.

The family tableau I came home to shocked me. I found all three of them - Mum, Dad and Gab - all sat in the lounge, watching TV. Mum ran to me as soon as I walked in, embraced me fiercely, and then slapped me hard, promising that if I *ever* got in trouble with the police again, she'd kill me herself. Regretful for being a bit harsh with her slap, she hugged and kissed me again, before returning to the sofa. Gab followed, giving me an awkward side hug. Dad glanced at me for less than a second.

'So the fuck-up returns,' he grumbled, returning his attention to the TV immediately. Nev shrugged at me. It was better than a beating, I supposed.

I sat myself down as far away from Dad as possible, near Gab. She didn't say anything but briefly squeezed my hand affectionately. Nev sat down next to Dad and helped himself to one of his six-packs of Stella on the floor.

The football match wound to a close and the ten o'clock news was set to follow it. As always, before the advert break, the newsreader came on with a preview of the evening's headlines. My heart leapt into my throat as I heard the night's top story.

'The remains of a body have been found in Grand Parade, York.

Police are yet to confirm the identity of the body but early sources suggest this could well be linked to the ongoing multiple cases of missing children and young people from this troubled area of Yorkshire.'

We all sat in silence whilst we awaited the proper news. As was typical of my father, he had dozed off in a drunken stupor as the adverts played. Not that he gave a shit about disappearing children. Nev, on the other hand, managed to stay awake and show an appropriate amount of interest in the news - but then, he was probably half a dozen cans behind my father that night.

The remains of a body. I promised Fred that I had never heard the mention of a body through his radio in the station. And I would keep the promise - I wouldn't breathe a word to anyone - apart from maybe Gab. But the body… the one that had probably arrived at the station at a similar time to me… a body that had been found in Grand Parade today… I didn't like this one bit.

The news started properly. The opening credits seemed to last for ages. I just wanted the bloody report! Dad remained asleep, snoring in the corner. Mum and Nev watched, half interested. Gab, like me, was transfixed on the screen.

'Hello and welcome to the news at ten,' the newsreader suddenly began, appearing on our screens. 'I'm Sophie Stark. Tonight on North Yorkshire News: police are investigating a body found near the shores of the River Ouse in Grand Parade. It is yet unconfirmed, but speculation links this body to the ongoing case of disappearing young people. Also tonight: campaigning continues in local elections across Yorkshire as voting day draws closer and closer, Hull and York Universities report further break-ins and thefts of educational equipment and the latest in the diesel CO_2 emissions scandal.'

The news report changed to a young man who gave a preview of what was coming up in sports news, including Leeds United's recent recurrent losses. My attention, however, was solely on the top story.

'Our top story tonight,' Sophie Stark resumed, as the camera moved back to her. 'Police have confirmed that a body has been found near the shores of the River Ouse near Toft Street in Grand Parade, York.'

I looked around my family. No one but Gab and I were paying attention.

'The body was found and called in by passers-by this morning and police immediately cordoned off the whole surrounding area.'

Dad's grunts interrupted the news as he stirred in his drunken state of unconsciousness.

'The body is currently in the possession of the police and medical examiner. The identity is yet to be confirmed, but we have preliminary police reports informing us that the body belongs to a female in her early twenties.'

Gab took a sharp intake of breath.

The news then played a video showing an eyewitness who had been walking their dog nearby. 'I didn't see much,' the man said, a thick Yorkshire accent making his words a little difficult to understand. 'Walking t'dog, then I sees this poor girl. Proper mess, like. Looked like she'd been underwater or summit. Dog didn't know what to do with herself!'

The screen flashed back to the reporter. 'We don't have any solid reports yet, but speculation and early police comments suggest that this discovery is being treated as suspicious.'

'No shit,' Gab mumbled under her breath.

'It is suspected that this could be the body of one of the many young women who have disappeared from Grand Parade over the past few years.'

Once again, the report cut to a different image, this time of a senior Police Officer - not Fred - giving an interview to the press.

'Obviously, as soon as we know any more, the public will be updated. Our medical examiners and forensics team are working on identifying the body and cause of death. We suspect this may be one of the missing women from Grand Parade. As her body was found near the river, there is a strong possibility of drowning. Quite when this took place is difficult to say, as we know it can take some time for a body to wash up out of the river. We urge all members of the public to be extra vigilant around the river, and, of course, if anyone has any information, we urge you to come forward immediately.'

Little more useful information was given, and my interest in the news immediately began to wane when the reporter moved on to local elections.

Around me, Dad was flat out, whilst Nev and Mum appeared to be in a world of their own. I looked to Gab, who looked shell-shocked by the news. We both knew this *had* to be one of the missing girls. The plot continued to thicken... disappearing kids, dark assailants chasing after them down Beggar Home Lane, a mysterious person called Key... and now a body in the river.

Something horrendous was going on and somehow, quite how we didn't know, but somehow... we were becoming more and more involved.

TWENTY-SIX

'WE'VE GOT to talk to Vicky,' Gab told me as we arrived at school.

'What do you mean?' I asked. Vicky, to be honest, had been the last thing on my mind. In the last 48 hours, I'd had a near-fatal fight with my father, beaten a bloke up (and smashed his car), been arrested by the police and discovered a body had been washed up worryingly near where I lived. My discovery that Vicky had been shagging a bloke called Key had fallen to the bottom of my priorities list and I didn't really see it as that important anymore.

'We've got to ask her about this bloke. This Key.'

'I don't think that'll go down well. You said it took all day for you to get very little out of her at the cathedral. We've got more important stuff to worry about, Gab.'

'Like what?'

'Oh, I don't know. Maybe the fact that Dad is one punch away from killing Mum, I got arrested, or that we've got a window under my bed that shows us the fucking past!'

Gab sighed. 'You're so overdramatic.'

I looked at her incredulously. 'You are joking, right?'

She didn't reply immediately as we filed into the crowd of pupils heading for morning registration. As the bustle and rush of students engulfed us, she looked me dead in the eye and said: 'I think it's all connected. Vicky. Key. The body they found. The window... all of it.' There was a look of fear in Gab's eyes that I didn't often see.

I was about to reply when a hefty grip took hold of my shoulder. I spun around to find myself face to face with Mr Arnold.

'Morning Chris,' he announced, cheerfully, steering me away from the crowd. 'We need to have a little chat in my office.'

Mr Arnold took me down to the senior leadership office, where we were met by my Head-of-Year, Mrs Taylor, and Ms Cross, who was my form tutor. Mr Arnold took a seat at his desk. I felt slightly surrounded as the three teachers looked at me.

'Chris, we're not here to tell you off, we just want to help.' It was Mrs Taylor that had started the discussion. I wasn't entirely sure what they were going on about. Was it about Dad? Had someone said something?

'We obviously find out when one of our pupils gets arrested,' Mrs Taylor went on. No luck here then. It was about my misdemeanours, not about the fact that my father was an abusive arsehole. 'We just want you to know that we will help in any way we can. You need to face the consequences of your actions, of course. But we want to help make sure this doesn't impact you going forward. Any form of criminal record or caution can, of course, influence your future career prospects, but there are lots of things we can do to help support you.'

I nodded, glumly, not particularly concerned about my future career prospects at this point. I was sixteen, who actually thinks about stuff like that at such an age? The irony of these thoughts, thinking back from where I am now...

'Is there anything we can do to help right now?' Mr Arnold took over. 'Do you need any help with particular subjects? Any help at home? Is everything okay at home?'

There was a knowledgable intonation to Mr Arnold's voice. Did he know what was going on? How my Dad was behaving? For a moment, I thought about sharing with the three teachers. I'd always been told these were adults I could trust. But if they didn't help... and it got back to Dad that I'd said something... that could be catastrophic. And were things really that bad? Grand Parade was known to be a shithole, with everyone abusing each other. It was probably pretty normal how my Dad behaved. I suppose in that very thought process, you can see just how messed up my perspective had become.

'No. It's fine. I just got angry at the guy. He...' I paused, thinking how silly the next sentence was. 'He ran over my cat. And nearly ran me over. I just lost my temper.'

Mr Arnold nodded, a concerned look still evident on his face. 'I'm glad you were able to admit it,' the Deputy Head said. 'It means you're starting to acknowledge your wrongdoing. It's the sort of attitude they'll like when you have your court date.'

'Just know if you need us, we're here Chris. You can always talk to us if you have any concerns or worries.' It was Ms Cross, my Form Tutor, who had spoken this time. I smiled at her, weakly. 'You can always speak to me in form time, or anytime I'm around. I've been teaching you a long time, Chris, you know we look after each other in our form.'

I didn't say anything, but nodded at Ms Cross, giving her a grateful smile.

'Can I go now?' I asked after a few moments of quiet.

Mr Arnold sighed. 'If you're sure there is nothing else you want to talk about, yes, you can get off to class. But any problems, my door is always open, Chris. As are Mrs Taylor's and Ms Cross'.'

'Thanks,' I grumbled, taking my leave. As I shut the door, I heard Mrs Taylor change the subject and paused to listen in.

'Mike, you're going to have to mention what the police discovered in assembly. It's more than likely it's one of the girls that came to this school.'

'I know, Jo, I will. It's just a bloody morbid thing to talk about in an assembly.'

I walked away, having heard enough. The thoughts of the dead body reported on the news last night returned to me. Gab and I had every right to be concerned - just like the teachers were saying, it probably *was* one of the girls who'd been missing for some time. Maybe Molly Atkinson. I hoped it wasn't Ellie James, the girl who had only been missing a few weeks - that would be a little too close to home. She was a classmate, a friend of Gab's. That would just be awful.

As I walked away from Mr Arnold's office and headed towards the classroom, I decided it had been the right idea not to tell the teachers about Dad's abuse. It wouldn't make a difference anyway. Teachers always said they would help but rarely did. It would only make things worse. The last thing we needed was for police and social services to get involved. That really *would* tip my mum over the edge.

Looking back now, I wonder how different my life would have been if I *had* said something to the teachers that morning. Would I still have ended up in this position?

I think there are watershed moments in our lives. Moments that will shape the path we walk down. Tiny decisions that, at the time, seem so insignificant, yet have drastic and cosmic impacts. Maybe one day you choose to turn left instead of right, and the entire trajectory of your life changes. In that moment, I chose not to tell my teachers - the responsible adults - about the abuse we were subjected to by my father.

It's weird. Generations have passed, wars have been waged, and I'm still standing, albeit, not where I anticipated I would be. But I look back to the events I write about, a whole lifetime ago, and ponder on just how different the course of my life would have been if I'd just told the teachers about my Dad in that one, watershed moment.

TWENTY-SEVEN

GAB HADN'T GOT anything out of Vicky, surprise surprise. She'd probably made matters worse if anything. The mere mention of Key to Vicky made her lose her shit. She went into a full-blown rage at Gab right in the middle of the canteen (she could have picked a more subtle place to question her, in my opinion), before descending into heart-broken sobs and running as far away from my sister as possible. So all in all, a fantastic performance from my twin.

Gab told me this whilst we walked home. As soon as we reached the house, she bounded upstairs, shouting a hurried hello to Mum, who mumbled a reply from somewhere in the kitchen. Fortunately, Dad was nowhere to be seen. Gab then proceeded to head into my bedroom.

'Just let yourself in,' I muttered sarcastically, as I joined her up there. I flung my school bag onto the floor and watched as she pulled the window out from its hiding spot under the bed. 'What are you doing?'

'We need to see it. It's going to tell us what to do next.' She spoke erratically, almost a little unhinged. I could hear the same obsession, the same draw to the window that I felt in my heart. What Gab was saying made no sense whatsoever - how could she know the window would show us what to do? And what were we even supposed to do? Had I been given some clandestine mission no one had told me about?

'What the hell do you mean?'

She pulled the window fully out onto the bedroom carpet, leaving the sheet over it for now. 'Think about it, Chris.'

'I'm thinking.'

Gab tutted and shook her head. 'You saw Beggar Home Lane. Then you saw the car. Then you saw Old Lady Lilly. It showed you how Tigger had died. It showed you something about Paul. It's drawn us in. It's telling us things we need to know. Don't you think that it's weird, with all these disappearing kids, on the same day they find a body washed up by the river, we see Paul being chased by someone? Paul who has *also* disappeared? The window is telling us stuff, Chris! It's trying to give us information. I don't know why or how or any of that shit! But we need to look. Maybe... maybe we can help.'

'Is this because Vicky wouldn't tell you about Key?'

'I think it's all connected, Chris. I reckon that whoever this Key is, he could be the one taking all these kids. Chasing them down, abusing them.'

'What would a sex pest want with a spotty teenage lad like Paul?'

Gab shrugged. 'People are into weird shit.'

My turn to shrug. 'I guess you're right.' Oddly, a lot of what Gab said was making sense. The window did seem to present itself to me as everything started to escalate with the disappearing kids and the craziness at school. Coincidentally, it seemed the abuse from my father had escalated at a similar time - maybe the window would show me how to get rid of my Dad once and for all... I chuckled to myself. *I should be so lucky.*

'Come on,' Gab implored, pulling back the sheet over the window.

I knelt next to her, looking into the glass. It seemed darker - murkier today than it had yesterday. Almost as if it had been smeared in dirt overnight.

Nothing was happening.

'Do you see anything?' Gab asked, impatiently, clearly not getting any images either.

'No,' I breathed, staring at the glass. This had happened before.

When the window was back in the garden, over that infernal cold frame, I had spent hours staring at it, wondering if I really had seen images. Since I had believed in it, though, images had appeared impossibly easily. Maybe that was it… maybe…

It sensed my doubt. I guess. Somehow? Possibly? If I was doubting what Gab was saying, that it *wanted* to show us stuff, so we could do something to help, then maybe it wouldn't give us anything. We had to *believe* in the window.

'It's me…' I whispered.

Gab looked at me. 'What?'

'It's me. It won't show us anything because…'

'Yes…' Gab urged.

'Because I don't believe in it. I don't believe what you're saying. That it's showing us things so that we can help. It knows I'm doubting.'

'Well, fucking believe then,' Gab hissed. 'You were the one who showed me this bloody thing. You've dragged *me* into it. The least you can do is trust me. You always have. We've always had each other's backs. That's unusual for sixteen-year-old twins, Chris. We're unique. We've never let each other down. Never.'

I closed my eyes, nodding, forcing myself to believe Gab. She was right. We'd never let each other down. We'd always been a team, whilst our mother and father failed at parenting on a daily basis. We were best mates. We were family. I *had* to trust Gab. I just had to.

'Thank you,' I heard her whisper. My eyes were still closed. But I knew something had appeared.

When I opened my eyes, I gazed upon a semi-familiar scene in the glass before me. Out of the corner of my eye, I saw Gab's mouth wide open, agape, once again enthralled by the majesty of the window's abilities.

We were looking directly into a living room. After a few moments, I realised it was the same living room where we had seen Old Lady Lilly. But now, the clutter and debris of old age and frailty had gone. Even the furniture had gone. We were looking at an empty room. Slowly, boxes seemed to materialise. Then tools and papers with huge drawings emerged into the image, forming from nothing but thin air.

Then walls were cracking... and collapsing. Sledgehammers moved around with construction workers as the room before us was obliterated. Finally, a figure appeared directly in front of the window, giving us both a fright. Our gasps were in sync as the figure seemed to adjust the edges around the window and began to move it from its position.

Then, in an instant, the image disappeared and the window immediately reverted to its dark, murky glass. The crack I had noticed in one of the corner panes seemed to have got bigger.

'What was that?' Gab breathed, still staring at the mysterious artefact before us.

'I guess...' I whispered, still trying to comprehend what we had seen. 'I guess it was the start of construction - the renovation they're doing to Old Lady Lilly's house. I think we just saw this window's last vision.'

'Does that mean it won't show us anymore?' Gab murmured, sounding rather scared by such a prospect.

I shook my head, knowing the answer even though I had no idea. 'No. It doesn't show us things in time order. I saw that Victorian scene after I'd seen modern-day images. And it showed me Tigger getting run over multiple times, in between lots of other images. No... I think it just shows us what we need to see and when.'

'It's doing something else,' Gab murmured, her voice little more than a ghostly whisper.

I followed her gaze once again to the window. Again, I couldn't help but notice the crack in the corner pane getting slightly larger like a dehiscent wound opening up more and more.

This time, the image was again of Beggar Home Lane. Like yesterday, it showed an image of nighttime. I wondered if we were about to see Paul again, running desperately away from his unknown assailant.

But no... we were privy to a whole new image.

This time, a girl walked along, her pace quickening with each step. Now and then she looked behind her, clearly running from someone. It was raining. She was sodden, her hair stuck to her face and neck. She wore tight-fitting jeans with holes around the knees and a loose-fitting top. A leather jacket topped off the outfit, doing little to protect her from the elements.

Whilst looking at the images we'd seen through the window, I had come to realise that it seemed to *choose* when to show us certain details clearly. Sometimes the images were ethereal, ghost-like, almost unreal. Sometimes, they were in brilliant, vibrant colours. Sometimes they were in slow motion, sometimes they were sped up. The window *chose* what to show us.

The detail we could both see there was fear. There was a primal terror in the girl's eyes. She was petrified beyond her wildest imagination. Every few moments, she stole another glance behind her… her pursuer was close.

I could feel her fear. Gab could too. Both of us were shaking, sweat pouring from our brows.

The girl stopped in the middle of the road. She was near the red car, still there, as always. The red light flashed on its dashboard.

The girl took a good look around. The street was deserted. Rain continued to pour in torrents. She knelt. Gab and I watched on, engrossed, horror-stricken. The girl's emotions poured into us… a gentle hurricane of unbridled panic.

Kneeling on the floor, the image seemed to slow down. She was moving something on the ground… a grate. A water drainage grate, where rainwater was flowing profusely. She reached into her pocket. From within it, she pulled a small, leather-bound notebook. Glancing around her again to check she was alone, she held the book over the grate.

She looked up, directly at us.

Gab shrieked. I nearly wet myself.

We saw her face. One that was vaguely familiar.

The notebook dropped into the grate.

And like that, it was over. The image was gone. Gab was crying. I wretched, feeling like I was going to vomit.

I think I blacked out for a moment then, the horrendous emotions of the poor girl fleeing from my body after they had captivated my soul.

TWENTY-EIGHT

DAD BEAT up my Mum proper bad that night. Gab and I had barely recovered from what we had seen in the window when we heard an almighty crash downstairs. We raced down to the kitchen to see what was going on. Mum was on the floor, her nose bleeding profusely. There was smashed glass all over the place. My Dad was swaying where he stood, shaking a little. Fresh vomit that I guessed belonged to him could be seen on the kitchen floor.

'Bloody hell,' I breathed as I watched my two parents. Never had I seen a more horrific scene. What we had just seen in the window paled in comparison to this. 'Dad…' I murmured, bravely stepping forwards. 'Just stop, leave her be.'

My Dad turned on me rapidly. Before I knew it, my back was against the wall. He approached with the ferocity of a ravenous lion, hatred shining in his eyes. I could smell the booze on him. It was rancid. Mixed in with it, I could smell some nasty chemical coming off his body - probably some other awful drug he had recklessly shoved into his body.

'Remember your place, boy,' he spat, blood-tinged saliva landing on my face. I held my ground. 'I am the boss of this house. You keep your fucking mouth shut.'

'Dad...'

It was Gab who courageously spoke up this time. 'Dad, just stop, I'll have to call the police.'

Gab probably shouldn't have said that. Len Keeler did not like being threatened. Slowly and menacingly, the beast that was my father turned on his heels and slowly began to prowl towards my sister. Gab cowered against the wall of the kitchen herself.

I saw red.

Just like when I'd attacked the boy with the red car, I lost control. I can't exactly remember what I screamed, but it was something along the lines of: 'Don't you touch her, you worthless piece of shit!'

Almost unaware of my actions once again, I jumped at my father, knocking him to his knees. With strength I was barely aware I had, I swung my knee around into his face. Dad roared like a wounded animal, swinging wildly at me with flailing limbs as he crumpled to the ground. I kicked him in the abdomen, hard, knocking the wind from his body. A stifled grunt and subsequent quiet confirmed that he was out - for a few minutes at least.

I ran to my Mum's aid, Gab getting over the shock of Dad nearly beating her to a pulp.

'Mum!' Was all I could manage as I knelt beside her. Her head and nose were both streaming with blood. Her eyes looked a little uneven and she appeared pretty dazed.

'Call the police,' I muttered to Gab as I tried to sit my Mum up. She grumbled in protest but eventually succeeded in sitting erect. Gab ran off to find her mobile phone.

How I wished I had asked for help at school. Maybe this could have all been prevented. Dad coming home pissed and beating the shit out of anybody or anything he could find had happened once too often. We needed help. This wasn't normal. And now, I was in no doubt that someone would have to help. Dad wouldn't be able to stop them once they saw this.

I heard our front door open.

'Gab?' I called. Had she got the police already? That was impossibly quick.

'Chris?'

It wasn't Gab's voice. It was Uncle Nev's. Thank goodness! Someone who could help.

My Dad's brother ran to the kitchen as I called for help, followed closely by Gab who was now on the phone to the police.

'Police and ambulance,' she announced, as the emergency services operator began to connect her call.

'Fucking hell,' Nev breathed as he saw the aftermath of Dad's most recent beating. 'What the hell happened here?' His eyes darted from my Dad's unconscious form to my increasingly drowsy Mum.

'He came home pissed or high or something again,' I panted, the adrenaline of the last few minutes rapidly draining from my body. 'This isn't the first time it's happened, Uncle Nev. It's just… never been this bad.'

My Uncle shook his head. 'Bloody hell, Len,' he murmured, looking at my Dad's supine form. He put a comforting hand on my shoulder. 'I'm sorry, lad,' he murmured, clearly at a loss of what to say or do.

We turned to Gab, who was now giving details of our address to the phone operator. 'Thanks,' she mumbled. 'No, we're safe for now. My Uncle is here. Yeah. Thanks.'

She disconnected the phone. 'The police will be here in a few minutes,' she announced.

'Good,' Nev murmured cautiously, looking at his unconscious brother on the floor. 'Come on, Karen.' He walked over and helped my Mum to her feet. Together, the pair began walking out of the kitchen, leaving my Dad alone on the cold floor. He was still breathing, thankfully, but a small pool of blood had formed around his head. Twice in one week, I'd knocked my Dad out…

The police arrived a few minutes later. They immediately declared that all of us needed checking out at the hospital (including Dad) and that he would be under arrest whilst he was a patient. We agreed. Gab and I got into the police car. Mum and Dad came behind in their separate ambulances. Nev completed the convoy alone in his old Ford Focus. Second day in a row I'd been in a police car… what a week I was having.

Once the Doctors had checked us over, they confirmed that me and Gab were, although a little shaken up, absolutely fine physically. Mum had a few nasty cuts and bruises along with a small bleed on the inside of her head, just on the outside of her brain. The Doctors said they wanted to observe her and maybe evacuate the bleed in surgery if it got any worse. So she was staying in.

Then came the debate of what would happen to Gab and I. We were technically minors, meaning we needed somewhere safe to stay. Thankfully, Uncle Nev agreed to temporarily care for us in our own home. As Nev was a close relative and much less likely to beat the living shit out of us, the hospital staff and police were more than happy for us to go home with him.

As for Dad, he was placed under arrest in a side room with two police officers. He was handcuffed to the bed, awaiting the results of a few scans before he could be formally taken to the police station.

We said a brief yet tearful goodbye to Mum before Uncle Nev drove us home. He instructed us to go straight up to bed and get some rest whilst he tidied up the mess of the house. Both of us were shaken to our cores, exhausted - both emotionally and physically - and heartbroken. We needed to sleep.

I lay on my bed, breathing heavily, looking up at the ceiling. *It's over.* I said it out loud. 'It's over.' My Dad's reign of terror was finished. He would be arrested and sent to jail for domestic abuse. Good riddance. That piece of shit deserved nothing more than to spend the rest of his days in a prison cell. It was done. He couldn't hurt us anymore.

I was mainly relieved but also terrified that my Mum wouldn't be okay. Hopefully, with Len Keeler gone, she might be able to get back to having a normal life. Maybe we could be a real, happy family. Just maybe.

I was so lost in my thoughts that I barely heard Gab sneak into my room. She had her pyjamas and a dressing gown on. She came and sat at the end of my bed. She didn't look at me or say anything. She just sat there. Was I supposed to say something comforting?

'It's over,' I murmured, echoing my inner thought process. 'He's gone. He won't bother us anymore.'

'I think it was Laurie.'

'What?' Was my sister in such a state after the night's events that she'd lost it?

'Laurie. Laurie Openshaw.'

'What are you talking about?'

'In the window. The girl. The one with the book.'

'Who the hell is Laurie Openshaw?'

'A girl who went missing a few years ago. I think we were about fourteen. She was a few years older than us. Went to Grand Parade High, down the street from our school.'

'Oh yeah.' It did ring a bell. And the face in the window had looked vaguely familiar. It would make sense. Not that it was my top priority tonight - my Dad had finally succeeded in putting my Mum in the hospital. He could have killed her. I didn't really care what the window had shown us.

But you do.

There it was. A voice in my head? The window talking to me? Gab bleeding into my subconscious? I had no idea. Even now, I don't fully understand it. I've had a lot of time to think about it, and never came up with a solution. But it was there. A single thought. Enough to remind me that the window had something it wanted us to do, if an inanimate object was capable of such thought.

Gab was grieving for Mum, and for Dad, and for all the awful shit we had gone through as a family. And I was too. But we still had a job to do, and maybe that job was exactly what we needed. We were resilient kids, I knew that much. Yet, to survive everything we had gone through, all the trauma, all the bullshit... we needed something to keep us afloat. And that something was right in front of us. Follow this bizarre trail of breadcrumbs, after the missing girls and Key and whatever the hell the window wanted to show us.

'We need to go and look for that notebook.' Once again, I was barely conscious of what I was saying.

Gab looked at me, her face laced with anxiety and anticipation. I noticed bags under her eyes. She was knackered. Despite all of this, I wasn't surprised when she said: 'Let's go now.'

TWENTY-NINE

IT WAS RAINING, exactly as it had been in the images we'd seen in the window.

We waited until the early hours, sitting awake in our bedrooms. Uncle Nev had come to check on us both before he retired to Mum and Dad's room, where I heard him putting on new bedsheets. He had been silent ever since, as if he wasn't there, fast asleep.

Silently, dressed in hoodies and tracksuit bottoms, we slipped out of the house, barely noticing how immaculately tidy Uncle Nev had left it. He was a good man, my Uncle. I wish my Mum had married him instead.

We jogged through the deserted streets, caring little for the rain that was pummelling down on our bodies. There was a cry of protest from my skin as it began to feel the icy bite of the springtime nocturnal downpour, but my mind pushed on.

We had a job to do.

It didn't take us long to make it to Beggar Home. It looked exactly as it had in the image. Dull, dismal, and, for the first time, noticeably full of dark mysteries. This was the street I had seen my cat die on. The street we had seen Paul running down, terrified. The street where Laurie had thrown away a notebook.

As we had agreed, we started our investigation standing directly outside Old Lady Lilly's previous residence. The skip was still there, now overflowing. From a glance, not a single light was on - even if the house now had inhabitants, they were sound asleep.

We tried to visualise the angle from which the window would have seen the images and stood for some time trying to work this out. Then, Gab remained in position by the skip, whilst I explored the other side of the road for any drainage grates. I couldn't help but notice the red car with masking tape over one window, where I'd thrown a brick through it. *Aiden Bennet, that little prick.*

In the end, we decided that only one grate could realistically be the one that Laurie had dropped the notebook in. I knelt next to it as Gab ran across the road to join me.

Similarly to how Laurie must have, we kept glancing around the deserted street, checking that we were still alone. No one. Not a soul. The rain continued to pelt down on our bodies as the world went on spinning silently around us.

The grate was loose. Of course it was. Without a word, we worked together to jimmy the grate up, pulling the old metal out of its hole with surprising ease. Within a few minutes, we had removed the grate. It was only about a foot by a foot-and-a-half in size, and not particularly heavy. Quietly, we lay it on the pavement next to us, careful not to cause a clang and wake any neighbours. Captain Knobhead (Aiden) wouldn't be far away, and I most certainly didn't want to encounter him at that point. I'd probably give him an even worse beating, the mood I was in.

So, without a huge amount of effort, we now had a hole in the ground before us, where we hoped to find the fabled notebook. Gab looked at me expectantly.

'What?' I whispered.

'Stick your head in.'

'Bugger off.'

'What do you mean?'

'You stick *your* head in Gab, this was your bloody idea.'

'It was both of our ideas.'

'Yes, but...'

'Just stick your head in,' Gab snapped. 'I'll hold on to you.'

'Cheers,' I grumbled sarcastically, accepting my fate. I lay flat on the soaking, freezing pavement, with my face and head looking down over the grate. I felt Gab grab my legs and hold on tight. Carefully, I eased myself forward and lowered my head into the hole before me.

It absolutely stank. A rife mixture of human excrement, dampness and animal shit assaulted my senses, making me gag. My eyes watered profusely. I swore loudly and tried to look around.

The shaft inside the grate was pretty small. To either side of me, a channel could be seen, where water collected by the grates ran down to a central collection point. It was only about two feet deep below the road level. A slow trickle of viscous-looking fluid ran down the channel, water mixed with the shit and filth of Beggar Home Lane's waste. Nothing particularly interesting could be seen.

'It's not here, Gab,' I shouted, trying to project my voice out of the hole. 'Nothing here apart from water and sewage. It must have been washed away when Laurie dropped it in.'

'I don't believe that,' came Gab's reply from somewhere above me. 'Why would the window have shown it to us if we weren't supposed to find the notebook?'

'Because it's a fucking stupid window and it wanted me to stick my head in a shitpipe?'

'Look harder!'

I sighed, resigning myself to my assignment. I felt Gab tap my arm and hand me her mobile phone with a light turned on at the back. 'Use this!' She called. It felt like she was miles away - a combination of being headfirst in a drainpipe and the ever-more intense rainfall.

Waving the phone light around furiously, I continued my desperate search. I disturbed a few rodents hiding a few feet down the tunnel, who hissed ferociously at me. I looked in detail at the crisp packets, plastic bottles and old condom wrappers littering the pipe. Nothing of any use.

Then, out of the corner of my eye… some paper.

I reached out, careful to avoid what I was pretty sure was a clump of faeces covered in (maybe human) hair. My hand closed on a damp clump of papers. I pulled at my discovery. It wouldn't budge.

'Have you got something?' Gab shouted down.

I didn't reply. I was too focused on what I was doing. I pulled harder. It still didn't move. It seemed to have moulded itself into the drainpipe, a mixture of dirt and grime holding it in place.

'Chris?' Gab called again.

'Shut up, Gab, I'm concentrating!'

She shut up.

I pulled again.

This time, I felt movement. My hands closed over what felt like the spine of a book. I pulled harder. More movement. One more pull...

I nearly dropped it as it suddenly came away from its resting place. I felt myself slip further into the pipe.

'Pull me out!' I shouted suddenly, holding on to my discovery for dear life.

I felt Gab's hand on the back of my jumper as she pulled me up. The front of my hoodie nearly choked me as I was wrenched back into reality.

Coughing and spluttering, my head and upper torso emerged from the grate. I rolled over, allowing the rain to wash over me, clinging on to the little wad of papers in my hand. I breathed heavily, greedily sucking air into my lungs. Escaping the smell of the pipe was a welcome relief.

Gab looked at me in shock. Carefully, I handed her what I had obtained. Only then did I feel able to sit up and look at it.

Both of us stared silently. What I had picked up was a tattered old notebook. One of the covers was missing, meaning some of the pages were ruined and completely unreadable. But, another cover was still attached. The book remained bound by the weakening spine. It was whole.

My heart leapt into my throat when I saw the initials L.O. on the cover.

L. O.

Laurie Openshaw.

Holy shit.

THIRTY

WE WERE SURPRISED to meet Uncle Nev as we returned to the house. He was sat at the bottom of the stairs, clearly aware of our absence and waiting for us. He was fully clothed and wide awake. Luckily, I'd shoved the notebook we'd found into the back of my trousers, meaning we were able to keep it well hidden.

'I was wondering when the pair of you would reappear,' Nev said, simply.

I wasn't entirely sure how to respond. Luckily, Gab was ready. 'We just needed some air, Uncle Nev. We're both pretty shook up after today.' She wasn't lying, to be fair.

Nev just nodded sadly. 'I get it, kids. No one your age - hell, any age - should have to go through what you two have. I'm so sorry that it got this bad.' He wasn't going to tell us off, that much was for certain. He stood up and began walking to the kitchen. 'Do the pair of you want anything?'

Reluctantly, we nodded, following him down the hallway. Nev had cleaned the kitchen up beautifully. You would never have known what had gone on in there just a few hours earlier.

We both sat down at the table whilst Nev boiled the kettle. I felt the notebook up against my bottom as I took a seat. It felt like it was burning a hole through my trousers. I was so desperate to see what was inside.

There will be time, Gab seemed to say silently through her eyes. She looked away from me and towards Uncle Nev, now pouring hot water into cups of instant hot chocolate. Without saying a word, he gave out the drinks and sat down at the table himself. He blew on his drink to cool it and then took a sip. I did the same. It was cheap hot chocolate but nice enough. There was a smoothness to it, soothing my soul.

'Why did you never tell me, you two?' Nev murmured, almost absently. 'Why didn't you tell me what was going on? I could have helped.'

Once again, I let Gab reply. She often took the lead in situations like this. 'It was never this bad. He's always been a miserable prick and a bit heavy-handed after a drink, but in the last few weeks it seems to have escalated.'

'How bad has his drinking been?' Nev asked.

'Bad,' I grumbled.

Nev looked at me expectantly.

'He's pissed more than he's sober,' I continued. 'I don't remember the last time I saw him without a drink.'

'He's come home and wrecked the house a few times recently?' Nev enquired.

'Yeah,' Gab confirmed, taking back control of the conversation. 'He came in and smashed up the garden after he lost a pub quiz. Then there was last night. But he's often not in. He just disappears off, probably to the pub or to find more shite to use in his woodwork shop.'

'So he's still building?' Nev replied, seeming surprised.

'Bloody loves it,' I muttered. 'It's the only thing that makes him happy.'

Nev nodded and didn't say anymore. The three of us sipped at our hot chocolates. They had cooled down a little and were slightly more enjoyable.

'What's going to happen?' I asked, after a few moments of quiet.

Nev sighed. 'I imagine your Dad won't get out of police custody any time soon. Once the hospital is happy, they'll discharge him into the police's care. He'll go to jail and wait for a trial I guess.'

'He has to go to prison,' Gab whispered, audibly distressed. 'He just *has* to.'

Nev nodded sadly. 'I know, Gab. Try not to think about it. I'm going to look after you. You and Chris and your Mum are my priority.'

'What about Mum?' I asked. 'Do you think she'll be okay?'

'A bleed on the brain is nothing to turn your nose up at,' Nev explained. 'It's a serious injury. But they're monitoring her, and they'll operate if she gets any worse. People recover. But she might need rehab - physically and mentally, after all the shit your father has put her through.' Nev clearly saw his words had saddened Gab and me, so he continued. 'I'm sure she will be okay though. Eventually. And until she is, I promise to look after you both.'

I forced a smile. I was grateful for Nev's care, but still heartbroken that it had got to this stage.

'You both have to be honest with me, though,' Nev murmured, his voice taking on a more serious tone. 'You have to tell me everything. What your Dad's done, what's been going on, how bad it's got, everything. I'll be asking, the police will be asking, and the courts will probably be asking. So you have to promise that you'll cooperate and tell the truth.'

Gab and I looked at each other, silently reminding ourselves of the window under my bed that was semi-controlling our lives. *That* was a secret we wouldn't be sharing.

Nev seemed to take our silence as an agreement to tell the truth and we spent the next few minutes quietly finishing our hot chocolate. Eventually, Nev announced he was going to bed. He hoped we would feel up to school tomorrow, he said, but understood if we needed some time.

Both Gab and I thanked him. It was genuine - we were grateful. He'd rescued us, in a sense. But there was so much more going on than Nev could know. Somehow, whilst our own world went to shit around us, we'd found ourselves caught in the depths of a plot, one that could lead us anywhere…

THIRTY-ONE

WE WAITED downstairs for about half an hour. Once we were sure that Nev was back in bed and unlikely to reappear, we took our opportunity to look at the notebook.

'Let's go in the garage,' Gab whispered. 'It's quiet there, he won't be able to hear us, but we'll hear if he comes down the stairs.'

I agreed but felt a little unsure about going into the garage. I was being stupid, I knew, but I hadn't been in there since the other night when I'd got arrested. That was when Dad was still here. It was always a bit disconcerting going into Dad's private space without him (unless we were stealing booze). Almost like there was a darkness at work there. Something that made you want to run from the room.

We settled at the workbench, lit dimly by the single lightbulb dangling down from the roof. Finally, with trembling fingers, I extracted the notebook from the back of my trousers and laid it on the workbench before us.

We stared at the book for a few moments. Now we could examine it more, and with a little more light (although not much more), we could see just what a mess the notebook was in. The missing back cover meant that nearly half of the pages had been soaked and ruined to the point of unreadable. Smeared ink seeped through the pages, obscuring any sense the pages had once held. The front cover, whilst still intact, was pretty ruined itself. The letters L.O. were only just visible - how we'd seen them in the relative dark of the street, I'll never know. As soon as we opened the front cover, the remains of the spine disintegrated with a quiet snap. Just like that, the book fell apart. The cover came away with the remnants of the spine and pages spilled out like blood from a wound. Carefully, Gab pulled the intact pages away.

The garage was silent. I was acutely aware of how loud my breathing was. I realised my heart was pounding, blood rushing to my head and throbbing painfully. I saw Gab's fingers tremble as she began to leaf through the pages.

'There's not much on these,' she whispered, her voice quivering. She was right. The first few pages held little of interest, aside from confirming who the book belonged to. Laurie had written her name several times in different fonts, maybe practising calligraphy or a signature. The text was still blurred and water-damaged, but at least it was partly readable.

Gab turned through a few more pages. Some were blank. Others had doodles of flowers or houses. A few more lists - maybe shopping lists or wish lists - an Amazon Kindle was mentioned on one page.

After poring through a few dozen pages, I began to lose hope. There wasn't much left of the notebook that hadn't been ruined by the contents of the drainpipe. Had all the important information been in those final, wrecked pages? And what important information was I expecting, anyway?

'Hang on,' Gab murmured, stopping her increasingly rapid page turns.

A date.

In the top right-hand corner of a sheet was a date and a single sentence.

15th Jan, 2010
Happy sweet sixteen!

Both of us held our breath as Gab turned to the next page. Then we gasped.

Finally, we'd found something.

Found this little book in my desk drawer - I've been wanting a diary anyway, and this is a nice notebook! Hello Diary! I want to write a little bit in my diary every day until I'm 18 because I have a lot I want to do before then! So, Diary, get ready to hear some great stories!

Over the next fifteen minutes, we read through about twenty pages of Laurie's writing. She regaled tales of her time at Grand Parade High and her journey to complete her bucket list. She managed to go and see Coldplay live, she did an all-nighter with some friends in the park, she attended Glastonbury festival, she swam in the river (successfully), and she drove a car without a licence.

'She had one hell of a year,' I muttered as the date moved towards her 17th birthday.

'Better than mine,' Gab replied, glumly. 'Hang on…'

A page had caught her interest. It started with an underlined title next to the date:

14th Nov, 2010
<u>Losing the big V!</u>

'What's the big V?' I asked, genuinely unsure.

'Don't be an idiot,' Gab dismissed me. Apparently, it was something I should have known. The subsequent diary entry, thankfully, cleared things up.

I needed to do it before I was 18, and I'm glad I chose him! He was soooooo fit. Like film star fit. I didn't think I'd enjoy it that much, but it's just like they say in the films… it's sooo good! I didn't think I'd want to do it with an older guy, but he just had so much experience. And he bought me such nice things. I'm seeing him again tomorrow and I just can't wait!

'This is interesting,' Gab murmured.

'This is creepy,' I muttered. 'Losing her virginity - her "big V"' (I said that ironically), 'to some random older guy? You don't think it's...'

'Shut up and keep reading!' Gab snapped.

16th Nov, 2010
What a night! Key was just amazing, once again! I think I'm falling in love... we've only been on a few dates! Is it possible to fall in love that quickly, Diary? I don't know, but I hope so.

'She said Key!' I exclaimed, a little louder than I had imagined.
'Shut up!' Gab hushed me, angrily.

19th Nov, 2010
Tonight we did it in his car behind the park. It's a BMW, so it's really really nice. He even let me drive it around a bit. Little bit upset though, tonight. He told me that he used to have a wife. He doesn't anymore, but it just makes me remember that he is a lot older than me. Will we be able to have a future?

'I don't like where this is going,' I breathed.
'Me neither,' Gab agreed, not dismissing me this time.

We read through the next few pages, which were all along a similar theme. It didn't get too graphic but highlighted the many places Laurie and Key had evidently had sex. Throughout, however, a tone of doubt continued to seep into the prose. Laurie's voice became more and more uncertain. There was an ever-increasing sense of foreboding.

11th Dec, 2010
I've decided I need to break it off with Key. I do love him, I know that much. But I've got to be sensible... I'm not even seventeen! Our love has to remain a secret... it's illegal! But I can't live like this. I love him, but I can't live keeping secrets. It'll just get messy. I'm going to break up with him tonight after we've done it one more time.

The next few pages were ripped out.
'Shit,' I whispered.
One page was half ripped, with *"Christmas Eve"* written in the top

corner, still visible. The page behind, which hadn't been ripped, showed smudges of ink.

We were running out of readable pages. The water had worked its way through the book at this point.

The final page we would read was the most harrowing of all. It made me feel sick to my stomach. I could see tears coming from Gab's eyes as she read, silently.

There was no date. The handwriting was a scrawl, a dramatic contrast to Laurie's previously calligraphic penmanship.

He wasn't happy about you, Diary. He said I put him at risk, writing about him. He ripped out a lot of pages whilst he kept me locked away. I'm out now and I'm going to hide, and I'm going to hide you too, Diary. I don't know if I'll get away from him, he's fast, but I might. Hopefully, someone will find you and know that they need to arrest Key, who didn't want me to know his real name but…

Water damage and dampness obscured the final few lines.

'That's ridiculous, as if it ends there!' Gab hissed, furious. 'How bloody typical. It's like something out of a *fucking* film, how the hell are we supposed to use this?!'

'Hold on!' I exclaimed in hushed tones. I was just as frustrated as Gab, and equally distressed by the diary entry. But I'd realised something.

I reached for the discarded pages - the ones that had been too water-damaged to read. Luckily, we hadn't messed up the order.

We were supposed to find this, I thought. *I knew it. The window has shown us. This book is the next part of the puzzle. We're being shown breadcrumbs… we're finding the answer. So the next clue has to be in here.*

Carefully, ensuring I didn't cause any more damage to the already wrecked pages, I examined the page that would have directly followed Laurie's final legible entry. The ink had seeped through.

It wasn't much, but it was something.

IKEA

'Ikea?' Gab whispered, incredulously. 'Ikea?'

'It's a Swedish furniture shop.'

'I know what it is, you twat,' Gab spat. 'But why the hell is that what she wrote?'

'I don't think it's all she wrote,' I said, motioning at the page that said Ikea. It was stained and ink had run all over it. Laurie clearly wrote with a fountain pen, one that was *not* very water-resistant. Ink ran all across the page like a dull Picasso. She'd written much more in what I imagined was her final diary entry before she dropped it into its hiding place.

'She'd been hoping someone would find it,' I concluded. 'So she wrote stuff to help someone identify Key. Then she dropped it in the gutter.'

'How the hell would anyone have found it in the gutter? Surely she could have picked a better hiding place.'

'I dunno,' I murmured. 'The window showed her looking around, all scared. Maybe Key was chasing her. Maybe it was the best place she could think of at short notice.'

Gab nodded, agreeing with me (surprise, surprise!). 'That makes sense. Maybe she hoped it would wash up somewhere. Or someone would see her do it?'

'Like us,' I whispered, my own words sending a chill through me.

'So we know we're after a guy called Key, and that Ikea has something to do with it.'

'Do we need to go to Ikea?'

'Don't be stupid. Surely it can't mean the shop.' Gab was back to straight talking.

'I think the nearest Ikea is near Leeds, anyway.'

'Well, we're not fucking going there.'

I shrugged.

'Maybe it's letters that have merged together with the ink running. It's got a K and an E in it, so does that link to Key?'

'What, I-key-a?' I asked, a sarcastic smile on my lips.

Gab ignored me. 'Don't be a twat.'

'I'm just making suggestions.'

'They're not helpful.'

'Fine then.'

We both sat quietly, confused and unsure what our next move was. Why had the window shown us Laurie and led us to the notebook? Had it chosen us to chase down this Key, whoever he was? The same Key that had abused Vicky and maybe other girls? Someone who was behind the disappearance of Ellie and Vicky and Molly and maybe even Paul?

It was just a bloody window! What the hell did it mean? We needed to know more about the window.

'We need to find out about this window.' I repeated my inner musings to my sister. 'That's where all this started.'

'Who's going to know about the window?'

I already knew the answer. 'Old Lady Lilly.'

THIRTY-TWO

GAB HAD *NOT* BEEN a big fan of my suggestion. She reminded me that Old Lady Lilly had been moved out of her house because she had dementia and needed to go into a home. Apparently, Mum had mentioned it to Gab a few weeks ago, when Dad had first brought the infernal window home with him. Lilly's son had some big well-paid government job, so had paid to put her into Village Hall Home - a very nice, plush nursing home on the nice side of York, near the Minster.

'She will be of absolutely no help,' Gab reiterated to me over breakfast the next morning. 'No help whatsoever. She's got dementia, Chris. She's senile. Crazy. She won't have a clue what we're talking about.'

'I think she will,' I argued. 'The window is crazy. It's messed up. Surely crazy knows crazy?'

'That's a ridiculous theory.'

We were sat having our breakfast. Uncle Nev had kindly cooked us some bacon sandwiches, before leaving us with a steaming cup of tea each and going for a shower. As a result, we were alone in the kitchen, watching as the morning news came on. Nothing too exciting was said in the national news, but my ears pricked up when BBC Yorkshire announced its headlines.

'In the latest update on the body found on the shores of the River

Ouse in Grand Parade, police have confirmed that medical examiners have successfully identified the body.'

I turned the volume up. Gab and I were both transfixed, almost seeming to know what was coming.

A senior policeman appeared on the screen, giving a press conference. 'We are sorry to announce that the body of Laurie Openshaw, who went missing over a year ago from Grand Parade, was found on the banks of the River Ouse two nights ago. We are not yet able to confirm the cause of death as drowning, as toxicology reports have come back inconclusive, with several substances in her system. Further investigations will be taking place. We extend our most heartfelt and warmest condolences to the Openshaw family at this unbelievably difficult time. We would also like to encourage anyone with any information about Miss Openshaw or any of the other missing young people to come forward immediately to help in this ongoing investigation. Thank you.'

The newsreader returned to the screen as Gab and I sat in stunned silence. This was all too much of a coincidence. Laurie's body had been uncovered at almost the exact same time we had seen the vision of her and found her diary. She had been linked to this mysterious Key, as had Vicky, and potentially, the other missing kids.

We sat musing over the revelation, white as ghosts, as the newsreader continued onto the next story of ongoing thefts from York and Hull Universities, particularly from the science labs. The news moved on to sports results before finishing and promising that Homes Under The Hammer was on next.

Uncle Nev reappeared after a few minutes, breaking our trance. He looked fresh - he had shaved and combed his hair nicely. He looked like a sober, more good-looking version of our father (although he enjoyed a good drink just as much as the next lad, if only in a little more moderation).

'Are you okay, you two? You both look ill.'

Gab stammered to answer. This time, I took the opportunity to speak. 'We're okay, Uncle Nev. Still just a bit overwhelmed from last night.'

Nev nodded, displaying his understanding. 'I get it, lad. You both will be for a while. And that's okay. It'll take a long time for things to get back to normal. But I can help you through it, your Mum will too, and so will the authorities.' He paused, taking a sip of his coffee that had just finished brewing. 'Are you sure you both want to go to school today? I said you didn't have to if you didn't feel up to it.'

'No, we're fine Uncle Nev,' I continued, Gab still sitting silently. 'It'll be a good distraction.'

Nev smiled encouragingly. 'Good on you both. Get back into it.' He downed the rest of his coffee and headed for the door. 'I'm heading up to the hospital to check in on your Mum and see what's going on with the police and your Dad. Do you both want to visit the hospital after school? I can meet you there if you want?'

'That would be good, thanks.' I tried to sound as normal as possible.

'Great. See you both then. I've got my phone if you need me.' He waved his ancient Nokia in the air and took off.

I turned to Gab, who was still silent, white and pretty scared.

'Gab,' I murmured. 'This is all getting too much. We *have* to find out more about the window. We have to know how we've got involved in this. Old lady Lilly will be able to help us. I know it.'

Gab finally looked at me. 'How?'

The window. Her staring at me. Almost beckoning. The window...

'I'll show you.'

I didn't know how I was confident, but I was. I had no idea how the window worked or how it connected to us. I just knew, in that moment, that it did. This bizarre, impossible, supernatural object that had somehow found its way under my bed was inexplicably linked to the two of us. Whether it was showing us a way or just playing with us, it didn't matter. I *knew* what I needed to do.

Without hesitation, I took Gab by the hand and dragged her upstairs. Hurriedly, I pulled the window out from under the bed and pulled away the sheet. I tried to ignore the fact that the crack in one of the panes of glass seemed to have grown - it now ran through the whole segment.

I looked into the window. My twin did the same.

I knew it.

Old Lady Lilly. In her normal setting. Conglomerations of useless junk all around her. Her frail, ghostly body still breathing… just.

And she was looking directly at us.

Straight to it this time. No absent staring. She was looking right at us.

And she was beckoning. A single, skinny, withered old finger, held out just a little distance from her body. I could see the bone with flesh hanging off it, all the elasticity of her skin lost in her deepening journey into frailty.

She stared right at us, finger slowly, painfully, moving backwards and forwards, calling to us, pulling us in, summoning us.

We both knew that we had to see her.

THIRTY-THREE

VILLAGE HALL HOME was situated on the west side of York city centre, not far from York Minster. In fact, York Minster was linked to this particular nursing home, helping raise money to continue its good work. The nursing home was already private, so any extra funding they got was a bonus.

Gab and I loyally left the house as if going to school. Uncle Nev wouldn't know any different. I doubted school would even call home. They would have heard about the absolute car crash that was our family life, and they would most likely assume the pair of us were having a much-deserved day off. If only we could be so lucky.

With a little help from the maps app on our phones, we managed to find our way to Village Hall Home. From the outside, it looked delightful. It was a beautiful, old, Victorian building, probably worth a good few million pounds. There was a very well-kept climbing wisteria going around the front entrance in addition to delightful flowerbeds and vegetable patches at the front of the building.

Gab and I had walked there in silence. We were both resigned to the fact that we needed to go and see Old Lady Lilly. We were both confused, exhausted and terrified, but we didn't know what else to do. Mum was in hospital, Dad was under arrest, and Uncle Nev was lovely but not the sort of person who could help. I doubted even Mr Arnold and Mrs Taylor could help, despite their promises the other day in Mr Arnold's office. So, we'd taken matters into our own hands and turned to an old lady with dementia as our source of wisdom. What could possibly go wrong?

The front door was open and led into a small reception area. An overweight lady in her fifties sat at a reception desk with the name SUE printed in big letters on a badge above her left breast.

'Are you visitors?' She asked curtly. She had the definition of a resting-bitch-face. I've still never met someone called Sue that I actually like - not that I see a huge amount of women these days.

'Yes, we'd like to see Lilly, please. She's an old neighbour of ours. We used to pop in and see her.' I thought my lie sounded pretty convincing.

Sue eyed us suspiciously. *What a bitch.* 'Lilly doesn't get many visitors.'

'We haven't had a chance to come since she moved out. Busy with school work and stuff, you know?' I smiled sweetly, getting nothing in return from Sue.

Still not convinced, Sue tapped away at the computer. 'What's Lilly's surname?' She asked us, dubiously.

'Uh...' Bollocks. Mum would have known.

'Mac something?' Gab cut in. 'McCollum or McCarthy or something like that?'

Sue grunted in response. 'Not quite but close enough.' We'd convinced her. She pushed a pair of visitor's passes across the desk. 'If she doesn't want you there, you leave straight away. Don't be upsetting our residents. Claire will take you through to her room and check she's happy with you.' Distrustfully, Sue motioned to a nurse - presumably Claire - who was equally overweight. Claire pulled herself to her feet and signalled for us to follow her as she waddled along the corridors of the nursing home. We followed loyally, muttering thanks to Sue (what a bitch).

We stayed mute throughout our journey. Private and well-funded or not, the place still stank like an old people's home. There was a musty scent of piss and poor-quality spaghetti bolognese heavy in the air. Even the walls seemed to groan with the age and frailty of the home's residents. We glanced into a few rooms as we walked past. No one looked very alive. The majority were in bed. The odd few were slumped in massive armchairs. Some had drips hooked up to them. Televisions played loudly across the whole building, from both the residential rooms and the social areas. It felt as if we were standing at the edge of life, death just a short journey down the road.

Finally, we stopped at one of the rooms. Claire toddled into the room and informed Old Lady Lilly she had visitors. Lilly appeared overjoyed and shouted something about a chocolate digestive. Claire gave us a grumpy nod of approval and left us alone.

We proceeded inside.

Lilly looked much like she had in the window, only worse. Her room was remarkably similar to the living room we'd been privy to. There was useless paraphernalia everywhere, as if someone had picked up everything the old woman owned and dumped it all back down in this much smaller room. Reams of magazines, books, photographs, empty tablet boxes and half-eaten snacks were strewn across the room. So much for private nursing care - the place looked like a dump.

Lilly herself epitomised a person in the final stages of life. Most of her wispy hair had fallen out, and she wore a poorly fitting woollen beanie hat to keep her head warm. Her skin was gaunt, clinging to her bones, exposing the contours of her skull and facial structure. Not a single tooth could be seen in her gummy mouth. Her whole body appeared to be shrivelled, like a grape that had been left out in the sun for weeks. She was covered in a multitude of blankets in a desperate attempt to keep her warm. I noticed a bizarre-looking device attached to the edge of her bed - a syringe inside a plastic case. Next to it hung a chart entitled "Syringe Driver Hourly Checklist".

We stood looking over her. I felt nothing but pity in my heart as I looked at this woman. Her eyes seemed to look straight through us, glazed over as she remained in her own little world.

'Is that you, son?' She croaked, reaching out an aged hand towards me. I'm not entirely sure why, but I took it. I felt like she needed some comfort. Maybe.

'No,' I murmured. 'No it's not your son, but we live on Ashlands Road, down the street from your old house. We're Chris and Gab Keeler.'

Lilly's eyes remained absent. 'I was promised three chocolate digestives last Christmas,' she groaned, unmoved by my introduction. 'I can't remember where I put them.'

'Lilly,' Gab murmured. The old lady didn't react. 'We wanted to talk to you. About your old house.'

'I don't have an old house,' Lilly announced. 'I've always lived in the same house. Right here, on Beggar Home Lane.'

I smiled sadly. Dementia was a truly cruel disease. 'Do you know where you are Lilly?'

'Of course I do, don't be silly.' Lilly seemed to chuckle a bit. 'I'm in my house. Beggar Home Lane. Where generations of my family have lived. My little lad was born here. He must be about fifteen by now.'

I somewhat doubted that Lilly's numbers were entirely correct, but I nodded anyway. It was better not to disagree. I tried to stay on topic. 'Lilly, have you ever seen anything unusual out on Beggar Home Lane?'

'I was there for the coronation, you know!' Lilly declared, proudly. 'I watched her Majesty Queen Elizabeth the Second take her throne! A few years ago now, I think, but I saw it. We danced! In the street! Mother was so mad at me... she still is!' She looked Gab dead in the eye and whispered: 'Mother's not here, is she?'

Gab shook her head. She was much more impatient than I was. 'Come on, Chris, we're not going to get anything here.'

'Gab...'

'Come on. Bloody waste of time.'

'Kathleen, is that you?' Lilly asked Gab, reaching for her hand. Gab recoiled a little. She was being a bit heartless, but we'd had a tough week.

'No, Lilly, it's not,' Gab snapped. 'And we'd best be going. It was nice to see you.'

Lilly began to babble about a party she had gone to as a teenager, rambling slightly incoherently.

I took a chance. 'Lilly, we need to know about the window in your house. The one that can see the past.'

Lilly froze. Her chatter stopped. Her eyes weren't glazed over anymore. They were alive, shining. She was staring right at me. She gripped my hand, tightly. Her gaze pierced into mine, invading my soul. Then she whispered, only just loud enough to hear. 'What do you know of that window?'

THIRTY-FOUR

I COULDN'T TEAR my eyes away. Her stare was captivating, seizing hold of my entire being. I was vaguely aware that Gab was looking on in shock, awestruck. I breathed deeply, trying to understand this transformed woman before me.

'We...' I stammered. I couldn't find the right words.

'Tell me, child. We don't have long.' Her entire tone of voice had changed. There was an urgency, a desperation. In a moment, this frail old being had become lucid and alert.

'They're doing construction on your old house. They threw out the window. We took it to build something in the garden...'

'What did you build?' Lilly's question was stern. Her mind had become unbelievably sharp.

'A cold frame... like a greenhouse for the plants.'

'You looked in the window?' She was insistent. Was that a note of fear?

'Yes.'

'What did you see?'

'A lot.'

'Tell me,' Lilly implored. There was a hiss to her voice. Almost as if she was possessed.

'It showed me Beggar Home Lane. In the past, like in Victorian times. Then in the present. I saw my cat get run over. And we saw you, in your house. And the builders in there after you'd left.'

'What else?'

'I...' I hesitated. The cat and the Victorian scene were one thing. The other visions... the darker visions... the ones linked to the missing children and Key and all the weird shit that was going on in my life... that was a different thing entirely.

'Tell me, boy!' Lilly hissed. She was sat up straight now, as if her atrophied muscle had suddenly been reborn.

'I... we...' I looked to Gab for help. I was a little lost for words. She was just as useless. For once, my sister remained speechless, her mouth still agape.

Lilly looked at me expectantly. I took a deep breath.

'We saw someone being chased.'

'Who?'

'A boy. A friend. Someone who's disappeared.'

'What else?'

'A...' Again, hesitation.

'Tell me!'

'A girl. I think she was being chased too. She hid something in a drain.'

'And?' Lilly's question felt loaded, as if she already knew the answer.

'And we went and found it.'

'What was it?'

'Just a notebook,' I confessed, trying to play it down. Lilly's sudden lucidity had terrified me. I wasn't sure how much I could tell her.

'The notebook led you to me?' She asked.

'No,' I mumbled, a little confused. 'No, we saw you beckoning us. In the window. Telling us to come.'

'You live on Beggar Home?' Her questions were coming quickly now.

'No, nearby,' I stammered. 'On Ashlands.'

'Hm.' Lilly relaxed back a little, finally tearing her gaze away from me. I gasped for breath. It was like I'd been throttled. She had occupied my entire being.

When I regained my composure, I finally asked her. 'What is the window?'

Lilly didn't say anything initially. Instead, she shook her head and sighed. Finally, she answered. 'I asked myself that same question countless times over the decades.' Her tone had changed again. It was low and monotone, but there was a conversational quality to it. 'And I still don't really know the answer.'

I took in a gulp of breath, still hungry for oxygen after the old woman's hold on me.

'I've lived in that house my entire life,' Lilly whispered, ethereally. 'It's been in my family for generations. That window was always a part of it, looking out onto the street from our living room. It's been changed and repaired and replaced multiple times. But it's always been the same...'

Gab and I were silent. I realised my sister was holding her breath.

'When I was a child, I thought it was just my reflection. The things I saw. It was just me, walking past. Or something in my imagination. I was only young.' Lilly's voice had a subtle Yorkshire accent, a quiet baritone lacing her words.

'Then, in the depths of night, when I was a teenager, I saw an image, as bright as day, shining in the window. It was as you described...' Lilly's eyes met mine once again and locked in firmly. 'It was a scene from Victorian England - a scene my parents would have been familiar with.' Lilly's eyes were glistening again as she tore her gaze away from my face, looking out into space... towards her *own* window, her small piece of existence in Village Hall Home.

'I was mesmerised,' she murmured, as if transported back to that moment. 'I stared at it for hours, the scene playing over and over again. So I kept coming back to the window, in the small hours, every night, without fail. And because I believed I would see...'

'The window showed you things,' I interrupted, somehow understanding some of the window's bizarre laws.

'Exactly!' Lilly exclaimed quietly, her tone taking on an erratic nature. 'At first, it was the same scene over and over again. Then... I suppose I wanted more. And it *gave* me more. Like it was connected to me.'

My whole body was sweating. Gab was noticeably shaking.

'The images began to change. I saw other things - people going past, children being led to school by their mothers, carriages, then automobiles, animals, sometimes just the street, looking a little different to how it did in real life.'

Somehow, despite the adrenaline and terror coursing through my veins, I managed to ask a question. 'How did you know that you were seeing visions in it? The window was already looking out onto your street... did you not just think you were seeing real life?'

'How many times have you seen a horse-drawn carriage come down your street, boy?' Lilly snapped, clearly irritated that I had questioned her. 'How many times does a thunderstorm appear in a single window on the clearest night you've ever seen? How many times do you see your dead grandparents walking around the street as bold as brass?'

I stammered, trying to come up with an answer... or an apology.

'Exactly as I thought,' Lilly spat. Her attitude had changed. She was angry now. *Don't question the window.* I knew that to do so was a cardinal sin, in Lilly's eyes.

'Replace the window frame, repair the glass, change the whole bloody thing... it never stops. A window, in that place, in that house... it will always show you things. And now the house has finally been demolished... the space for it doesn't exist anymore... but it has lived on, it seems... in its final form...'

It appeared to me that Lilly was rambling more to herself. She was lost in her thoughts, reflecting on everything she had known about the window over the years.

'You've come to me because the window has shown you something you don't know what to do with, is that right?' Lilly finally continued.

Numbly, I nodded. Gab remained a still statue.

'What has it shown you? Really?'

She wanted me to explain what the images we had seen meant to us. I knew it. Somehow, as I felt connected to the window, I felt connected to this old sack of bones lying in bed before me.

I took a deep breath, briefly glancing at Gab as if expecting her seal of approval. Still nothing. She was frozen in shock.

'The people we've seen… the boy running… the girl who hid her notebook… we think they're connected to a series of disappearing kids in Grand Parade, possibly linked to an older man called Key.'

Lilly said nothing in response, looking once again out of the window of her tiny little bedroom. For a minute, we all remained silent. I noticed that my legs were trembling violently. I looked around for a chair, saw nothing close by, and clutched the rail of Lilly's bed instead.

'The girl,' Lilly finally responded, her voice flat. 'The one with the diary. What happened to her? In the end?'

How did Lilly know something had happened to her? But I knew the answer. There was something greater and more powerful than us going on here. A connection between the three of us in that room and the haunting window currently wrapped in a sheet under my bed.

'She's dead,' I responded, plainly. 'She was called Laurie Openshaw. She disappeared a few years ago and her body washed up by the river the other day.'

Lilly's face turned back to ours. She reached out and put her skeletal hand on mine, holding it tightly, with more strength than I expected from this cachexic human.

'So it's started to show you death,' she murmured. There was a note of sadness in her words. 'Which means there's no turning back.'

THIRTY-FIVE

I GASPED, pulling my hand away as if Lilly had given me an electric shock. I was trembling again, even more so than before. Did I see a tear in the old lady's eye?

Gab had finally snapped out of her trance and grabbed me as I swayed. She pulled a small visitor's chair towards me and guided me into it. I gratefully took a seat and put my head in my hands, breathing deeply. I was drenched in sweat. I felt like I was going to faint. I don't know if it was the conversation or the bizarre, inexplicable connection I felt to the old woman and the window. But I felt like I was on the edge of reality.

'I saw death in the window,' Lilly continued. 'When I was sixteen years old. I saw a boy trampled by a horse. I was horrified but somehow understood that it wasn't that important. The scene I saw was old… Victorian England at the very latest. It was not a suspicious incident. I watched as the community of our street gathered around this young boy and decided the child had been at fault, not the horse. I suppose horses were worth a lot of money in those days and putting it down wouldn't have been an option.'

Lilly was still looking directly at me as if Gab was absent from the room.

'I think the window showed me that to gain my trust. Or to continue to build our relationship, or something along those lines. Because then it showed me more. I began to see a series of very dark events that had played out over the centuries in Beggar Home Lane. Arsons, robberies, rapes, abductions... *murders.* I saw children stolen from their homes and beaten to death in the dead of night. I saw houses lit on fire in broad daylight. And this continued throughout my whole life. The window called me in and showed me all. I knew everything that had happened on Beggar Home Lane. The whole street, not just outside my house. I was given almost a birds-eye view. I was given all.'

I said nothing as my body began to feel slightly more like my own again.

'My greatest sin, boy, is that I never did anything, even when I probably should have. I just watched the window. I watched with fascination, never entirely sure why I was seeing things, but watching nonetheless. You ask me what the window is? I don't know. All I know is that it calls you in, it takes hold of you, and it shows you things until you do something. And if you don't do something... you'll end up like me.'

I looked at her, confused.

She cackled. It was a sad sound, one of vocal cords long past their prime, used for too many years, raw and fatigued. 'I spent my life living in that house, boy.' She seemed to continue to ignore Gab, still standing next to me, trembling, but more responsive than before. 'I saw many things through that window. I watched in fascination as I went through the motions of life. Marriage, childbirth, jobs, retirement, funerals. Every night, I watched. I wondered why my house had a window that appeared magical. But never once did I think about taking action, even when I realised I could have.'

She paused for a moment, taking a few deep breaths, as if explaining her story had exhausted her.

'As I got older, especially in the last few years, I saw things through my window that depicted very recent events. The girl you describe, the one hiding something in a drain... it was dark, in the middle of a storm, correct?'

I nodded, barely able to process what she was saying.

'The girl kept looking around as if someone was chasing her, yes?'

Again, a nod.

'Did you see the man who followed her?'

This time, I shook my head, just an inch.

'Hm. You see, I did.'

I felt like I was going to vomit. I didn't need anyone to tell me that I looked like death warmed up.

'A man followed her. Just a little later.'

Silence.

'In the last year, I saw this scene many times. Many, many times. Never had an image played that frequently through the window. I'd certainly seen repeats... like reruns on the television. But this was different. It was almost nightly. The window was *telling* me something. I *had* to do something about this vision.'

She sighed, shaking her head, as if ashamed of herself.

'But I did nothing. As I had my entire life with that bloody window, I did *nothing*. I just watched as it played over and over.' She paused. 'About a year ago, I think, it hit me like a freight train. Dementia. Normally, it's a slow disease. It takes years to fully impact you, slowly deteriorating your brain function and memory. People can live for decades, they can even take medication to slow the disease down. Some people get it very gradually - that's the Alzheimer's type. Others get something called vascular dementia - a type where you go downhill in a stepwise fashion, usually because of lots of little strokes. For me, it was like I'd had a bloody massive stroke. My brain function just dropped off a cliff.'

Gab and I remained quiet, listening as Lilly continued her woeful tale.

'Within weeks, I was incredibly disorientated. I didn't know where or when I was. I was constantly confused, and out of sync with the rest of the world. I only knew one thing - the window. That was the *only* constant in my life. The remaining members of my family didn't care about me, I'd lived alone for years, my neighbours ignored me... I had nothing, no one. So, I gave my all to the window. For my final year in that house, I hoarded everything around me, sitting, looking out to the window, looking for guidance, comfort, anything that it could offer me. It was the only thing that brought me lucidity. Yet my grip on reality continued to slowly slip away.'

In my mind's eye, I could see the image of Lilly sitting in her living room, surrounded by reams of papers and mountains of medication, always staring in one direction... at the *window*.

'It was my fault,' Lilly reflected, quietly. 'All of it. I should have known... as soon as I saw the image of that girl hiding her notebook and the man chasing her, I should have known to do something about it. I think the window had been pulling me in all those years, gaining my trust, fostering an unbreakable relationship with me, just so that it could show me that image at the right time. Just so that I could *help*. And I didn't.'

'So you think the window gave you dementia?' Gab murmured, speaking for the first time in the conversation. The question wasn't one of judgement or scepticism. It was of genuine interest.

Lilly smiled, wryly. 'I wondered when you would speak, girl. You just think I'm a crazy old woman, don't you?'

'I did,' Gab confessed. 'Not anymore. That window is fucking weird. And it can do weird shit. I don't doubt what you're telling us.'

Lilly chuckled quietly. 'You're a strong woman, young lady. You will do great things.'

Nobody spoke for a few minutes. Lilly seemed to close her eyes and breathe deeply, taking a rest. I briefly wondered if she'd fallen asleep before she spoke again.

'I don't know if the window gave me dementia, children, I honestly don't. But that window has abilities beyond our imaginations and most certainly has a mind of its own. It may be full of darkness and evil, but I also believe good can be done through its power.'

She looked at us both, her eyes flickering between the pair of us. 'I didn't take action when I should have. I spent decades taking from the window but never giving back, never seeing how I could help. I was selfish. Obsessed... I think the window can do that. You can lose yourself in it and forget your purpose, your identity.'

I understood that. I remembered how, just before I decided to tell Gab and share the window with her, I'd been overcome with a deep, selfish desire to keep the window a secret. Keep it *my* window. Luckily, I'd pushed away these feelings. I'd shared the problem with the person I trusted most in the world. I hadn't let the window take a complete hold of me... not quite.

'You two...' Lilly gasped for breath, tiring. 'You two understand the window. You understand that it needs belief. Trust. And by the sounds of it, it has shown you many more important events in a few weeks than I have seen in decades. I don't know if it punished me for being indifferent and inactive... but I know that I don't want you two to take that risk. You have to trust the window. You have to let it show you *more*. You have to use it to help. I don't know how and I can't explain specifics, it's not my window anymore, but you *have* to use it. Find the missing kids. Find this Key. I get the sense that the window is using you both to put an end to the terrible events going on in Grand Parade... events that have been going on for years.'

Lilly coughed, continuing to fatigue. 'I want to believe that the window has been preparing me for such a time as *this* moment. To share with you two. To guide you. Now go and do some good with it. Or - and I can't promise this, but I have a good idea - you'll end up like me. Or worse.'

Old Lady Lilly took a deep breath and leant her head back, exhausted, falling into a deep sleep. Gab and I watched her for a few minutes as she rested, peacefully, her withered body moving every so slightly with her frail respiratory effort.

In that moment, surrounded by the peace of her room and the musty smell of the nursing home, we enjoyed a few seconds of quiet, before the inevitable chaos that was about to follow.

THIRTY-SIX

'SO YOU'VE BOTH CLEARLY *NOT* BEEN to school.'

Both of us were still reeling from our encounter with Old Lady Lilly and thus caught entirely off-guard by Uncle Nev's unusually stern voice as we walked through the front door.

'I've had Ms Cross and Mr Arnold on the phone, worried sick about the pair of you!'

'We...' Gab began before Nev cut us off. I'd never seen him this annoyed.

'Bloody hell, both of you! Enough is going on without you two disappearing off to God only knows where!' He sighed deeply and pointed towards the kitchen. 'In there, now. Both of you.'

He sat us down and began boiling the kettle. Time for another one of Nev's pep talks.

'Where the hell have you both been?' He continued, glancing at his watch. 'It's two o'clock, so you've been somewhere other than school for over five hours!'

'We were just walking around, Uncle Nev,' Gab replied, immediately.

'Where?' Nev countered, just as quickly.

'Just down the river,' I chimed in. Bad move.

'For *fuck's* sake you two!' Nev's voice was rising with every sentence. 'We've got kids going missing, bodies pulled out of that damned river, your Mum in hospital and your Dad banged up! What if one of you had fallen in? What if one of you had got into trouble? Why the *hell* could you not just go to school?' Nev was irate. I'd never seen him like this. He was normally the calm counterpart to my brute of a father. But, in my heart, I understood. Nev, like my Mum, cared deeply for us. He was worried. And he was right to be, considering everything that was going on, half of which he had *no* idea about.

'Sorry,' I grumbled, genuinely apologising.

'You damn well should be,' Nev retorted, moving over to pour boiling water into three mugs with teabags in. 'I gave you both the option of having today off. You said you wanted to go to school. It would distract you, etcetera. So why the hell did you lie? If you'd wanted to go out for a walk, I would have been fine with it! No one knew where you were! I thought the worst had happened!'

'Sorry, okay!' Gab shouted back, noticeably upset. Nev immediately softened a little. He'd always had a soft spot for the both of us but was particularly lenient with Gab. 'We won't do it again.'

Nev sighed and handed out our cups of tea. 'Damn right, you won't.' He sat down around the table to face us. Then, bizarrely, he asked a question I was *not* expecting. 'Were the pair of you with Vicky?'

'What?' I blurted, choking on my tea. What the hell did Vicky have to do with it?

'Vicky Crampton? The girl who went missing a few weeks ago? In your school?'

'No,' Gab said, carefully. 'Why?'

Nev sighed. 'Ms Cross rang me at about ten this morning to ask where you were. Then at lunchtime, I got a call from Mr Arnold asking if we'd turned up and whether you two were with Vicky. She didn't turn up to school either.'

'Shit,' I murmured. The plot continued to thicken. Surely Vicky hadn't gone missing again?

'Hm,' Nev replied, eying me closely. 'So obviously, I've been worried sick. Vicky's already disappeared once, I thought you two might have got yourselves into trouble with her.'

We both shook our heads in sync but were speechless. Neither of us, it appeared, knew what to say.

Nev moved on. 'Anyway,' he murmured. 'Before I got into a panic about you two, I went to the hospital, didn't I?'

My interest was piqued as I prepared to hear an update on my two parents.

'Your Mum is doing okay,' Nev began. 'She's conscious but confused. The Doctors want to keep an eye on her. The bleed on her brain is too small to warrant them doing surgery at this point and they're happy to just observe her. Any worsening, she'll get another scan and then maybe some surgery, although she would have to be transferred over to Hull for that. That's where they do neurosurgery.'

I nodded, mutely. I didn't much fancy the idea of Mum being carted off to Hull - the arse end of nowhere - but that wasn't happening right now. I didn't want to think too much about the prospect of my Mum having brain surgery.

'As for your father, he's medically completely fine,' Nev went on. 'The Doctors have cleared him. So, at some point soon, the police will be escorting him to the station where he'll be put in jail temporarily. Then I guess we'll be awaiting a trial.'

'What'll happen to Dad?' Gab asked, sounding serious. 'Will he go to prison for a long time?'

Nev shrugged. He looked a little forlorn. It was understandable - his brother was in police custody and faced some pretty serious charges.

'It's difficult to say,' Nev eventually answered. 'He's had a few minor offences before - assault, drunk and disorderly, and that whole thing with him having a seizure at work whilst driving a crane all those years ago - although he was never charged for that. But, the upshot is, he's known to the police. And there is probably evidence - and testimony, from yourselves and your Mum-' (the idea of having to testify in court sounded bloody horrifying, so I was glad Uncle Nev skirted over it) 'that this abuse has been going on for a while and has been recurrent. So it's unlikely he won't get sentenced. How long for, I don't know.'

Nev looked quite beaten up after his explanation. Somehow, I managed to empathise. This man, in his fifties, free and single, who had planned a casual visit to his brother's family had suddenly become a temporary guardian, whilst his brother awaited trial for domestic violence and assault. It wasn't a particularly brilliant situation.

We finished our cups of tea in silence before Nev offered to make us some lunch. We both gratefully accepted and were treated to ham and cheese toasties, which was just what we both needed. Afterwards, we decided to retire to our rooms and be alone.

At the top of the stairs, Gab and I looked at each other. Uncle Nev was still downstairs, cleaning up the plates from lunch.

'The window…' Gab began before I cut her off.

'We'll get to it. But not now. It's too risky with Nev here. I don't want him to see it. Adults won't understand.'

'Lilly did,' Gab argued.

'She's different. It's *her* window.'

'It's ours now.'

Gab's tone concerned me slightly. Was she feeling that same pull to the window that I felt? The obsession? That unrelenting draw?

'We need to look,' Gab insisted, trying to push past me towards my bedroom.

'Not now,' I implored, holding her back. 'Not with Nev here. And not after today. We've seen too much. Heard too much. I need… I need to process it.'

Gab looked at me, despairingly. 'Now, of all times, you're going to be a pussy?'

Her words stung. That was what Dad had called me, unkindly, many times before. Gab had never said such things - not seriously, anyway.

'Yes,' I snapped, pushing her away, a little more firmly than I had intended. 'Yes, I am.'

With that, I forced myself into my room and locked the door. I stood with my back to the door for a few moments, before going over to my bed and lying down, my mind swirling with all that had gone on.

I stayed there for the rest of the day and long into the night. I never went downstairs for food. Instead, I flitted between sleep and wakefulness, feeling the ever-constant, almost palpable pull of the mysterious window that now lived under my bed.

THIRTY-SEVEN

I ACTUALLY WENT to school the next day. I know, madness.

It was strange though. For the first time in as long as I could remember, Gab and I didn't walk to school together. I heard her get in the shower and then leave the house twenty minutes later. Normally, she'd shower, then I would shower, then we'd meet downstairs for a hurried breakfast and leave together. Today she wanted nothing to do with me. Nev was nowhere to be seen… probably at the hospital.

So I made my own way to school, hurrying through Beggar Home Lane as quickly as I could, trying not to linger physically or emotionally on that road for too long. Once off Beggar Home, I continued on my commute, trying to turn my mind off, focusing on the pavement ahead of me, desperate to forget all that was going on. I was barely aware of the people walking in the opposite direction, the cars driving past, the old lady shouting at a rude bus driver, or the car crash that had happened on the main road, now surrounded by members of the public and a dozen police cars.

When I got to school, Gab didn't even acknowledge me entering the classroom before registration.

Ms Cross mentioned how she was pleased to see both of us again as she did the register and hoped we were both feeling alright. I shrugged but gave her a grateful smile, trying to ignore the intense stares from my classmates, directed at both Gab and me.

Adam caught up with me after registration.

'Are you alright mate? People are saying your old man beat up your Mum?'

'Yeah, mate,' I grumbled, barely aware of what I was saying or processing that Adam was showing a genuine interest in someone else for a change. 'It's been a bit shit.'

'I'm sorry, mate. Really.' He paused, then: 'Lucy broke up with me, didn't she.'

The words washed over me. I was indifferent. But, I'm nice. I still managed: 'Sorry mate. That's a shame.'

'It is, Chris, honestly. Once you've had a shag, you can't go without! I'm sorting myself out four times a day!'

'That's lovely mate,' I grumbled sarcastically.

'It's not, lad, it hurts after a while!'

'You should see someone about that,' I mumbled absently, leaving Adam's side to try and catch up with Gab.

'Gab,' I hissed, coming up behind her. She was with some of the other girls, deep in discussion. She ignored me.

'Gab!' I raised my voice a little.

She spun and looked at me, angrily. Then she nodded her head slightly towards the girls she was with. One of them was upset and crying. Gab's eyes told me all. We were probably okay. We'd needed some space. She'd tell me all later. Something was going on with these girls. Something important.

I nodded and left them in peace. Was this to do with Vicky disappearing again? I'd heard nothing more about it since Uncle Nev told us - it hadn't been mentioned in school. Had she reappeared? Was she still missing?

I was due for my Religious Studies lesson. Alone, I joined the horde of sweaty teenagers working their way down a corridor far too small for the volume of students. A few members of teaching staff walked amongst the masses, shouting 'This is a one-way corridor!' in vain, as hundreds of kids went any which way they wanted. Being within the crowd was bizarre. I was surrounded by so many of my peers, all with normal school-kid problems - homework, part-time jobs, exams, detentions, girlfriends, boyfriends, extracurriculars, sporting results. Here I was, right in the midst of them, surrounded by their bodies and their problems, living a life that could not have been more different. A life full of abuse and violence and mystery and… magic. Because realistically, that's what it was. Magic. Very, very dark magic.

Ms Dooley began the lesson. We were supposed to be continuing our reports on our recent visit to York Minster. I could barely remember it, so much had gone on since then. The overwhelming memory of that trip was Gab and Ms Dooley counselling Vicky after her horrific experience with Key. Remembering the religious minutia of the trip was somewhat of a challenge.

In the end, I wrote what I could remember about the architecture of the Cathedral - something I thoroughly enjoyed learning about. I thought that my report would be enhanced with some pictures, so I did some rough sketches of the Cathedral, detailing its nave and transepts, and, of course, the Great East Window.

For just a few moments, I was lost in my thoughts. Unfortunately, this was short-lived. As you know, this story doesn't go well for me.

Ms Dooley stirred me from my trance as I completed a rough sketch of the Great East Window.

'Chris?'

She was right next to me, talking quietly as if to prevent the rest of the class from listening. 'We've just had a message that Mr Arnold wants to see you and Gab in his office. He'd like you to go now.'

What the hell is it now? I thought, nodding glumly at Ms Dooley. She gave me an encouraging smile, looking at my work. 'It's nice to see how imaginative you've been for your report.'

'Thanks, Miss,' I grumbled, handing her my pages. I picked up my bag and took my leave.

The long walk along the now deserted corridors to Mr Arnold's office seemed to take an age. It was a stark contrast to how the school had looked twenty minutes ago. Now there was a tranquility. A peace. No clump of human beings trying to live out their existence. Just me and these cold corridors. A beat of calm, before the oncoming storm.

I met Gab a few moments later as she entered the main school corridor from the floor above. She'd been in History, her preferred humanity for our GCSE studies, which was taught directly above the Religion classrooms. She smiled weakly at me as we met. I put an affectionate hand on her shoulder.

She mumbled an apology and I muttered an acceptance. There was a mutual understanding between us. The window was doing weird things to us. That much was certain. We *had* to stick together.

As we neared Mr Arnold's office, we heard raised voices.

'I just don't know what we're going to do! It's getting out of control, man!'

Strange... they sounded adult. Not like the childish shouts given off by teenagers.

'I don't know what you expect me to do, Carl. We can't keep tabs on every single child when they're not in our school. We're only responsible for them from eight-thirty until three-thirty each day!'

The voices were getting closer. Or were we getting closer to them? We continued down the corridor.

'The Crampton's are losing their shit!'

'Carl, it's not our fault she's run off again! She'll turn up. You know what Grand Parade kids are like. She'll be on a bender.'

'A midweek bender? Come off it, Mike.'

As we reached Mr Arnold's door, our suspicions were confirmed. The argument was coming from inside. By the sounds of it, Mr Arnold was arguing with Carl Roberts, the Headteacher.

'Stranger things have happened in Grand Parade.'

'We should be educating against this!'

'We are, Carl! There's only so much we can do.'

'And this body turning up. That's a whole other shitstorm. Was she one of ours?'

'From Grand Parade High by the look of it.'

A pause. 'Do you know what they're saying about her?'

'No.'

'Formaldehyde, Mike. Fucking *formaldehyde*. In her blood!'

I knocked on the door. Gab threw me daggers. Clearly, she wasn't done listening.

'Who's that?' Mr Roberts could be heard to say, quietly.

Mr Arnold could be heard to shout. 'I'll be with you in a minute, wait outside please!' Then, quietly, but still just audible. 'It'll be the Keeler kids. I asked them to come, their Uncle's on the way in. It's about this car crash.'

'Fuck's sake, Mikey,' Carl replied. 'Yet another balls up we have to deal with.'

No more was said. The next thing we knew, the door was opened, and Mr Roberts, Headteacher, stood facing us.

'Hello you two,' he grumbled, feigning friendliness. 'Sorry it's been such a difficult few days.' He didn't sound sorry at all. 'Mr Arnold will sort you out.'

He motioned us into the office, where we were greeted by Mr Arnold. He invited us to sit in the two chairs before him.

So we sat, and our lives continued their downward trajectory.

THIRTY-EIGHT

'CHRIS, Gab, I know both of you have had a really rough couple of weeks. I'm sorry about that, I truly am. I sympathise.'

Mr Arnold sounded genuine. It took me a moment to realise that I was shaking again. Gab, as she (almost) always did, remained calm and stoic.

'I'm not sure where to begin,' Mr Arnold went on. He hesitated. 'Your Uncle is on his way in to get you.' He seemed to be stalling, unsure what to say.

'Is Mum alright?' Gab blurted.

Mr Arnold looked as if he hadn't been expecting the question and was a little flustered. 'Your... your Mum? Yes, she's fine, as far as I'm aware. Still in the hospital, I think. I haven't heard any updates.'

'Oh,' Gab responded. 'Good.'

'No, it's... it's your Father I need to talk to you about.'

I hung my head. *What has he done now? Hasn't he been arrested?*

'Late last night,' Mr Arnold began, 'your father was escorted from the hospital by police, after being discharged yesterday afternoon.' Mr Arnold paused, watching our faces, which remained stony and emotionless. 'He was being driven in a police car down to the main station, where he was supposed to be put in a temporary jail cell before moving somewhere more permanent.'

I wasn't sure where this was going.

'Unfortunately, the police car carrying your father was in an accident.'

Shit, I thought. *Is he dead?* I look back now and wonder: *is it bad that I hoped for that outcome?*

Mr Arnold shook his head, almost to himself. 'Dammit, Chris, I wish you'd told us what was going on at home when I asked you the other day.' There was a hint of irritation in his voice. I got it. Mr Arnold had been trying to help, as had all the teachers. And I'd said it was all fine at home when it clearly was not. Watershed moment.

'Anyway.' Mr Arnold managed to get back on track. 'The police car carrying your father was hit side-on by another driver, who was driving very recklessly.' There was judgement in Mr Arnold's voice. 'The police car was driven into a lamppost. Unfortunately, two of the police officers in the car died at the scene.'

My heart was pounding. And my father? Bloody hell, Mr Arnold was milking this.

'Your father,' our Head of Year continued, his words sounding slow and slurred in my head as I processed what was happening, 'was not in the police car by the time the authorities arrived. It appears he has escaped police custody.'

'Shit,' I whispered.

Mr Arnold continued as if I hadn't spoken. 'Unfortunately, he hasn't been apprehended since. We also haven't been able to find the driver of the car that hit them.'

I breathed deeply. It was a lot to process. My Dad was now essentially a fugitive…

'The police contacted the school shortly after registration this morning,' Mr Arnold went on, his words now becoming a drone. 'They don't think that you're in any immediate danger, but they want you under supervision at all times, in case your father decides to try and take you away or…'

'You don't need to finish that sentence,' Gab replied, darkly.

Mr Arnold nodded, clearly grateful. 'Your Uncle Nev is on the way to get you. It's been agreed by the police, your Uncle and the teaching staff that it would be best for both of you to stay in the house under Nev's supervision until your father is apprehended again.'

There was quiet for a moment. Then: 'I'm sorry this has happened to you both. I'm truly sorry.'

'What about Mum?' Gab asked, bluntly. 'Is she safe? What if Dad goes after her?'

Mr Arnold hesitated for a moment, then spoke. 'The hospital will be made aware that your father is on the loose and may go and see your Mum... they'll be told to not let anyone meeting his description in, and to contact the police if he shows up.' He didn't sound very confident about this suggested plan, but I let it pass. In my mind, it was unlikely Dad would turn back up to give Mum another round of beatings. He only ever did that when he was angry. If he was on the run, he'd be thinking about himself and how to survive.

'And the guy who smashed into Dad's car? Killing the police officers?' Gab continued her harsh tone of questioning.

'The police are also looking for him. He's a young lad. They've traced the car.'

Gab nodded, apparently satisfied.

'Until the situation progresses further, we'd strongly encourage you both to stay at home with your Uncle. The police will be there at a moment's notice if you need them.' Mr Arnold, again, didn't sound convinced.

'Have you two got anything you want to ask?'

I shook my head. Gab remained mute, giving a small shake of her own head.

'Okay.' Mr Arnold tried to give us both a reassuring smile. It was useless. I felt numb inside. Like my body had been anaesthetised, but my mind had been left in overdrive. I barely heard Mr Arnold say: 'Mrs Hamilton will take you two to the staff room. You can stay there until your Uncle arrives.'

I felt my body moving, as I stood up and left the office. I was only vaguely aware of one of the reception staff - Mrs Hamilton - kindly showing us the way to the staff room, despite the fact we both knew full well where it was. It felt like I was walking on clouds, cut off from the world around me. So much was going through my head. I could barely hear my own thoughts.

'Anything you two need, I'm just down the corridor.' Mrs Hamilton's voice floated around my psyche. 'And there are teachers in both of the next-door classrooms if you need anything urgently.' I think she smiled sweetly, trying to be caring. I barely remember.

Next, I was sat in a comfortable moth-eaten armchair in the staffroom, with Gab sat directly opposite me. I was finally able to take stock of my surroundings. The main staffroom, deserted. A large kitchenette took over one-half of the room, boasting little more than a kettle and a mouldy-looking microwave.

I looked at Gab. She was stony-faced. There was almost an anger in her eyes.

'Gab?' I murmured. This was the first time we had properly spoken since the previous night, when we had been at odds. 'It's going to be okay, you know.' I was at a loss for what else to say.

Gab looked directly at me, her gaze piercing my heart. There was a hateful glare in her eyes. What was going on?

'Gab? What's wrong? Is it Dad?'

'I don't give a shit about Dad,' she murmured. Her voice was monotone. There was loathing in it.

'What is it then?'

She continued to glare at me, anger emanating from her very being. Then she spoke the earth-shattering revelation.

'His name is Mikey.'

THIRTY-NINE

MIKEY. Impossible. Absolutely no chance. Yet as Gab blurted out her unfathomable trail of thought, I couldn't help but realise it made perfect sense.

Gab babbled almost without breathing, speaking in urgently hushed tones, leaning forward in her chair in the deserted staffroom, casting fervent glances around her, intermittently ensuring we remained alone.

'It all makes sense!' She exclaimed, a desperation clinging to her voice. 'How the *fuck* didn't we see it before? Mikey. Key. Ikea. It all fits. Laurie had written in her diary that Key's real name was *Mike Arnold*. Smudge those two words together, lose a few letters, it makes *ikea*. Mike Arnold. That's what she had written.'

I breathed deeply, taking it all in.

'Clearly, Mr Arnold uses Key as a nickname. No one would ever have guessed it. Key isn't that common of a nickname for someone called Mike.'

'I don't think it *is* a nickname for someone called Mike,' I countered. 'Like you said last week, it's probably a jokey university name that someone came up with. Or a way for him to hide his identity easily, in plain sight.'

Gab nodded, edified by my contribution. 'And it all makes sense with Vicky as well! She wouldn't *dare* tell me and Ms Dooley who Key was - no wonder! It's a member of the teaching staff! He's been the one having relationships with students and abusing them!'

'And we saw Mr Arnold the night of Vicky's party...' I murmured, my mind suddenly cast back to my drunken walk home that concluded in vomiting on Mr Arnold's shoes.

'Exactly!' Gab exclaimed, flinching slightly at her increased volume and checking herself. 'Exactly,' she repeated, much more quietly. 'Shit, I can't believe we never realised before. He's always been so nice... but he's in a perfect position - a senior member of the teaching staff who is a bit good-looking-'

'Really?' I butted in, incredulously.

Gab shrugged but otherwise ignored me. 'And he's in a place of power. He's senior enough and clever enough to get away with it. He's Deputy Head, answerable only to the headteacher - and maybe he's in on it too!'

'Woah, let's not get ahead of ourselves,' I whispered, checking around the staffroom myself to ensure we were still alone. 'It's one thing to accuse Mr Arnold, but Mr Roberts as well? Come off it.'

'You never know!' Gab implored. 'They seemed pretty pally in his office.'

'They sounded like they were having a row,' I grumbled.

'Yeah, as if Mr Arnold had messed something up.'

'I don't know,' I argued. 'Mr Roberts seemed pretty clueless. He was annoyed that Vicky has disappeared again. He didn't sound like he had much of a clue.'

Gab shrugged again but didn't argue the point further. I seemed to have helped her move on to the next important issue. 'But if Vicky's gone again... surely that means Arnold's got her?'

Somehow, I nodded. 'I guess so.'

'And look what happened to Laurie Openshaw!'

I remained silent, trying to process what was going on.

'She tried to leave him, she ended up running, then disappeared for a couple of years and now she's dead! Arnold's fucking insane! He could kill Vicky if she doesn't do what he wants!'

Again, I was finding it difficult to argue with Gab's conclusions. The issue was, we had no proof. Only a haphazard story, put together through a bit of clever deduction and an impossible window that gave us glimpses of the past.

'I bet he's done others as well... Ellie James went missing a few weeks ago. And Paul!'

'Surely he's not taking boys as well?'

'Stranger things have happened, Chris. A paedo is a paedo.'

I was quiet.

'And Molly Atkinson last year!' Gab continued, remembering yet another missing girl. 'Shit, he's been at this for years!'

I didn't say anything. I just reflected on Gab's words. Everything she was saying made sense. I didn't want to believe it - Mr Arnold had always been very pleasant - nice even - to me. He was always supportive and seemed like he wanted to help us and look after us. Especially over the last few weeks, when all had been going to shit... he'd been nothing but lovely. He'd even paid for our taxi home after Vicky's party...

All so that there were fewer witnesses. Of course.

'This is what the window wanted us to know,' I murmured, barely aware of the words I was speaking. 'This is the mission it has given us. It's what Lilly could have discovered but didn't. And look at her now. Demented. Alone.' I paused, bracing myself for the next, inevitable words. 'We have to do something.'

Gab nodded, a determined smile forming on her lips.

'There's just one issue,' I continued. 'We have no real proof. Just a hunch, a smudged diary entry and a few visions in a magical window.'

My sister looked a little forlorn at my assessment of the situation, before offering a solution. 'Let's just tell the police we have suspicions. We saw Arnold near Vicky's party. We heard him say something. Anything like that!'

I shook my head. 'I don't think it'll be enough. It's a kid's word against his. It wouldn't be unheard of for a kid in Grand Parade to make a false accusation like that.'

'I guess,' Gab muttered, sounding disappointed.

I sighed. I didn't know what to do next. But we had to do something. And I had one source of guidance that we hadn't consulted…

'The window,' I breathed. 'We need to look at the window again.'

FORTY

UNCLE NEV DROVE us home in silence. The inside of his battered old Ford Focus felt dusky and damp, but there was a strangely warm comfort to it. A softness. I guess we both just needed a moment to sit quietly, comfortably, with the soothing hum of the old engine massaging our souls. For a few minutes, we forgot about the sins of Mike Arnold and we were calm... a moment of rest before the storm.

'I suppose I should give you some updates on your Mum,' Nev eventually said, after we'd been driving for ten minutes. We were nearly home. 'I spoke to the Doctors this morning.'

Neither of us said anything. Nev took that as his cue to continue. 'They said the bleed on her brain has got a little bit worse. They had to scan her head again last night because she had a seizure. They can't manage it "conservatively" anymore, whatever that means. They're going to transfer her from York to Hull, so they can do a little operation.'

'How little is the operation?' I said, bluntly, having had enough of things being sugar-coated.

'Not little,' my Uncle confessed, 'but apparently not that big either. They have to do something called "evacuate the bleed". From what they told me, they put your Mum to sleep, make a small cut in her head and suck the blood out.'

'How do they get through the skull?' I responded, my tone remaining stony.

Uncle Nev hesitated. 'Don't worry about that,' he responded. 'These guys are professionals.'

'Do they drill it?' I asked, having watched enough medical dramas to be vaguely familiar with what neurosurgery entailed.

Uncle Nev hesitated again, then reluctantly conceded. 'Yes. But it's only a little drill.'

I didn't respond this time, and simply sat back in my seat, looking out of the window. As we trundled down Beggar Home Lane, I couldn't help but reflect on how upside-down my life had turned in the past few weeks. Two twins from a normal, rough Grand Parade estate had suddenly been thrown into a whirlwind of abuse and kidnapping and mystery and magic. And no one else in the world - apart from Old Lady Lilly - had even the remotest understanding of what we were going through. Least of all Uncle Nev.

We pulled up at the house. A police car was stationed outside. I was vaguely pleased to see that Fred, the officer who had interviewed me on my arrest, was leaning against the bonnet.

'Morning, Officer,' Nev announced, getting out of the car. We followed suit. Fred gave me a pleasant smile.

'Morning, Sir,' Fred replied. 'Morning kids. Sorry about everything that's been happening.'

I shrugged. 'It's fine. Shit happens.'

Fred looked a little surprised by my response but eventually glossed over it. He turned to Nev. 'We still haven't apprehended your brother,' he muttered as if trying to stop us from hearing.

'The kids know everything,' Nev interrupted. 'You may as well tell them as well.'

Fred nodded stiffly. 'Shall we go inside?'

We followed Uncle Nev and the Police Officer into the house, making our way to the kitchen to sit around the table. Fred seemed slightly less relaxed than he had done at the station. He clearly was less comfortable in an unfamiliar environment.

'Len... your Dad,' he added, glancing at the pair of us. 'Is still on the run. We're planning to arrest him as soon as we see him. Unfortunately, he's now added running from police custody to his list of crimes. When we do catch him, a judge'll have a hard time not putting him away for a long while.'

'Good,' Gab spat, a little too harshly. Both Nev and Fred looked at her, obviously a little shocked by her heartlessness.

Fred carried on. 'We've also not found the other party - the one who crashed into your Dad. But we do know that it was a young lad called Aiden Bennet.'

My heart seemed to skip a beat. Aiden Bennet. The boy from Beggar Home Lane. With the little red car. Who had run over my cat. Whose car I'd smashed. Who I'd assaulted. He'd smashed into my Dad's police car...

Fred saw my look of horror. 'This does, Chris, happen to be the same lad that you have got in trouble with before. I know you told me he drove like a twat. Well, I can confirm, he does.'

'You should have arrested him when I told you that,' I grumbled.

Fred shrugged. 'Like I said, we can't arrest someone for driving like an idiot. It'll catch up with him eventually.'

'You said he'd get caught by a speed camera or the police,' I countered. 'Not involved in a crash like this.'

Again, Fred shrugged. 'Unfortunately, things like this happen.'

'Whatever,' I sulked. I didn't know what I was particularly angry about - I suppose it was everything. The dickhead who had nearly run me over and successfully run over my cat had ploughed into my Dad's police escort, sending him on the run. The fact that my Dad was on the loose terrified me. Who knew what he was going to do? To me, to Gab, to my Mum, to anyone? Aiden, that little prick... I hoped he was dead in a ditch somewhere.

Fred's words droned on in the back of my mind. I was barely paying attention. He was saying something about us staying safe in the house, not going to school, Nev keeping a close eye on us, that they'd do everything they could to find both Len and Aiden, etcetera, etcetera.

At some point, I stopped giving a shit. Midway through Fred's soliloquy, completely unaware of what he was saying, I stood up, walked away, and headed straight for my room, where I locked the door, lay on my bed and cried. For the first time during this whole messed-up series of events, I cried.

FORTY-ONE

GAB KNOCKED GENTLY on my door. I don't know how long I'd been lying on my bed, but it was long enough. I needed to get out of my angst. We had work to do.

I pulled myself up, slightly begrudgingly and went to open the door. Gab marched in, lacking any form of sensitivity, naturally.

'Let's get this window out then, we need to work out what to do.'

A ghost of a smile crossed my lips. No "How are you?" or "Do you want to talk?" Standard, in your face, "let's get on with it".

Obediently, I reached under the bed and pulled out the window, still wrapped in its faithful bedsheet. I still didn't speak. Gab ripped off the sheet and pushed the window in front of us, so we were both looking directly at it.

The behaviour was typical of my sister. Our world was collapsing around us. One parent was on the run from the police, the other was about to have her head drilled open. Our friends were being abducted by a paedophile school teacher. We had a magic window that showed us the past, with a harrowing assignment from a demented old lady. It was enough to drive anyone mad. Not Gab though. And, by extension, not me. We had to lose ourselves in this mission. We had to give it our all. It was the only way we would survive this.

We looked into the window.

Images appeared quicker than ever before. It was as if the window now knew that it could trust us. It knew that we had heard its call. We had accepted its authority. We would do as it told us. Or led us. Or whatever.

The image we saw was familiar. Rain, darkness, fear. Laurie Openshaw stood in the pouring rain, looking around her. Beggar Home Lane appeared before us, looking not dissimilar to how it did that very day. Even the little red car that, only last night, had ploughed into Dad's police car, was sitting on the road.

Once again, the visceral terror Laurie felt invaded my soul, bringing sadness and fear to my every molecule. I held my breath. Her spirit overwhelmed me.

A familiar scene played out before us. Laurie glanced around, before bending down and dropping her notebook into the drain. She looked up. Her eyes met ours. It felt as if our souls connected. She latched on to us, pulling us. I could feel the chill of the wind and rain around her. I felt damp on my hands, still flat on the dry, threadbare carpet of my room. A shiver went down my spine. I felt a trickle of icy water down my back. It was the most intense vision the window had given us.

This is where the story had ended the first time we watched it. Now, we pushed on.

Laurie stood up, looking around again. Her facial expression changed. One of fear and terror turned into unadulterated horror. Laurie wet herself - we couldn't see it, but we *knew*. He was coming. He'd found her. *Key.*

Laurie ran.

Still feeling inconceivably connected to the girl, I felt my heart pound in my chest as Laurie's heart rate increased. My breathing became shallow like I was breathless from running. Laurie was gone from the window, but the image remained. My heart continued to race, a dull ache spreading across my chest.

Rain hammered down and lightning crashed in the window. The world around Gab and I seemed to condense, the entire room shrinking around us, light being stolen as we were pulled further and further into the depths of the image before us.

Sweat dripped off me, dramatically countered by a freezing chill gripping my very being. My heart continued to hammer. My throat was raw and dry, my breathing was shallow. It felt as if I'd run a marathon.

Then...

He was there.

Everything seemed to pause. My heart quietened. Did it stop? I wasn't breathing. I held my breath in a terrifying moment of stillness.

He was like a dark sentinel, stalking his prey, a disgusting, perverse predator, filled with rage and hatred and lust. He wore little more than jeans and a hooded sweatshirt, his body barely protected from the elements. The hood shrouded his identity, but as ever, the window showed the truth.

His face was as clear as day.

Arnold. Mike Arnold. Mikey. Key.

And the face of Key bore an expression I had never seen on that of Mr Arnold. The usually supportive, kind facial expression had gone. This was one of anger and desire and greed. It was one that still haunts my dreams even to this day, every night in the cold silence.

Mr Arnold, the man who had abducted Laurie and Vicky and probably Ellie and Paul and Molly too. The man who was supposed to be our Deputy Headteacher, our protector, our advocate.

Here he was, plain as day, chasing after a petrified, underaged girl, with dark, forbidden desires in his heart.

And just like that it was over.

Reality slowly returned to us as the images in the window faded into nothingness. Light returned to the room and temperature was restored.

Gab and I looked at each other, panting.

A small sound broke the silence. It was little more than a whisper, but as I looked down, I saw the crack in the window moving down, now working into the second pane of glass. Somehow I knew that, soon, this window would cease to be. And if we didn't save the day soon, who knew what was going to happen to us?

FORTY-TWO

SO WE KNEW. We knew what was going on. We were the *only* people in Grand Parade - hell, the only people in the *world* - who knew what was going on. We knew who had taken Vicky - twice. We knew who had abducted Laurie - and probably killed her, or thrown her in the river, or some other dark shit like that. And we had a pretty good guess that Ellie James, Molly Atkinson, and maybe even my mate Paul Thornton, had all fallen victim to this abhorrent bastard's perverse scheme.

Was it for the sex? That would make sense. Vicky, Ellie, Molly and Laurie would all have been considered pretty attractive girls - I wouldn't have kicked any of them out of bed. So it made sense. Some crusty old schoolteacher decided he wanted some fresh meat so abused girls. Probably, initially anyway, with their consent. We knew from talking to Vicky and from reading Laurie's diary that the relationship, however taboo and inappropriate, had, at least initially, been consensual. Laurie even sounded like she had grown to love Arnold.

Unfortunately, it was clear that Arnold didn't like taking no for an answer. When Vicky tried to leave he had plied her with material goods to keep hold of her, then threatened to harm her family if she said anything. He'd kept her prisoner in his house, for crying out loud!

And Laurie... well, from what we knew, as soon as she wanted to break it off with Arnold it went south. She'd been terrified in the image in the window. And that was the last time anyone had seen her - until just recently when she'd turned up dead.

What didn't make sense was Paul. Surely, Paul couldn't be one of Arnold's victims? It broke the pattern dramatically. Why would Arnold suddenly be interested in a spotty little boy, when he had his hands full with plenty of young girls? No... that didn't quite fit.

We'd seen Paul being chased by someone in the window - most likely Arnold. Had Paul stumbled upon Arnold's secret, and the teacher felt like he had to take action and do something about it? Maybe silence Paul?

Just a few weeks ago, Arnold had asked me about Paul in his office. Why would he do that, if he'd been responsible for Paul's disappearance? Surely he'd just be arousing suspicion unnecessarily. No... something didn't quite add up. Something was still wrong.

'We have to confront him,' Gab announced that evening, this time sitting in her bedroom, having just shared a dinner of sausage and chips with Uncle Nev.

'But we have no evidence,' I reminded her.

'We have Laurie's book,' Gab said.

I shrugged. 'That's just a tattered notebook. There's no specific evidence. She never actually named Arnold. Not properly. And if he's been using the name Key with all these teenage girls, I doubt many other people know him as that.'

'I guess.' Gab looked crestfallen. She knew the answers. She knew what was going on. But that made it worse because we were helpless. Our only concrete evidence had been given to us through the window. We had nothing, apart from our word. There wasn't a shred of evidence that would get the police or the school staff even remotely interested, let alone get a conviction.

'This is what the window wanted us to know, though,' Gab reflected, quietly. 'So why can we not do anything about it?'

Gab was nothing if not a strong woman. She hated injustice, particularly against other women. The idea that a man in a position of trust and power was abusing young girls and potentially killing them was outrageous, that goes without saying, but to Gab, it was even worse. She'd grown up in a household where our abusive father regularly knocked the shit out of our mother and ruled over her with misogyny and hate. She hated men who abused women. And she knew that a particularly nasty one was out there, getting away with it, whilst helping run a school.

And we were powerless to stop him. It was like being paralysed. We had the knowledge, but couldn't do anything with it. How could the window show us this and not give us a way to fix it? It was infuriating.

'We have to get evidence,' I murmured, barely aware I was speaking.

'What?' Gab asked. Her eyes lit up. There was a hunger in her expression. A hunger for justice.

'We know what's going on, but we have no way to prove it. Yet. So we get evidence.' I spoke with a conviction I didn't know I had, a plan forming in my head that was so simple and clear. Would it work? Probably not. But we had to give it a try.

'How do we get evidence?' Gab whispered, daring to hope.

'We go straight to the source,' I explained, gently. 'We get a confession.'

'How?'

'We confront Arnold. Head on. In school. He'll be caught off guard. He'll give something away. He may even confess.'

Gab snorted. 'He's a pro at this. He's not going to give anything away. Even if he does, why would anyone believe our word over the word of the Deputy Head?'

This time, I smiled. 'Because we'll be recording the whole conversation on our phones.'

FORTY-THREE

WE WERE STILL TECHNICALLY under what could only be described as "Protective Custody", as the police had requested that we didn't leave the house. Uncle Nev was also supposed to be staying with us, supervising us. Fortunately, Nev had never been one to stick to the rules, meaning that, thankfully, neither did we.

'I'm going to Hull to check on your mother,' Nev explained the next morning. I was sure he'd been to the pub the previous night, as well. 'The Doctors want to speak to me and may need me to sign some consent forms on her behalf.'

We understood. Mum had no family, as an only child with both parents dead. Dad would have been next of kin. In his absence, the only functioning family member any of us had left - Nev - had stepped in.

Nev gave us strict instructions to stay in the house. He told us he would be furious if he found out we'd left. It was for our own good, apparently.

We reluctantly agreed, with absolutely no intention of following his instructions. We waited half an hour after his old Ford Focus had driven away before we pulled on hooded sweatshirts and caps to cover our faces. Then, we started on our clandestine journey to school, to confront the man himself.

We hurried through the journey, walking much quicker than we normally did. We were at school within 20 minutes. Luckily, the main entrance was still open and, as it was midway through lesson two of the day, there were mercifully few staff around.

It wasn't difficult to sneak in.

Immediately, we made our way to Mr Arnold's office. Both of us had our mobile phones hidden in our pockets. We'd pressed voice record just before entering the school. It had been agreed we would both record the conversation, just in case of a problem with one of the phones.

We made it to Mr Arnold's office without attracting any attention, thank goodness. The corridor remained deserted. We listened at the office door. Not a sound from the inside. We knocked.

No answer.

We knocked again.

Silence.

I tried the door handle. It didn't budge.

'Shit,' Gab hissed. 'He's not here.'

'Maybe he's teaching?' I offered, quietly.

I don't know if the window had been subconsciously guiding us, or if we were just bloody lucky, but the situation resolved itself almost at once.

'Chris? Gab? What are you two doing here?' Mr Arnold's familiar voice had a stern tone to it as he approached us down the corridor.

Thinking on her feet, Gab took control. 'Sorry, Sir. I know we're supposed to be at home. We just... we needed help. You said we could come to you if we needed anything.'

Mr Arnold seemed to hesitate. 'Where's your Uncle? Does he know you're here?'

'No Sir,' Gab continued, on a roll. 'We came by ourselves. We need your help.'

Arnold still looked dubious, but clearly, he was concerned enough to give us a chance. 'You'd both better come in then,' he said, cautiously, unlocking his office door. He held the door open for us and encouraged us into the familiar two seats that faced his desk. We took up our places, silently. The phone in my pocket suddenly felt as heavy as lead.

Mr Arnold sat down opposite us, on the other side of the desk. 'What's wrong, you two?' He wore a sympathetic smile on his lips.

I wasn't entirely sure where to start. As was typical for my twin sister, however, she immediately took control, clearly having silently prepped what she was going to say.

'They found Laurie Openshaw's body the other day.' She spoke bluntly. Her tone had changed dramatically from that of the sweet, innocent girl who had been standing outside Mr Arnold's office just a few seconds ago.

Arnold seemed to flinch with surprise. He hadn't been expecting the conversation to start this way.

'We found out something about her disappearance,' Gab continued, confidently.

Arnold's face had changed. His smile was gone. There was a blankness to his expression, mixed with just a hint of shock. Hesitantly, he said: 'Go on.'

'We think she was involved with an older man. Things got messy and she tried to break it off. He got angry, chased her down, and we think he killed her.'

Arnold said nothing, now more composed, actively listening with interest.

'Vicky Crampton was going out with the same guy,' Gab went on. 'And now she's disappeared again.'

Arnold still said nothing.

'Both of them called this man "Key". That was apparently his name.'

There was silence. Mr Arnold said nothing but gave a curt nod as if inviting Gab to continue.

Gab seemed slightly stuck, unsure how to proceed. She'd expected Arnold to say something.

My turn to take over. 'Do you know anyone called Key, Sir?'

I heard Gab exhale with momentary relief. My heart was pounding in my chest. It felt like staring at the window again.

Mr Arnold paused for a moment before responding. 'Key?' He asked, sounding very innocent. 'That's a very odd name.'

The tension was building.

'That's what we thought,' I replied, coolly. 'Do you think it's a nickname for someone?'

Arnold answered slowly again. 'It could well be, Chris. Although it's a bizarre nickname.'

Silence.

Arnold continued. 'Have you told anyone else about this, you two? The police, or your Uncle?'

'No,' Gab replied, immediately. 'No, you're the first person we're telling.'

'Hm.' Mr Arnold looked away from us and out of the window, apparently musing over the situation.

He knows.

'We wonder if this same guy knows anything about the other kids who've disappeared. You know, Ellie James and Molly Atkinson? Maybe even Paul Thornton?' I was pushing it now. I could feel the pressure in the room rising, like a keg of power about to blow.

Mr Arnold looked back to me, his brow furrowed, obscuring his moderately attractive features. 'That's a big assumption,' he said, plainly.

'It's a big problem,' Gab retorted, a brutality to her voice.

A look of fear seemed to flash through Arnold's eyes. In a second it was gone, replaced by something else.

Rage.

He knows that we know.

'Do you have any evidence of this Key? Anything that the police could use?'

He's feigning innocence. He's trying to work out our position. See our hand. This is just a game of poker now. Who can hold out the longest?

'No,' Gab said, slowly. 'But we know that Vicky was texting someone called Key.'

Mr Arnold nodded, carefully. 'And how did you come about this knowledge of Laurie? How do you know she was involved with someone and it got… unpleasant?'

Shit, I don't have an answer to that.

'A friend of a friend,' Gab replied, immediately, having clearly planned this. 'One of my friends told me she knew one of Laurie's friends. We were talking about it after the body had been found. Apparently, Laurie hadn't told many people.'

'Hm,' was Mr Arnold's response, again.

We all sat silently.

Everyone in this room knows exactly what's going on. And he's too clever for us.

'This is very serious information, kids,' Arnold eventually said, looking directly at us both. Was there a hint of malice in his eyes? 'But thank you for telling me. I don't know how much help it will be, but I'll certainly speak to the police about it. Do we know if Vicky's phone is still at her house, or did she have it with her when she disappeared? It could be useful to see who she was texting. The police can trace numbers and do all sorts like that.'

'I'm not sure,' I responded, carefully. *He's bluffing. He's holding back. And he's not going to say anything.*

'Maybe we should see if the phone can be tracked down. It could help… everyone.' There was a darkness to his tone. He was stalling. Waiting for us to make the next move.

My next move was made for me.

My phone beeped in my pocket.

FORTY-FOUR

HURRIEDLY, I wrenched my phone out of my hoodie pocket. It displayed a text from Uncle Nev, checking in and saying he'd got to Hull safely. I barely noticed Mr Arnold's inquisitive look as I fumbled with the phone, trying to silence it.

My fingers trembled, the shrill beep of the text message's arrival cutting dramatically and harshly into the tense atmosphere. I fumbled. The text went away. The recording stopped.

Then it started playing.

I was shaking more and more, panicking, terrified. I tried to stop the recording. But it was like I couldn't control my fingers. I was in such a panic.

The next thing I knew, the recording was playing at double speed, relaying our conversation with Mr Arnold in the hallway, before being invited into his office.

Finally, I stopped it.

It was too late.

Gab's face showed nothing but unadulterated terror. Mr Arnold's face was stony and full of loathing.

Carefully, and impossibly calmly, Arnold stood up, walked around to the both of us, and held out his hands. Reluctantly, but at a complete loss of what to do next, I handed over my phone.

Arnold looked at Gab expectantly, saying nothing. Also unsure what to do, Gab reached into her own pocket and extracted her phone.

Taking both phones, Arnold walked back around his desk. Painfully slowly, he sat himself back down. He started with my phone. I heard a few beeps, as he presumably deleted the recording. My phone was returned to its space on the desk.

Then Arnold picked up Gab's phone and similarly deleted the recording. Then he placed it on the desk, next to my own.

Still silent, he reached across his desk. His fingers closed around a large water bottle, probably over a litre in size, full to the brim.

Not a word was said. A horrifying silence filled the room, louder than any noise I'd ever heard.

Mr Arnold unscrewed the lid of the water bottle. Still not looking at us, he gently tipped the bottle to the side. Slowly, water trickled out of the water bottle and onto the desk, cascading over our two phones.

He held the bottle like that for some time. This was back in the days of non-waterproof phones. Many a time, I'd been caught with my pants down - literally - having dropped my phone in the toilet. A little bit of water on your phone and poof. It was gone. Irreparably damaged. Caput. It would cease to be.

For what felt like an age, we watched as Mr Arnold drowned our mobile phones, pouring the entirety of the bottle's contents out, soaking his desk and the surrounding documents and articles that littered it. Even from where I was sitting, I could see water creeping through the inside of my phone screen, obliterating the circuitry inside.

Finally, as the temperature in the room felt like it reached boiling point, the water ran out. Mr Arnold returned the bottle to its resting place. He then proceeded to pick up both of our phones, stand up, and walk back around to us. Drips of water fell to the ground from the waterlogged devices. Gently, he passed our now destroyed phones back to us and returned to his chair.

His eyes locked with mine. There was untold malice and hatred in them. It felt like we had been quiet for centuries. Then, at last, he spoke.

'Shall we have a more honest conversation now?'

His voice sounded completely different. The kind-hearted, encouraging nature of it had vanished. Now… it was *evil*. The true man had been unmasked.

We said nothing.

Arnold leant back in his chair and sighed deeply. 'My relationships with Laurie, Vicky, and whoever else you've conjured up have absolutely nothing to do with you. And not that it matters, but I most certainly did not kill Laurie. That stupid girl probably fell in the river or threw herself in.' He spoke with such heartlessness. 'And I have no idea what has happened to Vicky, or any of the other girls.'

'How many schoolgirls have you been with?' Gab asked, her hatred emanating through.

Arnold shrugged. 'It doesn't matter, child, and I most certainly wouldn't tell you, even if I hadn't lost count.'

Cold callousness. It was horrendous to see.

He leant forward over his desk, his elbows bathing in the puddle of water that remained. 'You will both keep your mouths shut.' He hissed the words with untold venom. 'You will say nothing. Not that anyone will believe you. You have no evidence. I will never confess, and I will never be caught. I have been doing this for years, and never have I made a mistake. You two have no idea who you are messing with. I would suggest that you both forget everything you think you know. You both remember your place. And you never breathe a word of what you think you know.'

Arnold's voice had sunk to nothing more than a whisper, but it was more petrifying than ever. 'You little *shits* need to remember who I am. I will *fuck you up* if you dare mess with me. I have powerful friends, and you two have made a powerful enemy. Now get the *fuck* out of my office. I *never* want to speak to either of you little scrotes again. Is that clear?'

For a few moments, we all stared at each other. The final battle of the day. In the end, we lost. Gab and I both looked away. We looked at each other, forlorn. We were beaten. We'd lost.

Without another word, the pair of us stood up, taking our defunct mobile phones with us, and left Mr Arnold's office, the weight of the world heavy on our shoulders.

FORTY-FIVE

NEITHER OF US said much on the journey home. It seemed that was becoming our way - silent journeys through the streets of Grand Parade, York, reflecting on the madness and audacity of our radically changed lives.

I suppose the overriding feeling in both of us was failure. Sure, we were scared and absolutely shaken to our cores, but that was a given. A grown man - one in a position of power, who appeared to be a master of manipulation - had given us nothing less than a death threat. I believed the guy. Arnold would destroy us if we challenged him again. And when he had discovered we were covertly trying to record him… the brutality of his response… the silent destruction of our phones… it was bloody terrifying.

But I don't think it was the fear that weighed heaviest on our minds. No, the biggest burden was one of failure. We had been shown a truth by the window. A sadistic abuser had been unmasked before us… and we were powerless to stop him. Arnold was right - we had no evidence. Nothing that could prove he was behind Laurie and Vicky and Ellie and whoever else. Laurie was dead. Ellie had been missing for weeks. And Vicky had vanished, once again, probably captive in Mr Arnold's house.

We could go to his house... find her! As soon as the thought crossed my mind, I dismissed it. It was too dangerous. Who knew what the guy was capable of? He'd seemed pretty callous in our meeting. No... turning up at his house to try and find Vicky wasn't a good move unless we could get the police to go... but why would they?

As was our custom, we walked a little slower as we turned onto Beggar Home Lane. I guess it had become natural to us, after all we had seen there. We paused briefly outside Old Lady Lilly's house, which was beginning to look like a real residence again, after weeks of building work. The skip outside had been emptied recently and was already being refilled.

Our gaze travelled across the road to the house that I had seen Aiden Bennet come out of before I gave him and his car a thorough beating. We looked upon the space on the road where that beat-up little red car had so often sat.

It was only right that our eyes finally turned to the drainage grate, just a few metres from where that car had once been parked. The same grate where Laurie had stowed the only clue to her disappearance. The disappearance we had failed to solve.

Dejected and miserable, we trudged back to the house.

I was vaguely pleased that Uncle Nev's Ford Focus hadn't yet returned to outside our house. We'd successfully gone about our mission without him ever knowing.

On entering the house, I headed to the kitchen, planning to make a cup of tea. Gab marched upstairs, without a word.

I put the kettle on. That's what you do when you're not sure what to do, or you feel like you're stuck or need a break. You make a cup of tea. Strong as you can, with a Yorkshire teabag (it has to be Yorkshire), left to brew for four minutes, before giving the bag a firm squeeze with a teaspoon and adding a drop of milk. Yep, that's how tea was designed to be drunk, in my humble opinion.

Absentmindedly, I also made Gab a cup. Whilst less of a tea fanatic than myself, she didn't mind a cup and drank it - of course - as it should be drunk.

I sat at the kitchen table, cradling my drink, looking out at the garden, to the remains of the box that had once housed the window. That *blasted* window. That damn thing had started it all.

I must have been sat for about ten minutes before Gab reappeared. She grunted gratefully as she saw her steaming mug and sat down next to me.

'I didn't see anything new,' she mumbled.

'What?'

'In the window?'

'When?'

'Just now?'

I snorted. 'You've been looking at the window just now? The one in my room?'

'I think we're well past whose bloody room it is,' Gab snapped, staring at her drink.

I smiled weakly. She was right.

'It just showed me the same thing,' she continued, sipping. 'Laurie hiding the diary, running off, then Arnold appearing a bit later. It seems to be speeding up, repeating itself. Like it's on a loop.'

I nodded, understandingly. 'Before I beat up Aiden, I saw the image of Tigger being run over on repeat. On a loop, like you said. Then I confronted Aiden and I haven't seen it since. It's like…'

'The window is stuck,' Gab interrupted. 'It's showing us what it needs us to fix. Or what it needs us to respond to. We just don't know how.'

'If we could show the window to someone else…'

'Chris!' Gab exclaimed.

I hung my head. I knew she was right. We couldn't. It was our burden to bear. Like Lilly had taught us. I doubt the window would even show someone else anyway… you had to *believe* in it. Like I had. Like we both did.

We sat for a long time, not saying much. After what could have been hours, we heard the door open noisily. Nev was home. He was chattering on his old Nokia mobile phone - a dinosaur in today's modern age. All it could do was make calls, send texts and play *Snake*. He was talking rapidly, making lots of 'hm' and 'I see' statements. He walked into the kitchen still on the phone, waved at us, and walked over to the kettle, checking if it was still hot. Holding the phone under his ear, he went about making himself a coffee. Finally, he concluded his conversation. The whole time, Gab and I had sat in silence.

'I understand. Thanks, Officer. Keep us updated.'

He put the archaic phone down and brought his coffee over to the table to sit with us. I recoiled slightly at the smell - Nev stank! There was an impressive stench of sweat and chemicals.

'Sorry lad,' Nev winked, noticing my disgust. 'It's the stink of the day. I've been running up and down all over the place, been to Hull and back. And those hospitals stink! Chemicals and bleach everywhere! I even slipped on a freshly cleaned floor!' He showed us his arm, which was wet and smelt appropriately clinical and clean.

'How is Mum?' I asked, changing the subject.

Nev's expression turned serious. 'She's going in for surgery this afternoon. The surgeons want to drill a *small*,' (he emphasised the word very carefully) 'hole in her skull and suck out the blood that's there. It will save her. They tell me it's a common procedure, and there shouldn't be too many complications.'

'Will she live?' Gab's question was blunt, as ever, but it was what we were both thinking.

Nev nodded, slowly. 'The surgeons seem confident. She's young and relatively healthy. They think she'll pull through, as long as they get on with it quickly.'

'They should have got on with it days ago,' I retorted, angry that my Mum's life had been left in the balance for the proceeding days.

'Apparently, it's normal practice to watch and wait,' Nev countered, not unkindly. He was explaining everything as best he could. This had been a difficult few days for him too. He was unshaven and had bags under his eyes. He looked tired - the stress of suddenly becoming the sole guardian of two teenagers was clearly an unexpected challenge. 'They try not to operate unless they absolutely have to because operations don't come without risks.'

I wasn't particularly satisfied with his argument, but it would do. Gab then took over the conversation, steering it in a different direction.

'Who was on the phone? You said "Thanks Officer".'

Nev nodded, taking a swig of his coffee. 'I did, Gab, yes. I was on the phone with Officer Andrews - Fred, the one who was over here the other day.'

'And arrested me,' I mumbled quietly, remembering Fred well.

Nev nodded. 'He's a nice guy, Fred. He's keeping us updated on progress with your father.'

'Is there any?' I asked, doubtfully.

'No,' my Uncle confessed. I was right to have been doubtful. 'Both your father and this Aiden boy are still missing. They suspect your father has tried to leave town, and this Aiden lad will probably turn up in a day or so, potentially after a bender. You know what Grand Parade is like.'

We nodded, acknowledging the truth in what was becoming a cliché.

'They've got some leads though,' Nev said. I didn't feel anything as Nev continued. I didn't really care about leads in my Dad's case. The prick was gone and could stay gone, as much as I cared. He wouldn't come after Gab or me, or Mum for that matter. He was too interested in saving his own skin.

'There is some CCTV footage from a shop camera across the road from the crash. The police are examining it to see if they can work out your Father's initial movements. There's also a speed camera snap, as the red car was going well over the speed limit. And apparently, there was a dashcam on Aiden's car. All of this together may give us some idea of which way your Father went and what actually happened in the crash.'

'What's a dashcam?' I asked, unfamiliar with such a device. I couldn't drive yet, remember? I was only sixteen.

'It's one of these fancy cameras some people have in their cars, on the dashboard. It records what's going on when you're driving, so if you're ever in an accident, there's video evidence. It helps improve road safety apparently.'

'Aiden drove like a prick,' I said, laughing at the absurdity of the situation. 'He wasn't interested in road safety! Why the hell did he have one of these cameras?'

Nev chuckled. 'I asked the same thing myself - I was surprised to hear Aiden had one. But apparently, his parents had one installed in that little red car the moment he passed his driving test. Having one installed makes your car insurance cheaper.' Nev smiled. 'Makes no sense to me though, considering how much the dashcam cost in the first place.'

'Why?' Gab asked, sounding incredibly uninterested. 'How much are they?'

Nev shrugged. 'I mean you could pick up a second-hand one for probably less than £50. But this one was all-singing-all-dancing. Loads of memory, backed up videos saved to the internet, motion activated. It must have cost them hundreds. It would have been cheaper to just get a more expensive insurance package.'

Nev continued to witter on, chatting away about police investigations, cars and road safety. Something didn't quite sit right with me, however. I became steadily more cocooned in my thoughts, reflecting on everything that had happened over the past few weeks. I felt like I had all the pieces to the puzzle, they just weren't exactly in place.

I could see a flash…

The rest of the day passed monotonously. Nev cooked us some pasta, which we all ate in silence, watching the news. Political drama dominated most of the report until Sophie Stark came on to present a quick five-minute local news segment. The missing children and body of Laurie were only mentioned in passing, the bigger story being the theft of equipment from Hull and York Universities. A thoroughly disgruntled professor was complaining angrily to the local reporter.

I still couldn't quite piece my thoughts together as I walked myself up to bed. I murmured goodnight to Gab as I reached the top of the stairs and went into my room.

Intermittent flashing lights…

Closing the door behind me, I sat down on my bed, noticing that the corner of the window, still covered in the sheet, was sticking out from under the bed. Gab clearly hadn't hidden it away properly. Cursing her carelessness, I made sure my door was locked and pulled the window out once again.

The first thing I noticed was that the crack was bigger. It had worked its way through three of the six panes of glass, traversing in a disorderly fashion like a tiny snake. It was growing more and more.

I couldn't stare long at the crack. The window was calling me.

Once again, the room around me dimmed. I found myself looking at the same familiar images of Laurie, hiding her journal, before running, only to be pursued minutes later by Mr Arnold. The images were moving faster than ever, repeating over and over, playing in a furious loop. The emotion of the scene felt amplified, overpowering my being once again, drenching me in sweat and fear and - somehow - the rain from the street.

In an instant, as the physicality of the experience threatened to overwhelm me, the image slowed to a pause.

I breathed deeply, examining the scene. Laurie was approaching the edge of the window, now attempting her escape. All that was left was the rain falling, beating down against the pavement and the road and the houses and that little red car, awaiting the predator round the corner.

Flashes… tiny, rhythmic flashes…

The image faded and light returned to my surroundings. I felt exhausted. Laurie's emotions slamming through my body had shattered me. Shaking and fighting off vertigo, I wrapped the window and shoved it under my bed, a little harshly. Then, I collapsed onto the mattress, knowledge and revelations far too dangerous for a boy of sixteen swimming aggressively through my mind.

What was missing? What was the clue?

I dozed.

My eyes opened to darkness. I slept again.

It was the early hours. I was awake.

It made sense.

The image. The car. The flashing on the dashboard… the *dashcam*. The *motion-activated* dashcam.

FORTY-SIX

THE NEXT MORNING, Uncle Nev came into my room to announce he was heading out to work. Uncle Nev, unlike my Father, had managed to maintain a successful career in a construction company. He may have been a bit of an alcoholic - like my Father - but at least he was a *functioning* alcoholic. Nev worked for a firm near Leeds, a good forty-minute drive from our house. I begrudgingly agreed to his request not to leave the house (I didn't particularly think I'd follow such a request, but it was a nice touch) and waved him goodbye.

After hearing his car drive away and waiting for a few minutes, I went over to Gab's room. I was beyond excited to tell her what I had worked out. Irritatingly, Gab did what she always did best.

'The dashcam,' she announced, proudly.

'Bloody hell, Gab, when did you work that out?' I answered, annoyed.

'Last night in bed. It suddenly came to me.'

'It came to me too,' I muttered, in a feeble attempt to salvage my pride.

'Yeah, but I bet you needed the window to help you work it out, didn't you?'

I didn't answer.

'We have to go and speak to Fred,' Gab went on. 'He can help.'

'You think he's going to take the word of a couple of kids? One of which he's already arrested?'

'Listen, we have evidence! We can show him the notebook. Say we found it in a bush when we were walking down Beggar Home. Ask him to look whether the dashcam was activated the night that Laurie disappeared.'

'How will they know what night that was?'

'I imagine they'll have a police record saying when she was reported missing and when she was last seen.'

Gab was making sense, but I was still hesitant. 'It's over a year ago. How do we know the dashcam was in the car a year ago? And how do we know that the video will still be saved?'

'I reckon Aiden has been driving for over a year. He's probably about twenty. And the car was there in the window. There's a good chance.'

'What about it still being saved?' I implored.

Gab shrugged. 'We'll have to be lucky. But if the window has helped us work this out, there's a damn good chance we will be.'

Somehow, Gab's bizarre logic made sense.

'Come on,' she went on. 'Get dressed. We need to go to the police station.'

And so we went to the police station. We said very little on the journey. Nev, thankfully, was nowhere to be seen, having made true on his promise to return to work. I suspect he knew we wouldn't stay home, despite the apparent danger of my Father being on the run. There seemed to be a mutual, silent understanding that as long as we were back home before he was, there was no harm, no foul.

We arrived at Grand Parade's local police station. It was a small building on the corner of a junction where two roads intersected. A corner shop was the only other establishment that seemed to show any life.

Anxiety began to well up inside me as we entered the station.

We hadn't exactly planned how we were going to play this - not explicitly. Maybe Gab had come up with a plan in her head, as she often did. She was a born leader. Thus, I let her take the lead. She walked directly up to the front desk, where a young, pretty woman sat leafing through papers.

'Hello,' Gab began, politely.

The young woman looked at her with a smile. 'How can I help you, young lady?'

'I'm Gabrielle Keeler,' she explained.

Straight out with it, I thought.

'This is my brother, Chris,' she continued, motioning behind her in my direction. I waved awkwardly. 'Officer Fred has been looking after us - I think he's in charge of the case with our Dad disappearing after abusing us and then getting into a car crash.'

Not holding back, I thought to myself. Gab's all-in approach seemed to have worked, though. The woman at the desk put down her papers and gave us both her full attention.

'Of course.' She smiled warmly, trying to be comforting. 'We've heard about you both, Gab and Chris.'

I bet we're the talk of the station, I thought, cynically.

'I'm so sorry for all you've been through,' the woman went on. 'Anything we can do to help, you both just let us know.'

Gab gave the woman her sweetest smile and presented her request. 'We'd like to talk to Officer Fred, if, of course, he's available.' She was being more polite than I'd ever seen her. 'We just want to talk to him about some things our Dad said to us, we wondered if it would help in the investigation. And we'd like to find out where he's up to - and what's going to happen to us. We're living with our Uncle at the moment, you know. Our Mum is in the hospital in Hull, having brain surgery.'

I wasn't sure if the quiver in Gab's voice at the end of her statement was feigned or not, but it didn't matter. The woman at the desk - gushing with genuine sympathy - nodded immediately and got to her feet.

'You poor thing,' she exclaimed, coming round the desk to put a comforting arm around Gab. My sister sniffed, apparently crying. 'Let me take you through to Fred's office. He's definitely in the station somewhere, I'll get him to come and see you. I don't think he's got a big caseload at the moment, aside from your case, of course.'

'Really?' Gab asked, through - fake? - tears. 'Surely he's really busy? All these disappearing kids?'

Keep fishing, Gab. She was doing so well.

The young woman began to lead us into the depths of the police station, shaking her head. 'Don't worry, Gabrielle. Fred's priority is your case. Other cases are dealt with by other officers.'

This could be a stumbling block, I thought. Would Fred be able to help? At this point, it was the best we had.

We arrived at an office at the end of a long corridor. The door sported a slightly weary-looking sign saying "F. Andrews, Sergeant". The woman leading our way knocked gingerly and waited for a response, of which there was none, before opening the door. She ushered us inside and indicated two comfortable-looking armchairs.

'Make yourselves comfortable. I'll let Fred know you've arrived. I'm sure he'll be pleased to see you both. Can I get either of you a drink?'

'No, thank you though.' They were the only words I'd uttered.

The woman smiled affectionately and left the room, closing the door behind us. I immediately turned to Gab.

'Fred's not on the "missing children" case,' I announced, voicing my earlier concerns.

Gab nodded with understanding. 'I know. But I think he's still our best shot. He won't be able to ignore this.' She withdrew a familiar, damp notebook from her pocket and lay it on the desk before her. 'He'll have to do something.'

I found myself desperately hoping he would, as I stared at the letters L.O. on the front of the notebook, and remembered the audacious fear that had swept through me as I had watched Laurie's fate play out over and over again.

FORTY-SEVEN

FRED DIDN'T KEEP us waiting long. He arrived at the office just a few minutes after the front desk woman had left us. He looked a little exacerbated, and maybe a little disgruntled that two children were interrupting his likely packed work schedule. Fortunately, he picked up a few moments after he saw us.

'Hi, you two,' he smiled, encouragingly. He worked his way around his desk, manoeuvring around stacks of files and papers, before plumping himself in his chair. 'I've not got too long to chat, unfortunately, but I can give you a few minutes. Are you both okay?'

We looked at each other, a little dumbfounded. Where did we start?

After a moment's silence, Fred carried on. 'I'm doing the best I can to track down your father. We've got some footage from local CCTV cameras and the Bennet boy's dashcam. We'll be able to see what direction your Dad fled in, and exactly how the crash happened. Did your Uncle tell you all this?'

We nodded silently.

Fred smiled in acknowledgement. 'Elise tells me you have some information that might be useful.' The police officer's eyes flickered momentarily to the notebook that had appeared before us. There was a flash of confusion at how the unfamiliar object had landed on his table. Then he looked at us, expectantly. 'Well?'

I looked at Gab. She seemed frozen. Typical. Just when I needed her to be bold and bolshy. It looked like it was down to me.

'Yeah,' I murmured. 'I guess we have some information for you.'

Fred looked expectant, gesturing for me to continue.

I paused and glanced at the notebook. 'It's not about my Dad though.'

Fred appeared confused. 'Oh?'

With that, I took a deep breath and launched into my soliloquy. It was a ramble, really. Finally, in an instant, I could release some of the pent-up emotion that had built inside me for so long. Leaving out no detail apart from the window itself, I unleashed a torrent of information and emotion upon Fred.

Within moments, Fred had sat back in his chair and listened intently and actively, holding my gaze impressively as I spoke. I told him everything, with a few little lies to hide the supernatural wonders that had brought us to this point.

I told him how we'd been at Vicky's party before she disappeared, how Mr Arnold had appeared on the street nearby, and how a friend had gone through Vicky's phone, finding explicit pictures she had been sending to a contact known only as "Key". I told him how Vicky had revealed to Ms Dooley and my sister that she had been involved in an inappropriate relationship with an older man, whose identity she refused to reveal. Then I told him about finding the notebook in a bush on Beggar Home Lane - a little white lie. At that point, and that point only, Fred's gaze moved once again to the sodden notebook on the desk before him, before immediately returning his eyes to mine, locking into what felt like my confession.

I went on to explain that we'd found the diary, assumed it was Laurie's (based on the initials and the diary entries), and that the notebook proved she was *also* involved in an inappropriate relationship with a man called "Key". I then moved to open the book and show him the final sentence that was legible: *"who didn't want me to know his real name but…"*. Subsequently, I turned the page to show the smudged and water-damaged ink that followed, with the mysterious message: "*IKEA*".

With that, I made it to my finale.

I explained that Mr Arnold - Mike Arnold, the Deputy Head of our very school, St Joseph's - was in fact, the allusive "Key". He was regularly known as "Mikey", and thus, "Key" seemed to be a reasonable nickname. I then went on to explain that, moreover, we had confronted Mr Arnold ourselves. This revelation brought the first look of surprise to Fred's otherwise blank expression. I relayed Mr Arnold's threats and destruction of our mobile phones - one of which I presented to Fred from my pocket, defunct and expired.

And then, the pièce de résistance - we knew where evidence of Arnold going after Laurie could be found. If Laurie had "dropped" her notebook on Beggar Home Lane, it was reasonable to deduce that she may have appeared on CCTV - namely, the video feed on Aiden Bennet's motion-activated dashcam. The all-singing, all-dancing dashcam that wirelessly uploaded gigabytes and gigabytes of video footage to The Cloud, to be used by an insurance company or the police if ever the opportunity arose.

I began to reach my conclusion. 'With all of this, we both believe that Arnold could well be responsible for *all* of the disappearing kids in Grand Parade over the last few years. He was involved with Laurie, and then Vicky over a year later. Who knows how many others? Ellie James? Molly Atkinson? *Paul Thornton?*'

Again, Fred displayed a hint of surprise.

'But you have to question him, officer,' I summed up. 'Surely there is enough evidence here and on the dashcam footage that he should be at least brought in for questioning? We are *sure* that he will have been caught on the dashcam.' I didn't actually have that much confidence in my final statement, but the window had brought us this far, and - part of me, at least - didn't believe it would let us down now.

The three of us sat in silence for a long minute. None of us spoke. None of us moved. Eventually, Fred reached forward and picked up the notebook. Gently, he leafed through the pages, careful not to rip any of the more water-damaged ones. Then he sighed deeply, put the book down and looked at us both. Finally, he spoke.

'That's a hell of a lot of information for me to process in the space of two minutes.'

FORTY-EIGHT

WE ALMOST LAUGHED at Fred's statement. The police officer himself displayed a ghost of a smile. Still, Gab and I sat quietly. We waited for Fred's response. Gab offered me a weak smile. She was happy with what I'd said. I could see that.

'Okay, you two,' Fred eventually began, speaking slowly and clearly. 'First off, let me remind you that these are very serious accusations you are making. If any word of it is a lie, that would not go down well at all. Especially not for you, Chris, with you still awaiting a court date for misdemeanour.'

I nodded in understanding. I was happy that everything we had said was true - to a degree. I'd left out parts about the window. And they'd probably find out that the notebook wasn't left in a bush when they went through dashcam footage… but that wouldn't matter. If they looked, they'd see Arnold. *That* was what mattered.

'Obviously, if you two are serious about this, I'll need you to make an official statement.'

Gab's mouth dropped open. 'You believe us?' She asked, incredulously.

'I'm a police officer,' Fred explained, neutrally. 'I believe facts. You have presented accusations. A point of view. I can't say that I believe it, but I *can* say I will take what you have said seriously. We will write this down as an official statement, it will be handed to the officers dealing with the missing children case, and it will be taken from there. Are you both happy with that? Remember, if you have lied about *anything* in what you have told me, it could land you both in a whole lot of trouble.'

We both nodded numbly, barely able to believe what was happening. Was this real? Did we have a chance to take down Arnold?

Fred reached into one of his drawers and brought up a few pieces of headed paper, with the words "WITNESS STATEMENT" emboldened in block capitals. 'Let's go through everything again, from the start.' Fred got out a pen. 'I'll write down the relevant points.'

Slowly, with Gab helping this time, we went back over everything I had said. We trod carefully around the slight inconsistencies in the story, subconsciously protecting the window's involvement. Fred periodically wrote sentences on the paper, condensing our testimony into bite-sized, understandable chunks.

As we finished, I felt overwhelmed by exhaustion. I was as if I had poured out my soul twice in the space of an hour. I was knackered.

Fred finished off writing as our story concluded once again. Then he folded up the paper and placed it in an envelope. Gingerly, almost asking our approval in his slow movements, he reached for the notebook once again. He hesitated, looking at us, then picked it up and placed it in a clear plastic bag with the word "EVIDENCE" emblazoned on the side.

'Okay you two,' he sighed, standing up. 'Thank you. If there's nothing else, you're both free to go.'

I looked at Gab expectantly. Was that it? Hesitantly, we rose to our feet.

'Fred,' I murmured. He looked me in the eye once again. A piercing, intimidating look, with a hint of kindness and mercy. They were eyes that wanted to do good and would stop at nothing to achieve this. 'Do you believe us? Do you think this will work?'

Fred sighed again, looking at the envelope and evidence bag in his hand. 'Those are two different questions, Chris,' he responded. 'And it depends what you mean by "will it work".' Once again, Fred sighed.

'Whether it will work - I assume you mean, whether it condemns Mr Arnold - will depend on the evidence presented, and if the dashcam in question helps prove your theory. You have, however, presented enough evidence for us to open a line of enquiry. I would be surprised if the officers presiding over this case don't seek an opportunity to speak to Mr Arnold - even if it is in the form of an informal chat. We take matters of people in power abusing their role *very* seriously. This will be taken seriously. I can promise you that.'

I was grateful. It was a nice feeling. Someone was on our side. Yes, we had Uncle Nev and a few of the other teachers at school, and even Old Lady Lilly. But Fred was on our side and could *practically* help us, on whatever bizarre mission we had found ourselves on.

We began to walk towards the door. Fred beat us to it and reached for the handle. Before he opened it, however, he turned to us both and whispered, so quietly that we only just made out the words. But we did hear them, and they meant more than words could say.

'As for whether I believe you... well, I must remain neutral in all police matters, of course, but on this occasion, I will say this... I believe you both. I think, somehow you have discovered the truth. And, as far as I am able, I'll help get to the bottom of this. I guarantee it.'

FORTY-NINE

WE SPENT most of the afternoon watching reruns of a 90s sitcom on the TV. We had already discussed everything that had happened with Fred. We'd gone over things a few times, thinking about different possible outcomes and our next move. In the end, we concluded our next move would be to wait. We needed to trust that Fred - and his colleagues - would act appropriately with the information we'd given him.

We were halfway through an episode ("The One with the Football") when Uncle Nev returned home. He shouted a vague greeting before trundling into the kitchen. He returned to the lounge to join us, a four-pack of beer in his hand. So much like his brother... just less of a prick.

He offered a can to me with a wink. I gratefully accepted, pleased to have something to take the edge off after the last few days. Gab, sensible as ever, declined our Uncle's offer. Nev shrugged and took a seat next to me, raising his can half-heartedly in a toast, before taking a generous swig.

'And how was your day, you two?'

'Fine,' I mumbled, trying to keep my attention on the TV. I wasn't a great liar... if he asked too much, I would crack.

'Get up to much?'

I shook my head.

'Interesting that, because Officer Andrews called me and told me you'd paid him a visit.'

Bloody hell.

'He said you wanted an update on his investigation. Maybe a bit of comforting.'

Interesting… Fred hadn't divulged what we'd actually spoken to him about. I guess there must have been a police-civilian confidentiality clause or something.

'I guess…' I began before Nev cut me off.

'I get that this has been tough on you kids. Your Mum in hospital, your Dad being arrested then disappearing… all the abuse…' He paused briefly, taking a sip of his beer. 'And then we've tried to keep you in the house - for your own safety, of course.'

I remained silent. Gab was equally mute, her eyes fixed on the TV screen, glazed over.

Nev sighed deeply. 'Fred and I had a chat about you both, and how hard all this is on you. I guess the immediate danger has passed. We haven't heard as much as a whisper of your Father's whereabouts for days. I doubt he's planning to hunt the pair of you down. You two need a bit of respite. Time to be kids again.' When we didn't respond, Nev continued. 'I guess what I'm trying to say is that we don't think you need to be kept in the house anymore. You can go back to school if you want. You can go out with your friends. Just maybe stay away from dangerous areas, and try not to go out after dark. It's getting a bit lighter anyway, so that shouldn't be too much of a problem. But just be careful. I know you both always are… but Grand Parade can be a dodgy place.'

I smiled weakly at my Uncle. 'Thanks for looking after us, Uncle Nev.' It was all I could manage. Gab remained quiet.

Nev grinned warmly at me. 'You'll both be pleased to know your Mum is doing well, though.'

Gab came back to life at this statement. Her eyes were finally torn away from the TV, and she looked at our Uncle. 'Yeah?'

Nev nodded, encouragingly. 'Yeah. Surgery was a success. She's back on the ward, she's woken up and is a lot more alert than she has been for ages. It's looking positive.'

'Can we see her?' Gab asked, immediately. I was equally as desperate to see her.

Nev looked hesitant. 'Yes,' he murmured, carefully. 'But maybe in a few days. She needs lots of rest. No stress or excitement.' He clearly saw the disappointment on both of our faces. 'But it won't be long. End of this week. I promise.'

Reluctantly, Gab and I agreed. We didn't want to make Mum any worse. Anyway, it gave us a few days to focus on seeing if anything happened to Arnold.

'Do you think you might both want to go back to school?' Nev enquired, changing the subject.

I shrugged. I wasn't that fussed. Gab, however, nodded eagerly. 'Please. I think it'd be a good way for us to distract ourselves.'

Nev finished his first can and opened another. How much he looked like my Father in that moment…

'I'm pleased to hear that,' Nev smiled. 'And I'm sure the teachers will be pleased to see you back in the classroom.'

Not too sure about that, I mused, as images of our brutal meeting with Mr Arnold flashed through my memory.

FIFTY

THE NEXT FEW days were an immense anticlimax.

We returned to school like nothing had changed. Friends knew our Dad had been arrested - it had been reported by Sophie Stark on the news several times, and Grand Parade was a small neighbourhood.

But no one seemed that fussed. I guess it was understandable. Teenagers have a lot to deal with whilst they struggle to reach maturity. Exams, friendships, relationships, peer pressures, university prospects, family drama... all these things are mixed together across the canvas of teenage years, splattered like a Picasso across the history books of our lives. Being a teenager is tough. You don't have time to worry about someone else. You become cocooned in your own dramas, with everybody believing the universe revolves entirely around them. Adam, John, Meg and Lucy were some of our "best" friends at school... even they didn't really give a shit. They had their own issues to deal with - the most pressing being Adam and Lucy's recent breakup, which kept being interrupted by their decision to have one last shag... and one more, and one more.

If Arnold was in school, we didn't see him. Even when quietly sneaking past his office, in the quiet corridors of the early morning, we heard nothing. Was he in school? Had he been arrested? We had no idea.

Lessons went on as normal. I swore profusely at Mrs Isherham, my witch of a Spanish teacher, as she punished me with detention for "daydreaming" in her lesson. Honestly, it's not like I had anything going on in my life, did I? Isherham eventually relented after a good long argument, clearly deciding that I'd been through enough recently without suffering from another one of her detentions.

For three days, life trundled on painfully slowly. We went to school, sat in our lessons, chatted quietly in the social areas during break and lunchtime, and then went home to Nev's increasingly poor dinners. Then we'd go to bed, and Nev normally popped out for a few hours to the Homestead, our local pub. A promise that we would visit the infamous Hull Royal Infirmary on Saturday to see our Mum kept us going.

We didn't mention Arnold to each other. We didn't even talk about the window. Gab and I just went about life like nothing had happened. I'm not sure why… but we were waiting. Waiting for what, I didn't know. Were we supposed to look at the window again? Wait for further instructions? I didn't feel as much of a pull to it as I had previously. Maybe we had done enough. Maybe.

Adam pulled me aside as we left the school gates on Thursday afternoon. School had been monotonous, but largely uneventful. We still hadn't seen Arnold.

'Alright dickhead?' A friendly greeting, as was Adam's custom.

'Hi mate,' I grumbled, not looking at him. I began to head in the direction of the journey home.

'John and I are going to the park near the cemetery for a bit with some of the others. You fancy coming? We've got a few bottles of vodka.'

I shrugged, seeing Gab not far from me. 'I guess if my sister wants to…'

'Do you have to do everything with your sister?' Adam mocked, trying to drag me away. Gab, having heard him, was quick on our heels.

'He doesn't, no, you knob,' she spat. 'What's going on?'

'He's going to the park with some of the others,' I explained. 'They've got some vodka.'

'Cool,' Gab declared, clearly happy to blow off a bit of steam. 'Shall we get moving?'

I grinned as Adam mumbled in a feeble protest before the three of us headed off to the park. A few others from our year joined us as we walked. When we finally arrived at the park, around fifteen of us had gathered.

Adam hadn't been lying. There were indeed a *few* bottles of vodka. But by the time a few glugs had been spilt and the most idiotic of our group had drunk more than their fair share, very little was left for us. I didn't really care. Gab appeared slightly put out but was happy to be out of the house and away from school just the same.

'How are you guys?'

The question came suddenly, from Lucy. She had approached us where we were sitting, slightly away from the rest of the group. She sat down and offered us a nearly empty vodka bottle, from which we took a grateful sip. It burnt my throat fiercely and tasted like cheap nail polish, but it was probably what I needed. I immediately felt a little more relaxed (although I suspect a lot of that was psychological).

'We're okay,' Gab confessed, coughing after her share of vodka. 'Just a lot going on, isn't there?'

'You guys are well brave,' Lucy said, taking back the nearly empty vodka bottle. 'Putting up with all that shit. Honestly, I'm impressed. The others don't appreciate it, but I do. Well done for standing up to your dad.'

I shrugged in way of a half-hearted thanks. I wasn't sure I had stood up to my dad, really, but it was nice to hear it.

None of us said anything for a while. Instead, our gaze moved across to the cemetery next door to the park. I remembered the gardener shouting at us a few weeks ago, asking if we'd been digging up graves. Bizarrely, it looked like a good number of graves had been dug up recently. Mounds of dirt were sporadically littered untidily around the usually neat cemetery. I could even see a few broken bits of wood, almost as if pieces of a coffin had been pulled apart. Very odd.

The sun began to set after a while. The group began to disperse.

Lucy bade us goodnight and headed off, again with Adam, their breakup apparently once again on hold.

'I don't fancy going home yet,' Gab mumbled as the sky began to turn a brilliant orange. 'Shall we go for a walk?'

'Nev said not to be out after dark,' I reminded her.

Gab punched me gently in the arm, before smiling. 'He did, but I don't think he'll give a shit. He'll probably be pissed anyway.'

'He's not Dad,' I muttered.

'He's not. But he still likes a drink. He'll be at the Homestead.'

I didn't argue with Gab any further. Instead, I followed her as we meandered out of the park and through the streets of Grand Parade. It wasn't long before we found ourselves heading into the city proper, towards the centre of York. Night had truly fallen.

We made it to Fulton, a small neighbourhood near the city centre. From there, we walked down towards the river and continued our quiet journey. Streetlights were sparse along the riverbank, but we knew our route well, having been walking these roads for years.

Everything was quiet. We were quiet. The world was silent around us.

We listened.

The sky above was clear. Stars could be seen dotted haphazardly throughout the sky, the majesty of the universe reduced to nothing more than an inky blackness with tiny, silver lights.

The riverbank was deserted.

I felt a chill.

Somehow, I knew this walk had been a bad idea. Immediately, in an instant, I knew why.

'There you are, you little pieces of shit.' The voice pierced through the night air malevolently, like the sound of a demon cornering you.

Unadulterated terror seized me.

'You shouldn't have been wandering alone... I am going to *fuck you up...*'

FIFTY-ONE

MY BODY SEEMED to pulsate in shock as Mike Arnold lurched towards me. His brutally rough grip momentarily overwhelmed my arm before I managed to manoeuvre and twist out of his way. Luckily, Gab was far enough away to avoid the initial assault.

'You little shits,' he hissed, advancing towards us. With an increasing sense of despair I realised that, despite us being momentarily out of Arnold's reach, he was forcing us towards the edge of the river. We were mere metres away from the water's cold embrace.

'You had to open your stupid bastard mouths, didn't you?' our Deputy Head spat, moving towards us with increasing aggression. 'Couldn't leave well enough alone? Well, I told you what happened to little pricks like you who don't know their place... I will make you wish you were dead. I will rip your sorry little forms from existence. I will *fucking end* you.'

'Fuck off, you pervert prick,' Gab's colourful response came. She sounded a lot braver than I knew she felt. 'You only got what was coming to you.'

I felt the consistency of the earth beneath my feet change as I took another step backwards. *Bollocks*. We were at the river's edge.

Arnold's arm extended towards us, painfully slowly. Was he about to push us?

No...

Arnold's proximity to us increased. He was unshaven. He stank of body odour and booze. His eyes were wide and red-raw. There was unbridled hatred in his face.

In an instant, he moved.

I yelped in shock as his arm shot outwards and grabbed Gab by the scruff of her neck. My sister yelled.

Flinging her as if she were nothing more than a rag doll, Gab was thrown along the bank of the river, coming to land right on the edge, inches away from falling into the icy waters. I was too busy watching Gab's landing to notice Arnold's other arm, hand now balled into a fist, aiming directly for my face.

I could only grunt in dismay as a meaty left hook connected with my cheekbone. Immediately, I hit the ground, dazed, the world spinning madly around me. The earth beneath me was hard and cold, the early spring having left it slightly frozen. I spat blood from my mouth.

'I got taken in for questioning... for QUESTIONING!' Arnold roared, kicking me harshly in my abdomen, knocking the wind from me. I saw Gab trying to sit up from where she had landed.

Arnold grabbed the back of my shirt and began dragging me across the floor towards my sister. 'There have been accusations made against me to the police,' Arnold continued, his voice laced with loathing. 'They asked me if I was ever known as *Key*...' He finally let go of my sweatshirt, throwing me at my sister, and knocking her backwards once again.

I looked up. Arnold towered over the pair of us. He looked dirty. He seemed... unhinged.

'Somehow, by some absolute *fucking* miracle, they have footage of me near one of the girls the night she disappeared... and somehow, I don't know how, but somehow, I think I know which two arrogant twats led them to that video...'

They have him... we did it! The thoughts of triumph were quickly overshadowed. *How the hell has he not been arrested?*

'How have they not put you away?' I asked, trying to sound much more courageous than I felt, just as Gab had.

'Not that it's any of your business, you little prick, but they haven't got enough evidence… yet. They're planning to raid my house, check my DNA, everything… so I'll have to disappear… but before I do, I have one last thing to deal with…'

He bent down towards us, reaching into his jacket pocket. Terror seized me once again as Arnold pulled out a large kitchen knife. The blade probably wasn't far off a foot long. Its metal was dull and grey, but it looked menacingly sharp - more than enough to do us fatal damage.

'I heard, once upon a time,' Arnold mused, 'that your father wanted to be a surgeon… ironically, you'll both die by being cut up…'

Arnold flourished the blade before him, a horrifying glee shining in his eyes as he examined it. He pointed the blade at us, then lifted it behind his head.

He swung it down.

Gab screamed.

Everything happened too fast.

FIFTY-TWO

ARNOLD'S BLADE swung down with menacing speed, aiming directly at me. With impossible speed and strength, Gab responded with equal vigour.

From her position on the floor, she kicked her leg forward, aggressively and hatefully, planting her foot perfectly into the front of Arnold's knee.

A sickening crack echoed out into the silence, followed immediately by a harrowing, primal scream erupting from Arnold's mouth. I watched in horror as the man's knee buckled underneath him, bent in the completely wrong direction.

Gab's kick had been brutally accurate and incredibly effective. Arnold's leg was bent completely out of shape - dislocated, broken, I had no idea, but enough to immobilise the prick.

'You little SLAG!' Arnold roared into the night, any subtlety of our encounter long gone. Still holding the knife, he swiped angrily at us from his position on the ground, but he was too slow. Gab had already leapt to her feet and was helping me to mine. How dramatically the tables had turned in the space of a few seconds.

Both of us moved back quickly, far enough away that Arnold's now feeble attacks were ineffective.

'You will *fucking* pay for this, you little shits!'

'Fuck you,' Gab hissed, still keeping a good distance from Arnold. 'You deserve to go away for a long time, you disgusting paedophile prick.'

'One day I'll kill you, you little bitch.' Arnold remained crippled on the ground, one hand grasping his deformed knee, the other still brandishing his lethal-looking kitchen knife. 'I will *end* you.'

'How many did you rape?' Gab spat. She was angry. The pure loathing in her was almost tangible. 'How many did you force your manky body on?'

Gab was nothing if not passionate. So was I… I shared her hatred and disgust for the human being before us. But there was a primal rage awakening within Gab. A burning anger towards anyone who abused women. In that moment, I had no idea what my sister was capable of.

'Go to hell,' Arnold's hate-filled reply came.

Gab edged closer to Arnold.

'Gab-' I began to warn her. She held up her hand angrily.

'How many was it, Arnold? How many girls, supposedly under your protection, under your supervision as their *teacher* did you abuse? Vicky? Laurie? What about Molly Atkinson? Ellie James? What about Paul Thornton? You batting for both sides, you pervert?'

'Fuck you, you little bitch,' Arnold's venomous reply came. 'I had nothing to do with Paul. I'm not some gay. I'm only interested in girls. The younger and sexier the better.'

Poor choice of words from Arnold there.

Gab lost her cool, darted forward, and kicked him mercilessly in the face.

Arnold cried out in pain and frustration, madly swinging his knife, whilst Gab nimbly jumped backwards and out of the way.

'I will KILL YOU!' Arnold bellowed, trying to struggle to his feet. Gab backed away towards me. She was panting, overwhelmed by the adrenaline pulsing through her body.

I took over. I reached down to the ground and picked up a stone - or more of a rock. It was about the size of a melon. I didn't know what I planned to do with it… but it made me feel like I at least had a weapon if I needed one.

'Alright, you bastard,' I began, trying to keep my voice level and cool, hiding the tremor. I knew that the best option would have been for Gab and me to walk away. We could have left the situation, with Arnold rotting on the riverbank, maybe escaping or getting picked up by the police. We could have gone straight to the police station and told them what had happened. Told them where to pick up Arnold, and told them that they should arrest him.

But we didn't. There, in that moment, we both knew that we weren't going to leave it like this. Neither of us could leave this bastard the way he was. He needed to pay.

Again, I wonder how different my life would be today if we had walked away at that moment. It was one of those decisions that - whilst it didn't seem tiny - didn't seem monumental. It was just how we felt in the moment. I wonder what would have happened if we *had* walked away…

Watershed moment.

'We have the upper hand,' I continued, calmly. 'Right now we can walk. You can't even manage that.' I didn't entirely know where I was going with this. I was improvising.

I knelt. I was still out of Arnold's reach, just far enough away that he couldn't swipe at me with his knife. 'Are they all dead? Laurie? Vicky? The other girls?'

Arnold spat in my face.

I threw the rock.

It hit Arnold directly in the face, connecting with his right cheekbone and eye. Our former Deputy Head shrieked in pain and dived towards me in response. I leapt to my feet and moved backwards, just enough to avoid a vicious swipe from the deranged man.

'Are they dead?!' I shouted, feeling the same anger that had possessed Gab pulse through me.

'The hell if I know, boy!' Arnold finally confessed, panting for breath. Rivulets of blood streamed down his face, several new wounds having now appeared courtesy of the rock.

Somehow, Arnold managed to get onto one knee, his other, redundant leg still bent off at an awkward angle. 'I'm no murderer, I can tell you that much… not yet anyway.' There was malice in his voice, as he brandished the knife once again. 'No... they must have done that to themselves if they are all dead. The Openshaw girl was pathetic... she probably threw herself in the river, crying about how shitty her life was, how horrible her boyfriends were, how damn awful she was in bed.'

That was enough for Gab. She screamed, sounding like a wounded animal, and ran full pelt at Arnold.

'Gab!' I shrieked, trying to stop her attack, which was now in full force.

Somehow, Arnold managed to stand on his good leg.

He swung the knife towards Gab in a fierce uppercut.

He missed.

Gab narrowly avoided the attack and dropped down into a tackle, grabbing the schoolteacher by his waist and knocking him back with all the strength she could muster.

All I heard was a grunt from Arnold.

The knife flew into the air and landed in the river.

Gab collapsed to the ground at the very edge of the riverbank, releasing her grip on Arnold and coming to the end of her tackle. Arnold's already handicapped form had no chance.

Mr Mike Arnold - Key - our Deputy Head, fell into the River Ouse, his already damaged body lost to the depths below and the relentless current.

He didn't surface.

After spending a few moments looking on in shock at what had happened, I ran to Gab at the riverbank and pulled her away from the shoreline, dragging her to relative safety. She was panting and crying and covered in dirt and sweat and blood.

She looked me dead in the eye. There was fear and sadness in her expression. But there was also a satisfaction. An anger that, at least a little, had been placated.

Had we killed Arnold? I had no idea. Neither did she. Neither one of us knew what to do next.

So I just hugged my sister, and let her cry into my shoulder. Because, essentially, that was all I could do.

FIFTY-THREE

I'M NOT sure how you're supposed to feel the morning after a potential murder. Surely there should be some form of remorse, or regret or guilt?

But I felt nothing.

I awoke in my own bed, comfortable, warm, and feeling good. I had no sadness. No regret.

I was pleased.

Do people deserve to die? I don't know. And I don't think it's up to us to decide. No one should have the power to choose who lives and who dies. No one on Earth, anyway. The power to decide life and death is far too great for any one person to hold.

But Arnold deserved it. I knew it in my heart. The window had told us.

For the first time in a long time, I realised I wasn't thinking about the window. I didn't feel it calling to me. There was no pull or hold. It was like it had turned itself off. Maybe its job was done. Maybe we'd brought the justice it sought.

Gab, having got over the initial shock and upset of everything that had happened last night, seemed remarkably chipper the next morning. It was Saturday, and we were going to see Mum.

We bundled into Uncle Nev's Ford Focus, which was looking more and more tired with each passing day. Nev chatted away at us for most of the hour-long journey to Hull Royal Infirmary. Gab and I said very little. We were quietly content. Happy that we had achieved justice over Arnold. He would never harm another girl again.

Admittedly, he could still be alive. But we doubted it. We had decided that the night before. Arnold's broken leg and head injury didn't stand in his favour. Additionally, an incredible amount of rainfall had graced York, making the river burst its banks and stoking the current. This fact alone made it almost impossible that he would have been able to escape the murky depths.

Should we have felt guilty?

Maybe.

But maybe we didn't because of the window… its assignment had been completed. We knew it could manipulate our emotions… it had done whenever we saw a vision. So maybe, just maybe, as thanks, it gave us the privilege of being guilt-free.

At the back of my mind, however, something didn't sit quite right. I couldn't say what it was. Last night had become nothing more than a hideous blur in my mind. But something was troubling me… not the potential murder, not guilt, not fear… just… something. Something was off… something Arnold had said to us. I mused in my thoughts for a long time during that journey, trying to work out why I was unsettled.

Hull Royal Infirmary is an eyesore monstrosity in the middle of Hull city centre. It stretches high into the sky with over a dozen floors piled on top of each other, boasting over six hundred patient beds. Mum's ward was on the fourth floor, where all the brain issues were dealt with.

Seeing Mum brought a bizarre mixture of relief and heartbreak to both of us.

She looked awful. Part of her hair had been shaved away, and a large bandage now covered where the surgeons had drilled into her skull. She was tired, partly due to her injuries and the surgery, and partly due to the painkillers and anti-seizure medications she was on. She didn't look like our Mum.

But she was alive. She had survived the horrendous reign of Len Keeler and was going to be alright.

She didn't say much to us but was definitely aware that we were visiting. The nurse told us that they hadn't seen my Mum smile before… but she smiled when she saw us. We both held her hand and she squeezed us tightly. She came in and out of consciousness whilst we sat with her, for about an hour. At one point, a young-looking Doctor came over to tell us she was making good progress. The extent of the bleed, she explained, had become much more severe very suddenly, which is why she had been rushed across to Hull. Almost all of the blood had been taken out, and repeat brain scans looked good. Unfortunately, the insult to her brain had been severe, so recovery would take a long time. They were confident, however, that she would be able to get pretty much back to normal, eventually.

They hoped.

Our journey home was more solemn. Our contentment had been replaced with concern and sadness. Not just for Mum's current state, but the sorry state of our family. Here we were, in a busted-up old car, being driven by our Uncle who, whilst very nice, was not our Father, and was a bit of an alcoholic himself. My Father was still at large, undiscovered and unfound.

And we had just - probably - killed a man.

Life's weird. Strange shit happens. Things can change in an instant.

And let me tell you, the messed up shit wasn't done yet.

FIFTY-FOUR

IT WAS Sunday morning when Sergeant Fred Andrews turned up at our house. Nev, conveniently, was out.

'Hi, you two. I was wondering if we could have a little chat? Informally?'

We nodded eagerly. Surely this was about Arnold? The idea that we would be in trouble for his assumed disappearance never even crossed our minds.

Fred came in and we offered him a cup of tea. That's what you do in Yorkshire.

'I'm afraid I don't have any news about your Father,' Fred began, as he sat down and gratefully took the drink and biscuit we offered to him. 'But I hear your Mother is doing well. Have you visited?'

I nodded. 'We went over yesterday. She's okay but tired. Apparently it'll be a long recovery.'

Fred seemed to understand. I guess he would have seen a lot of brain injuries during his time in the police.

'Anyway, I came on behalf of some of the other officers, partly to thank you, and partly to ask a few questions.'

Suddenly, a knot tightened in my stomach. If Arnold was considered missing, would we be suspected? Surely we wouldn't be in trouble? It was self-defence! In any case, how would they know?

'The information you gave us about Mr Arnold was taken very seriously,' Fred began. 'I passed on your statements and the evidence to the team dealing with the missing children. And we checked the dashcam footage for the last few days before Laurie Openshaw disappeared. You were right - we saw Mr Arnold chasing after her, although we also saw her drop her diary into a drain... so how it ended up in the bush where you found it, I have no idea.' At this point, he eyed us slightly suspiciously, before brushing over the point.

'We also found through social media that Key used to be a nickname he used when he was younger. So your story had legs.' He paused, watching our facial expressions. I tried to show no emotion. 'We brought him in for questioning, he held himself together well, but there were a few inconsistencies in what he said, the details of which I won't go into. We let him go - temporarily, as we didn't have enough evidence to warrant an arrest.'

I held my breath.

'Unfortunately, in the last few days, he's disappeared. He missed an interview with us yesterday.'

We said nothing.

'Has he, by any chance, approached either of you?'

Was this a moment where we should tell the truth? Surely Fred would be able to get us out of any trouble last night's conflict would bring us? If we told the truth, right then, surely we would be okay?

I also knew that if we lied in this moment, we could never take it back. Lie to the police, all we would do is continue making more lies to cover up our other ones, all until the truth unravelled. It always does. I'd watched enough crime shows to know that.

'No,' Gab responded, flatly. 'Even at school, we haven't seen him for days. I assumed he was avoiding us, after our encounter a few days ago.'

Fred seemed to understand and nodded. I think he genuinely believed Gab.

I knew why Gab had lied. Despite my inner turmoil, the window still pulled at me, although it had felt silent for days. The window had assigned *us* this task, in the most bizarre, supernatural and confusing way. It was our burden and our burden alone. We couldn't tell the police. I just knew it.

Something still bothered me...

As Fred continued to talk, somewhat pointlessly about the upcoming hunt for the now presumed fugitive that was Mr Arnold, something sat heavy on my mind. A feeling I couldn't shake that something didn't quite add up. I'd had the same abnormal feeling in the car yesterday on the way to Hull. Something was... off. Wrong. Something Mr Arnold had said to us in those final few moments. Something that I had brushed over in the heat of the moment, something that just didn't make sense...

"I had nothing to do with Paul. I'm not some gay."

I gasped, and blurted out words, interrupting Fred's droning voice. 'Do you think Arnold's the one who's been kidnapping everyone? All the kids that have gone missing?'

Fred shrugged, almost indifferently. 'I'm not sure, Chris. That's what the investigation will show. We're looking for more evidence as we speak.'

'Because Paul was never found,' I responded, quickly. 'Paul Thornton. He was a friend of mine.'

Fred looked slightly puzzled, then sympathetic. 'You're right, Chris. We've still not found Paul. He's just another kid in a long line that have gone missing over the years. And whilst the vast majority have been girls, the odd lad has gone missing now and then.'

'Who else?' I replied. My mind was racing so much that it felt like it was on fire.

Fred hesitated, clearly unsure how much he should tell us. 'I can't tell you specifics,' he eventually murmured. 'But a few years ago, there were several lads that disappeared. Some students, some older. An old bloke in his seventies was amongst them.'

'Do you think Arnold was responsible for them as well?'

Fred almost laughed. 'Chris, we unfortunately can't pin every missing person on Mike Arnold. From the look of things, he's probably more of a sexual predator than anything. If we assume Vicky and Laurie are the type he goes for, it's likely that he never really deviated from that. The vast majority of sex offenders have a *type*, so to speak. It's unlikely that he's responsible for the lads. Even Paul.'

'And he wasn't into lads…' I mused, quietly.

'What?'

'Nothing,' I recovered. 'I guess… he didn't seem like he was into lads.'

Fred smiled sadly. 'Probably not.'

Fred continued talking as my consciousness left the room. My mind swirled uncontrollably, going over and over Arnold's words. *He had nothing to do with Paul.* As I remembered more of the conversation, I realised he had even denied murdering Laurie… *"The Openshaw girl was pathetic… she probably threw herself in the river…"*

It wasn't over.

A horrible sense of dread and fear washed over me as I realised, to my horror, that Arnold wasn't the only bastard out there. There was someone else killing these girls, stealing these men… and somehow, deep in my heart, egged on by that blasted window… I was neck-deep in discovering who this was and stopping them.

FIFTY-FIVE

'WELL, I'LL BE DAMNED!'

The words came from Uncle Nev's mouth as we sat with our dinners on our knees, eating a hastily put-together dish of pizza and chips. The TV was blaring in front of us, a dramatic headline taking over the entire news report. Two minutes ago, we had been aimlessly listening to the host of *Pointless* announce the "pointless" answers to the question "Countries beginning with the letter L". In stark contrast, both local and national news demanded our attention, and not for a pleasant reason.

'Our top story tonight,' the BBC's main presenter on the national news announced. 'A schoolteacher is wanted in connection with multiple disappearances of young girls in the suburb of Grand Parade in York.'

Incredibly, in front of us, Mike Arnold's face appeared. It was a standard photo, probably taken from his HR file at school. He looked so normal. There was even a sort of kindness to his face. No one would have ever suspected what a bastard he was. We certainly didn't.

'Michael Arnold has been Deputy Head at Saint Joseph's High School in York for over ten years, a school that has been plagued with several incidents of missing children over the past few years. Recent evidence uncovered by police examining CCTV footage and searching the suspect's house has led to him becoming the principal person of interest in the ongoing investigation into the disappearing school children.'

The news report went on to give a bit more background on Arnold and summarise the long history of missing children in Grand Parade. Interestingly, I noticed they only mentioned missing girls… there was no mention of Paul or anyone who didn't meet the demographic of a 15 to 18-year-old female.

'Detective Staples, of North Yorkshire Police, made the following statement earlier today.' The BBC reporter's face disappeared from our screen to be replaced with a sturdy-looking policeman, likely in his fifties, and likely a little too keen on pork pies.

'Our investigation into the missing schoolgirls recently led us to Mr Arnold, and we brought him in for questioning. He denied all charges at the time, but some inconsistencies in his statement led to us seeking a warrant to search his home and question him further. Unfortunately, he failed to attend the police station for further interview and has not been seen for over 24 hours. We are now appealing for the public to immediately get in touch if they have any information on the whereabouts of this now-wanted man.'

'Should have arrested him when they had him,' Nev muttered gruffly, shovelling pizza into his face.

'I guess they didn't have enough evidence,' Gab murmured, quietly. This earned a suspicious glance from our Uncle, but he made no further comment. In the meantime, the TV had switched to footage of what we presumed was Arnold's house, with a reporter standing outside in front of some police vehicles. Absentmindedly, I noticed that the reporter was our very own local newsreader, Sophie Stark.

'The police searched Michael Arnold's house in his absence today,' Sophie explained. Was that a tone of excitement in her voice? Probably the biggest story she had ever dealt with, I supposed.

'Inside, police found computers with over one hundred images of child pornography, all of the images showing women under the age of eighteen. There were also several basic mobile phones that police suspect were for short-term use. Some of these mobile phones have been analysed and found to have text conversations and telephone history with at least three of the young women who have gone missing in Grand Parade over recent months: Vicky Crampton, Ellie James and Laurie Openshaw. It is Miss Openshaw's body that was sadly found on the shores of the River Ouse in recent days.'

There was no empathy in Sophie Stark's voice. She spoke matter-of-factly, clearly and with a slightly accusatory tone. 'At the moment, it is unclear as to what was the true extent of Michael Arnold's involvement with these girls, and police are asking for anyone with information to come forward.'

Once again, the screen jumped to a police officer, this one female, younger and considerably less obese than Detective Staples. She too was standing outside Arnold's house, with the banner on the screen below her identifying her as Officer Montgomery. 'Our primary conclusions suspect that Mr Arnold was at the very least involved in inappropriate sexual and possibly exploitive relationships with several young girls. This, in addition to the pornography found, carries a significant sentence, and we will be focusing maximum police effort on tracking him down. I am not currently able to speculate on whether he is also connected to the death of Laurie Openshaw, or whether he knows any more regarding the location of the other missing girls. We will keep families and the public updated at all times during our ongoing investigation.'

The rest of the news report droned on for what felt like hours. Uncle Nev, having finished his pizza, couldn't tear his eyes away from the screen. When the report finally concluded (with a lighter story about a monkey giving birth at the local zoo - wholly inappropriate in my opinion), Nev turned the TV off and faced us. His face was stony and serious.

'I am so sorry that this was a teacher you interacted with, kids.' He spoke very kindly as if he wanted to take away some of Arnold's blame and comfort us. 'Gab,' he continued, bluntly. 'Did he *ever* touch you? Or try something? Tell me now, and we can report it right away.'

Gab shook her head immediately. 'No Uncle Nev. He never did. He was always very kind to me.'

'I bet he was,' Nev murmured, darkly. 'Little scrote probably was lovely to all the girls. I hope he gets what's coming to him. He deserves nothing less than life in Strangburn.'

Nev paused for a second, before standing up, knocking over the pair of empty lager cans at his feet. 'Did you two know anything about this? Or see anything suspicious? Anything?'

We immediately denied it. 'Never, Uncle Nev,' I offered. 'Like Gab said, he was always very kind to us. Especially recently, with everything going on.'

Nev seemed satisfied. 'Good. I wouldn't forgive myself if either of you ended up involved with that bastard piece of shit.'

He said no more, leaving the room and heading into the kitchen, where I heard a third can of beer being opened. *Oh, Uncle Nev,* I thought, grimly. *If you only knew just how involved we both are…*

FIFTY-SIX

THE NIGHT WAS cold but clear. Moonlight cast a ghostly light into my room, penetrating through the smallest of cracks between my curtains. I lay on my back, covers pulled up close around me, eyes wide open.

We'd got Arnold. Sort of. He was probably dead, but there was a chance that he was on the run, and at least the police knew who they were after. We'd helped start the process of bringing justice. Maybe we'd stopped girls from going missing.

But it's not just girls.

Something still didn't sit right with me. In my gut, there was a tiny bit of something that was off, and it wasn't the slightly questionable pizza Nev had oven-cooked for us.

A chill passed over me. I thought I could hear a whisper. My thoughts turned to the bizarre, supernatural artefact under my bed. The one that had told us so much, yet kept so much hidden.

I'm not some gay.

When I was in primary school, I remember my teacher audibly telling the class how she forgot where she had put her notebook, but she had known just a few seconds before. "Go back to where you were!" Eleanor, one of my 6-year-old classmates had shouted. "You'll remember if you go back to the last place you thought about it," she declared. Lo-and-behold, my Year 2 teacher Mrs Jackson walked back to her desk, where she had last thought of her notebook and - bingo! - she remembered that she had left it in the staffroom.

Memories are bizarre like that. The complexity of how our brains remember and recall is beyond our deepest understanding. Brains can be the world's most powerful computers, yet at the end of it all, brains are just like mush. They're soft and friable, encased within the secure prisons of our skulls. They are capable of wonders. Yet they degrade and fail, riddled with dementia and strokes and cancers.

He didn't kill Laurie.

This was far from over. I knew that. But I had all the pieces laid out before me, an impossible puzzle that I was so close to cracking. Maybe Gab would know... but she'd been pretty nonchalant ever since the news broadcast. Did she feel like we were beaten? Arnold was dead or on the run... was that really justice?

Someone was chasing Paul.

I sat up abruptly.

Whispers.

Did the window call again?

Not the window. *A window.*

Another window.

Fred's words... *"A few years ago, there were several lads that disappeared. Some students, some older. An old bloke in his seventies was amongst them."*

Then another memory. Something so insignificant that I would never have noticed it.

The groundsman, near the park. *"Wasn't you digging at these graves was it?"*

Whispers in the night.

Suddenly, I felt like I was going to vomit.

I stood.

Listen.

Something moved in the darkness. A deep, burning chaos, red and blue and full of terror.

I went to the window. My *own* window. The crack of moonlight bathed half my body as I stood before the drawn curtains.

I breathed deeply. My heart pounded in my chest.

Aiden Bennet was still missing.

Trembling, my hand reached for the curtain. Inch by inch, I began to open it, slowly at first, then quicker, then in one sudden motion, like ripping off a plaster.

My window showed nothing but the street. This was not a mystical window. It did not show me the past.

But it did show the present.

Beneath me, at the edge of our drive, just a step away from Uncle Nev's battered old Ford Focus, there she stood.

At first, I felt terrified. I opened my mouth to shout for help or to scream, but no sound came. I was frozen, paralysed.

Then, as she moved - and it was the smallest, simplest of movements - I calmed. I knew she was real. I just *knew* it. Because I'd seen her do that same movement before. It was nothing special, nothing dramatic, but I knew it.

It was the movement of a single, deathly, spindly finger, with skin and tissue clinging helplessly to a bone that belonged to a hand that had lived far too long and seen far too much. It was the hand belonging to a woman whose mind and memories were turning to dust as her cerebral tissue mercilessly decayed, her family long since abandoning her to the cruelness of this world.

Before me stood Old Lady Lilly, who had once lived on Beggar Home Lane, and now lived in Village Hall Nursing Home. This was Old Lady Lilly, infirm, bed-bound, senile.

And somehow, she was standing at the end of my driveway, beckoning me forward with her ghostly appendage, as she had done once before, what felt like a lifetime ago, in the majestic horror of the window beneath my bed.

FIFTY-SEVEN

'HOW THE HELL ARE YOU HERE?'

'It doesn't matter Christopher Keeler.'

'How can you stand? Are you okay? Should I get you a chair?'

'Shut up and listen. It's cold and dark, and time is wearing thin.'

'What do you mean?'

'Is the window cracked?'

I froze. It wasn't just the weather. It was her questions. Her impossible omniscience.

A chill almost bowled me over. It wasn't just the icy air, although I had rushed out onto the street (as quietly as I could) and neglected to even put on a jumper, let alone a dressing gown. But whilst my thin, short-sleeved pyjamas offered no protection against the bitter night, my chill came from within. It came from the terrifying audacity and impossibility of her question. The damning fact that we were in way over our heads, free-falling through an impossible situation that we had no idea how to deal with.

'Answer me, boy!' Lilly hissed. 'Is the window cracked?'

'Yes. It…' I hesitated. 'It has been for a while.'

'I see.' Lilly paused. I could tell she was immensely lucid. There wasn't even a hint of the malignant dementia that I knew was eating away at her brain. 'Then we really are at the end of our path.'

Her whisper renewed a chill, which shot down my spine.

'It was only small, to begin with,' I explained, cautiously. Why? I suppose I didn't know what else to say. 'But it's got bigger. We didn't damage it or anything... it seemed to happen by itself.'

'Time is short, boy,' Lilly replied, hurriedly. 'The job is far from done, and the clock is ticking.' The old woman adjusted herself slightly. For the first time, I noticed the cane she leant on. It was old and withered, just like her, made of wood with a handle that curved around for her hand like a miniature Shepherd's crook.

'We followed what the window showed us,' I protested. *Why am I justifying myself to a demented old woman?* Nevertheless, I continued. 'It showed us Arnold. We confronted him. It pointed us to evidence. We gave it to the police. Now he's a wanted man, and they'll catch him before he abducts another girl, if he's not dead already. Case closed.'

It's not though, is it? I couldn't keep the painfully obtrusive thought from my head. And Lilly, apparently, knew it.

'It's not, Christopher,' she whispered, echoing my thoughts. 'I know it. You know it. Your sister knows it. You've only scratched the surface.'

'What do you mean?'

'You've completed your practice round. Now, you're ready for the final showdown.'

The boys. The dead. The graves. Stuff that just didn't make sense if Arnold was behind it all.

And there was something else... something deep down in the back of my memory, a detail so tiny that I probably hadn't even paid attention when I noticed it...

A theft...

'You must look at the window again.' The instruction given by Old Lady Lilly was plain, matter-of-fact and emotionless. She wasn't asking. There was no rejecting the mission. It was a command.

'Why?'

'It has one final thing to show you.'

'How do you know all this? Do you even know what the window is? How it works? Why the hell any of this is happening?'

'No, Christopher, I don't.' Her eyes bore into mine, cleaving their way into my soul. 'I know little more than you. I know what the window does and what it shows, and I suspect it shows us things that we could help with. I hope - and have often prayed - that it is a power to be used for good. As it has so far, showing us the truth of who Michael Arnold is. But it has more to give.'

She paused, her breath suddenly becoming ragged. 'If the window is cracked, and the rift is growing bigger, I fear we have very little time left. If you and your sister do not use it soon, for one last time, you will not be able to do what it wants you to do. And if you cannot complete its task... I fear we will never stop these disappearances. They will continue. Our nemesis is clever and crafty, but also pure evil. I know this, but I know not how. You must stop this. Before it's too late.'

'Why is the window cracking?' It wasn't a particularly relevant question, but it was the only one I could manage in that moment.

'I don't know, child.'

'Guess.'

'Why?'

'Because you know more about it than me.'

'Alas, I fear not. I have spent longer with the window, yes, this is true, but your experience has been more... intense. More powerful. Darker.'

'I don't care. Why do *you* think it's cracking?'

Lilly was quiet for a moment and looked as if she was pondering my question. Finally, she spoke. 'I believe this window has been around for a long time. Decades. Most of my life. Some of yours. I believe there is a power in this window... an energy that cannot even begin to be understood by the likes of humankind. Even my son, my wise and wonderful son... even he would not understand its mysteries if I told him, and he understands a lot.' She paused again, readjusting her position and grip on her stick. 'I do not think this energy can last forever. I think it is too much for a manmade inanimate object to hold. That window survived my entire life, and the glass wasn't even scratched when it was ripped from my house just a few weeks ago. But now, as it lies *under your bed*,' (a chill shot through me once again, ambushed by Lilly's foresight), 'wrapped in a sheet, protected by you and your sister, surviving an attack from your father...' (*impossible, how does she know that?*), 'now... it has cracked. The energy is too much. Soon it will be broken, and then I believe its mysteries and knowledge will be lost forever.'

Lilly appeared to feel she had said enough. She turned and began to walk away. I stood, a statue, paralysed by the depth of knowledge and the weight of the revelations this old woman had poured out before me. I was about to cry out when she turned back for a final time. Her face looked tired. Her wrinkles had become more prominent. Her eyes were absent.

'Look in the window, Christopher. Tonight. Before it closes forever.'

She never spoke to me again and hobbled away at an impressive speed in the direction of Beggar Home Lane, her old home. Surely I should have walked her home? Got her back to the nursing home? Called a taxi? An ambulance?

No. You have a job to do.

I didn't know if the voice was my own or Lilly's or the window's, but I knew it was right. I did have a job to do. And I didn't have much time.

FIFTY-EIGHT

'GAB, YOU'VE GOT TO LISTEN.'

I burst into Gab's room (as quietly as I could, cautious of not waking Uncle Nev) and shook her awake. She was less than impressed.

'Gab, please. I have to talk to you, the window isn't done with us.'

'Oh, fuck *off* Chris, I can't be arsed with this anymore!' She tried to pull her duvet back over her, ignoring me. I understood. She felt defeated. We'd busted Arnold and got the police involved. But we weren't any closer to him being behind bars, or the missing people being found. What had been the point of it all?

This. This is the point of it.

'Gab, Old Lady Lilly was just outside.'

'Bull. Shit.'

'Seriously. You've got to listen to me. We have work to do!' I spoke in a hushed whisper, but the urgency was heavy in my voice.

'Go away, Chris.' She was monotone. Exhausted. If I'm honest, so was I.

I paused. Thought carefully. Gab had always been the determined one. The sensible one. The one who cared for me, who motivated me. Now, I had to do the same for her.

'Old Lady Lilly told me our work wasn't finished. That this was just the warm-up.' I decided I would just talk at her. 'There is more to do. But now the window is cracking, she thinks it will break soon. When that happens, I don't think we'll be able to see things in it anymore. I think the window will be closed. Quite literally.' I hesitated, taking a deep breath. 'I think it's got something else to show us. Something we need to act on. Something that might lead us a bit closer to these missing people. Everything seems to revolve around this window... like it's the centre of the universe.'

My voice had taken on a ghostly tone, as I uttered the mysterious inner musings of my mind. Gab had stopped fidgeting with the quilt. She was listening. I thought so, anyhow.

'It's like some impossible force has been controlling events. Kids disappear from *our* town, with more and more vanishing as we find the window. Dad goes ape-shit, and Mum has brain surgery. Arnold was going after girls from *our* school. Girls that *we* knew. Vicky spoke to *you*. Adam told *me* about Vicky's phone and the text messages. The car that ran over Tigger was opposite the window. The same car smashed into Dad and let him escape. It had a dashcam catching Arnold. And it all seems to revolve around this fucking window... and, by extension, around *us*.'

Slowly, Gab pulled the cover back. I saw her face for the first time that night. Her face was plain, expressionless. She wore none of her normal makeup that was typical of a teenage girl. She also showed none of the innocence that a sixteen-year-old should. She had a hard-worn face that had seen too much already. Both of us, at that moment, knew we were inexplicably linked to that window. Somehow, a deep power somewhere beyond the depths of our understanding and the common sense of the universe had led to this moment. A moment where we were about to be shown something that would implode our reality.

A lot of things in this world can't be explained. Life, death, mutation, evolution, God, Buddha, Allah, the Big Bang. Life's mysteries that we can never fathom or even begin to comprehend. People claim to see ghosts, to be healed from terminal diseases, to know what someone else is thinking. Are these things real? I don't know. Life is nebulous and ever-changing. Creation is vast and inconceivable. Can we ever understand its complex intricacy? No. Did I understand why the window was with us, how it worked, or why it did what it did? No. Could I change it? No. Could I act on it?

Absolutely.

'How did Lilly get here?' Gab's question wasn't exactly the most pressing, but at least she had engaged.

'I don't know. She's got a walking stick.'

Seemingly satisfied with the answer, Gab sat up. Her expression was one of steely determination, laced with the tiniest hint of fear. 'We look again. Just once. A final look. One last time.'

I nodded. 'One last time.'

FIFTY-NINE

ONE LAST TIME.

The window sat before the both of us. The crack ran from the top right-hand corner, from where we both sat. It meandered untidily across the window, splintering out into the other panes. Of the six panes of glass, all but one displayed cracks. The paint around the edges, which my Dad and I had so carefully tidied up whilst building the cold frame was worn and decaying.

As soon as we had unearthed it from under the bed, we had felt the stench of death. It was a repugnant sense, intruding into our very beings. Pulling back the sheet that covered it had felt like ripping off a bandage. It was almost painful.

The window was dying. And, I suppose, a part of us was also dying. Our connection to this window had been so raw and intense and dark. Now, the connection was fleeing, and it wasn't doing so with ease.

Neither of us spoke. Everything was silent. Outside, the night continued. In my bedroom, time seemed to stand still.

We looked into the glass.

I felt cold.

Colour seemed to ebb out of the room around me. My breathing became thinner. I gasped, greedily sucking in oxygen. The air felt stale and old. Immediately, I realised this was going to be the most intense vision the window had ever given us. Looking at my sister, whose face was twisted in discomfort, I knew she felt the same.

It was as if a brick wall had slammed into me. I grunted. My eyes closed momentarily.

The following experience was the most bizarre, unexplainable and confusing of my life. I knew I was in my bedroom. I knew I was still looking through the window with Gab next to me. Yet, at the same time, I was within the image. This time, the window had brought me into the scene, providing the most visceral and disturbing vision yet.

I felt Gab next to me, as if she stood on the street by my side, on Beggar Home Lane, directly outside Old Lady Lilly's house, in the very spot where the rubbish skip now stood and where I had found a small pack of cigarettes.

The night was dark and cold. Rain fell (as was typical of these scenes, and the north of England).

Almost in slow motion, I saw Paul Thornton across the road.

This is the final image. We're going to find out what happened to my friend.

He ran, as we had seen before. As had been the case with many of the window's visions, I could feel Paul's emotions.

Pure terror. A sense of hopelessness.

I'm going to die. That's what Paul felt. Paul ran, terrified for his *own* life.

What the *fuck* was going on?

Paul's hood fell back, as I had seen it do in the last version of this vision. The horror in my heart (and I assume Paul's), intensified.

Then, running past where the little red car was usually parked (how bloody convenient that Aiden had clearly been out that night), came his pursuer. Paul's chaser looked the same as last time, clad entirely in black, hood pulled around their head and face tightly, obscuring any chance of identifying them.

Was it Mr Arnold? Somehow, I thought not. For one thing, up close, in the depths of the window's majestic abilities, it didn't look like old

Mikey. They weren't the right build. The assailant was shorter, slightly stockier, and inconceivably more evil.

More evil. I just knew it. The window was telling me. *Pure* evil. Hatred. Darkness. But not just that… not just darkness but…

Insanity. This pursuer was insane. The worst kind of evil, one driven by madness and a perverse, backwards version of what was right and wrong in this world.

The window was throwing all of this information at me, as I watched in morbid fascination. As we had seen, the chaser caught up with Paul and performed a perfect rugby tackle, bringing him to the floor abruptly and violently.

My body felt like it had been shocked, as I felt Paul's pain, the impact ricocheting through my very being.

I could smell the breath of Paul's attacker. It was rancid and putrid. Yet… familiar.

Dread like I had never known before welled up inside me.

Something horrendous was happening.

The vision continued, onwards past the point we had seen previously.

We heard the sound of a car.

Someone else was coming.

I tried to look to my right, where I could sense - no, hear - the car coming. I couldn't see. It was the edge of the image. The end of the window's scope. There was just a blurry blackness.

But the car was coming closer.

The emotion I felt went into overdrive. I was overcome with Paul's terror, my heart racing, feeling as if it was about to burst from my chest. Had I wet myself? Paul had. I knew it. I could feel a warm trickle stinging my leg, his feelings and physicality personified onto me.

Yet amongst all this fear and horror, there were other emotions inside me, battling it out in a mighty conflict. Regret. Sadness. Shame.

These weren't Paul's thoughts… they were mine. I was merging with the scene playing out before me, even as the images began to blur and I felt the pull of reality.

No… I don't have an answer yet…

The image was fading.

But the car was coming.

The car…

No…

Slowly, Beggar Home Lane was blackening around me. It wasn't going to show me everything… but it was going to be enough.

It all happened at once, in painfully slow motion.

The car came into view.

I recognised it straight away. The back of it seemed to glow, as if to attract my attention, highlighting the old busted rear bumper and dented boot.

Then, as the car stopped, Paul tried to fight off his attacker for a final time. He was instantly knocked unconscious by a brutal punch, but not before he pulled his attacker's hood back.

I could hear Gab crying.

Reality slammed back into me. I was sobbing. The image was over.

Crack.

I didn't need to look to know that the fracture slowly engulfing the window had expanded. Was the window done? Was it finally broken?

It didn't matter. Nothing mattered anymore. My world had come shattering down around me, wrenching me from my innocent little reality into a realm of darkness and chaos.

Because we'd known the car in the image. And more importantly, we'd known the face.

Paul Thornton, my friend, stolen from his simple life, had been picked up in a very familiar battered old Ford Focus, belonging to none other than my Uncle Nev.

And his attacker - holy shit, his attacker - had been none other than my abusive, alcoholic prick of a father - Len Fucking Keeler.

SIXTY

GAB DIDN'T STOP CRYING for a long time. I cried for a while too, but then exhaustion overwhelmed me and I laid on my back, looking up at the ceiling of my bedroom, stunned.

Dad. It was my Dad. *He* was the bad guy. The answer. And who had been helping him? None other than our friendly temporary guardian Uncle Nev. Who else would have been driving that shitty old car?

'All along,' Gab finally whispered, her voice breaking through the harsh sobs. 'All along it was him. Dad. Our own father. The absolute piece of shit!' Her last words were spoken in an intense hiss, venom and hatred spewing from her. 'That sadistic, miserable, dickhead bastard RAPIST!'

I shushed her quickly, acutely aware that my Father's presumed assistant was still asleep across the landing.

'Don't shush me, Chris!' She spat, her volume rising again. Rapidly, she had moved from one stage of grief to the other, now intensely angry and full of rage. 'That bastard is going to pay.'

'I know,' I hushed her. 'I know.' Not entirely sure what I was doing, I put my arms around her and held her.

There we sat, on the floor of my bedroom, the window in front of me, cracked almost - not fully, but almost - all the way through, with my arms wrapped around my sister as she gave into grief once again. She sobbed harshly into my shoulder, her body shaking in a brutal cocktail of fury and misery.

Finally, she asked: 'What do we do now?'

I thought about this for a long time. Suddenly, somehow, I was the leader of the pair. Gab had always been headstrong and forthright and the natural leader. Now, she was broken, but hellbent on revenge. So was I, but somehow I held it together better. Was it because of what Lilly had said to me? Was it the power of the window?

In my heart, I knew that it was much simpler than that. He was *our* Dad. I knew that it was *our* responsibility to deal with him. The police, for whatever reason, weren't going to be able to catch him. It was down to us. The window knew it, Lilly knew it, I knew it.

All along, it had been him. The thought enraged me and broke my heart all at the same time. Sure, Arnold had been a sex pest, but he hadn't been responsible for everyone. Not for Paul. Not for the missing males that Officer Fred mentioned. Probably not for Laurie's death.

Somehow - and looking back, I know that it must have been the window giving me this wisdom - I knew he was responsible for all of it. Arnold was just a red herring. A pawn, pulling us away from the bigger picture. I doubt my Father even knew that Arnold had acted as his scapegoat.

Was it surprising that it was my Father? He'd never said as much as a nice word to me unless we were building in his damn workshop. He'd spent most of his life inebriated, beaten my Mum within an inch of her life, abused Gab and I, escaped police custody and euthanised our cat.

No. It wasn't surprising. But that inbuilt connection, the one that tells you your parents are there to look after you and could never do a thing wrong and that they're superheroes - somehow, despite all my Father had done and continued to do, that connection had won out. It had blinded me to the truth.

But now, as Gab had said… *the bastard was going to pay.*

'Please Chris.' Gab's voice was full of pleading. 'What do we do?'

And I knew. In my subconscious, the window had told me. At the very end of the image, as the car had come into view, part of it had been highlighted. As if the window had drawn a huge, red circle around something saying "Here you go".

The boot of the car.

Uncle Nev, in the past few weeks, had often claimed he was off on trips to Hull to check on my Mum, or heading across to Leeds for work. In the evenings, he had often popped out, apparently to the Homestead for a few pints.

I called bullshit. He had gone to meet with Dad, for whatever sick operation they were running.

We had to get in the boot. Immediately. How often did he disappear in the night? How often did he run off whilst we were sound asleep, or away at school, or out with our friends? I had a feeling (no, I had been told by the window, but it was like a feeling), that we needed to be in that boot, tonight, because, like Lilly had said, time was running out, and shit was about to hit the fan.

'We need to get in his car, Gab. Now.'

'We should call the police.'

I was surprised to hear such a sensible suggestion from my sister, but I still dismissed it. 'No, we don't. We have no proof. Nothing.'

'They'll be DNA evidence in Nev's car? Surely?' She sat up, bringing her head off my shoulder to display her tear-stained face. She was tired and broken. But she was still determined.

Whilst I couldn't argue with her logic, I had too many doubts. And I was too transfixed on the fact that the window had *given us an assignment.*

'There might be,' I agreed, 'but I don't think it matters. They have no reason to suspect Nev. With Arnold we had evidence. The notebook. The dashcam.' The universe really had done a number on us, not letting the red car be there in this vision. The police could still check the dashcam just in case… they might have trusted us enough to do that, after what happened with Arnold.

No. It's us. We have to end this. And we have to do it now.

'No, we need to find out what the hell is going on,' I continued. 'We need to get in the boot of Nev's car and wait for him to drive off.'

'We could be waiting days,' Gab protested. 'Then he might start looking for us, and get suspicious.'

'I don't think so,' I responded, speaking with a confidence only afforded to me by the window. I was its slave now. That much was certain. 'In fact, I think he's going to go tonight.'

'How do you...'

As if on cue, we heard a hint of movement across the landing. The creak that was typical of the floor in my Mum and Dad's room, the old floorboard that groaned under the weight of someone getting up for the toilet. It wouldn't have disturbed us in the slightest if we'd been asleep. But now...

'We don't even have a phone to call the police once we find out what's going on,' Gab hissed, urgency and fear tangible in her voice. She was right - our phones remained waterlogged and destroyed after our encounter with Mr Arnold. 'It's too dangerous.'

I shook my head. *What am I doing?* 'Nev has a mobile. We can use that, once we find out what's going on.'

'How will we get it off him?'

'I don't know Gab!' I snapped. 'But we have to go, now. This is our window of opportunity.' I glanced at the cracked supernatural object in the middle of the room. 'Literally.'

Gab looked dubious.

'Please. Please, Gab. Trust me. Like I've trusted you.'

My sister looked at me for a long time. It felt like an age. She said nothing. Then, when another floorboard creak quietly echoed around the otherwise silent house, she nodded. 'We'd better hurry.'

I've had a lot of time to think over the last few years, as I've said. Often, I'll spend days just going through the motions, lost in my own thoughts, replaying the events I've written in these pages.

Do I have regrets?

I think of the days when I made a simple decision that may have led to disastrous consequences. What if I'd told Mr Arnold and the other teachers about my Dad abusing us that day in Arnold's office? What if we'd walked away and left Mr Arnold on the riverbank, instead of fighting? What if, that day, we'd decided to call the police and beg for help, instead of hiding in my Uncle's car and going to meet our nemesis?

Watershed moments. They change our lives, sometimes for the better, sometimes for the worse. That decision I made with Gab, in my little bedroom, just around the corner from Beggar Home Lane... I think that was probably for the worse.

SIXTY-ONE

NEV'S CAR was one of those old beaten-up ones, as I've said. It was a year 2000 Ford Focus, and the way you got into the boot was by using the key to turn a lock just below where the boot opened.

As quietly as we could, we'd pulled on some old tracksuit bottoms and hoodies, before stealthily sneaking out of my room. My parents' bedroom door remained closed, suggesting Nev wasn't ready yet. I did, however, see a slither of light underneath the door.

He was awake.

Barely breathing, we made our way downstairs. Nev's car keys were kept where they always were, on the side cabinet in the hallway.

This was the risky bit. We needed to get out of the house, to the car, open the boot, and then return the keys quickly and clandestinely enough that Nev would never know.

The house unlocked with an eerie quiet. Gab was the first to step outside and I followed quickly, keys in hand, the cold bite of the air barely noticeable as adrenaline pumped through our veins.

I could hear the pulse in my head hammering violently.

We made it to the car, where, just over an hour ago, Old Lady Lilly had delivered her harrowing instructions. Without hesitation or even a glance at my twin, I inserted the key into the lock and turned it.

A quiet pop told me we had achieved our first objective.

Gab pulled the boot open and began to clamber in. Without a word, I rushed back to the house, returned the keys to their rightful home and reached for my own keys, so I could lock the door.

Then I saw it.

Shit.

My bedroom door was open. I could see it at the top of the stairs. Nev could look in and see we weren't there.

I began to climb the stairs.

Nev's bedroom door opened.

I froze. Light flooded the upstairs landing. I didn't breathe.

I heard my Uncle make his way out onto the landing. Was he going to come straight downstairs? I braced myself, ready to come up with an excuse. *Bollocks.* I realised the front door was still open. Cold air was billowing into the house. How the hell would I explain that? We were nearly finished before we'd even started.

Then, mercifully, I heard the bathroom door open, close and lock. Nev had chosen the most perfect time to take a piss.

Rushing more than I probably should have, clumsily and loudly, I clambered up the stairs and pulled my bedroom door shut.

Then a sudden thought occurred to me.

We didn't know where we were going, or what we were going to find. We were just stowaways in Nev's car. We needed backup. Quite literally.

We still didn't have mobile phones. Arnold had made sure of that. And at sixteen, I didn't have the capital to buy one myself (neither did Gab), and I hadn't been particularly keen to explain to Nev how my phone had ended up so waterlogged.

I remembered how Nev had been talking to Fred Andrews, (the police officer who had arrested *me*) on his mobile phone a few weeks ago. The day he said they were still searching for Dad and Aiden.

Fred. A police officer we could trust… I hoped.

What I did next was incredibly risky. It made me more terrified than I had been that whole time.

I went into Nev's room.

His bed was unmade and untidy. The room was cluttered with the contents of a suitcase, roughly thrown all over the police.

Nev's trusty old Nokia was on the bedside table.

I picked it up and mashed a few keys (physical buttons, none of this iPhone shit for Nev, oh no). The phone instructed me to press * and "enter" to unlock.

I did just that.

Incredibly, it opened.

My fingers trembled as I tried to operate the clunky mobile. It felt like using a computer from the 90s. I went to contacts, praying that Nev would have Fred saved.

I was in luck. At the very top of his contacts list, filed under "A" for "Andrews", it said: "Fred Andrews (Police)". I selected "options", then "send SMS".

I paused briefly, frozen in time, listening for the sound of Nev in the bathroom. It was silent. No sound of taps running or piss flowing. Never before in my life had I hoped so much that someone was opening their bowels.

Texting on the Nokia was painfully slow. I had to press each number button several times to get particular letters. *I'll never take predictive text and the keyboard on my iPhone for granted again…*

As quickly as I could, I wrote, simply:

"fred it's chris keeler…. nev and dad are the kidnappers were following them 2 find missing girls plz follow us or trace phone or something or I think we might die don't text this phone its nevs please come"

It wasn't the best bit of prose I'd ever written, but it would be enough to get the old policeman's attention. I hoped. If it woke him up.

Trembling, and beyond amazed that Nev was still in the bathroom, I put the phone back and snuck out of the room.

The toilet flushed.

Slightly too loudly, I raced down the stairs and back towards the door. Somehow, Nev remained in the bathroom the whole time, as I successfully snuck out of the house and locked the door behind me.

At the car, Gab gave me a half-concerned, half-furious look as I leapt into the boot next to her. Still, she said nothing as I pulled the car shut and we were cast into blackness.

'Where the *hell* have you been?' There was a tarpaulin in Nev's boot that she pulled over the pair of us. 'Just in case he opens the boot,' she whispered, by way of explanation. I doubted Uncle Nev would be fooled by the two person-sized lumps under the tarpaulin but I didn't protest. We were committed now, come what may.

'I texted Fred off Nev's phone,' I breathed. I heard her gasp. Before she could tell me what an idiotic risk it was, I continued. 'Maybe he can trace Nev's phone. Maybe it will mean he follows us.'

'What if Nev looks at his sent messages?'

'It's an old Nokia, Gab. You have to actually go to the "Sent Messages" folder to manage that.' She said no more.

We waited for a long time. Neither of us had a watch on. We had no idea how much time passed.

Adam, my friend from school, had a dog. I remember asking him once if the dog could be left alone at home. Boring question, I know. He said yes, and that really, the dog shouldn't be left for more than eight hours. However, after the first hour, it is said that dogs lose track of time. They don't have an awareness of how long they've been alone unless their food is due. So, basically, leaving a dog for two hours was no different to leaving it for eight hours, as long as it had enough food to last. I felt like a dog that night. We could have been in that boot for thirty minutes. We could have been there for five hours. All I knew was that when the car eventually started up, it was still pitch black in the boot under the tarpaulin, and I'd been dozing slightly.

Gab whispered in the darkness. 'Are you okay?'

'Yes,' I grunted, but I wasn't.

'Here we go then,' Gab mused, barely making a sound.

I didn't reply. The vibrations of the car surrounded us, darkness our only friend, as we were driven further into the mystery we'd found ourselves in, and ever closer to our fate.

SIXTY-TWO

IT FELT like we were driving for a long time, but then again, we had no concept of time passing. It was like we had fallen into an alternate reality, where time stood still. The shaking movement of the car was almost hypnotic as we continued our journey in darkness, towards darkness.

We heard nothing from Nev, just the clunking of him pulling the car through various gears. At one point, we were definitely driving on a major road, maybe a motorway. There was a familiar roar of tyres on tarmac, going about sixty miles per hour. After a while, we noticeably slowed. The texture of the ground beneath us seemed to change, almost as if we were driving over a softer surface… maybe grass or dirt.

Finally, we stopped.

Neither of us dared breathe.

The car turned off. Nev's door could be heard to open. Footsteps drew closer. Was he walking away? No. He was walking around the car… towards the boot.

'Shit,' I heard Gab whisper, as we listened to the familiar sound of the boot being unlocked.

We lay, deathly silent, still as statues. We both held our breath, terrified that even the subtle movements of respiration would give us away.

It didn't matter.

The tarp was pulled away.

Both of us blinked, trying to see ahead of us. A torch in Nev's hand blinded and disorientated the pair of us. We lay frozen on the spot, unable to move, fear paralysing us.

'Bloody hell, you two,' Nev grumbled, almost conversationally. His voice maintained its soft quality. 'You really have got yourselves in the shit now.'

He stepped away from the car, taking his torch with him. 'Get out, please. Both of you.'

Gingerly, our balance slightly off, we clambered out of the car boot. Nev stepped forward and closed it, quietly. Then he motioned with his torch. We looked at him blankly. He shook his head in what I think was disbelief.

'You're idiots, both of you,' he sighed. 'You should have left this alone. Everything would have been fine. Now… fucking hell, now I have no idea how this is going to end.'

We looked at each other, then at Nev, the spots in our vision slowly fading after the torch had assaulted our eyes. For the first time, we realised we were in a field. Nothing but darkness, black as pitch, surrounded us, Nev's torch offering the only light in an otherwise dismal abyss. In the distance, I could hear flowing water… maybe we were near the river, or a canal.

'Come on then.' Nev motioned with his torch again. 'Don't make me force you.'

At a loss of what to do, and acutely aware that Nev was completely in control, we began to walk in the direction he had indicated. He followed us closely.

After a few minutes, he grunted, indicating that we should stop. We obeyed. The outline of a large tree could be seen before us, silhouetted against the moonlight. The sound of water was much closer now… it was a flowing stream… were we by the river?

'Go to the tree,' Nev murmured, pointing with his torch. We did as we were told.

He joined us and knelt at the tree's trunk. Moving some leaves and earth aside, his torchlight was cast over a wooden hatch, just big enough for a grown man to fit through. He grumbled to himself as he unlocked a padlock attached to the hatch, before gently opening it. He shone his light downwards, into the hole. 'Climb in. It's only a few metres down. There's even a ladder.'

I looked anxiously at my sister. She spoke her first words since exiting the car. 'We're not going anywhere with you.' Brave words. Pointless, brave words.

Nev sighed and reached into his jacket. I didn't have to be a genius to know he was about to bring out a gun. Even in the darkness, I saw the moon and torchlight reflecting off the metal surface of the firearm as he produced it.

'I don't want to use this, Gab. But you're both too far into this now. You're going to have to deal with it. Do as I say.'

'You won't shoot us here.' Gab remained confident. 'People will hear it.'

Nev shrugged. There was pain in his face. This wasn't easy for him. Whatever *this* was. 'We're about three miles from the nearest settlement,' he explained, casually. 'Out in the great north Yorkshire fields, near the canal. Past Strensall. We're in the wilderness now. No one will hear this gun. No one will ever know what happened. Now, Gabrielle, I really *don't* want to shoot my niece. But I will if I have to. Now, get in the hole.'

Again, Nev pointed at the open hatch, his gun now fully revealed to both of us. He motioned the weapon in the direction he wanted us to go.

Gab knew we were beaten. So did I.

We obliged.

The ladder felt cold and slippery on my hands as I descended. I had absolutely no idea what I was going into. I did have an idea, however, that I was descending towards my death. Maybe that was okay.

I went first, followed by Gab. Once we had made it down a few rungs of the ladder, we heard Uncle Nev follow, pulling the hatch shut behind him. Once again, we were cast into complete darkness.

Almost as soon as we were plunged into darkness, I felt the soft, loamy soil beneath my feet. A moment later, Nev's torch pointed downwards, dimly illuminating our path. I heard the steady clink of metal on metal, as Nev climbed downwards gun still in hand.

I helped Gab down as she reached the earth. Nev was hot on our heels.

I put my hand on the wall to steady myself. Nev's dim torchlight was the only illumination in the dank underground of the tree's roots. The space was barely wide enough to fit the three of us. A wooden door stood before us. Everything else was damp earth.

There was a smell down there... a smell of chemicals and iron and sulphur... and death. If you ever want to know what death smells like... well, you'll know it when you sniff it. And what we smelt was death, in its rawest, truest form.

'I'm sorry for what you're about to see,' Nev explained, stepping forward with a key for the door. 'And for whatever happens to you. I truly am.' There was a genuine apology in Nev's voice.

What the hell were we about to see?

For a moment, I thought of fleeing back up the ladder. From the look on Gab's face, I reckon she had the same idea. But I remembered the gun. Neither of us would make it up before Nev shot us down. No one would even hear it.

No, we were on our own. And this was our fate.

The door opened. We followed Nev through.

Terror revealed itself.

SIXTY-THREE

I FELT like I was going to vomit. Gab looked as sick as a dog.

The chamber we had entered was massive. It was a dome-shaped room, the ceiling caked with the earth of the ground above. Blood and entrails seemed to paint the walls. Vats displaying hazardous chemical waste signs were placed haphazardly around the room. Machinery and metal tables littered the chamber, some piled high with papers, others stained red with gore, others sporting… remains. The stench of blood and rotting flesh was overpowering.

But that wasn't what was most disturbing.

No, what was most horrifying was the life being kept in this chamber.

In the centre of the room, three rectangular, stone tables were situated. Upon them, three bodies lay. On the back wall of the cavern, there seemed to be display cases. I couldn't see in detail, but I was pretty confident the wall was filled with a display of body parts. Several rectangular, coffin-shaped boxes were littered around the room and covered in cloth.

And around the edges of the chamber were *metal cages*. Some were empty. Others had their contents hidden by dirty-looking sheets. But others... others had people in them. Weary, broken, abused people, still alive, at the very edge of existence.

I had never seen such an atrocious sight.

I vomited.

'What the fuck is this?'

That voice. That voice I knew all too well, that filled me with loathing and hatred and white-hot rage. The voice neared us, swearing and shouting, just like it always did. I didn't need to look up from my vomit to know who I was facing.

Len Keeler. My Father. Sadistic Bastard Number One.

'They followed me, Len,' Nev confessed, sounding - maybe - a little scared.

'Bloody hell,' Len spat. 'Bind them.'

Nev didn't utter a response, but the next thing I knew I was being held tightly, my hands pulled behind me. A cable tie was twisted painfully around my wrists and pulled tight. I fell to my knees. Gab barely had a chance to respond before Nev did the same thing to her, although her wrists were bound in front of her.

Finally, I looked up. There before me, Len Keeler stood. What the hell was he doing here? Why was there blood and body parts everywhere? What was this?

'You two could have escaped all of this,' my Father grumbled, grabbing me by the scruff of my neck. Out of the corner of my eye, I saw Nev similarly grabbing Gab. She was crying. Like me, she had never imagined we would find something like this.

'I won't be able to let you leave, you know,' Len went on. He spoke almost conversationally, his initial anger at our arrival gone. Interestingly, he seemed more sober than he had in years. 'You'll have to stay here. Whether you live, die, or become a subject is entirely up to the pair of you.'

My Dad shoved me forward towards an old, moth-eaten sofa at one side of the room. Gab was flung in next to me. I adjusted myself uncomfortably, the ties digging into my wrists and giving me the incredibly uncomfortable sensation that my shoulder was about to dislocate.

Nev and Len sat down opposite us. In an instant, the dynamic had changed. We were in a sort of meeting. An interview. Somehow, I felt like it was time for answers.

'What is this?' I grimaced. Acid burnt the back of my throat, the last bits of vomit still present. I spat onto the floor.

My father looked at us, curiously. 'You haven't worked it out?'

'It's some sick sex dungeon,' Gab sneered, her voice filled with venom. 'He rapes them, then chops them up. That's what this place is. Nev helps him. Probably has a go himself, you piece of shit.'

Nev was expressionless. Amazingly, a ghost of a smile broke across my Dad's face. He was different to how I'd ever seen him. I'd have guessed he was stone-cold sober. And - although it broke my heart to think it - he seemed - almost - happy. Contented. Like this was his happy place. However sick it was.

'You've always been a clever girl, Gabrielle,' Len Keeler finally said, paying a rare compliment. 'But you've got this completely wrong.'

'How? You're just some sadistic fuck who likes to screw young girls and then kill them. You chop them up and keep them here, in some sick museum. You *bastard*.' She hissed her final words, loathing spilling out of her.

'No Gabrielle, you're wrong,' Len repeated firmly as if he was teaching his daughter a lesson. In some messed up sense, I guess he was. 'It may surprise you, but I have little to no interest in sex. Ask your poor Mother.'

Gab made to move at the mention of our Mum, standing up off the sofa. Nev, never saying a word, leant forward, silently holding his gun out in front of him. Gab sat down. Satisfied, Nev lay the gun on the small table between them - almost a coffee table - alongside his car keys and old Nokia phone. It was perversely bizarre - here we were in some deranged laboratory out of a horror film, and we were sat as if in someone's lounge.

My Dad shook his head, then continued. 'No, Gabrielle, it's true. I genuinely have no interest in sex. That fool, Mr Arnold, he did. But being obsessed with sex is messy. The abuser always gets caught and can never quite hide his tracks. Me... I'm not interested in that. I'm interested in something much more pure. Much more satisfying. And my interest does not leave any victims. Once someone comes with me, they never see the light of day again. Unfortunately, that's just how it has to be.'

He spoke so indifferently. He was apathetic about whatever he did. No… he saw it as his *right*.

'So what *is* your interest? What the hell is this place?' Finally, I spoke. And, clearly, it was the question my Father had wanted to answer.

'My interest, Christopher, is the human body. All of it. How it works, how it changes, how it can be fixed, how it can be destroyed. That is what I am interested in. And this…' He held out his arms, motioning around the room. 'This is my anatomy lab.'

SIXTY-FOUR

'YOUR WHAT?' I stared at my Father, incredulously.

'My anatomy lab,' he replied simply. I watched with interest as my Father's hand shook violently and he looked across to his brother. Dutifully, Nev stood up, walked to a poorly built wooden cabinet (which looked suspiciously like one of my Father's woodwork projects), and opened it. From it, he brought a bottle of brown-looking liquid and two glasses. Without a word, Nev returned to his seat and poured two large measures of what I assumed was whisky into the glasses. He handed one to my Father, who steadied his shaking hand and accepted. He took a large glug.

'Still a pathetic drunk I see?' Gab spat, her voice laced with hatred and fury.

'He relief drinks,' Nev explained, apparently jumping to my Father's defence. 'He's been trying to come off ever since he was arrested. It's dangerous to stop boozing cold turkey. He gets withdrawal if he doesn't have something. So we've slowly been cutting down. Now that he's in his lab every day, he doesn't feel the need to drink. This place…'

'Fulfils me,' my Father finished, drowning the remains of his glass.

He shook his head when Nev offered more. 'Yes, this place brings me solace. It means I don't need to drink.'

'What the fuck is going on, you sick piece of shit?' Gab's next question came, still full of loathing. 'If you're not raping them, then what are you doing? What the hell do you mean, anatomy lab? What's that supposed to be?'

My Dad sighed, leaning back in his chair and looking at us both. There was a depth to him I'd never seen before. Almost... a wisdom. A dark, twisted wisdom.

'All of this is a long story, Gabrielle.' He paused, before smiling to himself. 'But I suppose that, actually, we have plenty of time. Unfortunately, you two won't be able to leave this place. It doesn't mean you'll become one of my subjects, I'm more than happy for you both to stay around and help... but you can't ever leave. I'm sorry. Now you've seen it, I can't risk my entire operation being blown.'

I shifted uncomfortably in my seat, the cable ties digging harshly into my wrists. How were we going to get out of this?

For a split second, my gaze passed over Uncle Nev's keys and phone, lying untouched on the table before us.

There is a way out.

'As you both know, once upon a time, I was a Doctor,' my Father began, speaking informally. It almost felt like a bedtime story. 'I was pretty frigging good as well. I had designs to specialise as a surgeon and made every effort throughout medical school and my early years as a physician to get there. I attended courses, made presentations, and won distinctions and prizes, all in the name of securing a job as a surgeon. Unfortunately, a few failed exams and job rejections later, my path to becoming a surgeon was becoming more and more difficult to tread.'

I knew all this. Mum had told us before.

'I'd always enjoyed a drink, ever since being a teenager. You two know what it's like up north, you grew up around here.' He eyed us knowingly. 'And I got into the drinking scene at med school. I was always partying. Medics were known for it... work hard, play hard. I guess I never fully appreciated I had a problem until I'd reached that stage where my surgical career wasn't progressing.' He paused, a dark look filled with sadness overtaking him. I listened with interest. We knew this story… but I felt there was more to it.

'Anyway, I was drinking a lot more when I failed exams and got job rejections. It got out of control, I'm not entirely sure how. The next thing I knew, I was turning up to work still drunk from the night before. That turned into drinking on the job. That turned into being pissed on the job.'

There was regret in his voice. This story hurt him. 'I'm not proud of what I did, kids,' he explained. There was genuine sorrow in his voice. I'd never heard it before. Len Keeler was a man of masculinity and aggression and power. Never before had I seen a vulnerability within him. 'But this kept escalating. Eventually, it ended badly, as it was always going to. I was helping deal with a kid in the Emergency Department. Nothing too complicated, just an asthma attack, something I'd dealt with hundreds of times before. But I was hammered. No one on shift had noticed. That was until I dropped the oxygen mask, couldn't hold the kid's airway open, and vomited in the trauma room.'

Gab and I looked at my Father, sadness and shame heavy on our hearts.

'The kid died.'

He said it so bluntly. So finally.

'And I was struck off. Obviously. I should have gone to jail for a fucking life sentence, but I had powerful medico-legal friends who got me out of it on mental health grounds. In the end, the hospital got sued for not looking after me properly. I was overworked, they should have seen the signs, they said. More the fool them.'

I felt anger well up at my Father again, as he betrayed a smile at his last comment.

'I had a short spell in Strangburn was all I got. I bet you two never knew that, did you?'

No, we hadn't known that. Mum had always skipped over Dad's prison stint, expulsion from medicine and butchering of a child. We'd always just been told he'd given up.

'You kept drinking didn't you?' I murmured, darkly. 'You went and got a construction job and had a seizure from your drinking whilst you were operating a crane.'

Dad gave that hateful little smile again. Almost as if he was proud of what he had done. 'I see your Mother filled in a few of the blanks?' He spat on the ground, his mood changing in an instant. The abusive mess of a Father we knew and loved had returned for a few seconds. 'Stupid whore, spreading rumours that aren't her business.'

I felt Gab tense next to me, her fury rising as our Mother was further insulted.

'Calm yourself, girl,' Dad murmured. 'There's no use fighting me.'

'Your Dad's drinking was out of control,' Nev explained calmly, as if trying to defuse the tension.

Fat chance of that.

'He needed help. So I helped him. We talked for a long time about what would help. What did he enjoy? What made him get out of bed in the morning, aside from the drink?'

'You know what the answer was, kids?' Len asked, taking back the conversation. 'My old job. The medicine. Specifically, the surgery. The thrill of the cut. The intricacy of the human body, its nerves and tissues and vessels and organs. The buzz of fixing someone. The rush of building a stronger bone or organ, your hands so deep inside a person's abdomen you can't even see them. *That* was what I loved. And I couldn't bloody do it, because of my drink.'

It had been a vicious circle my Father had never been able to escape. I was beginning to understand.

'He tried the woodwork,' Nev explained. 'That's why he loved it so much. It brought... some satisfaction. Enough that he kept the drinking moderately under control.'

'But it wasn't enough,' my Father continued, his speech becoming a little erratic. 'Woodwork was good, and I enjoyed building, but if it went wrong it didn't matter. I could give up and start again. I could throw away the mistakes. It didn't matter if I messed up. Nobody would get hurt.'

'It was difficult for your Father to find satisfaction,' Nev continued. 'His drinking worsened again. He was in danger of drinking himself into an early grave.'

'He should have,' Gab grumbled, repulsed.

Nev shook his head. 'I care about your Father more than anyone in the world, Gabrielle. He's my brother. The only family I have left!' He looked to my Father with nothing but fondness.

I was disgusted.

'I had to help him,' Nev explained.

'A few years ago,' Len continued, his voice taking on a husky tone, 'I got into a fight with some students. I'd been out drinking and they'd got in my way. Most of them ran away, but one lad stayed to fight. I beat him within an inch of his life, then didn't know what to do. I had a guy bleeding out on me in the middle of a deserted park. I called Nev for help and he came straight to me. Helped me hide the body. Cover it up.'

The missing students.

'Then, I realised something,' Len murmured, excitement rising within him. 'I realised that I suddenly had a human... a real-life human body, that I could... fix.'

'Holy shit,' Gab murmured, as she realised the extent of what my Father was doing.

'Nev helped me find somewhere hidden - an old warehouse, long since abandoned - and we did surgery on the boy. Tried to fix his injuries.'

'Fucking hell...' I whispered, my Father's actions also starting to fully make sense in my mind.

'He died, obviously, pretty quickly. But then we had this body... a *real* body. One I could dissect.'

'No, Dad no!' Gab roared, tears streaming down her face.

Len continued, unperturbed. 'So I did. I dissected him in his entirety. Obviously, his body started to go off pretty quickly, and I had to come up with a way to preserve my work... the pieces I had dissected and highlighted the anatomy of... pieces I called my prosections.'

'Injecting bodies with certain chemicals, like formaldehyde, will embalm them. Essentially freeze them and stop them going off.' Nev spoke with a similar simplicity to my Father. As if what he was talking about was the most normal thing in the world. 'We didn't have the equipment for the first boy. So, unfortunately, we had to burn his remains once your Father was done with them.'

'No, no, no,' I whispered, hating the word "first" that my Uncle had used.

'You know what, kids?' My Father asked, leaning forward towards us, his face displaying just a hint of joy. 'I had never felt so alive. I was doing what I loved again, even if it was in a different setting to that of a hospital.'

'It's pretty bloody different,' Gab murmured, her voice trembling.

Dad shrugged. 'Yes, it is. But that's not the point. For those moments, I had no interest in drink. I just wanted to dissect and fix and learn.'

'From that,' Nev concluded, 'this place was born.'

'Come,' my Father said, standing up. 'Let me give you the tour.'

Barely aware of what I was doing and horrifically shellshocked at my Father's revelations, I stood up and began to follow. Gab, who tripped getting up and paused for a moment to recover crouched by the coffee table, reluctantly followed.

SIXTY-FIVE

THE FULL EXTENT of the cavern was quickly revealed to us. My Father began by leading us to the back of the cavern, towards what I suspected was a display of human bodies. As we neared the edge of the cavern, death was indeed revealed.

Shelves ran the full length of the back of the cavern, sporting every body part one could think of. There were limbs and abdomens and chests and *heads*, all dissected within an inch of their life, clearly showing particular parts of human anatomy. All of the specimens were a dull, beige colour, as if the life had been sucked out of them. They almost looked like they were made of clay.

There were *hundreds* of pieces.

'This is my Prosection wall. I guess this is the first chapter of my journey down this path.' Dad continued to speak casually as if providing a tour of the Natural History Museum. 'After the first boy, Nev and I thought about how we could continue our work. As I say, doing such work fulfilled me. It helped me not want to drink. So, we expanded.'

Slowly, Dad walked us down the corridor, as we stared, aghast, horrified yet fascinated with the body parts on display. Nev brought up the rear. Our wrists were still bound.

'The first subject - a student - showed us it was possible,' Nev explained. 'And students are a very transient population. No one knows what they're doing or where they go. And they all love to party. So in York, it's only natural that a few would disappear, presumably into the river.'

'So that was the population we targeted,' my Father explained. 'Students. Males initially, because they were more likely to take risks and be out after dark alone. Not many female subjects to begin with.'

'There were a few oldies as well,' Nev butt in, a quiver of excitement in his tone. 'A few lonely old blokes that no one would miss. They could just as easily have fallen into the river.'

My Dad nodded in agreement. 'Our issue was preservation. Embalming, as we said, was essential. Bodies go off rather quickly. But York University had a dissection lab, where they embalmed with formaldehyde. A few cleverly coordinated attempts later and we managed to steal some of their equipment and used it to inject those we had taken.' Len Keeler gestured at the vats displaying hazardous waste signs, dotted around the room.

'Sometimes we injected whilst they were alive,' Nev murmured, darkly.

'Oh yes. That was when it got interesting.' My Father's voice was augmented by a terrifying excitement. 'To embalm a body for preservation, you inject formaldehyde into the subject's carotid artery in their neck. At the same time, you drain their natural fluids - blood, etcetera - from the jugular vein on the opposite side of the neck.'

'It's exquisitely painful.' Nev sounded like I had never heard him before. A malignant glee had taken over him. He was getting as much enjoyment out of this as my Father... disgusting bastards!

'They generally didn't survive that bit,' my Father continued, almost regretfully. 'But they were alive long enough to feel pain. And that was *good*.' Evil. Deranged. Insane. 'We initially underwent embalming of their chest and abdominal cavities,' Dad continued, casually. 'First, we aspirate the fluid and contents of the abdominal and thoracic organs, then we inject them with formaldehyde. Doing all of this stops the organs working, but it preserves them beautifully.'

Len then motioned to the specimens before him. Despite myself, I couldn't help but feel a hint of admiration. Although I had little interest in science or biology, I could not deny how impressive the Prosections were. Every part of the human body had been dissected down, showing the endless intricacies of the nerves and tissues that made us tick. For a moment, I marvelled at the dissected chest before me, showing the heart and its surrounding arteries, dyed blue to highlight their course. Alongside it, half a head was displayed, cut vertically down the middle of the face. The inside of the head was on display, showing half a brain, an eye, multitudes of nerves and vessels, and complex bony structures.

'You're disgusting,' Gab hissed, bringing me out of my trance. 'You abduct people, cut them up and put them on display. What the *fuck* is wrong with you?'

'A lot, I suppose Gabrielle,' my Father confessed. Again, that vulnerability. The complexity of my Father's psyche laid out before me. 'There's a lot wrong with me.'

'But he's trying, Gab,' Nev implored. 'He's trying to be better. It's better than being an abusive drunk. He's an addict, and he's found a creative way to control himself.'

'Bullshit,' Gab's venomous response came. 'You can't call this a creative way of controlling himself. It's illegal. It's murder. It's *sick*! And it's all for nothing, he's still an abusive drunk! You say you've been doing this for years and it makes you better, but you put our Mum in hospital just a few weeks ago! You're still a piece of shit!'

Dad nodded, almost ashamedly. 'You're right Gab. You see, I didn't have things under control. In the last few months, things started to escalate. Let me... continue to explain.'

And, because we didn't know what else to do, we followed my Father further into his insanity.

SIXTY-SIX

'WHERE THE HELL ARE WE ANYWAY?' Gab spat as we followed my Father. 'What is this place? How did you find it?'

Dad seemed a little irritated that the conversation had moved away from his little hobby but answered the question nonetheless. He was baring all tonight.

'We're in the depths of some abandoned farmer's fields out between Strensall and Sutton-on-the-Forest, north of the city.' He spoke as casually as if he was giving directions. 'We found it a few months ago when we were looking for a new location. We were sitting under that big tree, having a few cans, and found a hole in the ground. We went down and found this cavern. No idea where it came from or what it was used for, but we decided it was ours. Hence, our lab was born.'

Len seemed to grow bored of answering Gab's question and changed the subject back to his chosen topic.

'So I collected several bodies that I dissected in their entirety,' Len continued, leading us back out into the main body of the cavern. Nev continued to bring up the rear. 'Mostly male, students, old people… and a few girls.' His voice turned menacing again as he spoke the final words. 'Girls were more difficult to come by as, like I said, they're less likely to be alone in the dark. But then I discovered Molly Atkinson, and later Laurie Openshaw. Two girls who had been involved with a pervert at your school, Mike Arnold.'

I audibly gasped, amazed that my Father had held knowledge of Arnold's actions for a long time.

'I knew he would work well as a scapegoat if these girls disappeared... it would always lead back to him. As I said, it's harder to hide crimes of sex and passion. It always gets messy. This is clean. Clinical.

'Molly became the first female in my Prosection collection.' My Father walked us over to a rectangular shape, covered by a curtain. Without hesitation, he ripped away the sheet to reveal the horrors beneath.

I heard Gab vomit behind me as the gruesome sight was revealed. Within a glass display case, a full body was displayed. Molly had been essentially flayed, all of her skin gone and her musculature exposed. One breast had been cut away, displaying the muscle and fat beneath. Her abdomen had been opened, displaying perfectly preserved abdominal and reproductive organs. Her face... I'll never forget the face. All the skin was gone. One half of her face had kept the muscles and nerves and blood vessels. The other had been dissected down to the bone, showing nothing but her skull. The dull grey colour of formaldehyde was evident.

'You bastard,' I breathed, running out of words to call my Father. How was this happening?

'Laurie was next,' my Father continued, ever so casually, 'but something didn't feel quite right with her. I didn't want to dissect her. I suppose... I had achieved mastery of dissection. I had done so many bodies and explored every crevice of humanity. I only really needed to do a woman once... the anatomy is quite similar, apart from the obvious. I didn't have the desire to cut her up...'

'Your Father's... condition,' Nev interjected, 'means he needs to keep his interest in something, otherwise he turns to drink.'

'You say condition,' Gab panted, still retching, 'you mean he's an alcoholic. An abusive alcoholic, who can only be cured by slicing up any poor bugger he comes across? Come off it, Nev, he's a psychopath!'

Gab shrieked as Nev delivered a perfectly aimed slap to her face, almost knocking her flat.

I cried out in protest, only to feel Dad's hand on my shoulder, gripping firmly. I turned to see him shaking his head.

'Don't you call your Father a psychopath,' Nev said, looking down at Gab, who was struggling to get to her feet with her hands still bound. I felt my cable tie continue to dig harshly into my wrists. 'You're going to have to sort this bitch out, Len. She'll be too much trouble otherwise.'

Gab spat at Nev. Mercifully he didn't respond. Interestingly, my Father also didn't respond to Nev's statement.

'Nev's right,' Dad eventually continued. 'I needed to be kept busy. Interested. So I kept Laurie caged up for a while. Experimented. I injected her with different street drugs, to see the effects. Then I tied her up and inflicted injuries upon her - mainly knife wounds or blunt trauma - then worked on stitching her up and fixing her. All whilst she was still alive. I... enjoyed her pain. It made the whole process so much more fulfilling.'

Dad paused for a moment, looking thoughtful. His eyes moved across the cavern, towards the three stone tables in the centre of the room, displaying three supine bodies, currently unidentified. His eyes drifted around the room to the cages, far at the other side of the space, their inhabitants motionless.

'Eventually, she died,' my Father continued, calmly. 'I suppose her body gave out. But it allowed me to practice trying to bring her back, and when that didn't work, I embalmed her and dissected a little. I didn't get very far through the dissection though... as I said, I had grown bored of simply *dissecting*.'

Bloody hell... how much deeper did this go?!

'Over the last few months, however, something has changed. The way we do things... has changed.' My Father spoke with such great foreboding.

Slowly, he led us away from Molly's flayed remains. Gab, having just about recovered from Nev's slap, followed me in my pursuit of our Father.

'I was taking more and more people. Those who disappeared recently... Ellie Wright, Vicky Crampton, Paul Thornton... they were all me. The girls, after Arnold had broken them. Paul... just because he was in the wrong place at the wrong time.'

We were approaching the other side of the cavern, where dark cages stood like prison cells. Each was dimly lit and it was impossible to see the details of who was inside... but many of the cages were inhabited, each with a body that appeared to be breathing, but barely moving.

'The more we took, the more I realised that dissection just wouldn't fulfil me anymore. We didn't even bother trying. We just left them in cages, keeping them alive, waiting until I worked out what to do next.'

We stopped before another display case, this one smaller, yet still covered with a sheet. Nev stepped forward and unveiled the next revelation.

I think my emotions had taken enough of a battering that night. On any other night, the contents of this display would have broken my heart. Now, I was so emotionally dead and buried that it barely sparked sadness in me.

Tigger, my poor cat, run over by that prick, Aiden Bennet, in his *stupid* red car, was presented before us. What was left of him, anyway. Presumably, upon confiscating the cat from Gab and me, he had decided he would have a go at dissecting Tigger. The remains were barely identifiable, but I knew that tabby fur anywhere.

'I don't know why we hadn't thought of it before,' Nev explained. 'Animals were much more common and much easier to steal than humans. So your Dad dissected Tigger.'

'It didn't matter,' Len butted in, seeming to scold Nev with his eyes. The younger brother stepped away, almost in fear. 'It didn't satisfy me. If anything, it was more boring than humans. I always knew that was the case. I never went after animals because my interest is in the *human* form, not that of animals.' He sighed deeply, turned away from Tigger and continued walking. Again, we followed.

'I drank a lot more. You two probably noticed.' He didn't need to tell us that. We'd seen what he'd done to Mum, still recovering in Hull. 'And I made mistakes. I don't quite know how I did it, because I was so hammered, but Laurie's body ended up leaving this place with me. I must have dropped her in the river or something. I have no idea what happened, but even I realised my drinking was out of control.'

'No shit,' Gab spat.

Dad ignored her. 'That's why your Uncle Nev came down the other week. I told him I'd messed up. We were trying to work out how to fix it and get out of the shitstorm I'd created. By the grace of some higher power, we didn't have to do *anything*. Some evidence appeared against Arnold and now he's a wanted man. So I was lucky.'

I shifted uncomfortably, realising *we* were the reason that the police were hunting the wrong man… well, not the wrong man exactly, but certainly the lesser of two evils.

'If there was some higher power, it wouldn't do *shit* for a scumbag like you,' Gab grumbled. I had never seen my sister so full of hate.

My Dad smiled at this. 'Unfortunately, Gabrielle, we're not here to discuss the existence of a higher power. We are here to work out what we're going to do with the two of you. But first, I'm going to finish the story. Once I had escaped the police… again, by an absolute miracle of a car crash, suddenly, I worked out what to do next. As if completely by accident…'

SIXTY-SEVEN

'WHEN WE TOOK in a friend of yours - Vicky, I believe - we had some… issues. She put up a lot of resistance and caused herself a few injuries. Nothing serious, a few head wounds, some bruised limbs. But after a few days in one of our suites,' he motioned maliciously at the cages to the side of the cavern, still cast in shadow, 'she began to become drowsy. Unconscious. We examined her, and I realised that her head injury had been a bit more serious than we thought. I suspected she was bleeding into her brain.'

Ironically, just like our Mother.

My Dad continued to take us closer to what he had dubbed his 'suites'. I didn't look forward to what I was going to see next.

'That's when the next bright idea came. You see, you can dissect hundreds of bodies and, whilst they're all slightly different, they follow the same general patterns. You know ninety-nine percent of the time, you'll find a liver where there should be one. But injuries… diseases… *pathology*… that can vary in *so* many ways and have countless effects on physiology.'

I didn't like where this was going.

'I'd had some relief when I experimented on Laurie… fixing up her wounds, seeing the effects of drugs on her, etcetera. But Vicky's problem presented an interesting opportunity.'

We were nearing the cages... and in doing so, also moving towards the three stone tables, each bearing a body, unmoving.

'So I operated on her... with no anaesthetic, of course. I drilled a hole in her head, extracted the blood and stitched her up. Then I waited for her to recover. And she got a little better. I'd done it. I'd successfully operated. I was so proud. So happy.'

The grin that enveloped my Father's face was genuine. For a second, I almost forgot it was the result of being a psychopath.

'In that instant, we both understood what we needed to do and what would keep me at peace forever,' Len continued. 'Dissection only takes us so far... but surgery, pathology, *fixing*... that never stops bringing me joy.'

Nev took over as we neared the cages. 'So that is what we turned into. We turned into an operating room. Any injuries our guests had, we fixed them up. Some died. Some got better. But those that got better only presented more opportunities.'

'You didn't...' I began, working out where this was going.

'Of course we did,' Len interrupted. 'We inflicted injuries. We injected poisons and chemicals. We experimented on the bodies. Then we would cut. All whilst the patient was awake, bound to one of our operating tables.' He motioned to the stone tables at the centre of the room again, where I am sure we would find the conclusion of our tour.

We had arrived at the first cage. Nev flicked a light switch.

I immediately recognised Ellie Wright, pretty much unconscious, held to the ground in an uncomfortable position. Chains held her to the floor and sides of the cage, and heavy blocks of metal seemed to be placed at strategic points of her body.

Gab let out a strangled whimper. Ellie was her friend. They had been partying together just a few months ago...

Gab fell to her knees once again, tears flowing in waves. I just stood, stunned, barely able to process what was going on.

'Our current patient-' (*patient, did he really call her his* patient?) '-is a sixteen-year-old female. She is our pressure sore patient.'

'What the fuck does that mean?' Gab sobbed, anguishing.

'She is being held in a particular position,' my Dad continued, impatiently, 'so that excess pressure is placed on her thighs and back. Eventually, the skin in those areas will begin to break down, as will the fat and muscle. When that happens, she'll be at risk of infections in the bone and tissue. At that point, we will operate, and try to save her. Although I expect she'll lose at least one limb.'

A horrific smirk crossed the faces of the two brothers. I felt rage, hot as sin, burning up inside me. My terror was subsiding... I was angry now.

'Next patient,' Dad continued, still using that word blasphemously, 'is an older gentleman.' When the light revealed this man to us, I didn't recognise him but assumed my Father had kidnapped him at some other point. 'He has been with us for several months, but in the last few weeks, we have injected his abdomen daily with vials of bacteria and chemotherapy drugs, helpfully stolen by my faithful brother on his recent trip to Hull.'

Nev's evil smile showed all of his near-perfect teeth.

'We suspect that, soon, this gentleman's abdomen will become infected. He may even have some damaged abdominal organs. So, when we feel the time is right, we will perform an exploratory laparotomy - an operation in which we open his abdomen and try to find and fix the problem.'

This poor soul was lying on his back in the cage, his breathing shallow and laboured. He too, was barely conscious.

'Next patient.' My Father was moving quickly now. There must have been half a dozen cages. 'I'm sure you'll know well.'

Despite the fact I had guessed what I would see when my Father turned this light on, I was still traumatised when I saw Paul Thornton. This, so far, was also the most disturbing cage. Paul was strapped to the ground, his mouth covered by an oxygen mask. The tubing from the mask ran out of the cage, into the cavern walls, but seemed to be filled with a dark smoke.

'Paul is being given a mixture of oxygen and fumes from burning wood, tar, cigarettes, cannabis, and anything else you can think of. He's been a challenge to keep alive.' Dad sounded almost like a *real* Doctor, delivering a family bad news. 'Hopefully, he'll soon have severely damaged lungs. Then - and I'm excited for this one - we're going to transplant some new lungs into him.'

I could barely believe what I was hearing. My Father was insane. Categorically, certifiably insane. I'd never heard anything like this. Yet, bizarrely, the question that came to my lips was not one I really needed to ask.

'Where are you getting the other lungs from?'

My Dad smiled mischievously. 'Come and see our operating tables.'

SIXTY-EIGHT

SLOWLY, we followed my Father towards the three stone slabs at the centre of the room. Nev followed behind, pushing me roughly to encourage a little more speed.

My Dad had shown us a museum of dissection, a collection of caged victims, but this was possibly the most disturbing part of the cavern.

Three stone tables stood before us. Surrounding them, like tiny satellites, were trays suspended on metal poles, displaying a variety of gruesome-looking instruments. There were scalpels, retractors, and sharp, pointed metal rods. The odd butcher's knife and meat cleaver could be seen. Each was coated in dried blood and entrails.

Upon the tables themselves, three individuals lay strapped down tightly - two men and one woman. Their abdomens were bound by a tight strap, made of what looked like a reinforced car seatbelt. Leather straps held their arms and legs in place. Apart from cloths over their groins and the breasts of the woman, they were naked. Dark lines drawn with what looked like felt tips could be seen across their bodies, presumably marking my Father's planned incision sites.

The woman I didn't recognise. The two men, however, I recognised instantly.

The first was a man I thought to be dead, and whose supposed demise had left me riddled with guilt.

It was Mike Arnold.

He was out cold. His head was bandaged, and a section of his skull appeared to be caved in - a scar from the rock I had thrown at his face. His leg - previously bent out of shape by my sister's assault - had been pulled back to its natural position, and was now surrounded by an untidily assembled metal cage. His whole body looked unnatural... damp and swollen. I supposed that was the water damage of the river.

He was breathing. Just.

'Our good friend Mr Arnold here was recovered from the river. I wonder if you two had anything to do with his current presentation?' My Dad eyed us knowingly. Whether he did know what had happened, I still don't know, even to this day. Somehow, Len Keeler had a deep-seated wisdom that I couldn't entirely understand. 'Anyway, whatever happened to him, he has been a perfect specimen. He had head trauma, limb trauma, water-damaged lungs and flesh... I've had a fantastic time operating on him. I suspect he'll need some more surgery soon - although I haven't quite decided what yet.'

Interestingly, I felt no remorse for what had happened to Arnold. He was a pervert and a bastard. He deserved to die. Did that make me a bad person? I still don't know. I reflect on that a lot these days, as I sit alone... did all this make me a bad person?

We moved along to the middle table. This was another I recognised.

Aiden Bennet. The arrogant twat who lived on Beggar Home Lane had somehow found himself at my Father's mercy.

'I had to act quickly when the boy crashed into me,' my Dad explained, ever so informally. 'Luckily, I was pretty unscathed. He didn't crash into the side of the car I was in. I took the opportunity. The officers in the car with me were dead, I could tell. So I made my escape into the depths of the Yorkshire fields, bringing the unconscious boy with me.'

Gab and I continued to look at Aiden, aghast. Although he was an absolute knob, I did feel sympathy. He didn't deserve this. He deserved a bit of a beating up and putting in his place, but he didn't need this. I winced as I noticed the scars down both sides of his chest.

'This young lad was my first practice. I removed his lungs, then transplanted them into his neighbour.' He eyed the girl on the furthest table.

Something didn't quite make sense…

'If you transplanted his lungs, then…' I stopped as I realised the answer to my own question. My eyes were drawn to Aiden's unmoving chest. Only then did I realise that the poor lad was dead. 'Shit.'

My Dad shrugged, indifferently. 'That's what happens when you remove someone's lungs. They stop breathing.'

'Bastard!'

Gab suddenly lost it. I don't know if it was the horrific sights surrounding us or whether it was Dad's brutal lack of empathy - I suspect both - but she absolutely lost her rag. In a fit of rage, she ran at our Father.

With her hands still tied in front of her, she threw her whole body at him, knocking him to the ground. Gravity exerted its influence on her as well, and she crumpled on top of him, roaring in beastly anger. She lurched around on top of him, her tied hands making her look like a fish out of water, her efforts futile.

All Len Keeler did was laugh, as his daughter failed to cause even the slightest hint of harm. After a few seconds, my Uncle stepped forward and picked Gab up.

Whilst Gab was held in place, Len pulled himself to his feet. I stayed still, exactly where I was. I was assessing the situation, looking for an out.

Something in Gab's jumper didn't seem quite right… a bulge in one of her sleeves… had she broken her wrist or something?

'Nev,' my Dad announced, smiling maliciously. 'I think we've found the answer to our problems. One with just the right amount of *spirit*.'

'Oh indeed,' Nev replied, equally forebodingly.

'What the *fuck* is that supposed to mean?' Gab spat, as Nev pulled tightly at her hair.

My Father stepped towards her, moving his face within centimetres of Gab's. 'It means I have found my perfect subject. The one whose lungs might just be strong enough to be transplanted.'

'Don't you *fucking* dare!' I roared, myself advancing towards them.

Len moved quickly. He landed a brutally strong punch directly in my face. I felt a crack in my jaw and crumpled to the ground. Then Dad's foot was on my chest, holding me down.

'Strap her in, Nev. Then get your gun. We might need it for this one.'

Holding Gab harshly by a handful of hair, Nev moved towards the table with Aiden on it. Working quickly (and impressively with just one hand), he unstrapped the young man's corpse from the table and pushed it carelessly to the side.

It hit the ground with a deafening, horrifically final thud.

Without pausing for breath, Nev wrenched Gab by her hair up onto the table. My sister shrieked in pain, sobbing loudly. I struggled against my Father's foot, but he just pressed down harder. I could barely breathe.

Helpless, I watched as Nev manhandled Gab into position. With a scalpel from one of the nearby trays, he cut her ties (ensuring he sliced a decent chunk of skin, bringing even more anguished cries), and pulled her arms out to the side, strapping them to the table with expert efficiency. Moving seamlessly from one act to the other, he pulled the seatbelt over her abdomen and bound her legs. He performed this with an effortless grace, clearly well-versed in securing my Father's unfortunate victims.

'The girl to your right, Gabrielle,' my Father announced, delivering a good kick to my chin, sending shockwaves down my already damaged jaw and dazing me, 'was a student at the University. From Bulgaria. No one seemed to care she was missing. It didn't even make the news. Why would it? Just some other slut to fall in the river. Not worth reporting.'

Gab swore again at my Father, loudly and profusely. Dad ignored her.

'She was the recipient of the lungs we took from this young man.' He motioned at Aiden's body, his chest cavity opened up following his ejection from the table, bodily contents exsanguinating on the floor next to him. 'She did not survive the operation. And now, I need lungs to transplant into Paul Thornton. You, my daughter, will have healthy, strong lungs... strong enough to give you such a loud and dirty voice!' He spoke almost as if he was disciplining her.

'You can't, Dad,' I gasped, struggling on the floor, my hands bound behind my back. 'Please, stop. You just can't.'

'Nev, bring the fucking gun!' Dad shouted as Nev made his way across the room, back to the coffee table where he had left his firearm. 'One more word out of the boy and you can put him down.'

'With pleasure,' Nev's reply came from afar.

I panted on the ground, desperately trying to fill my lungs with air.

'I was wondering what we would do with the two of you,' Len murmured, almost to himself. 'If you had been cooperative, I think you could have stayed. Assisted me. Helped me. Unfortunately, I think we're far past that, would you agree? You are both too... combative. No matter, no matter.' He was muttering, pacing around the stone tables, seemingly lost in his own world. 'No, Gabrielle will serve as an excellent transplant provider. I'm sure of it. If not, we can try Christopher. But if Gabrielle's do work... well, Christopher could be part of another experiment... maybe we could shoot and stab him in his abdomen and practice trauma surgery... yes, that would be good. That would work well.'

I was listening to the ramblings of a madman. A deranged monster, who had me and my sister trapped, about to cut one of us open.

'Nev, what are you doing? I need to prepare for surgery.' Dad's voice echoed across the cavern.

Nev's reply came slow and monotone. 'I can't find my phone.'

'What?'

'My phone. It's gone.'

'Well, where have you put it? Does it matter? There's more pressing matters, boy.' Dad was getting irate. Interestingly, I remembered Nev putting his phone down on the table, next to the gun.

No...

'It was next to the gun. When we stood up. And now it's moved.' Now, Nev's tone was suspicious. Accusatory, almost.

'Is it on the floor?' Len asked, impatiently.

'No. It's been... taken.'

Len came to the realisation immediately of what was going on. Without warning, his foot slammed into my chest once again. I yelped in agony, the wind knocked out of me.

I watched as my Father drew his own mobile phone out of his pocket. A burner phone, most likely, now he was on the run. He dialled what I presumed was Nev's number.

'Voicemail. Straight to voicemail.' Len's voice was cold.

With Gab still tied to the table, Len crouched and began to roughly pat me down. 'Where is it, boy?' He hissed.

I said nothing. I could almost feel the fear rising in my sister. It made sense... the stumble and crouch by the coffee table... the specific questions about where we were... she must have stolen the phone and called for help.

But now...

Dad gave up frisking me. He stood up as Nev appeared back at the operating tables, and pointed at Gab. 'Search her.'

SIXTY-NINE

NEV WAS on Gab faster than anyone I had ever seen. It took him seconds to find what he was looking for.

Gab's left sleeve, the one I had thought looked a little unusual, had hidden the device. When she had stumbled at the coffee table at the very beginning of our tour, she had bent down. Incredibly subtly, she had clearly picked up the phone.

My Uncle's response was impossibly cruel.

He slammed the gun he had picked up from the table into Gab's temple, releasing a torrent of screams from her mouth. Then he retrieved a butcher's knife from one of the trays and swung it downwards in a fit of anger.

I'll never forget my Sister's scream.

The knife took Gab's arm clean off, just below the elbow. The noise that left her mouth was primal, like a caged animal suddenly fatally wounded. It reverberated around the cavern harshly, terrorising our eardrums.

Blood spurted from the wound as Gab rolled in agony, the right side of her body now a little more free following her dismemberment.

Meanwhile, Nev ripped the sleeve off the liberated limb and retrieved his phone. 'You little bitch,' Nev whispered, loathing filling his voice as he examined the phone. 'She's had the police on the phone this whole time.' He turned the phone over to my Father, showing the screen displaying the name "Fred Andrews (Police)" and the call time of twenty-two minutes.

'That's why you wanted to know where we were…' Len breathed, looking furious with himself. 'They'll be looking for us… maybe even tracing the call. They'll… they'll be here soon.' He stamped hard on my chest and I roared in pain, feeling something else crack. At least one rib was broken.

Whilst I flailed on the floor in agony (and Gab seemed to do the same on the stone table), Len and Nev stepped to one side, speaking in hushed yet urgent tones.

'We need to get the fuck out of here,' Nev began, a slight tremor in his voice. 'We'll both get life in Strangburn for this… if not the shitting needle.'

'They don't have the death penalty here, you twat,' Len chastised. 'And they'll never find us. We're fucking underground.'

'I don't know. The police these days are like the bloody CSI! They'll triangulate our position!'

'Don't be a fool,' Len spat. 'They called one frigging police officer. He's not going to be able to triangulate our call. You can't do that on such short notice.' He did, however, seem to contemplate his options. It wasn't beyond the realms of possibility that Fred had heard Dad explain our location and was on his way, with backup. After a moment, he made a decision. 'Lock her up. Then him.' He motioned at me on the floor. 'If either of them put up a fight, kill them.'

'Len, don't you think…'

'Shut up! I need to think about this.'

Len began pacing again, muttering to himself. I didn't hear a lot, but it suggested he was weighing up all his options. 'Police… no, they'll never find us… we're underground. But we have signal… I made it that way… maybe they *can* trace us. Shit, if they find us… no, Len, don't be an idiot, they'll never get down here. Even if they do, we can kill them. They'll be so shocked… no… they won't know what to do…'

My Father continued to pace and mumble, apparently losing all awareness of the events going on around him. I returned my attention to Gab, who was rolling around violently on the stone table, writhing in agony. My heart broke for my sister as my Uncle Nev approached her, gun still in his hand.

Gab moved more aggressively, succumbing even more to the pain. Although... was she? She moved rhythmically, almost tactically, as if... she was trying to break free her remaining hand!

Nev realised a second too late.

I pushed myself into a seated position, trying to get ready to help, despite my hands still being bound. I was far too slow.

In an instant, Gab's left hand had slipped underneath the strap that bound it - clearly not as carefully tied as Nev had thought.

Nev moved towards her, gun raised. Looking back, I wonder why he didn't fire. Maybe he was too shocked. Maybe he did and missed, and I just hadn't heard it. The whole night is a blur to me now.

Gab's left hand shot out to the side of her, reaching a tray laden with surgical instruments. As Nev descended on her, gun pointing vaguely towards her, I watched her fingers close around the handle of a scalpel.

With sickening accuracy, she swung her left arm around in an arc, directly towards my Uncle.

It had taken less than a second.

The scalpel bit into Nev Keeler's neck beautifully and smoothly. In an instant, a torrent of red was released, cascading down out of his neck as his artery wall was shredded. Light faded from his eyes in a second. The gun dropped from his hand and clattered onto the stone table. Blood gushed out of his neck, his body crumpled and life ebbed out of him before he even hit the ground.

My Father looked on in horror, frozen to the spot.

Gab moved with an inhuman speed. The scalpel moved to cut the seatbelt around her abdomen. She then moved to the straps on her ankles. Cutting them open impressively deftly, she clambered to her feet, the remains of her severed arm cradled to her chest.

Concluding her masterful performance, her left hand picked up Nev's dropped gun and pointed it at my Father.

'It's over, dickhead,' she hissed. 'Now get on your fucking knees.'

SEVENTY

DAD REMAINED frozen to the spot, looking on in utter bewilderment at what had happened. How dramatically the balance had shifted. How quickly the tables had turned.

Then he smiled.

It was a sickening smile, one full of evil and malice and insanity. One that forgot the fact his brother had just been murdered, or that he had massacred dozens for his own enjoyment, or that his two children were stood before him, dismembered and weak.

It was the smile of a demon.

'You've lost an arm, Gabrielle. You're still bleeding pretty badly. You'll pass out soon. Your brother is still bound. No... this is far from over, child. You cannot defeat me.'

Gab advanced, her grip on the gun unwavering. She did, however, look increasingly pale. Blood continued to spurt from her severed limb. Ever so slightly, she swayed in her stance.

'Get on your knees,' she hissed, edging closer to Dad.

Seemingly obeying, Dad dropped to his knees and raised his hands - half-heartedly - almost pretending to surrender. The smile on his face never faltered.

Without warning, Gab swung the butt of the gun into Dad's

temple, just as Nev had done to her. Len Keeler roared in pain and frustration, falling ungracefully sideways.

Now limping, Gab returned to me, dropped the gun at my feet and reached for the scalpel she had used to execute Nev, now on the ground next to the operating table. She was looking more and more unsteady, the colour draining from her rapidly. I knew we needed to stem the bleeding in her arm. We *had* to. Otherwise, she was going to lose too much blood and then...

Gab - her remaining hand now shaking uncontrollably - bent down and used the scalpel to undo the cable tie still binding my wrists. Mercifully, my hands were freed. No longer did I feel like my shoulders were about to dislocate.

Time seemed to freeze. Was I hearing things? Over Dad's grunts and curses and my sister's heavy breathing, a new sound rang through the night. A sound that, if it was real, brought relief to my heart.

Sirens.

Was Fred coming to our aid? Had he heard enough on the phone?

I held my breath. Gab's breathing slowed and she fell to her knees, scalpel clattering to the ground. Even Dad quietened.

The sirens stopped. There was noise up above. Voices. A shout.

It was coming from the entrance to the cavern!

'We're in here!' Gab managed, energy fleeing from her body.

The gun was still on the ground before me.

Dad moved with unparalleled speed.

Having recovered enough from a gun to the head, he had charged us. I didn't have time to react.

The next thing I knew, he had slammed into Gab, throwing her to the ground before straddling her. His hands closed on her neck and he began to squeeze.

'Get off her you BASTARD!' I roared. Summoning strength I didn't know I had left, I dived on top of my Father, beating at his back as hard as I could.

The life was fleeing from Gab.

Dad twisted his back rapidly, throwing me off him. I landed on the ground a metre away.

There was a commotion at the mouth of the cavern. Someone was there.

Please be the police. Please, God, let it be the police.

'We're in here! Help us! Please!' My voice was hoarse and shouting was painful. It felt like I had smoked a thousand cigarettes.

My eyes fell on the abandoned scalpel. I didn't even seem to notice the gun, just slightly more out of reach than the knife. No... the gun was invisible to me. I wanted Len to bleed.

I heard a door crash down behind me. People had entered the cavern.

I didn't care.

The scalpel was in my hand - even now, I don't remember picking it up. A force of nature had possessed me.

My vision blurring, only half conscious of what I was doing, I rounded on my Father again and dived onto him. This time, I plunged the blade of the scalpel into his back.

Dad let off a horrifying screech, his grip on Gab's throat releasing. I heard my sister gasp for breath - she was alive, for now - as Dad recoiled.

I pulled backwards with all my might, pulling him off my sister's helpless form. I stabbed again, catching him in the front of his shoulder.

More screams.

My vision began to blacken. My ears rang harshly.

I felt a strong pair of hands on me - not Dad, not Gab - pulling me back. The scalpel once again fell to the ground.

Then I was lying down, next to Gab, her arm still bleeding profusely. My vision sharpened again, and I watched her chest rise and fall. Her eyes were closed, but she was alive. Just.

There was a burst of commotion around me as my senses began to return to normal. Two men dressed in uniform were now next to Gab, one rapidly bandaging her arm.

I sat up, fighting vertigo, to see my Father now back on his feet, hands pulled tight behind his back. In a bizarre twist of fate, he mirrored how I had looked under his captivity just half an hour ago.

Two men dressed in police uniforms were with him. One I didn't know, but the other I recognised as Fred.

We'd done it. We'd got him.

The ringing in my ears began to settle and I heard words spoken in the cavern. 'Do not have to say… do not mention when questioned… rely on in court.'

I struggled to my feet, looking around. Five officers were in the room. Two were attending to Gab, two were with my Dad, and the fifth was wandering close by, looking around the cavern in horror.

Len was smiling.

I don't know why. I still don't. But he looked proud. Happy. He didn't care what happened next. He looked as if he had achieved what he set out to do.

And it made my blood boil.

The gun remained on the ground before me, forgotten in the melee of the last few minutes. Steadying myself, I bent down to pick it up.

It felt cold in my hand. Cold, hard, metallic, lethal.

It felt good.

'Chris,' Fred's voice came, sailing into my consciousness. 'You can put that down now, lad. You're safe. We've got him.'

I looked at the policeman - the one who had arrested me yet seemed to have a soft spot for Gab and me. One who had saved us. He stood just behind my father, securing his handcuffs. I saw care and sorrow in his eyes. He would help.

'What happens to him?' I managed. My voice was still raw.

'He's going to prison for a long time,' Fred's companion said, almost cheerily. 'I doubt he'll ever see the light of day again.'

'But he deserves to die.' I almost whispered it.

Fred nodded, finally happy with the cuffs. 'A lot of criminals do. But that's not how it works, unfortunately.'

'He's too dangerous to be kept alive,' I said, plainly. The gun was still in my hand. I looked at it closely, my thoughts turning to the path of the bullet, and how it would rotate and slice through the tissue it travelled into.

'It's okay, son,' Fred reassured me. 'He'll be going somewhere where he can't hurt anyone. Life in Strangburn.'

Dad was still smiling. Like he was egging me on. I suppose, in a way, he was.

I raised the gun.

'Chris, stop!' Fred shouted, concern now enveloping his face. 'This is not the way. I know what he's done to others. What he's done to you. And I know that people have already died tonight.' He looked to Nev's corpse, surrounded by a pool of blood, then to Gab's unconscious form. *She'd better not be dead.*

'He deserves to die,' I repeated. It was black and white in my mind.

Fred held Dad closely. He was standing just behind him, gripping the handcuffs that now bit into my Father's wrists. 'I know, son, but please, just put the gun down. We can talk about this. It's all going to be okay. I promise.'

My finger felt the trigger of the gun.

I felt a police officer close in behind me. It was now or never.

'Chris!' Fred shouted, his voice now stern. 'Put the gun down!'

Do we get to decide whether people live or die? Maybe we should. Religious people say God is the ultimate judge. "Judge Not Lest Ye Be Judged". Should we take life into our own hands? Should we decide who lives or who dies? Do people deserve death? The black depths of hell? I *knew* Len Keeler did.

Just a small squeeze of the trigger… all it would take.

I breathed.

As I look back now, all these years later, surrounded by cold stone, what would have happened if I had taken a different path? What if we had told someone about Dad's abuse? What if we had told someone about the window? What if we had ignored Old Lady Lilly? What if Dad had got where he wanted to in his career and not become a deranged psychopath? What if we had asked Fred for help sooner?

What would have happened if we hadn't got into Nev's car that night and just called the police instead?

No…

Watershed moments. They define our lives. In more ways than we can ever understand.

I fired the gun.

SEVENTY-ONE

BBC.CO.UK/NEWS/KEELER-JUNIOR-TRIAL-GOES-TO-VERDICT

CHRISTOPHER KEELER HAS BEEN SENTENCED to life imprisonment on two counts of murder.

Mr Keeler, 17, son of the now-deceased mass-murderer Leonard Keeler, has been the subject of a rigorous trial that has taken place over several months and has finally, today, concluded at York Crown Court.

Mr Keeler was found guilty by a jury of imperfect self-defence and manslaughter following the events of earlier this year, in which the whereabouts of several missing and murdered individuals came to light.

In the Spring of this year, an underground cave was discovered, housing multiple missing individuals including several under-eighteens, that had gone missing from the local area in the proceeding months. Leonard Keeler died at the scene, having been responsible for multiple counts of abduction, grievous bodily harm, theft, unlawful possession of firearms and murder.

When Leonard Keeler's children found him in this cave, they were threatened with death, the court heard. Mr Keeler's daughter, Gabrielle, faced significant assault and lost a limb. Her self-defence led to the death of Mr Keeler's brother, Neville. Miss Keeler was found not guilty of murder earlier this year, with both judge and jury finding her actions reasonable force considering the circumstances.

The jury heard, in Christopher Keeler's trial, that the police had arrived well before Mr Keeler fired his weapon. It is believed that Leonard Keeler had been handcuffed and was in the preliminary stages of an arrest when the gun was discharged. The weapon was only fired once but is believed to have killed both individuals with a single bullet.

At the trial, Mr Keeler's lawyer stated that the defendant had been "understandably furious, overwhelmed and heartbroken" by what he had found out about his father. The lawyer argued: "Although this doesn't make his actions right, it certainly makes them understandable."

When asked about his second victim whilst on the stand, Mr Keeler was overcome with emotion and unable to answer the questions. His legal representation, however, delivered a pre-prepared statement that read: "Mr Keeler is immeasurably sorry for his actions. The accidental death of Sergeant Fred Andrews is something he will regret for the rest of his life".

Sergeant Fred Andrews, a senior figure in the North Yorkshire Police, died at the scene as a result of the injuries inflicted by the bullet

Mr Keeler claims was meant for his father. Evidence given at the trial by the forensic crime department supported the claim that Christopher Keeler had aimed the gun at his Father and that the bullet continued its trajectory, through the exit wound, into Sergeant Andrews' neck.

Mrs Dawn Andrews, the late Sergeant's wife, whose legal representation led the charge against Mr Keeler, stated, in court that: "His [Christopher Keeler's] actions were selfish, irresponsible and disturbing. No boy who wants to kill his father should be allowed to roam the streets. If he had simply done as my husband had said and allowed the arrest, none of this would be happening. He is a devil."

When asked about whether he was regretful of his actions, Mr Keeler told the jury: "I was horrified and ashamed of all my father had done, and cannot begin to explain the pain he caused. He nearly killed my mum and sister and killed and abused so many of my friends. I think my father deserved to die. Jail was too good for him. Of course, I regret everything that happened. I wish that none of it had happened. But if you ask me whether Len Keeler deserved to die, I would say: yes, without a shadow of a doubt".

After several days of deliberation, the jury came to the unanimous decision that Christopher Keeler was guilty of murder on two counts: one of imperfect self-defence with unreasonable force against Leonard Keeler, and one for involuntary manslaughter causing the death of Sergeant Fred Andrews.

[WATCH THE MOMENT THE VERDICT WAS ANNOUNCED]

Christopher Keeler left the courtroom in police custody, with no further statement made. His head remained bowed throughout.

After the trial, his sister and mother (recently recovered from an aggravated assault by Leonard Keeler) were seen leaving the courthouse in tears.

The Keeler family's legal representative gave these closing remarks: "We obviously didn't get the result we wanted today. We believe that Chris had undergone an awful amount of emotional trauma and was in a state of inner turmoil. I believe the killing of his father is understandable. If it had just been his father who had been killed, I think we would have had a very different outcome today. Many would probably consider the boy a hero. The tragedy of all of this is the collateral damage. My continued condolences to the Andrews family, but I do wish they had been more understanding in court."

Mr Keeler was taken to Strangburn Prison in North Yorkshire directly from the courthouse and will begin serving his life sentence immediately.

[WATCH CHRISTOPHER KEELER BE LED OUT OF THE COURTROOM]

<NEXT STORY: THE EXPLOSIONS IN MAINE - WHAT WE KNOW SO FAR>

SEVENTY-TWO

'YOU LOOK GREAT.'

'Shut up.'

'Honestly. Blue suits you.'

'Bullshit, Gab. I'm wearing a bright blue jumpsuit so that I can't hide if I try and run away.'

'Still, looks nice.'

'Cheers.'

We were talking through phones on the wall. There was a pane of glass between us. Ironic really. All of this had started with a bloody glass window.

'How are you though?'

'Is that a real question?' I probably said that too snappily. It wasn't Gab's fault I was in here. Nor was it her fault she had got off for killing Nev. I *did* understand the difference between that and what I had done. Her life had been in immediate danger. Nev had cut off her arm, for crying out loud. Shoving a scalpel in his neck would probably be considered 'reasonable force'. That's what the jury had thought anyway.

'Sorry. But are you okay?'

'I mean, I haven't been stabbed or arse-raped yet. I get three meals a day. I'm keeping myself to myself.'

'Do you have any friends?'

'I don't know if I'd call him a friend. But my cellmate is alright.'

'What's his name?'

'Alistair.'

'What's he in for?'

'We don't really talk about it. I don't think you're supposed to. But I guess drugs.'

'Fair enough.'

Quiet. That was all there was now. Nothing more to say. I had little left to say.

I don't know how many times I'd gone over that night in my head. That single moment. That watershed second.

I remember it so clearly, as if it had all happened horrifically slowly, in a frozen moment of time. I remember the jolt of the gun as I pulled the trigger. It had ricocheted through my body like a bolt of lightning. I remember almost seeing the path the bullet took as it rotated and flew through the air - a deadly, merciless missile. I remember it hitting my Dad, square between the eyes, impressively accurate for my first ever go with a gun (and hopefully my last). I remember Len Keeler's head exploding into oblivion, his brains splattering gorily around the room, a firework of death and destruction. I remember his body crumpling to the ground, just as Nev's had minutes before.

And then I remember the overwhelming feeling of shame and guilt and horror at what I had done. I remember my vision blurring and my body giving out as I saw Fred Andrews, the police officer who had cared so well for Gab and me, collapse in tandem with my Father. He was clutching his neck as it spewed blood across the room, the bullet having left my Father's obliterated head and lodged itself into Fred's cervical spine, lacerating his carotid.

Life blinked out of Fred's eyes. I watched it happen before I passed out.

The next thing I knew, I awoke in a jail cell, where I remained, awaiting trial. Gab couldn't rescue me, and neither could Mum, even if she hadn't been in a hospital bed. I was a murderer. And there was no argument about it.

A tsunami of guilt and shame and regret washed over my every fibre. I sat in a slump for weeks, barely engaging with lawyers, police officers, and family. I kept going over that single moment and how, single-handedly, I had murdered two people, ruined Fred's family's life, ruined Gab's life and ruined my own life. A pit of despair had opened in my soul, and I didn't know if I'd ever get out of it.

'The window's broken.' Gab's words came through the phone, crackly and muffled. 'Completely.'

I nodded silently. It made sense, I suppose. If any of this made sense.

'I guess,' Gab continued, 'it's job was done.'

'Do you think it knew?' I asked. 'Was it always going to lead us down this path? Was this where we always finished?'

Gab shrugged. 'No idea. Do you think Lilly knew?'

My turn to shrug. Then… 'I guess Lilly never acted on what she saw. Maybe, deep down, she knew it would lead to bad places. Like she might catch the bad guy, but lose herself in the process.'

'It's like that quote in Batman.'

'What?' I snorted. First time I'd laughed in a while.

'The Dark Knight. You know, Batman.'

'I know what the film is. What do you mean, the quote?'

'You either die a hero, or you live long enough to see yourself become the villain.'

'Is that what I am? The villain?' I'd often wondered this myself.

'No. I think you were misguided. Led by a window and Lilly and by your own rage. But some people probably see you as that.'

'I don't blame them. I killed Fred.'

'By accident.'

'Still.' Nothing she could say would make it better.

'Lilly's died you know,' Gab mused, casually.

This didn't surprise me. 'I guessed that might be the case. She was like the window I suppose. Waiting until the job was done.'

'Dementia.'

'No shit.'

'I went to see her a few times, you know,' Gab murmured, absently. 'Just to talk to her.'

'Did she know who you were?' I wasn't particularly interested, but it gave us something to talk about.

'Not really. She seemed more confused every time I went. But I never mentioned the window. Even when it broke, I never mentioned it.'

I nodded, but none of it really made sense. Gab had only ever seen Lilly lucid the day we both went to visit her, at the mention of the window. I'd seen her lucid once more when she had visited me the night everything went to shit. Otherwise, her mind had been riddled with disease.

'I don't know why you bothered visiting her,' I grumbled, darkly.

Gab shrugged. 'I guess…' She paused. Then: 'It's the closest thing I could get to a bit of closure.'

We were quiet for a bit. Visiting time was coming to an end.

'How's Mum?' I asked, trying to change the subject.

Gab smiled. 'She's fine. Recovering well, lots of rehab. She misses you. Says she'll visit soon. It's just a long way to travel in her condition.'

'No, it's fine. I'm not sure I want her to see me like this anyway.' I didn't.

'You can't avoid her forever, Chris. You got life. You'll be here a while.'

'Maybe not with good behaviour,' I said, mischievously.

Gab smiled weakly. 'Don't get your hopes up.'

'FIVE MINUTES!' A Prison Officer shouted, reminding us that time with our loved ones was short, and that time *certainly* wasn't our own.

'Do you regret finding the window?' Gab asked.

It was a good question. I didn't really know. It had brought death and destruction and essentially the end of my existence. I missed my friends. I missed McDonalds and beer. I still hadn't had sex.

But what we had done… the lives we saved. The potential murders we stopped. Paul was home, recovering with the help of some of the best respiratory doctors in the country. Ellie was alive, and back with her family. Vicky was too.

So I guess... no, I didn't regret it. I wish things had gone differently... but in the end, I had made my bed. I'd chosen certain paths in watershed moments. I'd brought myself here. And no, I couldn't regret that.

This was where we finished.

'No,' I said, defiantly. 'No. It was meant to be. As is this. As is all of this.'

The Prison Officer began to move us away.

'Live your life Gab,' I murmured, as I was ordered up. 'Be the best you can be.'

SEVENTY-THREE

IT'S TAKEN me a long time to write this. The world has changed, the prison has changed and, most importantly, I've changed.

I like routine. I'm up at six for roll call, I go for breakfast, and then we're all off to "work", if you can call it that. I work in the kitchen, but only as a dishwasher. That's fine by me. It keeps me busy, lets me think, and I can keep myself to myself. Work only takes an hour or so, then I'm in the community room or my cell. Lunch follows soon after. Then more work. Then more sitting, either alone or with a few others. Sometimes we play cards. Other times, we sit.

More often than not, I write. Writing has brought me solace more than anything else. It's how I've been able to survive, furiously scribbling away in notebook after notebook that I bought from the prison shop, with the meagre wage of fourteen pence per hour I get from dishwashing.

I suppose, more than anything, writing has helped me reflect and process what's gone on. For a sixteen-year-old to go through what I did… it's no wonder I'm messed up.

We promised never to tell anyone about the window. As far as I'm aware, Gab has kept her side of the promise, enjoying her life with

Mum on the outside. I've never breathed a word of it, only written about it in these pages.

Gab comes to see me a couple of times a month. I guess it's become less frequent recently. She's got a life to live. Obviously, between 2016 and 2020 I didn't see much of her - understandable - but now at least there is some consistency. Occasionally, Mum comes with her. It's been years since her stay in the neurosurgical wing of Hull Hospital, but she's never quite recovered, even now. She has seizures pretty regularly, Gab tells me, and often gets confused. The neurologist who looks after her tells Gab she expects Mum will develop a sort of dementia-like syndrome quite soon, considering the damage to her brain and the lack of a full recovery. Unfortunately, my Mum was just another one of the scars left by the shit-show that was Len Keeler's life.

When Gab sees me, she tells me about the world outside. Grand Parade seemed to become a dramatically safer place overnight. Len Keeler died, and the kidnappings stopped. The grave robbing ceased. Mr Arnold, one of my Father's many victims, died in hospital soon after the night we discovered him. His injuries from my Dad's experiments were far too great. St Joseph's High School - my old stomping ground - has developed into an award-winning, OFSTED outstanding school. Pretty impressive really.

Oh, and Gab's getting married next year. Nice chap called Danny. I haven't met him, obviously, but I'm told he's lovely, and he looks after Gab well. They met post-2020, and have been together for years now. I'm happy for her. She's happy. And that's good. We had a shitty life for a time. I'm glad she's got some happiness.

As for me, I'm fifteen years into my sentence. I've been doing the same thing every day for the past decade and a half. I've got used to it. This is life for me. I've come to terms with what I've done. I've accepted that this was my fate. Whether the window knew it or Lilly knew it or some higher power knew it, this was always the way it was going to go. I was always going to choose a particular path in those watershed moments.

This is where I was meant to finish.

I got a new cellmate last week. Alistair has moved on, although I'm not entirely sure where. It's a shame - we got quite close, me and him.

But anyway, I've got this new cellmate, Ben. He's a young lad, probably early twenties, in for armed robbery. He's pretty naive and a bit of a twat, but he's a nice enough chap. He told me immediately what he was in for, which is a big prison no-no, but I'm a patient guy, with years of time behind me now, and I like to think of myself as one of the nicer inmates at Strangburn.

The first night he was here, he showed me some fruit he had stolen from dinner. Said he was going to start collecting it, put it in a plastic bag and make hooch - a dirty, super strong prison alcohol, made by pulping up fruit, adding a bit of bread and leaving it somewhere warm for a week to ferment. I warned him that such things aren't a great idea and he might want to think twice about doing something so risky this early in his sentence.

He ignored me. Like I say, he's a twat. But our conversation made me think.

'All my mates told me it's what you do in prison,' Ben told me when I questioned his decision.

I shrugged. 'Some of the lads do. That's up to them. But they've been doing it for years, and have got damn good at hiding it from the guards. I'm not going to tell you what to do, mate, but I will say I don't think it's a good idea. Not whilst you're still finding your feet in here. You've got a long time to start making hooch.'

Ben isn't one to take criticism well. I've learnt that pretty quickly.

'Nah mate, I'll be fine. I'm good at hiding stuff. Subtlety is my middle name.'

I shrugged again, finding it slightly ironic that he considered himself subtle after being caught for armed robbery. 'Do whatever you like, Ben,' I said, 'but don't even think about making or hiding it in this cell. I do pretty well for myself here, and if I get into shit because of you, I have some people who will fuck you up.'

Whilst I am well known and generally liked in the prison, this last bit was a bit of a lie. I don't have thug friends who will go around and teach people a lesson on my behalf. Prison doesn't really work like that, not in my experience, anyway.

'Well I won't be sharing any of it with you,' Ben huffed, sounding a little bit like a spoilt child.

Once again, I shrugged. 'Don't worry, mate. I don't drink.'

'You don't drink? Fucking loser.'

'It's what happens when your Dad's a drunk.'

Ben and I haven't had much more in the way of conversation so far, but I'm sure he'll open up. I'm a nice guy, and the young lads always need someone to help mentor them when they first start. Not in a weird way or anything. It's just that prison is hard to adjust to. Alistair helped me a lot. I suppose I should repay the favour.

So here I sit. Fifteen years into a life sentence. No hope of getting out, despite numerous appeals and continuing court fights by my lawyer. I've given up trying. Gab has as well. She needs to live her life. I made my bed.

I suppose I should end this story with some deep cathartic ideas, tying all of this together with some reflective rhetoric of what I have learnt about the complexities of life and the human psyche. Well, don't get excited, because here's my reflection: shit happens. Sometimes, bad things happen to good people. It's the way of the world.

All I will say is that every day, we are presented with hundreds of decisions. Some seem massive, like where to buy a house, some seem tiny, like what to have for dinner. I guess it's a fine balance of deciding how much thought we should put into the seemingly little decisions. I had some choices in my life. I made decisions. They defined the trajectory of my destiny.

I was always meant to find the window. What I did with it… I guess that was up to me. It definitely influenced events, but I had a much bigger part in that.

Now the window is gone, and so is Lilly and so is my Dad. My Mum too, to a degree. Lost to the chaos of my Father's insanity. And I guess, in a way, I'm gone too. I'm stuck here, simply existing, not living, doing what should have been my Father's time.

But I'm okay with that. This is where I was meant to finish.

19/06/24 // J.D.JONES // CHESHIRE, ENGLAND

AUTHOR'S NOTE

Wow. This one took a dark turn. I don't think I fully expected it would, but I'm pretty happy with how it turned out. Hopefully, it gripped you and surprised you right up until the very end. It certainly surprised me as I was writing it.

Early in my writing journey, I looked to the advice that comes from masters of the form. Any of you who follow my social media won't be surprised that Ken Follett, Brandon Sanderson and Stephen King are some of the many authors I have looked up to and listened to. One of the things I find fascinating is hearing the methods of other writers. I watched a talk by Sanderson where he explained how he is more of a "planner", with a reasonable outline for each of his books and an idea about what is going to happen in each part. Conversely, King famously often starts out with a simple idea and sees what happens as he writes, with less of a plan.

When writing *The Chaos Legacies*, I'm a bit of a planner. I think I need to be, with a planned total of six books across two trilogies. I know key events that need to happen and have a reasonable idea of how each part of each book will end. But I still like to leave enough room for my characters to have their own autonomy, so my imagination can run wild. In *The Chaos Legacies*, that freedom of writing has led to some surprises even for me - without giving anything away, The Viper's storyline in Book 2 was certainly not how I originally intended it, but I'm so happy it ended up that way.

For *Beggar Home Lane*, I adopted a much more "Stephen King" approach. I started off with an idea, about a bizarre window that showed the finder dark events of the past — from that developed what you've just read. I didn't really know how it would end, and I certainly didn't anticipate the twists, or where Gab and her brother would end up in the finale. But writing this book was an absolute joy. I loved the experimental, free-writing experience. It's definitely not how I'll write all my books, but I'm absolutely going to do it again.

Ironically, the single idea that sparked this story was not originally mine! Credit must go to my wonderful father, Howard. He enjoys woodwork in his semi-retired life, and (much to my mother's despair) spends far too many hours in the garage and on the front driveway building his latest project. Together, we've built a bar and decking for my garden, a wood shelter, and my baby's nursery. But one day a few years back, Dad found a window in a skip at the end of our road, to build a cold frame of his own. A throwaway comment followed its discovery: "I tell you what would be a great story. Someone finds a window, and it shows them everything that's ever gone past it. Maybe you should write that."

So you have Howard to thank for this story: Howard and his woodwork. However, despite their shared love of building things, that's where the similarities between my Dad and Chris Keeler's dad end. Howard is a hero, both as a family man and as a retired, yet decorated police sergeant. He's inspired my book, read and critiqued one of the early drafts, and been a bloody brilliant father. Cheers, Dad.

I'm grateful, my dear reader, that you have given this book a chance - and all my books for that matter. As an independent author, doing things on my own steam, having your support means the absolute world. It's not been easy, but my love of creating stories is enough to keep me writing, and hopefully keep you entertained in the process.

There's lots more to come. I hope you stick around.

J x

ACKNOWLEDGMENTS

This is a totally different book to anything I've written before. Hopefully, it's turned out well in your opinion! But, as always, the final version you hold in your hands would not have come into existence if it weren't for some truly wonderful people.

Let's start with the epic, wonderfully gifted proofreaders/editors that are Andy Wood and Ian Knight. I cannot thank the two of you enough. Not only did you both *speed* through it (Ian in less than 24 hours!) but you picked up things I never would have noticed - and evidently things that my computer didn't notice! I'm so grateful. Thank you both for being brilliant.

Howard - you were a massive part of this book. You gave me the initial idea, after finding a window in a skip that you would later use in a cold frame. Then, you gave me valuable insights into the police and legal world, fact-checking my work and highlighting my inconsistencies. Words can't thank you enough for everything you have done for me over the years - this is just a drop in the water, and I'm so grateful that you're my Dad.

Of course, as always I must thank the brilliant Tom Edwards, my amazing illustrator. I know that this story was well outside your normal genre and scope of work, but you produced a phenomenal cover nonetheless. I'm so lucky to have a cover designer who understands my vision and makes it ten times better. Thank you.

There is a good number of people in my hometown who have helped with the promotion of this and my other books. Thanks go out to our local newspaper for kindly featuring my work. And of course, thanks to Adam and Katy, for letting me host my launch nights in your fantastic bar, and for keeping me well-hydrated during my writing sessions there (on one of the few quiet afternoons when I get a chance to write!)

Ali, Lizzy - as always, your support and excitement for my books is never taken for granted, and I'm incredibly grateful for your support and unwavering fandom. Thank you both.

Annabelle, Samuel, Maisie - the silent partners of Wentworth Jones Publishing. I'm thankful for your support, encouragement, love and brutal honesty. The first draft of the blurb for this book led to Samuel commenting: "It doesn't grab me". As a result of his harsh - but true - feedback, Beggar Home Lane received a much more exciting blurb. You've got Sam to thank. Sam - please never stop being so honest. I need it.

As mentioned, Dad, you've been essential in this project, and I feel like you should be thanked again, alongside my wonderful Mum, who promises she's much more excited to read this one. Thank you both for your endless encouragement and love.

Words can never express how much I appreciate and love my wonderful wife. She, as always, is the first person to see the first draft, and the first to give me honest, detailed feedback. She tells me if the story is good or bad, and tells me which bits she thinks could go and what could stay. She is my best reviewer, my harshest critic and my best friend. And - good news - this is her favourite book I've written (so far). Love you.

And of course, I must thank the most important part of my life, our beautiful baby girl Nancy. This is the first book I've published since she was born, and I hope she doesn't read it for many years, considering the number of F-bombs I dropped. But she is my biggest inspiration, and I can't express how grateful I am that she is in our lives.

Finally, all thanks go to my Lord and Saviour Jesus, without whom, all of this would be for nothing.

Dearest reader, I cannot express how grateful I am that you have read the words I have put to paper. I truly hope you enjoyed them. Thanks for being on this journey with me. Always more to come.

J x

Printed in Great Britain
by Amazon